A Lady Never Lies

"Shakespeare meets *Enchanted April* in this dazzling debut. Pour yourself some limoncello, turn off the phone, and treat yourself to the best new book of the year!"

—Lauren Willig, national bestselling author

"Extraordinary! In turns charming, passionate, and thrilling—and sometimes all three at once—*A Lady Never Lies* sets a new mark for historical romance. Juliana Gray is on my auto-buy list."

—Elizabeth Hoyt, *New York Times* bestselling author

"Juliana Gray writes a delightful confection of prose and desire that leaps off the page. This romance will stay with you long after you have turned the final page."

—Julia London, *New York Times* bestselling author

"Charming, original characters, a large dose of humor, and a plot that's fantastic fun make *A Lady Never Lies* a fabulous read. Prepare to be captivated by Finn and Alexandra!"
—Jennifer Ashley, *USA Today* bestselling author

"Fresh, clever, and supremely witty. A true delight."

—Suzanne Enoch, *New York Times* bestselling author

"Juliana Gray has a stupendously lyrical voice, unlike anybody else's I've read—really just a gorgeous way with language. Some of the imagery made my breath catch from delighted surprise, as did the small, deft touches of characterization that brought these characters so vividly to life. The story feels tremendously sophisticated, but also fresh, deliciously witty, and devastatingly romantic."

—Meredith Duran, *New York Times* bestselling author

DISCARD

DISCARD

A DUKE
NEVER YIELDS

Juliana Gray

BERKLEY SENSATION, NEW YORK

THE BERKLEY PUBLISHING GROUP
Published by the Penguin Group
Penguin Group (USA) Inc.
375 Hudson Street, New York, New York 10014, USA

Penguin Group (Canada), 90 Eglinton Avenue East, Suite 700, Toronto, Ontario M4P 2Y3, Canada
(a division of Pearson Penguin Canada Inc.) • Penguin Books Ltd., 80 Strand, London WC2R 0RL,
England • Penguin Ireland, 25 St. Stephen's Green, Dublin 2, Ireland (a division of Penguin
Books Ltd.) • Penguin Group (Australia), 707 Collins Street, Melbourne, Victoria 3008, Australia
(a division of Pearson Australia Group Pty. Ltd.) • Penguin Books India Pvt. Ltd., 11 Community
Centre, Panchsheel Park, New Delhi—110 017, India • Penguin Group (NZ), 67 Apollo Drive,
Rosedale, Auckland 0632, New Zealand (a division of Pearson New Zealand Ltd.) • Penguin
Books (South Africa), Rosebank Office Park, 181 Jan Smuts Avenue, Parktown North 2193,
South Africa • Penguin China, B7 Jiaming Center, 27 East Third Ring Road North,
Chaoyang District, Beijing 100020, China

Penguin Books Ltd., Registered Offices: 80 Strand, London WC2R 0RL, England

This is a work of fiction. Names, characters, places, and incidents either are the product of the author's
imagination or are used fictitiously, and any resemblance to actual persons, living or dead, business
establishments, events, or locales is entirely coincidental. The publisher does not have any control over
and does not assume any responsibility for author or third-party websites or their content.

A DUKE NEVER YIELDS

A Berkley Sensation Book / published by arrangement with the author

PUBLISHING HISTORY
Berkley Sensation mass-market edition / February 2013

Copyright © 2013 by Juliana Gray.
Excerpt from *How to Tame Your Duke* by Juliana Gray copyright © 2013 by Juliana Gray.
Cover art by Alan Ayers. Cover design by George Long.
Interior text design by Kristin del Rosario.

All rights reserved.
No part of this book may be reproduced, scanned, or distributed in any printed or
electronic form without permission. Please do not participate in or encourage piracy of
copyrighted materials in violation of the author's rights. Purchase only authorized editions.
For information, address: The Berkley Publishing Group,
a division of Penguin Group (USA) Inc.,
375 Hudson Street, New York, New York 10014.

ISBN: 978-0-425-25118-8

BERKLEY SENSATION®
Berkley Sensation Books are published by The Berkley Publishing Group,
a division of Penguin Group (USA) Inc.,
375 Hudson Street, New York, New York 10014.
BERKLEY SENSATION® is a registered trademark of Penguin Group (USA) Inc.
The "B" design is a trademark of Penguin Group (USA) Inc.

PRINTED IN THE UNITED STATES OF AMERICA

10 9 8 7 6 5 4 3 2

If you purchased this book without a cover, you should be aware that this book is
stolen property. It was reported as "unsold and destroyed" to the publisher, and neither the
author nor the publisher has received any payment for this "stripped book."

ALWAYS LEARNING   PEARSON

As always, to the faithful ladies of the Romance Book Club, and especially to our dear and witty Abigail, who gets the duke.

ACKNOWLEDGMENTS

I'd like to think that Shakespeare, that great purloiner of history and legend, would not have minded my adaptation of *Love's Labour's Lost* into a romantic trilogy set in Victorian-era Italy. I've tried in *A Duke Never Yields* (as in the previous installments, *A Lady Never Lies* and *A Gentleman Never Tell*s) to honor my source with plenty of the servants' banter, mistaken identity, and magical realism he employed to such classic effect.

But I owe another debt to Giuseppe Verdi, who composed many of his greatest operas at the same time and in roughly the same corner of the world as the setting of this trilogy, and all three books are littered with references, large and small, to his life and work. My most blatant larceny, of course, is of the Curse of the Castel sant'Agata itself (named, by the way, for Verdi's estate in nearby Lombardy). Opera lovers will recognize at once that the over-the-top events taking place in the castle's courtyard in 1590 mirror those in the first scene of *La Forza del Destino* (itself an adaptation of earlier dramas by Schiller and Angel de Saavedra); my Leonora's flight to a religious sanctuary is based on that of Verdi's Leonora. The Convento di San Giusto is named for the convent in *Don Carlo*, which opera also inspired some of the dynamics of the love triangle in *A Gentleman Never Tells*, including one of its key scenes.

Both Shakespeare and Verdi loved the otherworldly, and their works seethe with ghostly spirits, with undercurrents of fate and destiny, with the redemption of sin as the beating heart of human drama. I've used these devices liberally in this trilogy, and I hope the masters would approve.

One final word of heartfelt thanks to cast and crew: my matchless agent, Alexandra Machinist; my keen-eyed editor, Kate Seaver, and her lovely assistant, Katherine Pelz; the wonderful people at Berkley who make magic with book covers, marketing, publicity, and sales; and most especially to my copy editor, Marianne Grace, who kept all the details straight in this complex three-book project, and who deserves a year-long Tuscan holiday of her own, dashing aristocrats included.

PROLOGUE

London
February 1890

The Duke of Wallingford, as a rule, did not enjoy the sound of the human voice upon waking. Not that of his valet, nor his mistress—he never, ever spent the night with a woman—and certainly not the one that assailed his ears just now.

"Well, well," said the Duke of Olympia, to the prostrate form of his eldest grandson. "For an instrument that has cut such a wide swathe of consternation, it appears remarkably harmless at present."

Wallingford did not trouble to open his eyes. For one thing, he had a crashing headache, and the morning light already pierced his brain with sufficient strength, without his giving up the additional protection of his eyelids.

For another thing, he'd be damned if he gave the old man the satisfaction.

"Who the devil let you in?" Wallingford demanded instead.

"Your valet was kind enough to perform the office."

"I shall sack him at once."

Olympia's footsteps clattered in reply along the wooden floor to the opposite end of the room, where he flung back the curtains on the last remaining window. "There we are! A lovely day. Do examine the brilliant white of the winter sun this morning, Wallingford. Too extraordinary to be missed."

Wallingford dropped an arm over his face. "Rot in hell, Grandfather."

A sigh. "My dear boy, may I trouble you to consider a dressing robe? I am not accustomed to addressing the unadorned male member at such an early hour of the day. Or any hour of the day, as a matter of habit."

Arthur Penhallow, Duke of Wallingford, twenty-nine years old and assuredly not a boy, flung his unoccupied arm in the direction of his dressing-room door. "If the sight offends, Grandfather, I recommend you to the wardrobe. The dressing gowns, I believe, are hanging along the right-hand side. I prefer the India cashmere, in wintertime."

"I must decline your gracious invitation," said Olympia, "and ring for your valet instead. Have you never considered a nightshirt?"

"When *I* am sixty-five, and without hope of tender feminine attention upon my withered person, I shall remember the hint." This was not quite fair. Wallingford knew for a fact that his grandfather's person, withered or not, currently enjoyed the tender feminine attention of Lady Henrietta Pembroke herself, who did not choose her lovers for mere whimsy.

On the other hand, the opportunity was too tempting to pass up.

"And yet, Wallingford, your own person exhibits no evidence of feminine attention of any kind." A delicate pause. "Quite the contrary, in fact."

"Bugger off."

"What a crude generation my children have spawned. Ah! Shelmerstone. You perceive His Grace stands in need of a dressing gown. In a manner of speaking, I hasten to add."

Wallingford heard the door close behind his valet, heard the soft tread of the man's feet across the thick Oriental rug toward the dressing room. "Shelmerstone," he said, "once you have dressed and shaved me, you may collect your things and vacate your position. I am not to be disturbed before nine in the morning, and certainly not by so intolerable a character as His Grace, my grandfather."

"Yes, sir," said Shelmerstone, who was accustomed to being sacked several times a day, as a matter of course. "I have taken the liberty of putting out the gray superfine, sir, and your best beaver hat."

"Why the devil? I ain't contemplating church this morning."

"I chose it, sir, as being more suitable for calling upon a lady, on a matter of such unprecedented delicacy."

This caused Wallingford to sit up at last. "What lady?" he demanded, shading his eyes against the merciless abundance of light. Was it his imagination, or did everything smell of stale champagne this morning? "What . . . *delicacy*?" He said the word with a shudder of distaste.

"Madame de la Fontaine, of course." Shelmerstone emerged from the wardrobe's depths with a dressing gown of fawn brown cashmere and an air of irresistible moral authority, laced with cedar.

"See here." Wallingford rose from his bed by the sheer force of habit and allowed Shelmerstone to fit his arms into the robe.

Olympia, impeccable as ever in sleek morning tweeds and riding boots, squared his arms behind his back and cast his grandson his most withering sigh. Wallingford had loathed that sigh in childhood; like an ill wind, it blew no good. "My dear boy, there's no use pretending ignorance. The entire town knows of last night's charming little farce. I don't suppose you'd consider *belting* that robe? At my age, one's digestion is so easily upset."

Wallingford lashed his robe into modesty with vigorous jerks of his arms. "There was no *farce*, Grandfather. The Duke of Wallingford does not condescend to *farces*."

"Shelmerstone," said the Duke of Olympia, his bright blue eyes not leaving Wallingford's face for an instant, "may I beg your indulgence for a moment of private conversation with my grandson?"

"Of course, Your Grace." Shelmerstone set down the shaving soap and departed the room without a sound.

Wallingford attempted a smile. "I'm to be scolded, am I?"

His grandfather walked to the window, fingered aside the curtain, and gazed out into the forest of white pediments that was Belgrave Square. The light fell across his features, softening the lines, until he might have been taken for a man twenty years younger were it not for the shining silver of his hair. "I don't object to your taking the woman to bed," he said, in the preternaturally calm voice he reserved for his most predatory moments. "French husbands are tolerant of such things, and as a diplomat, Monsieur de la Fontaine must be aware of the advantages of the liaison. It is why such a man marries an alluring woman."

Wallingford shrugged. "He has been all that is accommodating."

"Yes, of course. And in return, one expects that you would demonstrate a certain degree of respect. A *modicum*"—here Olympia's voice began to intensify, signaling the approach of the attack—"a *modicum* of good breeding, which would prevent your indulging that wayward prick of yours with another diversion, whilst you remained the acknowledged lover of Cecile de la Fontaine." He turned to Wallingford, eyes ablaze. "Under her own roof, of course, and at her own party. How else to humiliate her so thoroughly?"

"I never made Cecile any promises." Wallingford's insides were turning rapidly to stone, defending him against onslaught. Of course he had been wrong; he'd known it even as he was committing the very act—up against the wall of the de la Fontaines' elegant conservatory, quite efficient, quite pleasant, if rather oppressively drenched with the scent of Cecile's prize orchids—and to quit the lady in question (what the devil was her name, anyway?) with so little ceremony had represented the height of stupidity. Every lady, even one willing to take an uprighter with her hostess's own lover against her hostess's own conservatory wall, required a little ceremony.

But who would have expected her to confront him so publicly, and so half-nakedly, and with such quantities of fine French champagne flung at his head? His hair was still sticky with it.

"No, of course you did not. I'd have expected nothing else," said Olympia, in a voice laden with scorn. "But there's a promise implicit in taking such a woman as Madame de la Fontaine to bed, a respectable woman, a woman of position. Indeed, a woman of any sort, though I should hardly expect you to possess the chivalry to go so far as that."

No one wielded scorn so brutally as the Duke of Olympia. Wallingford felt it pound against the hard stone of his innards in a familiar rhythm, searching for weakness. He added a few buttresses for support against the assault and hardened them into granite. When he had finished, and felt sufficiently confident of the results, he idled his way to the carved wooden bedpost and leaned against it, arms crossed. "A bit of the pot calling the kettle black, isn't it, Grandfather?"

"I don't deny I've taken many women to bed," said Olympia, "and, on the whole, a far more interesting lot than *you* have troubled yourself to assemble, but I have always had the decency to finish with one lover before taking another."

"Except your wife."

The words snapped and spun in the pale morning light. Wallingford regretted them instantly.

Against Olympia's hand, where it fisted atop his waistcoat, a gold watch chain caught the sun with a sudden glitter. "In the future," he said evenly, "you will avoid any mention of Her Grace in vulgar context. Do you understand me?"

"Of course."

"I have often wondered," Olympia went on, relaxing his fist, "whether a wife might not have civilized you, or at least contrived to soften your worst instincts."

"I am perfectly civilized. I am a perfectly good duke. My estates are in excellent order, my tenants prosperous . . ." Like a schoolboy, Wallingford thought angrily, desperate for some crumb of approval.

"Yes, for which I give you full credit," Olympia said. "Your father, that scapegrace, was not capable of so much. I often wonder at my daughter's lack of sense in marrying him. A duke, to be sure, and a handsome one, but . . ." He shrugged his shoulders expressively.

"I beg you to remember that the scapegrace in question was my father."

Olympia lifted the watch and flipped open the case. "You have an abundance of natural qualities, Wallingford. It grieves me to see so much promise go to waste."

"I beg your pardon," drawled Wallingford. "Am I keeping you from an appointment? Do not stand on ceremony, I implore you."

"I will come to the point. I understand Mr. Burke has laid a certain proposal before you."

Wallingford rolled his eyes and left his post at the bed to sprawl in an armchair. "What, his mad scheme to retire to Italy for a year of monastic reflection?"

"You cannot imagine yourself capable of such restraint?"

Wallingford leaned his head against the forest green damask and laughed. "Oh, come, Grandfather. Why should I? What use would it be? I have never understood this religion of self-sacrifice among the Burkes of the world."

"Have you not? Have you never contemplated the peculiar difficulties of his life?"

"His life as your bastard son, do you mean?" Wallingford said.

Again, the silence echoed about the room; again, Wallingford wished his words back. Phineas Burke was an excellent fellow, after all: a bit tall and ginger haired and taciturn for some, but a genuine scientific genius, an inventor of the highest order, building electric batteries and horseless carriages and whatnot the way other men tinkered with watches. A colossus, really. Moreover, he had none of the usual tempers and thin-skinned resentments, the vain strivings and artificial manners so common in well-bred bastards. Burke simply went about his business and did not give a damn, and as a result he was received everywhere. In his heart, Wallingford counted Burke as his closest friend, though of course one could never publicly admit such a thing of one's natural uncle.

Really, Burke was so steadfast and clever, so stalwart in any crisis, Wallingford could almost forgive him for being the apple of Olympia's eye.

"You see," Olympia said softly, "I know how it is. You've always been a duke, or else in daily expectation of a dukedom. You have been blessed with a handsome face and a sturdy figure. You take these things for granted. You think that you have *earned* all this around you"—his arm, at a wave, took in the splendid furnishings, the army of servants moving soundlessly behind the walls, the rarefied pavement of Belgrave Square outside the windows—"instead of having it dropped in your lap like an overripe peach. You think you deserve to enjoy sexual congress with some mere acquaintance, against the wall of your own mistress's conservatory, simply because you can. Simply because you are His Grace, the Duke of Wallingford."

"I recognize my good fortune. I see no reason not to enjoy its fruits."

"Its *fruits*? This woman, this lady of good family, with a

mind and soul of her own—she is reduced to a mere vegetable, in your calculus?"

Wallingford turned his attention to the sleek cashmere sleeve of his dressing gown, searching for a piece of lint at which he might brush, laconically, to show his disinterest. But Shelmerstone was far too efficient a valet to allow any flaws to disturb the impeccable line of the ducal sleeve, and Wallingford was reduced to brushing phantom lint into the dustless air. "I seem to recall," he said, "that the lady in question was enjoying herself."

"Really?" Olympia's voice was cold. "I rather doubt you would have noticed either way. In any case, I've decided that all this nonsense has gone far enough. You are nine-and-twenty, and a duke. With regret, I must demand you *not* to accept this proposal of Burke's, however edifying, and turn your attention instead to marriage."

Wallingford looked up, certain he'd misheard the old man. "*Marriage?*" he asked, as he might say the word *castration*. "Did you say *marriage*?"

"I did."

"Are you *mad*?"

Olympia spread his hands. "Surely you recognize the necessity."

"Not at all. We still have Penhallow, who would make an extraordinarily decorative duke, should I have the misfortune to choke on a chicken bone at dinner this evening."

"Your brother has no interest in your title."

Like a pitcher turned upside down, Wallingford found his patience had run abruptly out. He rose from the chair in a bolt of movement. "Have we come to the point at last? Is *this* why you came to see me this morning? I am to be a stud? My ability to breed another duke constitutes the sum total of my usefulness to you, does it?"

"My dear boy," Olympia said, "has the entire conduct of your adult life ever suggested your usefulness for anything else?"

Wallingford turned to the tray of coffee and poured himself a cup. No cream, no sugar. He wanted the drink as black as his mood. *Marriage*, indeed. "I have many talents, Grandfather, if you ever bothered to count them."

Olympia waved that away. "Don't be a child, Wallingford. In any case, you need not concern yourself with the tiresome matter of choosing a wife. I've done all the work for you. I have, in my deep and abiding regard for you, found you the perfect bride already."

Wallingford, in the very act of lifting the cup to his lips, let it slip instead with a thump to the rug below. Such was his astonishment, he did not bother to retrieve it. "*You* have found *me* a bride?" he repeated, in shocked tones, clutching the saucer as if it were a life buoy.

"I have. Charming girl. You'll adore her, I assure you."

"I beg your pardon. Have I gone to sleep and woken up two hundred years ago?"

Olympia patted his coat pocket and withdrew a slim leather diary. "No," he said, examining a few pages. "No, it remains February of 1890. Thank goodness, as I've an immense number of appointments to make today, and I should hate to have to wait so long to complete them. If this is all agreeable to you, Wallingford, I shall invite the girl and her family around at the end of March, when they return to town. A private dinner would be best, I think. Allow the two of you to get to know each other." He turned a few more pages in his diary. "A wedding around midsummer would be ideal, don't you think? Roses in bloom and all that?"

"Are you mad?"

"Sound as a nut. I must be off, however. I'll send in Shelmerstone on my way out. No doubt he stands ready at the keyhole. And Wallingford?"

"Yes?" He was too stunned to say anything else.

"Do contrive not to embroil yourself in any further scandal before then, eh? The Queen don't like it, not a bit. Oh yes! And orchids."

"Orchids?"

"Orchids to Madame de la Fontaine. It seems they're her favored blooms."

Olympia left in a flash of tweed coat and silver hair, and Wallingford stared at the door as if it were the gate to hell itself.

What the devil had come over the old man? He'd never so much as mentioned the word *marriage* before, and all at once it was brides this and weddings that and bloody *roses*, if you will!

He looked down at his hand, holding the blue and white porcelain saucer, and saw it was shaking.

The door slid open in a faint rush of well-oiled hinges. "Your shave is ready, sir," said Shelmerstone, and then the slightest intake of breath at the sight of the pool of coffee settling into the priceless rug, surrounded by long, ambitious streaks of brown and, at their tips, the final tiny droplets, still winking atop the rug's tight woolen weave. Without a pause, he snatched the linen napkin from the coffee tray and fell to his knees, blotting, going so far as to murmur a reproachful *Sir!* in the depths of his distress.

Wallingford set down the saucer. "I beg your pardon, Shelmerstone. His Grace has delivered me the devil of a shock."

"What was that, sir?" Shelmerstone asked, covering a sob.

"Marriage," Wallingford said. He added, for clarification, "Mine."

A dreadful pause. "Sir."

"Yes. Most distressing. He's picked out the bride, the date, the damned flowers. I daresay he's chosen her a dress already, and embroidered the pearls himself, God rot him."

Shelmerstone cleared his throat. His face was white, either from the coffee or the bride or some combination of the two. A funereal gravity darkened his voice. "Her name, sir?"

Wallingford squinted his eyes. "It was . . . something like . . . By God. Do you know, Shelmerstone, I don't think he even saw fit to tell me."

"Sir."

"Not that it matters, of course. I shan't do it. I shall tell my grandfather exactly where he can stash his arranged brides." His words sounded hollow in the great cavern of a bedroom, and he knew it. He could hear Shelmerstone's thoughts, as the valet bent over the coffee stain.

Ha. Like to see him try. No going against His Damned Bloody Grace Olympia, when he has one of them ideas in his noggin.

"I believe I shall fetch the bicarbonate," Shelmerstone said faintly, and rose to his feet.

Wallingford fell into the armchair, staring blankly at the room around him. His familiar room, grand and yet with a certain worn comfort, bare of unnecessary decoration, not a flower in sight, his favorite books piled on the nightstand, his aged single-malt Scotch whiskey at the ready. The very notion of a woman inhabiting this sanctum made his mind vibrate with dissonance.

No. No, of course not. Not even the Duke of Olympia would dare such a thing.

True, he'd hand-selected more than one prime minister in the last half century. And the Queen herself had been known to change one or two of her notoriously firm opinions after an hour of private conversation with His Grace.

And there *was* that time he had traveled to Russia aboard his private steam yacht and told the Tsar in no uncertain terms . . .

Good God.

Wallingford leaned forward, put his elbows on his knees, and covered his face with his hands.

There had to be a way out.

He spread his fingers and peered through them. The scent of last night's tossed champagne still hung in his hair, pressing against his nostrils, making him feel slightly queasy. Champagne. Orchids. His brain sloshed about with the memories of last night: the impulsive coupling, banal and sordid, the work of a mere minute or two, and then the sour distaste as he had wiped himself with his handkerchief and looked at the lady's flushed face and perspiring bosom and tried to recall her name.

He needed more coffee. He needed . . .

Something caught his eye, in the stack of books atop his bedside table, next to the coffee tray. Something that was not a book at all.

A tickle began at the base of Wallingford's brain, as if a pair of fingers were nudging him. It felt . . . it felt . . . almost like . . .

An idea.

He rose, paced to the table, and lifted the three topmost volumes.

There it was, beneath the Dickens, atop the Carlyle. A folded newspaper, given to him a month ago, the edges already beginning to yellow under the inexorable poison of oxygen.

Wallingford picked it up and smoothed the page. There, circled in thick black ink, the print as crisp as it had been when Phineas Burke had handed it to him in the breakfast room downstairs, read an advertisement:

*English lords and ladies, and gentlemen of discerning
taste, may take note of a singular opportunity to lease a
most magnificent Castle and Surrounding Estate in the
idyllic hills of Tuscany, the Land of Unending Sunshine.
The Owner, a man of impeccable lineage, whose ancestors have kept the Castle safe against intrusion since the
days of the Medici princes, is called away by urgent business, and offers a year's lease of this unmatched Property at rates extremely favorable for the discerning
traveler. Applicants should enquire through the Owner's
London agent . . .*

A year, Burke had proposed. A year of study and contemplation, free from the distractions of modern life and the female
sex. Four weeks ago, Wallingford had laughed at the idea, once
he had overcome his initial shock that such a notion should even
occur to a sane and able-bodied man, in full possession of his
youthful animal spirits.

A year, free of the interference of the Duke of Olympia, and
his brides and his June weddings. A year—it must be said—free
of recriminations from Cecile de la Fontaine and her vindictive
French temper.

A year free of temptation, free of ducal trappings. In a
remote Italian castle, where nobody knew him, where nobody
had even heard of the Duke of Wallingford.

Wallingford slapped the newspaper back down on the books,
causing the topmost volumes to tumble to the floor in surprise.
He poured himself a cup of coffee, drank it in a single burning
gulp, and stretched his arms to the ceiling.

Why, it was just the thing. A change of scene from gray and
changeless London. He could use a change. He'd been dogged
with a sense of dissatisfaction, of restlessness, long before his
outrageous indiscretion last night, long before Olympia's unwelcome visit this morning.

A year with his brother and his closest friend, both decent
chaps who minded their own business. Tuscany, the land of
unending sunshine. Wine in abundance, and decent food, and
surely a discreet village girl or two if absolutely necessary.

What could possibly go wrong?

ONE

Thirty miles southeast of Florence
March 1890

At the age of fifteen, Miss Abigail Harewood had buried her
mother and gone to live in London with her older sister, the
dazzling young Marchioness of Morley, and her decrepit old
husband the marquis.

Within a week, Abigail had decided she would never marry.

"I shall never marry," she told the stable hand, as she helped
him rub down the wet horses with blankets, "but I should like
to take a lover. I have just turned twenty-three, after all, and it's
high time, don't you think?"

The stable hand, who spoke only a rustic Tuscan dialect,
shrugged and smiled.

"The trouble is, I can't find a suitable prospect. You have no
idea how difficult it is for an unmarried girl of my station to find
a lover. That is, a lover one actually wishes to go to bed with. I
daresay Harry Stubbs down the pub would be delighted; but you
see, he has no teeth. Real ones, I mean."

The stable hand smiled again. His own teeth glinted an
expectedly bright white in the lantern light.

Abigail cocked her head. "Very nice," she said, "but I don't
think we should suit. I should like the sort of lover I could keep
for at least a month or two, since it's such trouble to find one,

and my sister and I shall depart this fine inn of yours tomorrow, as soon as the rain lets up."

The stable hand gave the horse a last pat and reached up to hang the blanket to dry on a rafter. She could have spoken to him in Italian, of course, though his dialect did not quite match the classical version in which she was fluent, but then it was so much easier to speak to people when they couldn't understand one.

The man settled the blanket on the rafter, arms flexing beneath his woolen shirt. Rather a strapping fellow, in fact. And his hair: such a shining extravagant coal black, a little too long and curling just so. Exactly what one wished for in a rustic Italian chap. Abigail's hands stilled on her own blanket, considering.

"I beg your pardon," she said, "may I trouble you for a kiss?"

He dropped his arms and blinked at her. "*Che cosa, signorina?*"

"You see, when I made the decision, on my twenty-third birthday, that I would find myself a lover before the end of the year, I determined to make the search as scientific as possible. One can't be too selective for one's first lover, after all." Abigail gave him an affectionate smile, a smile of shared understanding. "I canvassed the maids and the housekeeper—only the women, you see, for obvious reasons—and they were quite unanimous that the kiss should be the determining factor."

The stable hand's brow furrowed like a field under the plow. "*Che cosa?*" he asked again.

"The kiss, you understand, as a sort of test of each prospect's skill. Tenderness, patience, subtlety, sensitivity to one's partner: All these things, according to my friends, can be divined from the very first kiss. And do you know?" She leaned forward.

"*Signorina?*"

"They were right!" Abigail slid the blanket down the horse's hindquarters and handed it to him. "I kissed two of the footmen, and young Patrick in the stables, and the differences in style and technique were astonishing! Moreover, the manner of kiss, in every case, exactly matched what I might have guessed, judging from their characters."

The stable hand took the blanket from her with a bemused air.

"So you see, I thought perhaps you might be so obliging as

to kiss me as well, in order to round out my experience more thoroughly. Would you mind terribly?"

"*Signorina?*" He stood there, with the blanket in his hand, looking wary. A lantern swung near his head, making his thick black hair glint alluringly. Next to her, the horse gave an impatient stamp and snorted profoundly.

"A kiss," she said. "*Un bacio.*"

His face cleared. "*Un bacio! Si, si, signorina.*"

He tossed Abigail's blanket over the rafter, next to his own, and took her by the shoulders and kissed her.

A tremendous kiss, really. Full of raw enthusiasm, a thorough sort of embrace, his thick lips devouring hers as if he hadn't kissed a girl in months. He smelled of straw and horseflesh, lovely warm stable smells, and his breath tasted surprisingly of sweet bread.

What luck.

Abigail felt his tongue brush hers and, as if it were a signal, she pulled away. His eyes shone down on hers, dark with urgency.

"Thank you," Abigail said. "That was very nice indeed. I suspect you're the ravishing sort, aren't you?"

"*Che cosa?*"

She slipped out of his arms and gave his elbow an affectionate pat. "What a darling fellow you are," she said. "I assure you, I shall remember this forever. Every time I recall our year in Italy, I shall think of you, and this enchanting, er, stableyard. Such a splendid start to an adventure, if rather a wet one."

"*Signorina . . .*"

Abigail switched into Italian. "Now, the other horse, named Angelica, she is a fine mare, but you must watch her for the biting, and make sure she has enough of the oats."

"Oats?" He seemed relieved by the appearance of Abigail's Italian, however flawed.

Abigail picked up her shawl and placed it back over her shoulders. The rain drummed loudly against the roof of the stable, nearly overcoming her words. "I can stay no longer, what desolation. My sister and cousin have been waiting for half an hour, and Alexandra makes objection when I smell too strongly of the stables. She is a very fine lady, my sister."

"That one . . . the great lady . . . she is your sister?"

"Yes. I, too, am astonished. She is a marchioness, though her husband the marquis died two years ago, God forever rest his soul. And you have perhaps seen my cousin Lilibet, who is a countess, very beautiful and virtuous, traveling with her little boy. *She* wouldn't kiss a gentleman in a stable; no, never. But I must be away."

"Signorina . . . I will not see you again?" His voice wavered.

"Tragically, no. But you must be accustomed to such heart-break, working at an inn, isn't it so?" Abigail's gaze fell upon the corner, where an enormous lumpy pile stood covered by a series of thick wool blankets. "Why, what the devil's this?" she asked, in English.

"This?" he replied, in despondent Italian. "Why, it is only the machine left by the English gentleman."

"English gentleman? Here?"

"Why, yes. They arrived not an hour before your party, three of them, great English lords, and left this . . . this . . ." Words failed him. He gestured extravagantly. "Signorina, you will not stay?" he pleaded.

"No, no." She took a few paces toward the pile. "What is it, do you think?"

"This? What does it matter, next to my poor heart?"

"Your heart will recover with great promise, I am certain. The season for foreign travelers has hardly begun." Abigail took hold of the corner of one blanket and lifted it.

A sob wracked the air behind her.

"Well, well," she breathed, in English. "What have we here?"

The Duke of Wallingford's temper, never the docile sort, began to growl about his ears like an awakened terrier. No, no, not a terrier. Like a dragon, a fine fire-breathing dragon, a much more suitable beast for a duke.

Bad enough that the train from Paris to Milan should have no accommodation for his private car, forcing the three of them to travel in a common first-class carriage with decidedly coarse company and execrable sherry. Bad enough that the hotel in Florence should have sprung a leak in its old roof, requiring them to change suites in the middle of the night, to a floor alto-gether too close to the milling streets below. Bad enough that the final leg of the journey from Florence to the Castel sant'Agata should be awash with rain, the bridge ahead swimming, so they should be forced to put up in this . . . this inn of the worst rustic sort, filled with stinking travelers and flat ale and—the final insult, which no merciful God should dare deliver—the forever-damned Dowager Marchioness of Morley and her suite of assorted relatives.

Demanding his own private rooms for *her* party, no less.

The Marchioness of Morley. Wallingford had kissed her once, he remembered, on a long-ago London balcony, when she was a debutante and ought to have known better than to find herself in a shaded corner with a notorious duke. Or perhaps she *had* known better. She had certainly looked up at him with a rather knowing eye for a nineteen-year-old.

She was looking up at him now, with those same warm brown eyes, turned up at the ends like those of a particularly smug cat, doing her best to look beseeching. Her hands wrung away in front of her immaculate waist. "Look here, Wallingford, I really must throw myself on your mercy. Surely you see our little dilemma. Your rooms are ever so much larger, palatial, really, and *two* of them! You can't possibly, in all conscience . . ." She paused and cast a speculative glance at Wallingford's brother. "My dear Penhallow. Think of poor Lilibet, sleeping in . . . in a *chair*, quite possibly . . . with all these strangers . . ."

Just like Lady Morley, to play on poor Roland's schoolboy affection for her cousin Elizabeth, now the Countess of Somerton: that peach-cheeked beauty, that siren of sirens. The devil's own luck, that Lord Roland Penhallow's long-lost love should lurk in this godforsaken Italian innyard, waiting to launch herself back into his tender heart.

If indeed it *was* mere luck.

Next to Wallingford, Burke seemed to sense the threat. He cleared his throat with an ominous rumble before Roland could answer. "Did it not, perhaps, occur to you, Lady Morley, to reserve rooms in advance?"

Lady Morley turned to him with the full force of her cat-eyed glare. She had to look upward, and upward, until at last she found his face. "As a matter of fact, it did, Mr. . . . ." She made a terrifying rise of those eyebrows, which could lay waste to all fashionable London. "I'm so terribly sorry, sir. I don't *quite* believe I caught your name."

Wallingford smiled. "I beg your pardon, Lady Morley. How remiss of me. I have the great honor to present to you—perhaps you may have come across his name, in your philosophical studies—Mr. Phineas Fitzwilliam Burke, of the Royal Society."

"Your servant, madam," Burke said. His voice betrayed no intimidation of any kind. A rock, old Burke, despite his shock of ginger hair and his unnatural height. He stood there, in the bustling common room of the inn, as if he were still in his workshop, surrounded by machine parts, lord and master of all he surrounded.

It was the Olympia in him, Wallingford thought with pride.

"Burke," Lady Morley said, and then her eyes widened an instant. "Phineas Burke. Of course. The Royal Society. Yes, of course. Everybody knows of Mr. Burke. I found . . . the *Times*, last month . . . your remarks on electrical . . . that new sort of . . ." She gathered herself. "That is to say, of course we reserved rooms. I sent the wire days ago, if memory serves. But we were delayed in Milan. The boy's nursemaid took ill, you see, and I expect our message did not reach our host in time." She turned her displeased gaze toward the landlord, who cowered nearby.

Wallingford opened his mouth to deliver a thundering ducal set-down, but before he could gather his words into the appropriate mixture of irony and authority, the warm voice of his brother Roland intruded, rich with the full measure of its damned puppylike friendliness, cheerfully surrendering the fort even before Lady Somerton had appeared for battle.

"Look here," said Lord Roland Penhallow, a golden joy shining through his words to match the gleaming golden brown of his hair. "Enough of this rubbish. We shouldn't dream of causing any inconvenience to you and your friends, Lady Morley. Not for an instant. Should we, Wallingford?"

Wallingford folded his arms. They were sunk. "No, damn it."

"Burke?"

"Bloody hell," muttered Burke. He knew it, too.

Roland flashed his hazel eyes in that ridiculous way of his, the way the entire idiot female half of humanity found unaccountably irresistible. "You see, Lady Morley? All quite willing and happy and so on. I daresay Burke can take the little room upstairs, as he's such a tiresome, misanthropic old chap, and my brother and I shall be quite happy to . . ."—he swept his arm to take in the dark depths of the common room—"make ourselves comfortable downstairs. Will that suit?"

Lady Morley clasped her elegant gloved hands together. "Darling Penhallow. I knew you'd oblige us. Thanks so *awfully*, my dear; you can't imagine how thankful I am for your generosity." She turned to the landlord. "Do you understand? *Comprendo?* You may remove His Grace's luggage from the rooms upstairs and bring up our trunks at once. Ah! Cousin Lilibet! There you are at last. Have you sorted out the trunks?"

Wallingford turned.

There she stood in the doorway, the source of their trouble, the dear and virtuous and terribly beautiful Countess of Somerton. Did it matter that she was married to that beast Somerton? Did it matter that her scrap of a son clung to her hand, visible proof of her sexual congress with that same earl? It did not. Roland turned his besotted gaze toward her, and everything fell into shambles, the entire plan, a year of hiding away in the Tuscan hills beyond rumor, beyond the reach of the Duke of Olympia. Roland would make a fool of himself, and the tale would reach London, and within a week Olympia would be pounding on the door of the Castel sant'Agata, no doubt dragging Wallingford's intended bride by the hand.

Lady Somerton unbuttoned the boy's coat and said something to Lady Morley about the luggage. She rose in a lithe movement and began to unfasten her own coat.

Roland stood transfixed. A breath of air escaped him, rather like a pant.

"Oh, for God's sake," muttered Wallingford.

"I take it they know each other?" asked Burke, in his driest voice.

Wallingford gave Roland a sharp poke in his ribs. "Keep your tongue in your mouth, you dog," he began, and stopped short, because an apparition had just appeared behind the prim dark wool shoulder of Lady Somerton.

Wallingford could not say, afterward, why the young lady should have struck him so. He could not have said whether she was beautiful or not. She danced into view, her delicate features sparkling with rain, her eyes and face alight: a sprite of some kind, a fairy, full of some mysterious energy that seemed to burst from her skin.

Wallingford stood immobile. The buzz of voices hollowed out around him.

The apparition hovered for an instant next to Lady Somerton and gave her head a little shake. A fine spray of rain scattered from the brim of her hat. She cast about, and for an inexplicable and boundless instant Wallingford felt that she was looking for *him*, that this strange fairy had entered a remote Italian inn for the express purpose of discovering his soul.

But her gaze did not meet his. She instead found an object to his left, and her face, if possible, lit further. She darted forward, right up to Lady Morley, and said, in a voice of purely human excitement: "Alex, darling, you won't believe what I've found in the stables!"

Alex, darling?

The words snapped Wallingford back to consciousness. He started. He stared at Lady Morley. He stared at the girl. Lady Morley was wrinkling her nose, saying something about the stables, unbuttoning the girl's coat, calling her *Abigail* in a voice of deep familiarity. They stood in profile to him, outlined by the golden glow of the fire, and he could trace the two straight noses, the two firm little chins, in exact replica of each other. Lady Morley removed the girl's hat, and out sprang a nest of unruly chestnut hair, the same shade as her own.

Alex, darling.

Burke's hand landed on his shoulder. Burke's voice said something about sitting down to dinner. Wallingford said, "Yes, of course," and dropped upon the bench. His brain was burning.

Lady Morley's sister. This dainty fairy, this sweet apparition, like nothing he had ever seen before, was Lady Morley's little *sister.*

He was damned.

Abigail Harewood sat in a hideous bile green paisley armchair in the corner of the bedroom, her feet tucked up under her dress, and contemplated her sketchbook.

Not that she meant to sketch anything. Not, in fact, that she had sketched much at all during the voyage to Italy, despite her best intentions, which had loosely imagined a portfolio bursting with atmospheric depictions of towering Swiss peaks and rough-hewn peasant faces. No, the sketchbook lay in her lap with nearly all of its sheets still blank, except for an abandoned pencil drawing of the Milan cathedral (defeated by the gargoyles) and the pristine paper before her, which contained two words: *La stalla.*

"Philip, darling," said Lilibet, from across the room, "do stop unbuttoning your pajamas and get into bed."

Her voice was strained. Philip, who had been penned all day in a jostling coach, its windows streaming with rain, showed no particular inclination for sleep just yet. He leapt atop the mattress and began to jump. "Look, I'm an acrobat, Mama! Abigail, look!" His unbuttoned pajama shirt flopped against his lean five-year-old chest.

"Very credible, Philip," called out Abigail. "Let's see a somersault."

"Oh, jolly fun," said Philip.

"No!" Lilibet reached out and secured his arms with her hands, just as the boy bent his knees for a particularly bold and somersault-inducing jump. "Abigail, really. You know he does whatever you tell him."

"My mistake, Philip," said Abigail contritely. "No somersaults, unless your mother is quite out of the room."

"*Abigail.*"

She stretched out her toes to the nearby fire, simmering with intense and comforting heat in its nest of charcoal ash, and returned to the paper in front of her.

The Duke of Wallingford. She had never met him before. He had never come around any of Alexandra's salons and parties, and Abigail rarely went out in society. Conventional society, that is. When Abigail had vowed not to marry all those years ago, she had not stopped short at a mere negative promise. (Abigail, as a rule, did not stop short anywhere.) She had not been satisfied with resolving not to make a conventional marriage; she had vowed, in fact, to do her utmost to live the least conventional life available to her.

It had not been easy. In the early days, most of her allowance went to bribing the footmen and the housemaids: losses that she attempted to recoup through gambling, to mixed success. She was generally hopeless at cards, for she could not attempt to hide her emotions behind the appropriate mask of expressionless indifference, but eventually she found a reliable bookmaker and discovered she had a talent for picking horses.

Still, between the bribery and the hackney fares, the rounds of pints to keep the drunks at her local happy, and the occasional spectacular loss when her horses failed to gallop home in the correct order, she lived on the constant edge of bankruptcy. And then, occasionally, her sister Alexandra would remember her existence and call upon her to attend some shopping expedition or private dinner party, and she had to scramble to cancel her low engagements, and dress in the required white dress and pearls, and remember not to swagger or to profane the Lord's name or to discuss tomorrow's card at Newmarket.

Dukes, therefore, had not often appeared at her right hand and sat down to dinner with her. They were generally glimpsed from afar, and were generally of the white-haired, weak-chinned, short-and-stooping variety, cane handles hooked over their arms, silk top hats shining in the Ascot sun.

Wallingford was not short, nor did he stoop. He had not exactly invited her to dinner, either; that was his brother's doing, that darling Lord Roland with the golden brown hair and melting hazel eyes, who was evidently dying for love of her beautiful cousin Lilibet. (Not that Abigail could fault him for *that*.)

No, Wallingford was a different sort of duke altogether, a duke of the old order, tall and dark-haired and fierce-eyed, crackling with power and magnificently disagreeable. She had troubled him for the salt, and he had glowered at her with all the thunderous astonishment of a feudal lord addressed unexpectedly by his serving wench.

Oh, the shivers.

He was the *one*. There was no question that the Duke of Wallingford should be her first lover. Physically, he possessed every possible advantage: she particularly admired his lush dark hair, which would twine very handsomely around her fingers during the act of love, to say nothing of the uncompromising width of his shoulders, which might prove useful should he be forced, for example, to carry her across a raging river at some point in their liaison.

Moreover, Wallingford undoubtedly had the experience to

pull off the affair in a most satisfactory fashion. Abigail had made considerable research into erotic literature—an astonishing amount of it in circulation; staggering, really—and concluded that a man of experience was infinitely more master of the task at hand than some sweet but green young fellow, who would almost certainly become overexcited and make a short-lived mess of things.

Abigail could not conceive of the Duke of Wallingford in a state of overexcitement.

The air split with the sound of Philip's voice, raised in a series of hooting calls. Abigail looked up and found him racing around the room, pajama shirt flapping, Lilibet in helpless pursuit. His hand beat against his mouth, creating the hooting call.

Abigail stuck out her leg and brought him to a halt. "Philip, what on earth are you doing?" she asked.

"I'm a wild Indian!" he shouted, straining against her leg.

"Oh! Of course you are. Carry on, then." She retracted her leg and set him free, just as Lilibet swooped in to capture him.

"*Abigail!*" Lilibet said desperately.

Abigail fiddled her lead sketching pencil around her fingers. "Lilibet, dear, he's been stuck in a carriage all day. You ought to have made him run laps around the innyard, directly when we arrived. He wants a little exercise, that's all."

"I shall remember this, Abigail, when you have children of your own." Lilibet gave up and sat on the bed in a great tangle of petticoats and heavy dark blue wool, watching Philip circle around her.

Abigail looked down at the paper before her. The trouble, of course, was that the duke and his party only meant to stay here the one night, before trudging off through the dank late-winter gloom to whatever oasis of pleasure awaited them. One night was certainly not enough. Brazen she might be, but Abigail still required a little wooing to get things off on the proper footing, and besides, she wanted a real love affair: a matter of several months, full of passion and pleasure and clandestine arrangements, before it came to a dramatic end when she caught him in some infidelity, or when he was forced to marry and breed more dukes, at the exact moment when all that passion and pleasure began to fade into routine. She would throw a few vases at his head, he would grasp her by the shoulders and kiss her one last desperate time, and she would order him from the room and weep for days, or at least hours.

It would be perfect.

But damned difficult to arrange, when she was on her way to a year's exile in the Tuscan hills.

Well, what was the point of anything, without a little challenge to keep one on one's toes?

Abigail chewed thoughtfully on the end of her pencil, considering various scenarios, constructing mental images of a naked Wallingford in various attitudes, and at last scribbled a single Italian sentence on the paper. (The duke, she knew, would be much more inclined to accept an amorous invitation from an Italian serving maid than from the maiden sister of the Dowager Marchioness of Morley.) She folded the paper, placed it in her pocket, and rose from her chair, just as Philip shot by on his way to the door.

She caught him in her arms and rubbed his taut little belly with her nose. "Naughty boy," she said, laughing. "Naughty, wicked, despicable boy."

"Abigail, you'll overexcite him," said Lilibet, looking indescribably weary.

Poor Lilibet. If Abigail needed any further persuasion that she should never marry, she had only to look at her cousin: betrayed and belittled and God knew what else by a promiscuous husband who regarded her with rather less interest than the cut of meat for his dinner. All this, despite her beauty and charm and good nature, despite her implacable virtue. Lilibet's faithless beast of a husband was the very reason they were fleeing to Italy in the first place.

Abigail blew another raspberry into Philip's tummy and tossed him atop the blankets. "You don't deserve a story, you dreadful rascal, but I'll tell one anyway," she said.

A quarter hour later, Philip's eyes were closed, and his chest rose and fell in the steady rhythm of an exhausted sleep. Lilibet, looking equally exhausted, sank into the bile green chair and gazed with her weary blue eyes at her resting son. "Go back downstairs, Abigail," she said. "I'll watch him."

"And leave you by yourself?"

Lilibet looked up at her with a gentle smile. "Abigail, darling, I know very well that you're desperate to go back down to that common room. Don't think I didn't see the way you were examining poor Wallingford."

Abigail felt an unfamiliar surge of defensiveness. "I wasn't. He's a perfectly ordinary duke. There are *princes* in Italy, Lilibet. *Princes.* Much more interesting than dull English dukes."

Lilibet waved at her. "Go, Abigail. I'm all done in, really. Go, for heaven's sake."

A thump rattled the floorboards beneath them. The faint sound of merry voices raised in a scattered and unmistakably drunken chorus, quite improper for impressionable young English ladies. No responsible matron ought to send her cousin into the scene of such iniquity, and yet Lilibet seemed not to notice, or to care. Her eyes remained steady on the bundle of blankets in the bed.

Abigail knew better than to push her luck.

"Right-ho, then," she said cheerfully, and hurried out the door.

TWO

At least his horse was happy to see him, thought the Duke of Wallingford, though the apples likely had something to do with it.

"A greedy old fellow, aren't you, my love," he said, observing the steady disintegration of the apple in his gloved palm. When it had disappeared, he removed the glove and scratched the horse's forelock. "I shouldn't be here, of course. It's liable to lead to all sorts of trouble."

The horse snorted and pushed at his chest, leaving a dribble of apple specks on his coat.

"Easy for you to say, old fellow," he said. "You've got no balls to speak of."

A whuffle, low in the equine throat.

"It's a blessing, I assure you," said Wallingford, scratching his way down the horse's forehead, leaving no spot of exquisite sensitivity untouched. The animal stretched his neck with pleasure. "They're nothing but bother, women, excepting only a few brief and fleeting moments. And with this one, not even that, unless I'm an even greater blackguard than my grandfather makes out."

Above his head, the rain drummed against the tile roof of the stable, but inside the air was filled with damp warmth, with the familiar smells of straw and horseflesh and manure: simple earthy smells, the smell of youth and contentment.

"I wonder what she means by it," Wallingford continued, in a low voice. He moved his hand to the horse's neck and stroked the thick winter coat, its reddish bay color subdued to brown in the dull glow of the dark lantern hanging nearby. "She's got no business making appointments in the stables. Do you know, she wrote the note in Italian? As if I might think the serving maid had written it?" He shook his head. "I'm a damned fool, aren't I? Too long without female companionship. Four weeks, Lucifer."

Lucifer sighed with pleasure and lowered his head.

"Lost my head, I think. Nothing but an ordinary girl. Brown hair, brown eyes. Well, not brown exactly. More of a golden sort of color, dark gold, like sherry. Lighter than her sister's. And her face! The features are like enough, but it's a completely different effect, a sort of freshness and delicacy I can't quite describe . . ."

"Signore?"

The voice lilted through the dusky air.

Wallingford placed his forehead against the horse's neck and inhaled deeply. "You needn't bother, Miss Harewood. I know who you are."

"Oh, dash it," said Miss Harewood, with considerably less sweetness. "Why did you come, then?"

He inhaled once more, straightened, and turned.

There she stood, the dust motes floating about her, a fine woolen scarf wound around her head. She looked at him inquiringly, her light brown eyes widened into impossible roundness, tilted just so at the corners, exactly the same shape as her sister's; except while the slant of Lady Morley's eyes had always reminded Wallingford of a particularly stealthy cat, on Abigail Harewood those eyes took on an elfin grace, a mischievous fairy charm. She lifted the scarf away from her head, and the hair beneath caught the lantern in a gleam of rich chestnut.

"Your Grace?" she prodded.

He shook himself. "I came," he said, schooling his voice into ducal deepness, "in order to educate you on the wholesale impropriety of making appointments with strangers in the stables. Since your sister, it seems, is unequal to the task."

"But you're not a stranger," she said, smiling. "We spoke for quite an hour at dinner."

"Don't even *think* to match wits with me, young lady."

"Ooh!" She shivered. "Say that again, *do.*"

"I said, don't even . . ." He stopped and folded his arms across his chest. "Look here, what are you really doing here? You know the rules as well as I do."

"Oh, I know the rules as well as anyone. One has to know the rules perfectly in order to break them." She was still smiling, still unearthly, lightening the very air around her.

Break them.

Wallingford's groin, that seat of instinct rather than reason, tightened unto bursting in a single instant.

"Good God." The words struggled out. "You don't mean . . ."

She laughed and held up her hand. "Oh no! Not so far as that. I understand that anticipation is vital in these matters."

"Anticipation?" he said dazedly.

"Yes, anticipation. Of course, you're the expert, but I think we should go no further than a kiss tonight, don't you think?"

"A kiss?"

She laughed. "You sound exactly like the stableboy, before dinner. '*Un bacio,*' he said, in exactly that tone of voice."

Wallingford took a stumbling step backward. "*Stableboy?*"

"Oh yes. He was rather startled, I suppose, but he recovered quickly . . ."

"I daresay."

". . . and stepped up to the mark quite nicely. I say, is that your horse? He's a jolly splendid animal, aren't you, darling?" She brushed past him and took Lucifer's face between her hands. "Yes, a dear love, a remarkable great beast you are, a splendid, lovely animal."

Lucifer, enraptured, pushed his nose against her chest and whuffled.

Wallingford shook his head. "Look here, Miss Harewood. Do you mean to say you kissed the stableboy? *Here?*"

"Yes, and a lovely embrace it was. Much nicer than the stableboy at home."

"The stableboy at *home?*" The floor seemed to be dropping away beneath Wallingford's booted feet. He put out a hand to steady himself against the wooden wall of Lucifer's stall.

"Yes. Patrick was his name." She turned to him. "The brother of one of my sister's housemaids. Oh! Ha-ha. I see what you're thinking. No, no. I assure you, I don't go about kissing stableboys willy-nilly, hither and yon. Heavens, no!" She laughed. She had her arm up around the side of Lucifer's face, stroking him, and Wallingford could have sworn that the animal winked at him.

"Forgive me, Miss Harewood, for jumping to such an unwarranted conclusion."

"Oh, how forbidding you are! You must keep your brow exactly like that. How did Shakespeare put it? *'Let the brow o'erwhelm it as fearfully as doth a galled rock o'erhang and jutty his confounded base, swilled with the wild and wasteful ocean . . .'"*

"Are you quite mad?"

"No, no. Only a *little* mad, I assure you. No, as I said, I don't go about kissing stableboys as a rule. It's more in the line of an experiment."

"You *are* quite mad."

"Well, that's easy for you to say. I daresay you've had the unceasing attention of dairymaids and housemaids from the moment your trousers were first lengthened."

Wallingford opened his mouth to object, but nothing came out.

"You see? Whereas I, as a gently bred young lady, reached my twenty-third birthday a month or so ago . . ."

"Twenty-three!"

"Yes." She sighed. "I know, this ridiculous face of mine. In any case, there I was, twenty-three years old, by my sacred honor, and the situation seemed desperate. I determined to find myself a lover before the year was out."

"A lover? Why not a husband?"

"Oh, I don't plan to marry. Not unless I'm forced to wed some odious millionaire banker by my evil and impecunious uncle, who has kidnapped Alexandra and dangled her above a pit of poisonous vipers in order to gain my acquiescence . . ."

"A pit of vipers?"

"Or cobras. They're quite poisonous, I believe. Or one of those snakes native to the antipodes; do you know, I read once that six of the ten most venomous reptiles in the world are found in Australia. It makes one wonder why anyone would live there, though I suppose many of them hadn't any choice."

A little silence.

Wallingford cleared his throat.

"And barring such deadly maneuvers, you wish instead to lead a life of infamy, to degrade yourself before God and man . . ."

"Oh, listen to you!" She stroked Lucifer's ears and smiled again, a little wistfully this time. "Tell me, Your Grace, how old were you when you took your first dairymaid?"

Fifteen. The answer nearly left Wallingford's lips, so accurately had she assessed him, before he recollected himself and bit it back. Fifteen, and spending the summer at the family seat in the north, his mother convalescing by the seaside from her latest miscarriage and his father drawing his last ragged breaths in the ancient bedroom of the Dukes of Wallingford, done in by drink and excess and a bad fall from a horse that had punctured his already ravaged liver. Fifteen and quite alone, left to himself, his older sister married and his brother staying with an aunt. He had wandered about the estate every day, with the giant specter of impending dukehood staring him in the face, lonely and randy as only an adolescent boy could be. The dairymaid—yes, it was a dairymaid, blast that Miss Harewood—had secured him without any trouble.

Afterward, he had not felt degraded at all, neither before man nor before God. That had all come later.

"Do not attempt that argument with me, Miss Harewood," he said. "We are not here to debate the differences between men and women."

"I quite agree. We should be here all night, I daresay, for you seem as thickheaded and stubborn as any man I ever met. In any case, my maid assured me that if I wished to find the best sort of lover, I must try out a few young men with kisses in order to understand what sort of chap I was looking for. I began with John the footman . . ."

"John the *footman*?"

"And then his brother James, also a footman . . ."

"Of course."

She was counting on her long gloved fingers. "And then Patrick, just before we left. So you see, it was hardly a campaign of licentiousness, by any means. Merely curiosity."

Wallingford looked down at her slim figure, the fairylike delicacy of her face, and slammed his fist against the old wooden pillar holding up the roof. "But the risk! Good God! No man wants to stop at a mere kiss!"

"Why not?"

"Because there's no point. It's nothing but preliminary, which is why respectable young women don't engage in it."

"Nonsense. Kissing's very nice by itself, it seems to me, if done properly. Do you mean to say you've never kissed merely for the sake of kissing?"

"No," said Wallingford, but as the word left his mouth he knew it was a lie. There had been a time, of course, when kissing seemed like the sweetest pleasure known to man. When the dairymaid had drawn him down into the summer-ripened grass of the meadow and brought his mouth to hers, and they had kissed and kissed, and he had not dared even to put his hand beneath her skirts to touch her leg, had not even dreamed of pulling down her dress to see her bosom. No, he had thought of nothing but her mouth, and her sweet little tongue touching his, and they had lain there kissing for an hour until overrun by the cows.

Of course, she had taken his virginity in the hayloft a week later, which quite eclipsed all that came before. But for that first innocent hour, her kisses had been enough. They had been everything to him.

"No," Wallingford repeated, "and no man stops at kissing, when he can get more, by persuasion or by force, if he's desperate and blackguardly enough. You were quite out of your depth, Miss Harewood, and it's a wonder you weren't ravished and ruined."

"Why, as to that, Harry Stubbs showed me a tidy little maneuver to render a man unconscious instantly, so I'm quite . . ."

"Who the devil's Harry Stubbs?"

"One of the chaps down the pub. Kind old fellow, taught me all I know about picking horses. He used to be a forger, you know, before he took up bookmaking."

Wallingford struggled for air. He wrapped his hand around the pillar and gazed down at the sincere sherry gold eyes of Miss Abigail Harewood, at her full lips curved in a little smile, at her skin glowing like sunlit cream.

"Miss Harewood," he said, in a voice just above a whisper, "you are quite the most extraordinary person I've ever met."

Her eyebrows lifted; her eyes shone. "Why, thank you! I take that as a great compliment. I daresay you've met all sorts of interesting people, in your position."

"I didn't mean it as a compliment, in fact."

"Oh, Your Grace." She turned and placed a kiss on Lucifer's broad nose. "You have so much to learn about women."

He felt affronted. "I know all I need to know, as it happens. I know, for example, that you've no business skulking about unchaperoned in Italian stableyards in the middle of the night, and ought to be making your way back to your room this instant."

"I can't do that." She tilted her head a fraction and looked up at him from the corner of her eye, and Wallingford was lost, *lost*, the entire world dissolving around him and leaving only this beautiful and bewitching creature with her turned-up sherry gold eyes, regarding him as if she knew his every secret.

"Why not?" he gasped.

"Because you haven't kissed me yet." She turned slowly to face him. "Unless you don't mean to kiss me at all, of course."

A wave of rain passed over the stable roof, a distant rumble of thunder. The lantern wavered; the entire building seemed to groan around them. Lucifer shifted his feet, turned his long neck, and trained his pointed ears in Wallingford's direction.

As if to say, *Well, old chap?*

There was no question, was there? He had no choice at all. Not from the moment Miss Abigail Harewood had first danced into the shelter of the inn, shaking the rain from her hat in a halo of sparkles.

He took a step forward. "Has no one ever told you, Miss Harewood," he said, in a growl, "you must be very careful what you wish for?"

She tilted her head back. "Oh," she said, faintly, rapturously, and put her palms against his chest. "Bergamot."

"Bergamot?"

"You smell of bergamot. I'm absolutely *mad* for bergamot."

For an instant, he gazed down at her face, almost dizzy at the way she strained upward in delight and anticipation. When was the last time a lady had looked at him like that, so natural and unfeigned? He loved her face; he loved her expression. He lifted his hands and cradled her head, his palms holding the curve of her jaw and his fingers reaching up into her hair.

He bent down and kissed her mouth, and quite without warning he—*he,* the stately Duke of Wallingford—was fifteen again, and the sun warmed the back of his head, and the summer-ripened grass tickled his face with its sweetness, and a girl's full lips moved ardently against his as if he were an object of priceless value, as if she never meant to stop. As if kissing were all that existed in the world.

But *these* lips tasted of wine and dessert, *this* skin smelled of wool and soap instead of cow dung and sour milk. This was Abigail Harewood, enchanted little elf, shimmering with life and youth and imagination enough for both of them, and she pressed herself into his chest, wavering slightly, as if she were standing on her toes in an effort to close the gap between them.

Wallingford lifted his head. "Miss Harewood," he whispered.

"Abigail," she said.

He brought his hands to her waist, lifted her, and carried her a few tottering steps to the wall next to Lucifer's stall. She felt light and supple in his arms, her bones fine and strong beneath her coat and dress and petticoats. He let her slide gently down the wall as he kissed her again, passionately now, running his tongue along the crease of her lips.

"Oh," she breathed out, and in the opening of her mouth he deepened the kiss.

She lay flat against the wall now, her feet resting on the floor. He brought his forearms on either side of her face, bracing himself as he kissed her, because she met him with such eagerness he could not hold himself steady. Her arms reached up around his neck; her mouth opened up and shivered at the intrusion of his tongue. His legs were planted on either side of hers, and she twined one booted foot around his calf, linking them together at every point.

Dimly, Wallingford heard Lucifer snort in disgust.

"Bugger off," he said, from the corner of his mouth.

"What's that?" gasped Miss Harewood.

Lucifer's nose shoved at his arm.

"I said, *bugger off,*" growled Wallingford; then to Abigail, "Nothing, darling," and he set back to work, immersing himself in the caramel sweetness of her mouth, the tender give-and-take of her tongue and lips. At the back of his brain, an alarm was beginning to pound out, that Miss Abigail Harewood was no dairymaid, no restless wife of a foreign diplomat, and he had better obey the sage advice of his own horse and cease this nonsense directly.

But the back of his brain was very, very far away.

"Oh," said Miss Harewood, pulling her lips away a fraction. "Oh, Wallingford." The words brushed his mouth, absorbed into his skin. "Oh, that was lovely. Thanks ever so much."

Her booted foot unwrapped itself from around his leg.

"Thanks?" he repeated stupidly. His brain whirled in an eager spiral of desire and bliss.

"That was quite the nicest kiss yet." She slipped her hands from the nape of his neck and patted one cheek, as she might reassure a lapdog. "You will do splendidly."

"Do . . . *splendidly*?"

Wallingford's arms were still braced against the wall. In a graceful movement, she ducked beneath them and slipped her shawl over her head. Her eyes, he noted without thought, sparkled beautifully beneath the shifting glow of the stable lantern.

"Yes. But I must fly, before the others wonder where I've gone. It's very useful to have a reputation for absconding, but even Alexandra's patience has its limits." She gave his cheek another pat. "Dear me, you look quite dumbfounded."

"I am not . . . I am . . . What the devil?" he said helplessly.

She smiled. "Never fear. I'm quite sure we shall find each other again soon. I'm a great believer in fate, and why else should our paths have crossed? You *shall* be my first lover. I'm certain of it. Oh dear! Half past ten already! I must fly."

"Look here . . ."

But she was already kissing his cheek, already securing her coat collar about her neck. She dropped a kiss on Lucifer's nose and bent to pick something up from the doorway: an umbrella, large and practical.

"Miss Harewood!"

She turned and put her finger to her mouth. "Don't follow me! What if someone should see us?"

And she was gone.

Wallingford sagged back against the wall, every muscle slack and stunned. Lucifer pushed against his arm, gentler now. The horse's large brown eye regarded him with liquid sympathy.

"Don't even think it," said Wallingford. "Nothing's changed. I did not flee a thousand miles from one scheming young lady only to fall victim to another."

Lucifer blinked his large eye.

"After all, she's not duchess material. Not at all."

Lucifer reached for his net of hay and snagged a few stalks. Wallingford lay breathing against the wooden boards, gazing at a point just to the left of the lantern.

"I don't know what came over me. Lost my head entirely."

Lucifer made no answer. He was entirely absorbed in his hay.

Wallingford straightened and drew a deep breath. "In any case, that's that. I shall never see her again, or at least not for years, when we're all back in London and married off and all that. Shall be quite happy to be her first lover *then*, ha-ha." His hat had fallen from his head; he fished around on the ground and replaced it on his head, pulling the woolen brim snugly down his forehead. "Mad as a hatter, that one."

Lucifer lipped his hay ruminatively.

"That's that," he said again, and started forward through the stable door. His muscles, he found, had a rather curious feel: almost like jelly. And his lips seemed burned, swollen, impossibly sensitive.

The rain pattered down against his back; the inn loomed like a black shadow across the yard. He shoved his hands in his pockets and hurried forward, looking down to avoid the puddles, and collided with a resounding thump against the familiar brown wool chest of his brother.

"What ho!" said Lord Roland. "Out for a walk?"

Wallingford's swollen lips opened and closed. "Yes, a walk," he said. "Fresh air."

"Fresh air, that's the thing," said Lord Roland, as the rain poured off the brim of his woolen cap.

They stared at each other.

"Well, I'm off," said Wallingford, dodging to Roland's right.

"Right-ho!" said Roland, dodging left.

In the common room, there was no sign of her. Not that he was looking, really; one's eyes naturally searched about a room, on entering. One's ears naturally tuned for the sound of a human voice. It didn't mean one was looking, or listening, for any person in particular.

Heavens, no.

The landlord and his wife were bustling about in the corner, setting up straw pallets and spreading wool blankets. Wallingford gazed in dawning horror.

His straw pallet. *His* wool blanket.

A few men still huddled about one of the trestle tables, muttering and laughing. At another, Phineas Burke sat by himself, flaming ginger head in his hands, staring at a glass of grappa as if he expected it to shake itself off and perform a jig.

Wallingford sat down next to him with a rainy plop.

"You're wet," said Burke, without looking up.

"I daresay."

The bottle sat next to Burke's left elbow. Wallingford eyed it, picked it up, sloshed it about. Not much left. He tipped it up and drained the last drop. The wine tingled against his kiss-swollen lips.

"I daresay the women are setting up quite comfortably upstairs," Wallingford said.

"No doubt."

"No straw pallets for their ladyships' precious backsides."

"No, indeed."

Wallingford set his wet hat down on the table before him and gazed at the woolen houndstooth. "Well, it's just one night, I suppose," he said. "We'll be on our way tomorrow, and won't have anything more to do with them, praise God."

"Except for the wager." Burke drank the rest of his wine and set down the glass with a precise and deliberate stroke of his wrist. "The wager you proposed with Lady Morley, over dessert."

There was something accusing about Burke's tone, something foreboding. Wallingford staggered backward in his mind to dessert, only a couple of hours ago, at this very table. Miss Harewood and Lady Somerton had retired with the boy, leaving him oddly out of sorts. Lady Morley had been as baiting as ever and he—as ever—had risen to the bait. It seemed like another age, another Wallingford. "Now, look here," he said, feeling defensive. "You had something to do with that wager, remember? You proposed the stakes."

"So I did." Burke stood abruptly, swinging his long legs over the bench, and picked up his hat.

"Where are you going?" Wallingford demanded.

Burke settled the hat firmly on his forehead. His face was grim, his green eyes dark with determination. In fact, exactly the way he looked when Wallingford was foolish enough to interrupt him in his mechanical experiments.

"Out," Burke said, in a voice as grim as his face. "For a walk."

Wallingford drew a long sigh. "In that case, I'd suggest an umbrella."

THREE

People, Abigail knew, were rather like horses. Some were mudders, and some were not.

Her sister Alexandra was decidedly *not* a mudder.

Abigail—who prided herself on a cheerful willingness to plow through whatever weather was thrown in her direction—endeavored simply to ignore both the rain and Alexandra's complaints, and took refuge in warming thoughts. Specifically, the warming thought of the Duke of Wallingford kissing her in the stables last night.

She hoped he hadn't noticed how flustered she was. Flustered? She'd been in a transport, shocked and shimmering, her entire body overturned by the mere action of his mouth on hers, by the way his long and immense body had flattened her against the stable wall, by the scent of bergamot from his skin and the taste of wine on his lips. She tried, now, to remember exactly what had happened—which parts of her had tingled, where she had ached and melted—but the sensations defied description.

She had simply been alive.

Alive.

And now?

Well, a little numbness, a little anticlimax, was only to be expected.

Abigail trudged on into the dank Tuscan morning. Her boots sucked valiantly against the mud. The rain was letting up, a mere drizzle now, but the mud remained: heavy and viscous, snatching greedily at her feet with every stride. Before her, the baggage cart slowed. The horses, poor beasts, were straining into their harness. Somewhere ahead of them, the Castel sant'Agata rose up from the remote and rocky hills, refuge and sanctuary, their home for the next year. Untroubled, so the plan went, by visitors of any sort, and by lovers most particularly.

What now, then? She had slipped away in the nick of time last night, flushing and trembling, throwing her scarf up around her head so he wouldn't see how thoroughly his kiss had affected her. The Duke of Wallingford had probably kissed dozens of women, if not more. He would laugh if he knew what effect he'd had on Abigail's inexperienced lips. No, far better to leave and recompose herself. It would never do to let such a man gain the upper hand.

It would never do to let *any* man gain the upper hand.

But in fleeing, had she not given up her last opportunity? Last night, with Wallingford so warm and real beside her, their next meeting had felt so inevitable, the logical act of a fate desperate to bring them together. Here, amid the wet rocks and cold mud, the drizzle and the mist and the laboring horses, the Duke of Wallingford and his iron arms and his mad ardent kisses seemed as distant as the other side of the world.

As distant as the sun itself.

What on earth had she been thinking, running away like that, expecting him to . . . *what*? To pop on over to the Castel sant'Agata next week? Rap on the door and drag her to some convenient tapestry-draped bedroom and complete his seduction?

What a fool. What a silly, frightened fool she'd been. Now, she might wait for another year before such an opportunity arose again.

An unfamiliar sensation invaded Abigail's chest. She couldn't name it. It crept across her heart, cold and hollow and lonely, and yet as heavy as a blacksmith's anvil. It seemed to weigh her very footsteps, to suck against her boots like the mud itself. Could it be . . . no, it could *not*, this was not at all in Abigail's nature, she *never* succumbed to such things and wouldn't start now. Yet there was no other word but . . .

Melancholy.

Oh, God. Perhaps even . . .

Despair.

Buck up, Harewood, she told herself. A solution would be found. She just had to think, to discover a plan, to break free from this ungodly and wholly unnecessary sense of inertia, of . . .

"Bollocks," said Alexandra, next to her elbow, yanking her boot free from an unexpected hollow of mud.

Abigail jumped. "Oh! It's you!"

"Good heavens, my dear. Who else would it be?" Alexandra looked sadly at her ruined boot and carried on walking.

"I beg your pardon. I was lost in thought."

"Evidently. I'm rather out of sorts this morning myself. I've a dreadful headache, for one thing." Alexandra drew a massive sigh and glanced over her shoulder at the cart, in which Lilibet and Philip sat among the trunks, playing some sort of a game with a string. "Lilibet had us up at such a shocking hour. Quite exceptionally uncivilized, though I suppose it was for the best. The earlier we reach the castle, the better. If only we could have taken the coach."

"It would have been stuck in the mud at the first turn," said Abigail. "And we couldn't take such a chance. Coaches are so easily traced."

"Instead it's our own feet that will be stuck in the mud. Heigh-ho. It might be worse. We might be forced back into the insufferable company of Wallingford's party."

"I thought they were rather nice," ventured Abigail, jumping over a puddle.

"*You* weren't there over dessert." Alexandra's voice went dark. They were climbing a short rise; the mud had diminished, replaced by small sharp rocks. She kicked at one of them, sending it skidding and leaping across the road. "*You* retired with Lilibet and Philip."

"What happened at dessert?" Abigail asked.

"Nothing in particular." Another kick. "Well, Wallingford was an ass, of course, and poor Penhallow sat there in a daze of love for our cousin."

"And Mr. Burke?"

"Oh, the ginger? I hardly noticed him at all." Alexandra

looped her arm through Abigail's. "Dear sister. Do you know, that wretched Wallingford and his friends are embarked on the very same mission as we are? A year of academic retreat, for the betterment of their souls. If they had any to speak of, that is."

Abigail tightened her arm around Alexandra's thick wool-coated elbow. "What's that?"

"Oh yes." Alexandra nodded vigorously. "It's true. They've got their own secluded villa somewhere about. Wallingford even had the temerity to suggest that we weren't up to the challenge. That we should be running back home to England by Easter."

"Did he?" Abigail tried to quash the excitement that rose up from her belly, lifting the black anvil of despair and tossing it effortlessly overboard, into the muddy track beneath her boots.

"Quite. The cheek. I put him in his place at once, of course. I insisted we'd outlast their party with ease." Alexandra made a little cough. "I . . . well, that is, I even accepted a wager on the matter."

"Alexandra! You *bet* him?"

"Of course not. Ladies never *bet*, my dear," Alexandra said, pronouncing the word *bet* with distaste, as if referring to some unmentionable function of the body that ladies never committed, either.

Abigail laughed. "But how marvelous! You darling, Alexandra! I could kiss you. What are the stakes? A hundred pounds? A thousand?"

"Heavens, no." An injured air. "Nothing so crass as money, my dear. I'm amazed you would even think such a thing. Where do you get such ideas? No, no, the thought of money never once crossed my mind." She smoothed her coat with one hand and clenched Abigail's forearm with the other.

"What, then?"

"Oh, Mr. Burke suggested something. A newspaper advertisement of some sort, I believe, conceding the superiority of the other sex. It doesn't matter. The important thing is that we made our point."

"What point?"

"Why, that women are equally as capable as men in academic endeavors, if not more."

A pit of mud lay before them. Without a pause, Abigail dragged her sister around its rim, her mind racing, melancholy quite banished, ideas and possibilities and *hope*—oh, blessed hope—making her very sinews vibrate with delight. A wager with Wallingford! Of course! Here it was, the intervention of fate, bringing them together again as inevitably as the dice collided on a gaming table. Or perhaps that was not quite the right metaphor. In any case: "But I thought the academic superiority of women was quite self-evident. Why else would men require entire universities to further their studies, whereas we have always made do with a room and a few books?"

"You should have seen the look on his face," said Alexandra.

"I'm sure His Grace was positively thunderous." Abigail sighed longingly.

"Not Wallingford," said Alexandra. "Mr. Burke. He was silent about it, of course, but I could tell he was enraged at the idea. He left the table in an absolute *state*."

"And Wallingford? What did he say?"

"Oh, the duke? I don't recall. I left myself, directly after."

Abigail laughed aloud.

"What is it?" Alexandra said crossly.

"I was only thinking. Wouldn't it be jolly fun if the gentlemen were bound for the same castle as we are? All unknowing?"

"That's quite impossible. I have the lease right here in my pocket." Alexandra patted the breast of her coat with satisfaction. "All signed and sealed and airtight. I shan't allow so much as Mr. Burke's right toe upon the property, I assure you. Besides," she added, "there must be dozens of other castles about. The odds of such a coincidence are therefore . . . something like . . . er . . ."

"Yes?" Abigail said eagerly.

Alexandra patted her pocket again. "Incalculable."

Several hours later

The Duke of Wallingford stood in the middle of the drizzle and stared at the two papers in his hands. He looked back and forth. His heels dug into the stony earth, seeking further security; his back stiffened into iron.

In the course of his duties as head of one of Britain's most august families, Wallingford was often called upon to adjudicate disputes of one kind or another. He found the ritual more bemusing than anything else. The faces trained upon him, eager and anxious. The weight of respectful silence, suffusing the air with expectancy. The universal belief that he, Arthur Penhallow, had somehow been endowed by nature with a greater share of wisdom than the ordinary run of mankind, simply by virtue of having been born the eldest son of a man who happened, by that same lucky accident of birth, to hold the title of duke.

He took the responsibility seriously, of course. Whether sitting in judgment of some fellow peer in the House of Lords or deciding the rightful ownership of a peripatetic village sow, he understood the gravity of the charge he'd been given by his Creator. He endeavored to be impartial. He endeavored to consider all sides of the matter, every piece of evidence. He endeavored to give his full attention, the full weight of intellect at his disposal, to delivering a just decision.

But *this*? This was quite outside the realm of his experience.

He hadn't seen the lease agreement until now. Burke had taken care of all that, all the legal arrangements for the yearlong rental of the Castel sant'Agata. Burke was a clever fellow, a genius, with plenty of money and lawyers at his disposal. Wallingford hadn't given the matter a second thought. It had never occurred to him that he might, on the very day of their arrival, with the Castel sant'Agata rising nearby from the wet hillside in a jumble of yellowing walls and red-roofed turrets, hold not one but *two* copies of the lease agreement in his hands, exactly and word-by-word identical to each other, signed and notarized in perfect order.

Identical, except for the names of the leaseholders.

One agreement let the castle to Mr. Phineas Fitzwilliam Burke, R.S., and the other named, in plain black ink, one Alexandra, Dowager Marchioness of Morley.

The wind blew cold against his cheek, ruffling the papers. He wasn't looking at the words now; he knew precisely the nature of the problem before him. He was wet and cold and cross, having walked ten miles along the muddy Tuscan road while the ladies, curse them, had ridden in comfort atop his horses; he had found the fortitude to keep marching only from the knowledge that this would soon be over, that they would reach the castle and the women would be on their way, and he would no longer have to bear the siren call of Miss Harewood's floating laughter, the heartbreaking image of her graceful, straight-shouldered outline against the gray rock and brown winter grass.

And then they had arrived at the castle itself, and the horrible truth—the truth he had half suspected, perhaps unconsciously expected, from the moment he had first spotted the ladies at the inn—had at last been understood.

One castle. Two legal leaseholders.

Roland coughed gently, next to his elbow. The horses began to move about, hooves cracking restlessly against the pebbles of the track. Wallingford cleared his throat and looked up. To his right, Miss Harewood looked down at him from her lofty perch atop Burke's handsome chestnut; he could feel her gaze upon his face, her whole attitude bursting with eagerness.

To his left rose the castle itself, a distant shadow against the clouds. An odd frisson touched the back of his neck, a sense of otherworldliness.

"Well," he said. "Rather awkward. It appears Signore Rosseti is either a senile fool or . . . well, or a scoundrel."

Another gust of wind battered against his back. Lucifer, carrying Lady Somerton and her boy in the saddle, gave a vigorous nod of his head, jingling the metal rings of his bridle.

Wallingford held up both papers before him and went on, in his best judicial boom. "The letters are nearly identical, except that the ladies appear to have negotiated a better price for the year's lease than you have, Burke."

Burke scowled. "I was told there was no room for negotiation."

"Oh, rubbish, Mr. Burke," said Lady Morley, with a little laugh. "Merely tactics, as anyone knows."

"We have paid for a year's lease on the castle, and we intend to take it," Burke shot back, crossing his arms against his chest.

Wallingford frowned at them both. The day was growing late, the light already fading against the gloomy landscape. He thought for an instant of Miss Abigail Harewood trudging through the night, seeking shelter, chilled and hungry, and a shaft of pure instinctive horror bolted through his heart.

A solution would have to be found, and straightaway. Was there some alternative housing nearby? A village of some sort? Surely the castle oversaw a village; that was in the very nature of castles. The people there would know where this Rosseti might be found, and the matter could be cleared up. If necessary, the gentlemen could leave the ladies in possession of this particular castle and find something else. Something—he cast a glance at the ancient building, the unkempt row of cypress wavering precariously in the bitter wind—something perhaps a trifle more welcoming.

He was a fair man, after all. As long as his opponent played by the rules, he could do the generous thing. Perhaps it was all for the best.

He opened his mouth to speak, but in the same instant, Lady Morley made an impatient noise, a little grunt of decision, and wheeled her horse about.

"What the devil," he began, but his words were lost in the thunder of her departing hoof beats, galloping down the drive toward the castle.

Everyone stood frozen, even the horses, staring at the departing hindquarters of Penhallow's borrowed horse, which grew smaller and grayer in the mist, until both steed and rider faded into a shadow.

"Good God!" shouted Burke, breaking the spell. "Come back here!"

"What the devil," Wallingford said again, in an awed whisper. He looked at Miss Harewood, whose face was lit with amusement, her elfin eyes round and large in her pale face. "What the devil does she think she's doing?" he demanded.

Miss Harewood glanced down at him and smiled. She gathered the reins in her hands and nudged her horse with her heels. "Taking possession, I expect," she said, over her shoulder, as Burke's chestnut moved her down the track at a merry canter.

FOUR

Abigail knew something was afoot the instant the great hall opened up around her.

She had felt it already. When the smudged outline of the Castel sant'Agata had at last emerged from the drizzle, she had thought it seemed to shimmer, to waver against the clouds like some unearthly creation. She had sensed some mystery stirring in the air in the courtyard, in the abandoned lichen-crusted fountain and iron gates. A sort of expectancy, a holding of some invisible breath.

She let her gaze travel slowly about the bare stone walls, the great staircase curving up to the gallery, the mighty timbers crossing the roof above them. Not a stick of furniture obstructed her view; not a rug covered the flagstones beneath her boots. Abigail's imagination expanded with a whoosh, taking in the stark splendor around them and filling it with history. With life.

She crossed the room to the casement window, protected by a set of long and mildewed curtains. With one hand she pushed aside the fabric and peered out. "What a splendid adventure. Such delicious grime! I daresay it hasn't been washed in years. Do you suppose there's ghosts?"

"Of course not," Alexandra said sharply. "The very idea."

"I expect there's dozens of them. An old pile like this. And

Italians! Always poisoning one another and so on. I shall be very much disappointed if I don't discover a ghost in every corridor." Abigail turned from the window to find Philip standing in front of her, gazing owlishly about the room. Lilibet wandered about behind, settling her woolen scarf more closely about her neck, her fair brow deeply creased.

"Really, it's the wonder of the world you haven't found a husband yet," said Alexandra.

"I never wanted one. Come, let's explore." She took Philip's hand and led him across the great hall at a brisk trot, heading for the passageway at the other end.

"Slow! Slow!" said Philip, laughing, struggling to keep up.

"Hurry, hurry!" Abigail urged, and he broke into a run, filling the air with his giggles. From behind them came Lilibet's voice, begging them to wait, but Abigail, full of delight and anticipation, had no intention of waiting. Her lungs drew in the damp, musty air; her mood lifted and soared into the ancient stone and wood of this extraordinary castle.

"*Abigail!*"

Abigail skidded to a stop and looked up.

A figure hovered before her in the shadows of the passageway, its white apron catching the feeble light from the hall with a preternatural glow.

"Hello there," said Abigail. She kept Philip's hand firmly within her own.

"*Buon giorno,*" the woman said, stepping forward. She wore a dress of homespun wool beneath her long apron, and her hair was covered by a plain white headscarf. She had pleasant features, deep-set and regular, and her dark eyes regarded them warily.

Alexandra came up next to Abigail and spoke briskly. "*Buon giorno.* Are you the owner?"

The woman allowed a smile and a modest shake of her head. A warm scent drifted in the air around her, as if she'd been baking bread all day. "No, no. I am the . . . what is the word? I keep the house. You are the English party?"

"Yes," Alexandra said. "Yes, we are. You're expecting us?"

Lilibet walked up and quietly took Philip's hand from Abigail, leading him into the shelter of her arms.

"Oh yes," said the woman. "We have much pleasure to see you. Though I think you are a day before? We are expecting you tomorrow. You like the castle?" She made a broad motion with her arm, indicating the vast emptiness of the great hall behind them, the hard sweep of the stone staircase to the right. Her face seemed to light with pride, as if a candle had been set aglow beneath her skin.

"Who could resist such an inviting scene?" said Alexandra.

"Is so long when the family is live here," said the woman, with an expressive Italian shrug. "Is only me to keep the house."

"Haven't you any help?" asked Alexandra in horror.

"Oh, the maids, they stay in the village. They are not staying here, when there is no master. Is so lonely. Giacomo, he keeps the . . ." She rubbed her fingers together. "The earth?"

"The grounds," said Alexandra. "He's the groundskeeper. Very well. And what is your name, my good woman?"

The woman curtsied. "I am called Signorina Morini."

Signorina Morini. Something about the words caused a little shiver to spread down the length of Abigail's spine. Something about the woman herself, with her kind, almost lyric voice, the glow of her skin, the dance of her dark eyes. Something about the way the still, expectant air of the hall seemed to gather and lighten around her.

Here. The mystery, it was *here*, all bound up somehow in this woman's serene presence, shadowed with the faint scent of baking bread.

Abigail burst out. "Oh, what a lovely name. I do so like Italian names. I'm Miss Harewood, signorina, and I think your castle is perfectly magnificent. Could you perhaps show us about?" She waved her hand at the staircase. "Are our rooms upstairs?"

"But yes, they are upstairs." She frowned and cast her eyes about the great hall behind them. "But . . . the gentlemen? Where are the gentlemen?"

Alexandra went rigid. "The gentlemen? What about them?"

"Do you mean you were expecting us both?" asked Abigail, in excitement. Oh, this was better and better. "Signore Rosseti did it on purpose?"

Signorina Morini lifted her shoulders and spread out her hands, palms upward. "I only know there come three ladies, three gentlemen. They are not your husbands?"

"I should say not!" Alexandra snapped.

"Your brothers?"

Abigail laughed with delight. "Oh no. Not at all."

Lilibet broke in. "It was all a great mistake. We understood . . . we thought we had taken out a year's lease, but it appears the three gentlemen made a similar arrangement, and . . . perhaps you can find Signore Rosseti, and he can explain . . ."

Morini's brow had furrowed in thought. She tilted her head to one side and pushed at a few strands of black hair that had escaped from her headscarf, looking as if she were attempting to solve a large and complicated puzzle. "I see, I see. Is very strange. The master, he is very careful, very particular. Is very strange mistake." She straightened and clapped her hands. "But is good! Six English is very good! We have talk, laughter. The castle will be . . . transform. *Buon.* I will find your rooms."

Morini turned with an air of unshakable purpose and headed for the staircase, homespun skirts swishing against her legs. She lifted her arm and summoned them to follow her.

Abigail leapt after her.

"But, my good woman!" Alexandra called out desperately. "What about servants? Has the place been readied for our arrival? Is there dinner?"

Signorina Morini, striding across the hall at a brisk pace, did not stop to answer. She turned her head and said, over her shoulder, "We are expecting you tomorrow. The servants, they arrive in the morning, from the village."

"In the morning?" Alexandra demanded. "Do you mean there's no dinner? Is nothing ready?"

"Where is Rosseti?" added Abigail.

"He is not here. I make all arrange. Come, come. Is growing late!" Morini had reached the staircase and was positively bounding up the stone steps, propelled by purpose.

Not here, thought Abigail, leaping up after her in a surge of excitement.

Then where the devil *was* Rosseti?

The lantern cast a shimmering glow around the stable entrance, causing the very stones to move about in the walls.

Or so it seemed to Abigail.

For the first time, it occurred to her that it might perhaps not have been her cleverest notion, to steal out of a strange castle at midnight and across a courtyard to a building she had never before entered. One, moreover, that she suspected to contain ghosts and specters of all sorts, to say nothing of some eternal mystery that hovered just out of her brain's perception.

But what else was she to do? She had clearly seen a light wobble across this courtyard from her bedroom window; she had clearly seen it enter the stable. If she meant to discover the source of the mystery, she might as well begin now. The thought of danger hadn't entered her head. This was not a malevolent sort of mystery, she was sure. Mischievous, perhaps even tragic, but not cruel.

Still, she couldn't deny the shiver that coursed down her body just now. And her body, Abigail knew, was seldom ever wrong.

She reached out and pushed open the stable door anyway.

She was, after all, Abigail.

"Who's there?" someone snapped, in a loud and commanding voice.

Abigail felt her shoulders sag in relief. "Oh, it's only you," she said. "I might have known you'd be skulking about the stables at midnight."

"I might have known you'd be doing the same, Miss Harewood."

Abigail worked her way toward the pool of lantern light at the far corner of the space. Around her, the horses whickered in subdued welcome. "We seem to share the same habits, then. Is he settling in all right?"

"Quite all right."

His shape was visible now, tall and dark, covered rather romantically by a long cloak. His face turned away from hers, toward the dark shape of Lucifer's head, with its long white blaze gathering the feeble light.

"He was a very brave fellow tonight, weren't you, my lad?" she said, stopping just short of them, breathing in the comforting scent of horses and hay. "Bore up like a trooper."

"What are you doing here, Miss Harewood?" Wallingford asked with a sigh.

"I saw your lantern, heading for the stables. I wasn't sure what it was."

"So you decided to investigate? At midnight?" He turned at last. "In your nightgown?"

She shrugged and smiled. "Was I supposed to put on my stays and petticoats?"

"You're a fool. It might have been anyone."

"But it was you, after all. You'd never hurt me."

He breathed steadily, one hand curling around Lucifer's neck. "How do you know that?"

She shrugged again and hung her lantern on the hook, near his. "My instincts are never wrong. You're full of bluster, Wallingford, but you have a kind heart."

"A kind *heart*?" he asked, incredulous.

Abigail stepped forward and placed her hand on the other side of Lucifer's neck, stroking him gently. "Look at you, here in the stables at midnight, checking on the horses."

"Horses are one thing. People are another." His tone was bitter.

She let his words sit there between them in the damp air. The strands of Lucifer's mane, stiff and wiry, brushed against the back of her hand. She combed them thoughtfully with her fingers. "Do you feel it?" she asked, in a whisper.

"Feel what?"

"Around us."

He paused. She felt his breath near her ear, warm and spreading, carrying the faint hint of the old wine they'd drunk at dinner. "I don't know what you're talking about."

Abigail couldn't tell if he spoke the truth or not. There *had* been that pause, after all. "Don't you think there's something odd about this place?" she ventured.

"Yes. Damned odd. Starting with the fact that the three of you are here with us."

"It's fate, obviously. We're meant to do something extraordinary together."

"*Together* is out of the question."

She turned and smiled. "You're not still thinking about that silly wager, are you? Vows of monastic seclusion and all that? We're civilized beings, after all. We can rub along quite well with one another. We sorted everything out so agreeably over dinner, after all."

"That agreement is not meant to be permanent, Miss Harewood," said the duke. "Only until Rosseti can be found, and our rights asserted."

"Oh, I don't know. Women in the east wing, men in the west. Why shouldn't it go on all year, if we mind our language and manage to keep our laundry separate?"

He sputtered. "Because it's impossible. Because three ladies and three gentlemen cannot go on in close proximity without . . ."

"Without what?"

"Without driving one another mad!" he burst out, stepping back and turning away.

"Oh! Are you talking about carnal urges? Because I do think . . ."

"Miss Harewood," Wallingford said, into the stable floor, "I assure you, I don't wish to hear your thoughts on the subject of carnal urges, at the moment." He lifted his woolen hat, brushed his dark hair, and replaced the cap in an angry jerk.

"But why should it bother you? Why is it so necessary that we resist our natural inclinations?" Abigail asked. "Are you really so desperate to win your silly wager? I assure you, I don't care two hoots . . ."

"Damn the wager! Damn the whole silly project! I must have been mad." Wallingford leaned his forehead against the stable wall.

Lucifer gave a sympathetic whicker.

"Then why don't you simply turn about and go home?"

"Can't," came Wallingford's voice, from the stable wall. "Too late."

"Too late for what?" Abigail scratched Lucifer's forelock and gazed at the duke's dark form against the wall, at the curious way his head bowed, as if in despair, exposing a sliver of his nape to the damp air of the stable. When he made no reply, she went on gently: "Why are *you* here, Wallingford? The last place in the world anyone would look for you. No comforts, no ceremony. Not even your valet."

He said nothing.

Abigail said softly, "What are you hiding from, Your Grace?"

His hand formed a fist against the wall.

"My grandfather," he said, very low. "Myself."

She wasn't sure she'd heard him properly. He had muttered the words into the wood, and they seemed quite unlike him, quite unlike what she expected from him. "I don't understand," she said.

"Of course you don't. Innocent Miss Harewood."

"That's nonsense. I'm not innocent at all. I've told you all about my kissing adventures, and you don't know the half of what I get up to when my sister's not paying attention. I wager on horses, I sneak out for pints down the pub, I read the most shocking literature, I . . ."

He laughed and turned, crossing his arms, leaning against the wall. "Heinous crimes indeed."

"I dress myself as a boy when I visit the racetrack. I might be arrested for that."

Wallingford shook his head. "Go home, Miss Harewood. Go home and marry some suitable young chap, some pleasant smooth-cheeked fellow from a decent family. There are dozens of them about. I daresay you'd lead him around by the nose, and he'd never think of straying."

"If you were as bad as you say, you wouldn't have such scruples. You'd take me regardless and send me on my way."

"Don't tempt me."

"Why don't you, then?"

"Because you *are* innocent. You're impossibly innocent, the most innocent woman I've ever met. Because I'd like to think . . . the point of all this, you see . . ." He waved his hand, stood away from the wall, took a step or two down the stable aisle. He shoved his hands in his pockets and stared into the darkness. "Just go."

She rubbed Lucifer's muzzle and wrapped her arm around his contented neck. His head dropped, resting on her shoulder. "What if I don't want to go?"

Wallingford reached with his long woolen arm and took his lantern from the hook. He didn't even look at her. "Then I'll have to be disciplined enough for both of us," he said. "Which is, I suppose, no more than I deserve."

Abigail stood for some time after he left, caressing Lucifer's motionless head. Her eyes were closed. She was absorbing everything: the whisper of straw as the horses moved about, the creak of wood, the tiny currents of air in the humid chill, the rich horsey smell of Lucifer's black coat. The tingling at the back of her head, curling the roots of her hair.

"You can come out now," she said. "I know you're there."

The air went still, as if holding its breath.

"Who are you? Giacomo, I suppose? The groundskeeper. Morini told us about you. You're ghosts, aren't you?"

The lantern flickered.

"I'm not afraid. Look at Lucifer, here. He's almost asleep. I know you won't hurt me, or else you *can't* hurt me, because otherwise the horses would be upset."

Lucifer nodded against her shoulder, lipped her collar.

"You can show yourself. I won't say anything to the others." She paused. "Do you speak English?" There was no answer. "Can you tell me why you're here? What's going on? Have *you* brought us all together, here at the castle?"

From some corner of the stable, beyond the reach of the lantern, a horse neighed softly. Abigail waited without moving, almost without breathing, every sense open. It seemed she could feel each particle of air as it touched her skin.

At last she stepped away from Lucifer and gave him a pat. She lifted her lantern from the hook and gave it a last sweep about the space. The horses blinked at her from the cobwebs. Something rustled rapidly through the straw.

"You know I won't give up," she said. "I *will* find out. You've met your match, Mr. Giacomo, or whoever you are."

She walked out through the stable door and closed it carefully behind her. Ahead loomed the castle, black against the charcoal sky, hints of light gleaming distantly from a window or two. At the doorway stood a cloaked figure, dangling a lantern from one hand. The fire crossed his face in harsh streaks and shadows.

He was waiting for her.

Abigail crossed the wet courtyard. The drizzle had let up, leaving behind a clinging mist. Wallingford held open the door and followed her silently into the great hall and up the staircase. On the landing he parted from her, bound for the west wing.

The gentlemen's wing.

FIVE

April 1890

For a man of known libertine tendencies, the Duke of Wallingford was proving remarkably difficult to seduce.

Abigail had thought it would be a simple matter to begin her first love affair, once she had chosen her subject. She was ready, she was willing, she was reasonably appealing, at least to the indiscriminate male palate. She had found the perfect spot, a boathouse near the lake, and equipped it with everything necessary for one's passionate defloration: cushions and a fine wool blanket, stored in the cupboard; wine and glasses, tucked inside the splitting hull of an ancient flat-bottomed dinghy; the best beeswax candles in abundance. She had done it all in stealth, piece by piece, and waited until April had turned (March was far too cold for alfresco assignations, even in Italy, and even with a duke) before donning her most flesh-baring gown and making herself available of an evening.

The trouble was, the duke was making himself distinctly unavailable.

It was all the fault of that silly wager, Abigail thought crossly, dragging the goat across the stableyard to its pen before breakfast one morning. (Like Wallingford, the animal had proven unwilling to go where he was told, but in the matter of stubbornness no goat yet bred could outmatch Abigail Harewood.) What had Alexandra been thinking, heating up the competitive male juices like that? A *bet*, of all things: The one matter calculated to bring out every medieval masculine tendency toward pride and gamesmanship and bullheaded thick-wittedness.

And who would have thought the Duke of Wallingford—so decidedly, deliciously unchaste—would take the matter all so dashed seriously? Instead of gazing enraptured at the curve of her bosom, he had glowered fiercely. Instead of dragging her into a passionate embrace when he had encountered her in the twilit shadows of the spring-warmed garden, he had turned on his heel and stalked back into the house.

Really, was it something she'd said?

Abigail turned around the corner of the stable, and the wooden pen appeared before them. The goat set its cloven hooves firmly into the pale dust of the stableyard and let out an alarmed *maaa-maaa*.

"Now look here," said Abigail, "it's a fine old pen. You've got an olive tree all to yourself, and I shall personally undertake to see that the geese don't bother you."

The goat administered a firm knock to her buttocks.

"Well! There's gratitude for you." Abigail tugged at the rope. "Come along, then. You know you can't win. Besides, it's only for the rest of the morning, while I have breakfast and then help Maria and Francesca with the cleaning. We can't have you running about while the sheets and things are out to dry."

Maaa-maaa, said the goat.

Abigail tugged again. "You do realize that we're cleaning the house for the priest's Easter blessing tomorrow? Think of the infamy, if nothing is ready. You'll be damned forever, I'm quite sure, and consigned to some hideous circle of hell with only those bad-tempered geese for company, pecking at you incessantly."

A breeze drifted through the stableyard, shivering the goat's beard.

"Don't look so pathetic, Percival. I haven't a sympathetic bone in my body for recalcitrant goats who won't go where they're told," said Abigail. She looked up and shaded her eyes against the radiant morning sun. "Oh, look! Clover!"

The goat's head shot up.

"Right over there! Hurry!"

When at last Percival was secured in the pen, sulking under the olive tree, Abigail allowed herself a moment of triumph, stretched against the fence post, soaking the early warmth into her bones.

The hillside tumbled away before her in walls and terraces, rioting with the growth of spring: long gnarled rows of grape-vines, just shooting out their pale green leaves, bordered by the trace of what would soon be cornstalks; the peach orchard erupting into bloom to her right; and beyond it, the path down to the lake, surrounded by olive and apple trees. To her left, the laborers plowed long furrows into the vegetable gardens, their white shirts reflecting the watery sun. She could not see the vil-lage, nestled at the bottom of the valley, but she felt it there, a warm jumble of sand yellow buildings, red roofs glowing against the green hillside.

She loved them all. She loved everything about the Castel sant'Agata. She had loved watching it all stir into sudden life in the second half of March, in sprouts of pale green against the browns and grays of the wet earth; she loved standing here now, absorbing it all, the scent of the peach blossom and of rich, newly turned dirt, the distant lazy shouts of the laborers.

She loved the sight of the duke, swinging around the corner of the stable as he did every morning (she slipped her watch from her pocket, just to be sure) at exactly seven o'clock.

"Good morning," she called out cheerfully.

"Good morning," he said, rather less cheerfully. He did not bother to look in her direction.

Abigail leaned against the fence and let the faint spring sun absorb into her hat. The duke was standing quite still, about twenty feet away, and the clear light seemed to dust him with gold. He wore his well-tailored tweeds, his riding boots, his flat wool cap, and he gazed with penetrating ferocity at the fence ahead of him, as if blind and deaf to the beauty of his sur-roundings.

"Is there something wrong?" she asked politely.

He turned at last. "My horse," he said. "Where the devil is my horse?"

"In the pasture, I believe."

"In the pasture?" Wallingford said, as he might say, *In the starting line at Epsom?* "Why the devil?"

"The Devil, the Devil. You keep saying that. I assure you, the Devil has nothing to do with Lucifer grazing calmly at his leisure. Quite the opposite. Oh, ha-ha!"

He looked at her as if she were mad. "What exactly is so amusing?"

"The Devil. Lucifer. You've rather an affection for the old scratch, haven't you? A sort of occupational affinity?"

Wallingford slapped his riding crop against his boot. "My horse is supposed to be saddled, bridled, and waiting for me at seven o'clock each morning, in this very spot. I don't suppose you have any idea why today should be any different?"

Abigail shaded her eyes and looked out across the fields. "I suspect it's because they've starting sowing this morning at dawn."

"Sowing?"

"The fields, you know. Food for our tables and all that. It's spring, or hadn't you noticed?"

"And why should this affect the readiness of my horse for a morning ride?"

She turned back to him and smiled. "I suspect that's because the stable hands are needed for the plowing."

"For the *plowing*?" Wallingford looked at the fields, at the antlike industry of the distant laborers, with palpable astonishment.

"Look, I don't mean to cast aspersions," said Abigail, "but are you certain you've had your coffee this morning?"

He cast her a dark look. "As it happens, I have. I am in every way prepared to meet a pending appointment in the village, except that I *have . . . no . . . horse!*" He said the last words with deliberate force, which ought to have sent a dozen ducal retainers flying to do his bidding.

Except that no ducal retainers existed, here in the Tuscan hills.

Abigail smiled again. "Then I expect you'll have to saddle Lucifer yourself."

"Saddle him *myself*?"

She lifted herself away from the fence. "You appear flummoxed, Your Grace. Fortunately, you have me at your service, quite happy to extend my hand in assistance. Fetch your horse, and I shall burrow into the tack room and find your saddle."

"Fetch?" Wallingford roared, but Abigail had already skipped off across the stableyard.

The tack room was at the back of the building, shadowed and smelling strongly of leather. Abigail had been there often for one errand or another, and she knew exactly where Wallingford's equipment was kept. She hoisted the bridle over one shoulder, hooked her arm under the saddle and pad, and snatched the wooden box with the brushes.

At the door, she paused in contemplation. "In for a penny, in for a pound," she said to herself, and she set the box back down and jerked her bodice a little lower.

Lucifer regarded his master with a bemused dark eye, his jaws working away at a mouthful of tender spring grass.

"I hate to interrupt your idyll, old boy," said Wallingford, "but I require your assistance on the road to the village."

Lucifer stretched down his neck for another bite.

"Damned cheeky brute." Wallingford grasped the horse's worn rope halter and urged him into motion.

He should have been on his guard from the beginning, of course. The groundskeeper had even warned him. "The girl, she is waiting for you again," Giacomo had said, shaking his head, leaning against the stable wall. "She is trouble, that one."

Wallingford quite agreed, but he wasn't about to let Giacomo tell him so. "There's nothing troublesome about her," he'd said, slapping his crop impatiently against his boots. "She's simply a girl, going about her business. I daresay she's watching the goats, isn't she?"

"She pretend to watch the goats. She is watching for you."

"Rubbish. Good day, Giacomo." And he had stridden arrogantly into the stableyard and Abigail Harewood's cheerful tidings.

Point to Giacomo.

Lucifer, quite unlike himself, would not be moved from a leisurely stroll, and by the time the two of them achieved the pasture gate, Abigail was already standing there, bright and shining and full-bosomed, the sun gleaming gloriously in her chestnut hair and her slender arms groaning with equestrian equipment.

"Perhaps I should have chosen to walk instead," Wallingford muttered.

Abigail beamed at him. "Ah, excellent. I see you've gotten into the spirit of things directly."

"Just give me the saddle, Miss Harewood, and let us be done with it."

Abigail set down the box and tossed the saddle atop the fence rail. "Oh no, Your Grace. We must brush him first."

"Brush him. Of course."

She selected a brush from the box. "If we each take a side, we shall finish ever so much faster. I hope I need hardly tell you to brush in the direction of the hair growth."

"I believe I understand the mechanics." He snatched the brush from her hand and started to work.

"I don't understand why you're so cross. I think it's good for you, to escape all your ducal trappings and whatnot. Saddling your own horse is a fine start."

"I have not traveled all the way to Italy to learn how to saddle my own horse. I might have done that quite comfortably back at home."

"But you wouldn't have, though, would you? I daresay all that London nonsense, all the drinking and women and so on, has eaten into your soul. Hasn't it, Wallingford?"

"Rubbish." He worked his way across the line of Lucifer's girth, brushing with intense concentration, observing with a certain grudging pleasure the way the sun came to life upon the sleek dark hair. In the upper periphery of his vision, Abigail's hair bobbed alluringly above Lucifer's hindquarters. He was glad she couldn't see him. He felt bare, stripped to the bone by her matter-of-fact words.

"You needn't be so circumspect," she said, in that same unflappable tone. "I've been observing you, you know, since we first arrived at that wretched inn. I suspect we're more alike than you realize, except that I have rather a clearer view of things. Not having been thoroughly spoilt by unlimited power and riches, you see."

"I am not spoilt." He concentrated on the steady stroke of the brush, on the way the physical rhythm of the task restored his equilibrium.

"Here's the saddlecloth," said Abigail, popping up from under

Lucifer's neck. She handed it to him. "You spread it . . . no, the other way . . . yes, very good. Now flatten out the creases, or he'll be annoyed. No, I'm quite in agreement with you, about wanting to flee all the nonsense of social expectation back in England. I have an aversion to marriage and that sort of thing myself."

Wallingford smoothed away at the saddlecloth, arranging it just so. "Indeed. So you told me, that first evening at the inn."

"But you never asked me why."

"I daresay I didn't wish to pry into your private affairs. You, of course, have no such scruples. I daresay half London knows your views on marriage." He glanced over the top of Lucifer's back, where she stood quietly, both hands on the saddlecloth, smoothing her side.

"That's not true at all. I believe you're the first person I've spoken to on the matter, except that dear stableboy at the inn. And he didn't speak any English, so it doesn't signify." Abigail went to the fence, where the saddle straddled the top rail. He couldn't see her face; it almost seemed she was hiding it from him. She paused, drawing her hand along the saddle seat. "I'll tell you why. You see, I never wanted to marry. I promised myself I wouldn't. When I moved to London, and saw Alexandra's life, saw how my carefree and mischievous sister had transformed into this . . . this very amusing but rather . . . unadventurous wife of a great man, I told myself I should rather die than let that happen to me."

Wallingford stared at her helplessly. An absurd sensation invaded his chest: hollow and warm, all at once.

She lifted the saddle, and instead of handing it to Wallingford, placed it on Lucifer's back herself. She went on, in a subdued voice. "Her life had no purpose; it was all salons and parties, talking and flirting and never doing anything, only inventing more amusements. Oh, the occasional charity junket, of course; she's not so shallow as that. But I don't think she was happy, either, not really. She was restless and bored, though she pretended to have the time of her life. And Lilibet! Well, I'm sure you've heard the stories about Somerton. Her marriage was nothing but the blackest misery."

"Perhaps she should have chosen differently," Wallingford heard himself say, entranced all at once by the nimbleness of Abigail's fingers as she arranged the saddle and straightened the girth, by her gentle, candid voice, by the way she revealed herself to him without fear.

"Yes, but the institution itself! Would you mind going around the other side, Your Grace, and catching the girth?"

Wallingford went around obediently and found the girth strap, hanging down from Abigail's side of the saddle. He grasped it and drew it upward, toward the buckles.

"You, for example. You're one of the greatest men in England. If I married you—I speak hypothetically, of course—I should have to be a model of propriety, a . . . a pillar of society! It's exactly what ruined Alexandra."

Wallingford slipped the straps into the buckles and tightened them. "If I asked you to marry me—I speak hypothetically, Miss Harewood, and purely for the sake of argument—I daresay it would be because I liked you well enough as you are. I wouldn't want you to change." The reckless words left his lips before he could pause to think about them.

"But I couldn't help it. We couldn't help it. It would be inevitable. All this lovely freedom, to do and say as I please, to live here in this marvelous crumbling pile and milk the goats in the morning . . ."

"We are still speaking hypothetically, I trust. The bridle, Miss Harewood, if you will." Something light and airy seemed to be invading the region around his heart, filling the warm hollowness. His pulse was smacking away with unexpected force in his neck. He held out his hand for the bridle and was shocked to see his fingers trembling.

"Oh, of course. I don't want to be your wife. I've told you that already." She placed the bridle in his hand, and foolishly he looked at her face, at her dancing tip-turned eyes, at her radiant smile. "Aside from the stifling effects of marriage itself, there is your character to consider."

He snatched the bridle away. The airiness in his chest collapsed upon itself with a puff. "My character is perfectly good."

"Oh, of course. You're quite the most interesting libertine I've ever known. Here you are, after all, making a determined effort to study and so on. You're marvelously intelligent, really. And for all your bluster, you do have a genuine . . ." She paused. "A genuine power to you. An inner dignity, quite apart from your title."

"And how do you think you know all this?" He fumbled awkwardly with the leather straps, concentrating with fierce intent on the physical puzzle in his hands instead of the metaphysical puzzle standing before him.

"I've watched you. With your horse, with your friends. At dinner, when we're all together. As I said, you're a nonpareil among libertines." She sighed and shook her head. "But you are, after all, a libertine."

Lucifer snorted wetly into Wallingford's gloved hands.

"I am not a libertine."

"And rakes don't reform," she went on, as if she hadn't heard him. "It's the greatest and cruelest myth perpetuated on womankind, by nature and by literature. A man of libertine nature doesn't change his ways, not even if he falls in love, not even if he marries for love. Sooner or later, his instinctive natural craving for new female flesh overcomes whatever love and loyalty he feels to his wife. Look at your own father."

"God, I hope not," Wallingford muttered. "He's been dead these fifteen years or so, and wasn't much to look on even when alive."

"You see? To a duke, who can obtain any woman he likes with a snap of his fingers, regardless of his personal charms, sexual fidelity isn't simply beyond his capability. It's beyond his comprehension. The spreading of valuable ducal seed isn't simply his right, but his duty to humankind. I say, are you quite all right?"

"*What* did you just say?" Wallingford gasped out, between spasms of coughing.

"I suppose that was rather an unsuitable thing to say, for an unmarried lady." She did not sound repentant.

Wallingford closed his eyes. He drew in a calming breath.

"Better?" Abigail asked cheerfully.

He lifted up the bridle. "How the devil does this go on?"

"Oh, just offer it to Lucifer. I daresay he knows where to stick his nose." Her voice was full of laughter.

Ducal seed. Had she really said that?

Wallingford blinked at the arrangement of leather and steel in his hands and forced his mind to concentrate. That must be the bit, there at the end; evidently the nose went there. He offered it to Lucifer with suitable humility.

Lucifer stared, incredulous.

Abigail sighed. She came up behind him, fragrant with the scent of lemons and blossoms, as if springtime itself had soaked into her skin. He tried not to breathe, but it was no use. She was still warm and supple next to him, her delicate female hands closing over his crude male ones, and his chaste body leapt to prominent life, his ducal seed clamored for release.

"Like so, Wallingford," she murmured. "Lift the headstall, that's it. Now fasten the buckle behind his cheekbones. There we are."

His fingers fastened the buckle clumsily. The ground was tilting slightly underneath him. Abigail's hair brushed against his cheek like a caress.

"I hope I haven't offended you. I didn't mean any insult. Your nature is your nature; it would be like blaming a lion for being a lion."

"Of course."

"I wouldn't want you any other way, in fact. You suit me perfectly."

The blood drummed in his ears. "Miss Harewood," he said, turning.

She was even closer than he thought. A choke rose up in his throat.

"Yes, Wallingford?" she asked, a little breathless.

He opened his mouth and closed it. She waited patiently, while the sun turned her skin to gold, and tilted her face toward his.

Wallingford squeezed his eyes shut against her. "The reins, Miss Harewood," he said. "If you will."

Wallingford rode beautifully, like a man who knew his horse inside and out. Abigail loved that about him, too. She had expected him to ride well, having already seen him with Lucifer in the stables, but it had still been a pleasure to watch him that first morning, moving without a trace of effort, like a centaur in the early light. She watched him now, as he made his way down to his appointment in the village, whatever it was. Some willing widow, perhaps.

Something tickled her hand. She looked down at Percival,

who was nibbling her sleeve with a goatly mixture of hunger and curiosity. "He's awfully handsome, isn't he, Percival? I don't think he even knows how handsome. Everyone's always gone on about his brother, and of course they're right, Roland's terribly beautiful, but . . ." She scratched the goat's head and watched Wallingford appear and disappear among the olive trees. "But Wallingford, it's as if he's carved from granite. All that beauty, and he hides it among the stone. Do you know what I mean?"

Abigail looked down at Percival, who had stopped chewing her sleeve and simply stood there with his eyes closed, savoring the scratch of her fingers between his ears.

"Of course you know," she said. "You've a lot in common, goats and dukes."

The Duke of Wallingford kept his shoulders straight and his gaze fixed on the road before him, until he was quite sure Abigail could no longer see him through the trees.

She was far away, quite at the other side of the stables, and yet he could feel every detail of her: the gloss of her hair in the morning sunshine (she never wore a hat until midday), the yellow of her dress as it wrapped about her slender body, the strength of her gaze as she followed him along the track. The remembered feel of her hands upon his, her scent in his nose.

Trouble, Giacomo had said.

"As if she were sent by my very grandfather, expressly to test my will," said Wallingford to Lucifer, as they walked down the track into the sunshine. "To see how long I can hold out before misbehaving once again. To show me how incapable I am of restraining myself."

The very fibers of his body seemed to stretch back down the track toward her.

You think you deserve to enjoy sexual congress with some mere acquaintance, against the wall of your own mistress's conservatory, simply because you can.

They passed a few olive trees, spotted with nascent fruit, and as each shadow passed over his skin, Wallingford felt with pain the shutting-off of Abigail, and then the relief of restoration an instant later. He had, by now, ceased to wonder at the sensation.

He accepted it as a temporary affliction, another inconvenience to endure.

"That's why I can't quite banish her from my thoughts," he went on. "Because I can't have her. A quite natural human response. The situation's comical, really. The girl, the artless virgin, wants to have an affair with me, and I—*I*, Lucifer—am the one adhering to virtue. It's a trial of the most bitter kind. And yet . . ."

They were past the trees now, and turning around the bend. Just like that, she was lost to him.

And yet at least I have the satisfaction of refusing her. He thought the words, rather than said them aloud. They didn't quite make enough sense to put out there, into the world. He had come to this wilderness in order to avoid his grandfather's medieval notions of arranged marriage, but he had also come to avoid temptation itself, to see if his grandfather were in fact right. To see if he *could* last a year without self-indulgence of any kind; to see if he could find some cure for the dogged dissatisfaction haunting the recesses of his soul; to see if there were some finer, better, stronger-souled Wallingford lurking beneath. Someone like Finn or Roland; someone whom people might actually like rather than merely respect; someone whom a woman like Abigail Harewood might actually love rather than collect as a trophy.

That last thought had sprung without warning from the depths, and Wallingford actually started in the saddle with the shock of it.

"Going mad," he said aloud.

He put Lucifer into a canter.

The wager. At the time, it had seemed like the worst kind of stupidity, the kind of pride-driven impulse to which dukes should not be subject. He had blamed that damnably provoking Lady Morley and her teasing. She had sounded almost exactly like his grandfather.

Now he was grateful. Whenever he felt himself slipping, whenever the temptation of Abigail's rosy round bosom threatened to poleax his last tottering pillar of willpower, he remembered the wager.

He had transformed his private promise into a public one.

He was committed.

Lucifer cantered around the curve in the road, and the red rooftops of the village came into view, nestled below him like a cluster of russet flowers.

My dear boy, has the entire conduct of your adult life ever suggested your usefulness for anything else?

"I can do this, old boy." He could not say whether he was addressing the horse or himself. He slowed Lucifer down to a trot, the better to negotiate the rocky slope of the final stretch of road.

By God, I'll show the old bastard.

SIX

Abigail adored every aspect of her life at the Castel sant'Agata, but she especially enjoyed breakfast.

"Jolly splendid of them, to find kidneys and kippers for us," she said, tucking in half an hour later with all the gusto of an Englishwoman eating her morning ration of organ meats. "I wonder how they managed it."

Lilibet was chewing her toast with all the gusto of an Englishwoman eating roof shingles, seasoned with coal dust. There were just the three of them at the moment, Abigail and Lilibet and Philip, three tiny outposts of humanity set around the broad swathe of the ancient trestle table. The gentlemen made a point of breakfasting early, and Alexandra made a point of breakfasting late. "I suppose one can order these things," she said. "There are hundreds of English in Florence."

"Yes, but how would they *know*?" Abigail rested her cutlery against her plate in a pregnant pause. "Don't you think there's something a bit odd about the old place?"

"I don't know what you mean. It's an old castle, that's all." Lilibet lifted her teacup and closed her eyes.

Abigail tilted her head and observed her cousin's face, which seemed rather pale and ghostly itself at the moment. She could not understand why no one else sensed the undercurrents drifting about the Castel sant'Agata; to Abigail they were as obvious as the sunshine in the morning.

"Really? You don't feel it? As if there are ghosts hanging about every corner?"

"Ghosts!" Philip bounced in his seat. "Real live ones?"

"No, darling," said Abigail. "Ghosts are generally dead. But real *dead* ones, certainly."

Lilibet sent her a quelling frown. "What nonsense. Ghosts, indeed."

As she spoke, a parcel of air seemed to brush the back of Abigail's neck, making it tingle.

She turned to the doorway, where Signorina Morini stood quite still, headscarf like a bright red slash against the shadowed corridor behind her, teapot and toast rack in her hands. She was regarding Lilibet with a pensive expression.

"I have more toast, Signora Somerton, and more of the tea," she said.

"Thank you, Morini. Are the gentlemen about yet? Lady Morley?" She asked the question with casual indifference, as if it were not common knowledge that the gentlemen and the ladies never breakfasted together, rarely lunched together, and only dined together because of the supreme inconvenience of having dinner at any other hour.

Morini stepped forward into the dining room, sparing not a glance for Abigail. Abigail was not surprised. She'd been trying for weeks to hold a private conversation with the dark-haired housekeeper of the Castel sant'Agata, to no avail. Every time Abigail entered into the kitchen, Morini slipped away on some urgent task, her skirts swishing behind her, the faint scent of baking bread dissolving into the empty air in her wake. Like a wraith, Abigail thought, with just a touch of pique: pique, because surely no one else in the house was better suited to speaking with a wraith—to getting to the bottom of her wraith-like secrets, as it were—than Miss Abigail Harewood.

Even now, Morini was focusing all her solicitous attention on Lilibet. She placed a fresh rack of toast on the table next to the countess's plate, tilted the teapot above her empty cup, and answered her in a private tone. "Signore Burke, Signore Penhallow, they both had the breakfast, it is an hour ago. Of the duke, I see nothing."

Abigail set down her fork. Enough was enough.

"Morini," she said, quite loud, "I wonder if I could have a few words with you on the subject of ghosts."

Morini's hands froze in place around the teapot.

"Morini! The tea!" exclaimed Lilibet.

Morini straightened the pot just in time. She stood for a moment, holding the pot with both hands, and glanced at last at Abigail. A short glance only, a tiny stroke of lightning, and then she turned back to Lilibet.

But still, a glance. That was progress.

"Ghosts," she said. "Of ghosts, there are none."

Abigail smiled. "Something else, then? Because I think the air's humming with them."

"Is nothing, signorina. Only the old stones, the wind rattling the old walls. You are wanting more tea?" She offered the pot, and this time her eyes met Abigail's with resolution, with intent and dark-eyed meaning.

Abigail tapped her finger against the table and returned the housekeeper's gaze. Not a muscle moved in Morini's face, not a flicker. The teapot in her hands, the clothes on her body: everything was still and focused on Abigail.

The tingling began again at the nape of her neck.

"I see," she said. "Yes, more tea. I like your blend extremely, Morini."

"But what about the ghosts?" Philip broke in cheerfully, reaching for his mother's toast.

"Darling, don't reach. There are no ghosts, Morini says." Lilibet took the toast from Philip's fingers, spread it thickly with butter, and returned it to him.

"No ghosts," said Morini. She shot another glance at Abigail and swept from the room.

Abigail lifted the teacup and rested it against her chin. The shadowed passageway outside the door seemed full of secrets. "She's lying, of course. Did you see the look she gave me?"

"Nonsense. Philip, for heaven's sake, don't lick the butter from your toast. It isn't considered at all polite."

Abigail leaned back in her chair and tapped her finger against the rim of her teacup. "Very interesting."

"I assure you, he doesn't do it often . . ."

"Not the *butter*, Lilibet. I mean Morini."

"Why? Surely you don't think she's *hiding* something." Lilibet wiped her hands on her stiff linen napkin.

"Of course I do," said Abigail. She set down her teacup and rose from the table. "And I mean to find out exactly what it is."

Upon his return to the castle, the Duke of Wallingford found himself obliged, for the first time in his life, to unsaddle his own horse.

He found he rather liked the exercise, though he should never have let it become known among his acquaintances at the club.

He liked, for example, the little sigh Lucifer gave as the girth loosened and the saddle and cloth slid from his smooth back.

He liked the way Lucifer's coat quivered and shone, as he brushed it afterward.

He liked the quiet of the stable, the slow drone of passing flies, the scent of hay as he refilled the net in Lucifer's stall. He liked leading the horse outside and setting him free again in the paddock, to enjoy the sunshine and the clean, new-washed air, the soft early grass underfoot, the scent of growing things.

"Rather a nice holiday for you, isn't it, old chap?" he said, latching the gate and setting his elbows atop the edge. Lucifer tossed his head and took off, giving his hind legs a little kick, frolicsome as a colt in the limpid spring morning. His hooves thumped the turf in a reassuring beat. Wallingford felt his lips stretch slowly into a . . . what was it?

A *smile*.

"Signore Duca," came a petulant voice behind him.

Wallingford heaved a resigned sigh. So much for peace and solitude.

"What is it now, Giacomo?" he asked, without turning. Lucifer had settled himself in the shade of a tree and began to snatch at the tender new grass.

"Is the women, signore."

"It's always the women with you, Giacomo. What have you got against the poor creatures?"

Giacomo's voice slid into an abject whine. "They are trouble, signore. They are always making the trouble. The signorina, the young one, she . . ."

"Stop. I don't want to hear it."

"She is spreading the stories, signore. She is saying we are . . . I am not knowing the word . . . the castle, she is saying, has the spirits . . ."

That chill again, tickling the base of Wallingford's neck. He set his booted foot squarely on the lowest bar of the gate and ignored it.

"Of course there are no spirits," he said. "We poured out everything in the library, directly we arrived. Except the sherry, of course."

"Not the spirits for the *drinking*, signore! The spirits, the souls . . . you are not understanding?"

"Oh, as to that, I've been told many times I have no soul at all, on good authority."

"Signore!" Giacomo's voice was reproachful. "You are making the joke."

Wallingford sighed and turned at last. "I never joke, Giacomo. I am much too dignified for something so vulgar as humor. I suppose you mean the castle is haunted?"

Giacomo nodded his head vigorously. "*Haunted*. Is the word."

The damned chill again.

Wallingford folded his arms. The sunshine struck Giacomo's gnarled body like a bolt of clear gold, illuminating the very fibers of his clothing with eye-watering detail. He stood with his legs planted far apart, as if withstanding a flood, his hands attached to his hips. He was wearing a queer old-fashioned jacket, made of some sort of rough wool, and the same flat cap he always had on his head, obscuring his hair and most of his forehead, leaving only a pair of broad ears that looked as if they meant to lift him off into flight at any moment. He seemed quite solid, quite corporeal. Quite un-ghostly.

"Well, is it?" Wallingford inquired dryly. "Haunted?"

Giacomo swallowed heavily. "Of course the castle is not being haunted! Is a story, an evil story spread by the devil-woman . . ."

"Devil-woman! Look here, Giacomo, Miss Harewood may be a mischievous little sprite, but she's hardly the spawn of . . ."

"Not the girl! The . . . the kitchen, the house . . . she keeps the house . . ." Giacomo snapped his fingers impatiently.

"The housekeeper? Who the devil's that?"

"Signorina Morini. You do not see her. She is staying in the kitchen. She tells the stories to the girl, and the girl, she . . . she . . ."

"She what?"

"She tells them to everyone!"

"She hasn't told *me*." Wallingford felt a hard nudge at his back: Lucifer, prodding him with his muzzle. Wallingford was surprised he'd left his grazing to come over again. "At least, not since the first night."

Giacomo frowned. "What is she saying, then?"

"Only that she felt something odd lurking about. Female vapors, nothing more. Look here, old man, you're making the old mountain out of a molehill, as they say. Simply ignore the women. It's what I always do."

Giacomo's black eyes cast down to the beaten earth. "Is making the trouble."

Wallingford uncrossed his arms and waved his hand dismissively. "What's a few ghost stories, after all? Merely a little fun. I daresay nobody takes it seriously. I've never believed in ghosts, and I don't intend to begin now."

"Is true, signore?" Giacomo looked up at him anxiously. "You are not believing?"

"Of course not. Silly feminine twaddle." Lucifer pushed right between his shoulder blades, with such force Wallingford nearly stumbled forward. "Look here, old chap," he said, turning back to the horse.

"You are not listening to the stories, signore?" Giacomo asked, behind him.

Wallingford rubbed between Lucifer's eyes, right in the center of the white lightning strike. "God, no. I never listen to women, as a matter of policy."

Giacomo sighed deeply. "Is good. You are wise, Signore Duca. Is no wonder you are duke. Very wise, very good, very . . . very *wise* man."

Wallingford closed his eyes and pressed his forehead against Lucifer's long nose. The warmth, the solid clunk of bone soothed the tingling along his spine.

"Yes," he said. "So I've been told."

Then he straightened and turned to dismiss the groundskeeper, but the man had already disappeared.

"I f you leave this room, signorina, I shall tell everybody my suspicions. *Everybody*. I shall tell them the place is haunted, inside and out."

Signorina Morini, in the very act of swishing her skirts through the doorway at the opposite end of the kitchen, halted herself in mid-swish. "*Che cosa?*"

"You know exactly what I mean. You understand English perfectly well." Abigail had no idea how one ought to interact with ghosts, but she imagined it was best to speak with self-command. After all, *she* was the one made of good, solid, respectable living flesh.

Though that flesh was quivering rather disgracefully, at the moment.

Morini turned, and Abigail experienced an instant of doubt. The housekeeper was so full of color, her red headscarf burning against the shadows, the few escaping tendrils of her hair gleaming black against her pale skin. "Your suspicions. What are these . . . suspicions?"

"Why, that you're a ghost, of course. If that's the word."

Morini shook her head. "I am not a ghost, signorina."

"You're not a regular person. Not a . . . mortal person."

Morini's shoulders moved, a kind of flinch. She turned her face away, looking at the great hearth with its low-simmering fire, its fire irons in place nearby, its black long-handled utensils hung with care alongside.

"I'm sorry. I don't know how to describe any of this. I've never made much study into the occult. Now, Tom Thomason, down the pub, he's a regular expert, sees spirits everywhere, even in the lavatory, which is quite unnerving when you think . . ."

"Why you are saying these things, signorina?"

". . . and more than a little unsanitary, though I suppose if one belongs to the spirit world one's quite above worries about germs and . . ."

"You are not making sense, signorina."

"Yes, I am." Abigail took a step forward. "Please, Morini.

Tell me what's going on. I know there's something, I can sense it; I've sensed it from the beginning. There's some mystery, I know it."

Morini stood there across the room, her arms still crossed above the neat homespun of her dress, the white linen of her apron. Beneath the loose material of her sleeves, her chest rose and fell in a slight but rapid rhythm.

Did ghosts actually breathe? Or was this movement simply some mimicry of human activity, some half-remembered reflex?

Was the woman alive, or not?

Something gave way in Morini's face. Her black eyes softened, in sympathy or perhaps defeat. She sighed, lifting her arms up and down on her chest, and stepped toward the fire. "Signorina, you are perhaps wanting some tea?" she asked, over her shoulder.

Abigail let loose a breath she hadn't realized she'd been holding, and tottered forward to sink herself into a chair at the rough-hewn table in the center of the room. "Yes, signorina. I believe I should like some tea very much."

I s many years ago," said Morini, bustling about the fire with the black teakettle.

"It always is. Once upon a time and all that." Abigail propped her elbow on the table and leaned her cheek into her palm. Morini's slender body wove before her in practiced movements, as if she'd been making English tea for English visitors for . . . well, for how long? "*How* long ago?" she asked.

Morini sighed and glanced back at her. "You are not believing me, if I say."

"Oh, I'll believe whatever you say. My mind is quite open, I assure you. Amaze me."

"Is . . ." Morini paused and looked up at the ceiling, as if the years were marked on the heavy wooden beams above. "Is three hundred years."

Abigail's elbow gave way, nearly crashing her head into the table. "Three *hundred years!*"

"Three hundred. Very long ago. The castle, it was almost new, built by the great lord, the Signore Monteverdi, who . . ."

"Signore Monteverdi! But the castle's owned by a fellow named Rosseti, isn't it?"

Morini spooned the tea leaves into the teapot. "Now, is different. Then, is the castle of the Monteverdi. He and the Medici in Firenze, the great prince, they are friends, they make much gold together. The signore's father, he start the castle, and the signore finish it. He comes with his new bride, the daughter of the Medici . . ."

"A princess!"

"No, not the princess. She is the daughter of his lover, his mistress, not the daughter of the wife. But she is . . . how do you say? The apple of his mouth?"

"His eye, I believe."

"She is his apple, his best-beloved, and he give her in the marriage to Signore Monteverdi, his great friend, so she will live not far away." The teakettle sang; Morini took her cloth and wrapped it around the handle and poured the water into the curving blue and yellow teapot. "She is beautiful, she is charming, she is kind and wise. Everybody love the new signora. Signore Monteverdi, he is mad for her, he has the frenzy of love, he adore the stones because she put her feet on them. It is nine months, she give him a beautiful baby son."

"Of course she does."

Morini was bustling about, fetching the pot of fresh cream, the sugar, the silver spoon. The air seemed to swirl around her in the warm, fragrant kitchen, made of old stone and old wood. The same stone, the same wood, that this long-ago Signore Monteverdi and his lady would have known; the same hearth that had cooked their food. Abigail laid her hand against the table and traced her finger along the grain.

"The signore is so happy. The baby is strong, the mother is safe. He buy her many jewels, many clothes. His love grow and grow. It fill the castle and the vines and the village below. It is not a year, and the signora's belly is great again with another baby."

"Oh, the brute!"

Morini shrugged and poured the tea through the strainer into Abigail's cup. "He love her. She is young, she is beautiful. Is the way of nature. Her belly grow, the summer come. Her time, it is upon her, and the signore wait in the library all through the night, while she has the labor."

Abigail's hand began to tremble as she lifted the teacup to her lips. "I take it this birth was not so straightforward?"

"No, signorina. It is not." Morini's voice roughened. "The beautiful signora, she has much pain, much struggle. The sound of her scream, her pain, it fill the castle. The signore wait and he wait in the library, and he hear her screams all the night. He lock the door, he let in nobody."

"How dreadful! Though of course he had only himself to blame, the unruly satyr."

Morini shot her a quelling look. "In the morning, there is a tiny baby, a little girl, but the mother . . . the dear signora . . ." She choked and swallowed.

"Bled out, I suppose. The poor thing." Abigail bowed her head. "And her babies never even knew her."

"She is carry to Firenze, where the Medici and the signore, they put her in the tomb in the Duomo and have a great . . . a marble . . ." She shaped her hands.

"A statue?"

"Yes! A statue for her tomb. Is very beautiful, they say. And the little girl . . ."

"Did she live?"

Morini eased herself into the chair opposite Abigail. "She live."

"I suppose Signore Monteverdi hated her for it. Your great men are all alike, blaming everyone but themselves, holding grudges and whatnot. You'd think a simple mea culpa would kill them . . ."

"No, he is not hating her. He love her. All the love he is having for the signora, he give to her. He say, the signora give her her spirit, she is like the signora reborn."

Abigail frowned. "Isn't that a little . . . well . . ." She twirled her finger in an expressive circle.

"She look exactly like the signora, her mother. Leonora, he name her, just like his bride. She is beautiful. She smile, she laugh, all the day she is happy and filling of joy. The signore, he spend every minute with her."

"Do you know, I rather dread to hear what comes next," said Abigail, drinking her tea.

Morini's eyes drifted to the wall behind Abigail, as if she could see the castle's ancient occupants dancing in the distance.

"The years, they pass, and the Signorina Leonora grow and grow, until she is nearly a woman. The most beautiful girl in all Toscana. When she is turning sixteen, the signore, he take her to Firenze, they stay with his old friend the Medici."

"Oh, haven't those two fallen out by now and poisoned each other?" Abigail said dryly.

"No, they are still the friends, by the grace of God," said Morini, quite seriously. "Now, the Medici, he has a young man staying at his palazzo, a young Englishman, making his travels. He is a great man in England, they say. A lord. The lord of . . . I forget the name . . . Copperbridge?"

"Haven't heard of him."

"He is a great man, a handsome man, tall and strong and brave. He travel to Italy to learn, to study the art."

"A perfect Renaissance prince. How charming for Leonora! I expect they fell in love directly," said Abigail.

Morini's gaze returned, shining, to meet Abigail's. "Oh, the love! It is instant, like this." She snapped her fingers. "They are in love, they dance all the night, they cannot take the eyes from the other. Everyone watch them together, everyone is happy. Everyone except . . ."

"Monteverdi, I expect, the old letch." Abigail sighed. "Men, *really*."

Morini's eyebrows lifted. "What is this letch?"

"Generally speaking, a chap who . . . well, never mind. Carry on. I suppose Signore Monteverdi ordered the poor Englishman away, forbade him to visit, locked up sweet Leonora in a nunnery . . ."

Morini's eyes grew round. "You are hearing the story already?"

"Call it intuition."

"It is not this nunnery, however," said Morini, settling back in her chair. "Is only the castle, the Castel sant'Agata, these stones." She waved her hand at the walls. "But it is prison to Leonora. She is not going outside, she is not leaving her room. The signore, he lock all the doors, he sit in his library, he drink the wine and the grappa . . ."

"But hold on a moment." Abigail set her teacup in the saucer with a clatter. "Didn't he have a son, as well? Didn't he care about the boy at all?"

Morini looked down at her hands, spread like fans across the worn wooden table. "The young Monteverdi, he is like other boys. He is strong and brave, he studies with the tutors, he is sent to Firenze. He love his sister very much."

"Then he must have felt things dreadfully."

"He does not say. He try to speak to the signore, to allow the marriage. He is the friend, the great friend of the Englishman, you see."

"Oh! Well, that's awkward."

"But there is not hope. The signorina, she is a prisoner, and the young English lord, he is growing mad with his love, he is desperate. He find a house in the village, he put on the clothes of the peasant, he watch the castle day and night. He find the signorina's maid when she is outside, he beg her to help." Morini reached for the teapot and refilled Abigail's cup. "The maid, she say she will help, she take the signorina a note."

"Plucky maids! Clandestine correspondence! Oh, marvelous," said Abigail. "Did she get the note, or did old Monteverdi waylay the maid first?"

"She has the note. She is so happy! She dry her tears, she write back to her English lord. She will change the dress with her maid, they will meet in the night, when the castle is sleeping."

"Oh, heavens! Say no more, Morini. You must recall my virgin ears." Abigail paused. "So *did* they? Meet?"

"*Si*, signorina. Young love, it must have its way. All the spring, they meet, they have comfort in the other, until it is June, and the signorina, the poor Leonora, she find out . . ." Morini's voice trailed off. She looked down at her hands.

"Copperbridge is courting another girl? He's drinking in the village tavern all night, gambling away his fortune?"

Morini whispered, "She is with child."

"Oh." Abigail, who did not generally blush, felt an unaccustomed warmth rise into her cheeks. "Yes, quite. Midnight meetings have that effect, I suppose."

"Leonora does not want to tell to her lover the baby," Morini went on, "but the maid, she has much worry, she write a note. The Englishman read the note and he say, it is enough, Leonora must be mine now. They will run away together. He will come at midnight on the evening of the Midsummer, when the castle and the village have the *festa*, and take her away."

"Midsummer's Eve! I swoon," said Abigail. "Did they manage it?"

Morini rose and picked up a fire iron and nudged at the fire. "The signorina, she dress as a servant, she put on her mask. The maid, she steal the key and let out the signorina from her room at midnight, as she has done all the spring. Leonora, she wait in the courtyard for her English lord. She is happy, she is sad. She love her English lord, but she is hurting her father, who love her, too. She is making dishonor for him. Her heart is so soft, so tender."

"She's a better woman than I am, by God. I'd have stuck a dagger between his ribs by now," said Abigail.

"At last her lord come to the courtyard to take her. She say to him, wait, I must say the good-bye. The Englishman say to her no, if you say good-bye, the Monteverdi will never let you go. Then the maid, the maid of the signorina, she run into the courtyard, she say to hurry, the Signore Monteverdi is coming! *Hurry*, she say to them. *Hurry!* But . . ." Morini replaced the fire iron and stared at the coals. "Is too late."

"Of course it was. All that dithering about. What were they thinking?"

"The signore rush in, he see the lovers. He insult the Englishman, say to him, he is a dog, a mongrel. He will call the guards for to take him to prison. The English say he will not go to prison like a criminal, he is a man of the honor. If the signore wish to have the duel he will meet him."

"How medieval."

"The Signorina Leonora, she tell him no, no! She cannot see her lover do the duel with her father. Then Signore Monteverdi, he turn to his daughter and call her terrible names, names of dishonor. So the English lord, he . . . he . . . oh, the good English lord." Morini shook her head. "He tell Signore Monteverdi his Leonora is the angel from heaven, she is pure, that the sin is all to him. He take out his pistol, he say to the signore, see? I give you my pistol, do what you will to me. And he throw down his pistol to the ground." She made a motion with her hand. "Right down to the stone of the courtyard."

"Well, that was downright silly," said Abigail. "What use is he to Leonora without a pistol?"

"He mean to do the honor, to make himself sacrifice for the lady. And do you know what is happen?"

"Something horrible, I'm sure."

"The pistol, it *fire*. It hit the ground, and it fire, right into the chest of the old signore." Morini pointed her finger like a gun, and fired it off against the wall.

"What? That's impossible!" Abigail leapt to her feet.

"No, signorina. Is possible. It happen. Signore Monteverdi, he fall to the ground, crying the murder. He is dying. With the last of his breath, he curse the poor signorina, he curse my poor Leonora. Her father, the last of his breath, and he curse her and her English lord. He say, they shall never again know the true love, shall never be free, until his soul is revenge."

Morini's face was pink, her eyes glittering. Her hands clenched into fists at her sides. Behind her, the fire gave a little pop of sympathy.

"Oh, Morini," breathed Abigail. "Oh, signorina."

"He curse her," whispered Morini. "She and the English lord, they run into the night, and no one hear the word from them. The young Signore Monteverdi, her brother, he search and search for her. And the castle . . ."

Abigail wiped her cheeks. "What of the castle, Morini?"

"The castle, ever since, it hold the breath. It wait and it wait for the curse to end."

"The curse? Her father's curse?" Abigail looked back up at Signorina Morini.

Morini eased herself back into the chair opposite Abigail and reached one hand across the table. "The servants, they leave. The brother, the young signore, he never return. Is only two left, waiting and waiting, until the curse is no more."

"Two left?" Abigail reached out her own hand and touched Morini's fingertips. They were solid flesh, real beyond question. "You and Giacomo?"

"*Si*, signorina," said Morini. Her eyes were still brimming. "Me and Giacomo. I have the indoors, he has the outdoors. I have the ladies, he has the gentlemen."

"What does that mean?"

"Until the curse is lift. Until the debt, the blood debt of the young lovers, is made to pay."

"But what is the debt? What must be paid?"

"Signorina, is impossible. You must not ask. For three hundred years, we try and we try, we wait and we wait. Is impossible."

Abigail leaned forward and took Morini's other hand in hers. "Please, Morini. Tell me. I swear, I'll do everything in my power. I'll bring you justice, I swear it."

Morini stroked Abigail's fingertips and looked into her eyes. She sighed, so deeply it seemed to come from the very center of her soul.

"An English, signorina," she said softly. "An English lord give his true love, pledge his life, to the lady who live in the castle."

Abigail felt her heartbeat slow, as if time itself were dragging to a halt. "*Which* English lord, Signorina Morini?" she whispered.

Morini closed her eyes and spoke so quietly, the words nearly dissolved into the air before Abigail could hear them.

"Who is to know, until the deed is done, the curse is broken? I say only, the English lord and his lady, to join in faithful love, before the end of the midsummer moon. To give life again, to give back to the Monteverdi the life it lose."

SEVEN

A bigail walked back from the stableyard in a daze.

She had been in a daze since leaving the kitchen; the usual morning session with Lilibet and Alexandra, in what they politely termed the salon, had proved a complete failure, interrupted mercifully by Percival when he stepped through the crumbling wall in search of lunch.

An English lord and his lady, joined in faithful love, before the end of midsummer moon.

Abigail looked down at her dress, which was stained with the contents of Percival's promiscuous mouth. Her shoes, crusted with stableyard detritus. Her fingernails, worn down, the right index finger even ringed with a trace of dirt.

Is impossible, Morini had said, shaking her head in the warm castle kitchen.

A movement caught Abigail's eye, near the peach orchard. A flash of blue, right where the path went down through the terraces toward the lake. She put up her hand above her narrowed eyes and thought, for an instant, she saw the unmistakable profile of her sister outlined against the trees.

Well, perhaps not impossible. Wasn't Mr. Burke's workshop hidden down there, amongst the olive trees near the lake?

And Lilibet. Even a blind fool couldn't miss the lovestruck

gazes Lord Roland Penhallow cast her way, nor the flush that burned the lady's cheeks in reply. Lilibet was free of her dreadful husband now, or nearly so.

But even if Mr. Burke fell in love with Alexandra, even if Lilibet and Lord Roland found their way at last into each other's arms, it might not break the curse. There was no way of knowing which English lord could redeem the doomed lovers.

Which left only one other English lord at the Castel sant'Agata.

Could she?

Could *he*?

Undying love for *Wallingford*?

Wallingford, faithful lover?

She felt a powerful attraction for him, of course. Not to put too fine a point on it, but she could hardly think of anything else, these days. But physical attraction, once satisfied, was the most fleeting of connections. Everything she'd read, everything she'd observed, everything she'd reasoned through in her sensitive and perceptive brain, supported this conclusion. And even if she *did* love Wallingford, even if this dizzy urge to join her body with his obscured some deeper and more affectionate connection, there were Wallingford's own inclinations to consider.

Rakes, after all, did not reform.

Abigail pivoted briskly to the castle walls, and there stood Morini in the doorway, shimmering, her head ducked against the sun, tears glittering on her cheeks. At Abigail's gaze, she turned away and disappeared into the shadows.

The hair prickled at the nape of Abigail's neck.

She stepped forward, heart lurching, to follow Morini, but another sight arrested her eyes: Francesca the maid, in her blue dress matching the sky, with her white headscarf bobbing against the dun-colored stone of the castle, pushing what appeared to be a great wheel across the yard to the stable.

Abigail blinked.

"What in the name of heaven are you doing, Francesca?" she asked, in Italian, putting one hand on the wheel. It was quite solid, quite cool, and smelled strongly of cheese.

In fact, on close examination, it *was* cheese.

Francesca straightened and pushed at her headscarf. "It is the *pecorino*, signorina. Signorina Morini, she wants to clear the attics, she asks us to move all the cheese to the stables for to ripen there."

"What a dreadful task. Do you need help?"

"Oh no, signorina. Maria is helping with the cheese. But there is . . ." Francesca paused doubtfully, her black eyes narrowing against the sun.

"Yes? I am happy, more than happy, to help. The studying, it is all done for the morning."

Francesca gazed back at the castle, its high rooftops lit by the climbing sun. "We were just beginning the filling of the mattress and the pillows. Is only halfway done. We have still the gentlemen to finish."

"Oh, what fun! Filling them with what?"

"With the new feathers, the goose feathers. Is all upstairs, in the bedrooms."

The bedrooms. The bedrooms, where once the Monteverdis had slept and kept their secrets. The bedrooms where the Englishmen slept now.

A sense of inquiry and curiosity, a very Abigailish tide of mischief, rose up in her chest.

"The gentlemen's bedrooms, you say?" She smiled. "I will go at once."

Francesca bit her lip and knit her brow, the very picture of regret. "No, signorina! Is not your place! Is so messy, so full of the feathers. I should not have said."

"Francesca," said Abigail, putting her hand to her heart, "I would not miss these feathers for the world."

Abigail began with Mr. Burke's room, in order to get the proper hang of things. Practice makes perfect, her mother had told her, seated before the long-ago old piano in the study, shortly before dying in childbirth (at which, ironically, she'd had a great deal of practice indeed, though Abigail and Alexandra were the only survivors).

As it turned out, stuffing containers with goose down required a certain specialized set of skills, in company with vast amounts of fortitude. Abigail, lacking any skill whatsoever, relied solely on her fortitude, and the result was a downy white mess of apocalyptic proportions, covering all of the plane surfaces of Mr. Burke's room, as well as a number of the irregular ones.

But at least the pillows were stuffed.

She cleaned up every last feather and moved on to Lord Roland's room, where she stuffed the bedding with somewhat more speed, though an equally profligate excess of feathers. She snooped efficiently as she went along, noting the presence of a travelers' lap desk in the chest and a false back in one of the drawers, filled with books with titles like *Cahier de Mathematiques*, apparently written in code and with no resemblance to any mathematics Abigail had yet encountered.

Interesting, Abigail thought, but hardly useful.

In any case, Abigail's primary interest lay elsewhere. She tidied up the feathers and marched down the hall, sack in hand, to the chamber occupied by the Duke of Wallingford.

It was locked, of course, but Francesca had given her the master key. A beautiful thing, that master key, done properly in some ancient bronze alloy, engraved and curlicued within an inch of its life. She lifted the chain over her neck and fitted the scarred end into the lock.

Abigail half expected the duke to be sitting inside, thunder-faced, demanding to know what the devil she thought she was doing. To which, of course, she could have no proper answer other than a cheerful, "Snooping, Your Grace! Do step aside whilst I open these drawers."

But the room was quite empty, quite anticlimactic. Also disappointingly un-ducal, with its rustic furnishings and austere gray bedspread. Wallingford's two chests sat side by side under the window with brass locks gleaming in the diagonal slash of late-morning sunlight; a few books sat stacked on the chest of drawers, and a closed shaving kit rested against the bowl on the dressing stand. How humbling, how decidedly human of the duke, to shave himself every morning without the help of a valet.

Though she had searched Roland's room without compunction, and fully intended to do the same here, Abigail felt a curious reluctance seize her hand as she reached for the handle of the chest of drawers. She ignored it, of course. In this state of war, which was all Wallingford's fault and none of her doing, everything was fair.

The left-hand drawer contained neckties and collars,

starched into undreamt-of heights of stiffness by the industrious Francesca, as well as a great many plain white handkerchiefs embroidered with the ducal crest. Abigail picked one up and sniffed it. Laundry soap, and perhaps a trace of something else, the ancient wood of the chest itself. She tucked the handkerchief in her pocket and opened the right-hand compartment, which contained the ducal undergarments and which she promptly closed again.

There were limits, after all.

Clean white shirts, breeches, stockings: Really, did the duke conceal nothing interesting among his laundry? No, she was quite certain Wallingford was hiding something, somewhere. The entire notion of the Duke of Wallingford traveling to Italy for a year of academic study—an entire year without his accustomed comfort and privileges—beggared belief.

Besides, a man with nothing to hide must be very dull indeed, and hardly worth the trouble of seducing, let alone sacrificing oneself in undying love for the sake of some mysterious and unproven curse.

The very thought caused a pang of emotion in the region of her belly. Or perhaps it was merely a lingering indigestion from Morini's copious breakfast.

She moved on to the chests, and found them filled with books: scholarly sorts of books, Greeks and Romans, philosophical tracts, most of which Abigail had already studied with the tutor Alexandra had so expensively hired to keep her occupied during her London days.

Wallingford's wardrobe contained the usual complement of an English gentleman, with morning tweeds next to neat wool suits next to smooth black dinner jackets. Abigail slipped her hands into the usual pockets, and found no signs of billets-doux, no clandestine correspondence of any kind. Another little pang: disappointment, or relief?

She stood in the center of the room and turned in a circle, frowning.

Surely she had missed something.

If she inhabited this room and had something to hide, some secret passion, something worth traveling across Europe to keep concealed, where would she put it?

Abigail ran her eyes over the floor, the windows, the furni-

ture. The thick solid walls, made of stone, covering with crumbling old plaster. She stepped to one side and ran her fingers
lightly over the rough surface.

Quite old. No sign of having been disturbed or of hasty
replastering. In any case, what did the Duke of Wallingford
know about such things?

At last, Abigail turned to the dresser, a dark old-fashioned
hulk near the window, and with one finger drew aside the opening of Wallingford's shaving kit.

Bergamot.

Oh, heaven.

Abigail sank into the chair next to the dresser, sighing. His
shaving soap. That was it. She leaned over, inhaled again,
slumped back again, sighed again. In her mind, she had flown
instantly back to the stable at the inn, with the rain thundering
on the tile roof above, and Wallingford's velvet mouth covering
hers, and the stone wall pressed against her back, and—oh,
another sniff, oh, delight—and the duke's stone chest pressed
against her breasts, and . . .

"What the *devil* are you doing in my room?"

Abigail's half-lidded eyes flew open.

He filled the entrance, her Duke of Wallingford. His arms
lay crossed over his chest, and his broad tweed-swathed shoulders nearly touched the sides of the doorway. He was wearing
his riding clothes, and his shining boots lifted him to unspeakable authority. In her bergamot-drugged mind, he seemed as
handsome as a god, his cheekbones jutting proudly over mortal
man and his dark hair curling in a darling question mark upon
his forehead. His eyes blazed at her, lit by the sunlight from the
window, and for the first time Abigail realized that they weren't
black at all, but rather a deep midnight blue. She had never been
close enough in full daylight to see it before.

"What a question," Abigail said, rising, fighting the urge to
fling herself into his arms or else lie down on the floor with her
legs spread, "when it's perfectly obvious I'm only changing the
feathers in your bed."

She waved a demonstrative hand at the burlap sacks in the
middle of the floor, and the trail of down surrounding them.

Wallingford looked at the feathers, and at Abigail, and back
at the feathers. His arms remained crossed. He spoke slowly, as

he might to a person of known idiot capacities. "Changing . . . the feathers . . . on my bed?" he inquired in a measured voice, eyebrows raised.

"It's very hard work, though I don't suppose you have any idea," said Abigail. The scent of bergamot began at last to clear from her head in the gust of fresh air from the doorway, though oddly enough she still wanted to fling herself into his arms. Instead, she picked up a sack of goose down. "I was only taking a moment's rest in your chair."

Wallingford stepped forward and cast a suspicious glance around the room. "Aren't there servants for that sort of thing?"

"They're busy with the cheeses, of course."

"The cheeses?"

"It's a very long and domestic story, I'm afraid, and you don't strike me as the sort of fellow who takes much interest in domestic stories. Would you mind helping me with this mattress?" Abigail pulled off the blankets and sheets in a relentless tug.

"What the devil are you doing?" exclaimed the duke.

"Changing your feathers, of course."

"My feathers don't need changing, and certainly not by you."

His hand closed around her arm. An enormous hand, she thought, quite surrounding her with room to spare. She wanted to lean back in his shoulder, but it hardly seemed appropriate when they were arguing like this. "Of course your feathers need changing," she said. "I daresay these ones date from the last papal visit, which is to say centuries ago."

"Your presence in my bedroom is a direct violation of the terms of the wager."

"It is not. I'm on a housekeeping errand, quite innocent. You're the one with your hand around my arm, which strikes me as decidedly more seductive in intent."

Wallingford's hand dropped away. "I must ask you to leave."

"I must ask you to stand aside while I complete the re-feathering of your bed."

"You're the sister of a marchioness. It isn't your business to be re-feathering beds, or feeding goats and chickens, for that matter."

Abigail turned. "What the devil does that mean? What business is it of yours? I think a great many marchionesses would be improved by feeding goats on occasion. Dukes, too, come to think of it."

Wallingford glowered down at her. "You've no sense of propriety at all, do you?"

"No, I haven't." She stared up at him, as fiercely as she could, feeling suddenly small and frail next to the wide heft of Wallingford's shoulders, the unending length and breadth of him. She'd known large men before, of course, but this was different. Beneath those well-cut tweeds lay a fine latent energy, a seething will. She could sense it roiling inside him, ready to flood all that civilized bone and muscle with the warmongering energy of his ancestors, the ones who had first earned those titles that now trailed after his name and made him so irresistible to women.

All that uncivilized power, with nothing to lavish it on in these civilized modern times.

He stared back at her, quite close, his breath brushing against her face in quick gusts and his midnight eyes narrowed in concentration. His immense hands rose up and closed around her shoulders. "Why not, Abigail?" he asked.

"Why not . . . what?" She was a little breathless. A trace of bergamot drifted from his skin and touched her nose. Somewhere in the back of her mind, Morini's words were hammering, hammering, a confused tangle of fate and curses and vows of undying love, but she could not quite keep them straight.

Wallingford's voice deepened and softened, both at once. "Why haven't you any sense of propriety?"

"Because it gets in the way."

"In the way of what?"

She tried to think. "Of becoming an interesting human being. A real person, instead of a cleverly dressed doll."

"No one," said the Duke of Wallingford, lifting the back of his hand to her cheek, brushing her with his knuckles, "no one would ever mistake you for a doll, Miss Harewood."

Oh *yes*. Never mind the boathouse and its wine and candles. Never mind the possibility of a mistress in the village. Never mind Morini's silly curses. This was perfect. This was the moment, as the sunlight flooded the window and Wallingford's handsome face looked down at her with exactly that expression of longing and passion.

Oh *yes*.

Abigail put her hands on his chest and went on her toes.

His lips brushed hers, as soft as goose down.

"Oh," she said, and "Oh!" more like a gasp this time, when his hands slid up to her jaw and his mouth nudged again, so gently.

"Abigail," he murmured, kissing her, cradling her.

She wobbled, stepped backward to catch herself, and tumbled over the burlap sack of goose down.

Wallingford followed her, catching her, and somehow they were on the hard stone floor and not caring a bit, kissing madly, her hands tearing at his buttons and his hands tearing at hers. "Oh, *Wallingford*," she said.

"For God's sake," he growled, from somewhere in the hollow of her throat, his fingers popping apart her bodice, "it's Arthur."

"*Arthur?*"

"Arthur." He pulled open her bodice at last and breathed into the lace of her chemise where it frothed above her corset.

"But I can't possibly call out, *Oh, Arthur!* in the throes of passion."

He looked up. "What the devil do you know about the throes of passion?"

"Nothing at all, except that one doesn't share them with chaps named Arthur, if one can help it." She wiggled herself comfortably underneath him and lifted her head for a kiss. "But don't worry. I'll think of something. You don't mind if I call you something else, like Wolfgar or Tristan or . . . well, even Roland is rather nice for purposes of passion, but that would be awkward . . ."

Wallingford lifted himself away. "It would be *bloody* awkward!"

"Oh, come back here. You mustn't mind me. I've a habit of saying unruly things like that. Just ignore me. Arthur's fine; really it is. I'm sure I'll get used to it straightaway." She reached for his jacket, unbuttoned at last, and pulled it over his shoulders.

He opened his mouth to object, but his eyes fell back on her bosom, and his head followed. His fingers brushed along the lace, tugging it downward, raising sweet little goose bumps of anticipation on her skin.

"Oh, Arthur," she said, experimentally, and then, "Oh, *Arthur!*" with forced conviction.

"Abigail, you're so lovely, you're like a fairy, my own lovely fairy. I'm afraid to touch you," he whispered, kissing her again.

Oh, he tasted so delicious. She kissed him back, ran her hands over his shoulders. "Arthur," she said again, because she was determined to get used to it. "Oh, Arthur. I don't think I've ever enjoyed winning a wager so much."

Wallingford's body froze above her.

She gave his shoulders a little push. "Arthur?"

His head lifted. "What did you say?"

"I said, *Oh, Arthur!* Didn't I?" She thought back wildly.

"The *wager*. You said you'd won the wager."

She smiled and touched his beautiful lips, which were so soft and full, so incongruous in that hard, glowering face. She loved his lips. "Oh yes. Isn't it lovely? Such a silly idea, that wager. I'm so glad it's off the table, so to speak."

Wallingford jumped to his feet. "What the devil's going on here?"

Abigail blinked. She sat up, letting her bodice sag shamefully to her waist. Her hair had come loose from her pins and tumbled about her shoulders and down her back. She felt rather deliciously like a strumpet. "Isn't it obvious?" she said with happiness. "We're making love. At last!"

Wallingford's brow compressed to its most thunderous scowl. His beautiful lips thinned. He reached for his jacket. "You did this deliberately, didn't you? Who put you up to it? Lady Morley, I suppose?"

"Why, no one. No one suspects a thing. They believe I quite hate you." She pushed her hair away from her cheek. "What's the matter? Why are you putting your jacket on?"

He was already fastening the buttons with his dextrous fingers. "I perceive I am being made a fool of," he said.

"Oh, don't be ridiculous." Her skin was still tingling, the tips of her breasts aching against the uncompromising pressure of her corset. She was filled with want, filled with desire, and the impossible object of her need was even now straightening his collar into impeccable lines, erasing all signs of the man who had whispered passionately in her ear a moment ago and called her his lovely fairy. Abigail opened her arms desperately. "Come back here. I told you I'm given to unruly comments. There's no need for . . ."

"Feathers," he said. "What an idiot you must think me. I daresay you meant to shame us all into leaving the castle entirely."

"That's not true. I'd die if you left." She scrambled to her feet.

Wallingford stared at her coldly. He reached for her bodice, and she gasped, thinking he meant to rip it from her body and start anew, but instead he pulled the ends together. "You look like a strumpet," he said, and began fitting the buttons through their eyelets. Abigail was too stunned to stop him. "What a sacrifice you planned. Noble creature. Were you planning to take things to the ultimate conclusion, or are your friends even now waiting outside, ready to burst in and interrupt us in flagrante?"

He fastened the last button with such a violent jerk that she took a step backward. She crossed her arms over her chest. She was flushing all over, not with desire now, but anger. An unfamiliar sensation: Abigail hardly ever felt a genuine temper. Fury was as foreign to her nature as jealousy. She had no experience of dealing with it, no way to control the red-mist film that covered her sight and the words that tumbled from her mouth.

"I was planning to make you my lover," she said. "I was planning to make you the gift—a gift, you stupid man, I can only give once—the gift of my innocence. I was hoping it meant to you what it did to me, that this moment was as beautiful to you as it was to me, but I see I was mistaken. I see you're nothing more than the coldhearted seducer of reputation. I see I ought to have chosen Mr. Burke, or dear old Penhallow, except I'd never do that to my friends, and oh! Now you've made me cry, you dreadful duke, and I *never* cry!" She grabbed the sack of feathers.

"Wait, Abigail . . ."

"I hope you *never* find someone to love you. I hope you die alone and childless and *miserable*!" She took the sack by the bottom and let loose the contents at his head. "It's no more than you deserve."

Abigail did not stop to admire the results of her handiwork.

She turned and marched out of the Duke of Wallingford's bedroom, not even bothering to hear the apoplectic shouts that followed her down the hall, muffled by goose down.

There were feathers in his eyelashes. Feathers in his hair,
feathers in his jacket, feathers in his mouth, which he had
foolishly opened to remonstrate with her, even as the cloud of
goose down swept upon him.

"Abigail!" Wallingford roared, or as much as a man could
roar with a tiny speck of goose feather tickling the back of his
throat. He spat it out and tried again. "Abigail!" he roared, a
proper ducal roar of the sort designed to bring opposing armies
and rebellious tenants to their trembling knees. The very stones
of the castle should have bowed in obeisance before the authority in that roar, but Abigail Harewood did not stop, probably did
not even hear him.

She had disappeared without trace into the shimmering
spring air, like the fairy he'd called her.

Of course he hadn't meant to call her that. Like everything
else this morning, it had slipped from him without conscious
thought, as if he'd been inhabiting another life. For the past
several weeks, he'd done his rigid best to avoid her, to accost her
with scowls when meetings were inevitable, to close his mind to
the very idea of her. He had come dangerously close to forgetting himself earlier in the stableyard, and he could not allow
that to happen again.

He must not slip. He must not weaken.

But all those considerations had fled from his brain at the
sight of her, of Abigail, of the delicate bones of her clavicle
just peeping from the collar of her yellow dress and the black
eyelashes lowered over her impossibly large eyes. And then
those eyes had risen and taken him in, had regarded him with
such teasing warmth, such innocent knowingness, and he was
finished.

Oh, she had said, and *Arthur*, and the sound of his given
name on her lips had melted his ears and the brain beyond; the
sight of her skin, of the tender smoothness, the promising
plumpness rising above her corset, had driven him wild. His
lovely fairy, his angel-perfect Abigail, arching and sighing

beneath him. Damn the wager, and damn his grandfather, and damn the whole world except this one stone room and this one absurd and exquisite woman, designed just for him.

And then, amid her moans and sighs: *I don't think I've ever enjoyed winning a wager so much.*

It had all come crashing down. His pride, the budding, nameless feelings in his chest, the words he had been about to say.

She had played with him, set him up, used him.

Him, the Duke of Wallingford.

He stood in the center of the empty room, raising a small flock of scudding feathers with every heaving breath. Everything neat and in its place, except the bed, and the feathers, and his own disordered brain.

His scowl deepened. The door of his room seemed to mock him, standing open to reveal the yawning hallway into which Abigail had disappeared in a swing of yellow dress, and the glimpse of a window overlooking the verdant new-spring valley below.

Wallingford growled, deep in his throat. He started forward, swept through the door in two long strides, slammed it closed, and locked it. He paced to the stairs and leapt down them, making for the door, his riding boots striking like flint against the stone floor.

Dukes, after all, were not made for contemplation.

A bigail sat on the rocks with her arms clasped about her knees, watching Wallingford's long white arms propel his body across the lake.

He was quite naked. She glimpsed his lean back sliding just below the surface, his churning feet, even the flash of his buttocks at various points in his progress. Unfair, that a man with every advantage of birth should possess such a fine and perfect figure, such a graceful power of motion. With every fiber, Abigail longed to unbutton her dress, to unfasten her wretched stays and her chemise, all the civilized layers of clothing that separated her from Wallingford. She longed to dive into the water and join him, to see his face when she did, to force him to acknowledge the truth that lay between them.

But she did not. She went on sitting quietly, half shaded by the nearby olive trees, the sunlight warming her skin in tiny patches. In the distance, she heard a few childish shouts: Lilibet and Philip, probably, having a lunchtime picnic, avoiding the temptation of Lord Roland.

Why did Wallingford's silly vows mean so much to him? What was he really struggling against?

There *was* no great secret, she realized. There were no clandestine articles hidden among his belongings, no secret mistresses in the village. The Duke of Wallingford simply meant to test himself, and the motivation lay entirely within his own skin.

Wallingford had nearly reached the opposite shore now. She could no longer make out the details of him, the black gleam of his head in the sunlight, but his arc of movement remained as rapid and vigorous as ever, as if he could swim all day in the chilly early-spring waters. She gazed at his striving body with tenderness, with an entirely unaccustomed possessiveness, with pride in his strength as if he had pledged it to her.

They were all a little broken, weren't they? All six of them, not quite whole.

She rose from the rocks and shook out her skirt, and then she skipped up the path through the terraces and into the castle, where she found Signorina Morini at the broad table in the kitchen, sorting an enormous pile of beans for the evening soup.

The housekeeper did not look up. Her attention remained focused on the beans, her red headscarf radiant in the subdued colors of the kitchen.

Abigail sat down next to her and reached for a handful of beans. "All right," she said. "I believe you. Tell me how I can help."

EIGHT

As schemes went, it was certainly more promising than the time Abigail had disguised herself as a young man in order to take the entrance examination at Merton College.

Then, she had not gone half an hour out of Paddington Station before the nervous perspiration between her crushed breasts (like her sister, she had inherited the legendary Harewood Chest) had developed into such an intense and irritating rash that she was forced to disembark at Chiltern and take the next train home. The housemaids (who had chipped in with cast-off clothing from brothers and cousins) and the cook (who had packed her lunch with such care) had all been so disappointed at her early return.

But this scheme did not involve crushed breasts and stolen trousers. She and Signorina Morini were merely facilitating the proper course of nature, bringing together ladies and gentlemen who were falling in love already.

Abigail looked across the table at Lord Roland, dear and handsome Lord Roland, his hair picking up gold from the candles and his expressive hazel eyes gazing dreamily into a nearby dish of olives. Why, he was already expiring for Lilibet. He would be *grateful* for the friendly nudge of Abigail's helping hand.

Wallingford's fist interrupted her reverie with a brutal plate-rattling crash against the table. "Look here, Burke. Haven't you heard a word of this?"

Abigail glanced at Phineas Burke. She could hardly blame Alexandra for her fascination with him. Such a handsome fellow, too, with his great height and radiant color and perfect bones, almost an architectural duplicate of . . .

Abigail set down her wineglass and looked back at Lord Roland, and then at Wallingford, and then back at Mr. Burke.

Good God.

"I'm afraid I haven't," Mr. Burke was saying. "I've a problem with the battery to sort out, and all this ranting of yours isn't a bit of help. Penhallow, my good man, may I trouble you for the olives?"

Lord Roland gave a little start. "Eh what? Olives, you said?"

"Olives, sir. To your left. Yes, that's the one. Good chap."

Wallingford struck the table again with his judicial fist. "Burke, you insufferable sod . . ."

"Really, Your Grace!" said Lilibet, in properly shocked tones.

". . . I beg your pardon, Lady Somerton, but the man deserves it. It's his own miserable hide I'm attempting to protect."

Abigail watched Wallingford drink his wine, watched him shoot a fierce glance in Mr. Burke's direction. Fierce, and yet protective, too; why hadn't she noticed that protectiveness before?

"My hide is in no danger whatsoever, I assure you," Finn said.

Alexandra set down her knife and fork. She was sitting next to Abigail, so her face was invisible, but Abigail could imagine how it looked: skin smooth, eyebrow cocked, eyes gleaming with confidence. She said to Mr. Burke, in her bewitching drawl, "His Grace thinks I mean to seduce you, in order to win this silly wager of yours."

Abigail cleared her throat and spoke. "But that's absurd. If you seduced Mr. Burke, successfully I mean, the wager would technically be a draw, wouldn't it?"

Everyone turned to her, faces stretched in astonishment, as if they'd forgotten she existed, as if she'd said something to explode every known law in the physical world. She looked from one to the other. Had this fact never occurred to any of them? It seemed rather obvious to her.

Mr. Burke spoke at last, in a stunned voice. "Yes. Yes, I believe it would."

Abigail turned to Wallingford and gave him a smile of particular meaning. "You see? You may put your mind entirely at ease on the subject of seduction, Your Grace. No reasonable person would contemplate such a scheme. Two advertisements in the *Times*! It wouldn't do."

Wallingford returned her gaze with unspeakable rage. The color climbed up his face to flood the skin atop those magnificent cheekbones. What would he do, she wondered, if she rose from her chair and walked around the table and clasped those dear burning cheeks between her hands, just as she had that afternoon?

"Dear me, Wallingford," said Alexandra. "You really must endeavor to calm your nerves. I fear you will bring on an apoplexy. Have you any medical training, Mr. Burke?"

"Only a few rudiments, I regret to say. Hardly enough to loosen his cravat."

Wallingford regained his power of speech. "I am happy to be the source of such endless amusement. But you"—he stabbed his finger at Mr. Burke's broad chest—"and you"—ditto Lord Roland—"have no idea at all what these women have in contemplation. From the moment of our arrival last month, they've been scheming and harassing us, in order to make our lives here so hellish as to drive us away entirely, and leave them the castle to themselves. Do not, Lady Morley, be so insulting as to deny it."

"I should be very happy to see the last of you, Wallingford," said Alexandra. "I make no attempt to hide the fact."

Wallingford narrowed his eyes. Abigail had the uneasy impression that her sister had walked straight into a chessboard arranged with care by the duke himself. The flush had disappeared from his cheeks, and in its place a film of ice seemed to have frozen his features into severity. "Very well, then, Lady Morley," he said, in deliberate tones. "I should like to propose an amendment to our wager. To increase the stakes, as it were."

Increase the stakes. Now this was interesting. Abigail leaned forward a fraction of a degree: Would this plan of Wallingford's disrupt her own carefully wrought schemes this evening?

"Oh, good God," said Mr. Burke. "Haven't you a better use of your time, Wallingford? Reading some of that vast collection in the library, perhaps? It *is* what we're here for, after all."

Alexandra ran her finger around the rim of her wineglass. "He's welcome to join our literary discussion in the salon. We should be pleased to hear an additional perspective, although I would suggest bringing an umbrella, in case of inclement weather."

"No, damn it all! I beg your pardon, Lady Somerton."

Lilibet sighed, so quietly Abigail could scarcely hear her. "Not at all, Your Grace."

Wallingford straightened forward, gaining another inch or two of authority in his robust shoulders. His voice took on an absurd degree of resonance. "My proposal is this: that the forfeit, in addition to Burke's excellent suggestion of an advertisement in the *Times*, should include an immediate removal of the offending party from the castle." He sat back again, with a look of immense satisfaction.

Silence yawned among them, until Abigail thought she could hear the very flicker of the candles.

Lord Roland whistled. "Hard terms, old man. Are you quite sure? What if it's *us* that's given the old heave-ho?"

Wallingford gave him a superior smile. "You are, I admit, the weakest link in the chain, but I believe I may rely upon Lady Somerton's honor, if nothing else."

"Really, Your Grace," said Lilibet, in a faint whisper.

"This is beyond absurd, Wallingford," Alexandra said sharply. "All this talk of conspiracies and whatnot. I assure you, I haven't the slightest intention of seducing poor Burke, and I daresay he has even less desire to be seduced. This is all about this business of the feathers this morning, isn't it? You're trying to have your revenge on us . . ."

"If I'm wrong, Lady Morley, you should have no reason at all to object to the increased stakes." Wallingford reached for the nearby bottle and poured himself half a glass. "Isn't that so?" He drank, watching Alexandra from above the rim.

Next to Abigail, Alexandra seemed to vibrate. Abigail wanted to tell her not to worry, that everything would work out, that nobody would be rousted out of the castle, that this was all nothing more than the friction of their six unruly bodies as they found their proper places with one another. But what could she say? Alexandra—and though her sister had never spoken a word of it, Abigail made it her business to know these things—lay just now on her beam ends, after financial disaster had visited the jointure left her by Lord Morley; she had nowhere to go from here, no other home except this leaking Italian castle. And Lilibet! Even worse for Lilibet, were she to be forced from this remote seclusion: Brutal Lord Somerton awaited her in London, and was probably even now flooding Europe with his emissaries, searching for his absconded wife and son.

No wonder Alexandra hesitated at Wallingford's offer. The men might leave the Castel sant'Agata with no more injury than a badly bruised pride; for the ladies, the stakes (as Wallingford put it) were altogether higher.

But he'd backed them so neatly into a corner. Alexandra could hardly refuse, could she? Abigail stole another glance at Wallingford, who sat straight-shouldered at the head of the table, looking quite smug and handsome and pleased with himself.

"Of course I shouldn't object," Alexandra said at last, clenching her fingers around the stem of her empty wineglass. "Other than a sense of . . . of the absurdity of it all."

Mr. Burke cleared his throat and came to his lady's rescue. "Really, Wallingford. It's hardly necessary. I don't see any reason why we can't continue to muddle on as we are. A tuft of goose down, here and there, doesn't much signify. And I'm fairly confident I can resist Lady Morley's charms, however determined her attempts on my virtue."

Wallingford leaned back and cast his eyes around the table. "None of you, then, not one of you has the fortitude to meet my offer? Lady Morley? Your competitive spirit can't be tempted?"

"You always were an ass, Wallingford." Alexandra shook her head.

Oh, the hell with it, thought Abigail. Someone had to speak up and settle things, or dinner would never end, and her plans would be spoilt.

"Why not?" she said, into the silence.

Once more, all eyes turned to her in shock. Really, it was good fun, stunning the table with her pronouncements like this. She turned to Wallingford and gave him the full force of her gaze. "Why not? I can't speak for your side, Your Grace, but we three are simply going about our business, studying and learning just as we intended. If it amuses you to turn this into a game, to raise the stakes, consider the wager accepted." She gave her shoulders an insouciant shrug and turned to Alexandra. "It means nothing to us, after all. Does it, Alex?"

Alexandra blinked and took a deep breath. "No. No, of course not. Very well. We accept your stakes, Wallingford. Though it hardly matters, as your suspicions are entirely wrongheaded. In fact, your head *itself* seemed to be wrongheaded at the moment, and I suggest you turn away from your wild speculations and put it firmly to work as you intended in the first place. We're on Aristophanes ourselves, just now, and my dear Abigail has already reviewed it twice in the original Greek. I'm certain she would have some useful insights for you. Perhaps she can assist you with your alphas and omegas."

Oh, what a trump she was! Abigail stretched her hand beneath the table and gave Alexandra's wrist a little squeeze of support.

"My alphas and omegas are quite in order, I assure you, Lady Morley." Wallingford dabbed his lips with his napkin and dropped it by his plate. He rose, with a graceful motion of his lean body, and made the briefest of bows. "And now, ladies, if you'll pardon the unpardonable. I must excuse myself, and leave you to the far more appealing company of my fellow scholars."

Off he went, leaving the silence to settle in the echo of the shutting door.

And now, Abigail thought, folding her own napkin atop the ancient linen tablecloth, *let the games begin.*

G iven the cavernous size of the great hall of the Castel sant'Agata, the Duke of Wallingford, crossing it with energy and conviction, hardly expected to collide with Abigail Harewood's breasts.

Strictly speaking, of course, he had collided with her right shoulder, but when he threw out his hand to steady them both, it had landed—whether by accident or with the reflexive instinct of a homing pigeon—directly into the plush cushion in the center of her silk-covered chest.

"Why, Wallingford!" she exclaimed, not backing an inch. "What on earth are you doing here, at this hour?"

He couldn't remember. Something to do with a book. The kitchen. A large bronze key floated rather confusingly in the air before his eyes.

"What the devil are *you* doing here at this hour?" he growled instead, stalling for time. He couldn't even see her properly, with only a thin shaft of moonlight angling its way through the distant windows, but of course it was Miss Harewood. No mistaking that cheerful voice, that delicate scent of sweet floral soap, of lemons and blossoms. That curving flesh, fitting his broad palm to overflowing . . .

He dropped his hand, as if from a scalding teapot.

"I was just coming downstairs from putting Philip to bed," she said, without a trace of self-consciousness. "He made me read several stories from a great book on warhorses, which he'd purloined from the library, quite unsuitable for bedtime of course, but what can one do when a little boy takes an idea into his head, especially when . . ."

The library.

Wallingford's head cleared.

"Never mind all that," he said. "Do you know where I can find this housekeeper of yours? The kitchen, I presume? The door to the library is locked." He paused. "I suppose that boy of yours did it accidentally, on his way out. Left the light on, too; most dangerous."

"Strictly speaking, he's Lilibet's boy."

"Regardless. I require the key at once."

A little pool of silence opened up between them. Wallingford had the sense of fidgeting, there in the darkness where she stood.

"Well," she said slowly, "in that case, I shall go and look for Morini. But I've little hope of success. I quite expect she's abed by now."

"It's only eight thirty."

"She keeps country hours."

Wallingford shifted his feet impatiently. "Then you must wake her up. We can't leave the lamps burning in the library all night. It's dangerous, for one thing; and for another, I require a book."

"What book? I'll find it for you."

"Miss Harewood," he said, with deliberate scorn, "I need hardly remind you that the library remains in the territory of the gentlemen's side of the house. It is not your business to be fetching books for me from its shelves."

"I daresay you're used to having books fetched for you," she said. "I daresay you haven't fetched your own books since you were a boy, and probably not even then."

"Then you'd be mistaken. I'm quite capable of finding my own books. I . . ." Wallingford paused. In the silver gilt darkness of the hall, surrounded by cool stones and still air and the faint warmth of Abigail's invisible body a few feet away, he felt once more a sense of fidgeting nervousness, a dangling of Abigail's spirit. "Are you trying to distract me, Miss Harewood?" he said quietly.

"Of course not," she said, too quickly. "I always speak this way. Never could keep to a single topic. What were we discussing? Keys, or books? Or both?"

"Specifically, the key to the library," said Wallingford.

"Oh. Well, there's your problem, right there." She made rustling movements, as if smoothing her dress.

"Problem? What problem? The library is locked, and therefore we find the housekeeper and obtain the key. Perhaps you might care to lead the way, Miss Harewood." He spoke with stern authority. He was quite sure, now, that she was hiding something. The very hairs on his skin seemed to know it. Miss Abigail Harewood might flummox the rest of them, but *he* knew her cunning. He knew her, inside and out. She couldn't hide a single flutter of that ebullient manner from *him*; no, not a single hesitation of her voice nor wasteful movement of her hand.

"Ah, well, you see, Your Grace," she said, "and perhaps you ought to know this already, if you were properly familiar with the library in question, but you see . . ."

"Yes, Miss Harewood?"

"It locks from the inside."

Check.

Wallingford folded his arms. His eyes were growing more accustomed to the ghostly light, and he thought he could pick out Abigail's smile, just tipping the corners of her mouth, as if she were fighting to control it. Her dress rustled slightly, a shifting of petticoats around her slender legs. His right hand, he realized, was still warm from the accidental meeting with her breasts.

"What are you suggesting, then, Miss Harewood?" he said. "That the library door has locked itself?"

"Why, no. Of course not. But perhaps your brother has locked himself in. Did you think of knocking?"

"Why on earth would my brother lock himself in the library?"

"Why, for privacy, of course. To keep himself safe from interruption." She leaned forward and warmed his collar with her sweet breath. "From Lady Somerton's treacherous attempts at seduction, perhaps."

Was she *laughing* at him?

"Lady Somerton hasn't a treacherous bone in her body," he said confidently, and leaned forward, too, ostensibly to intimidate, but really because he wanted to catch once more the sweetness of Abigail Harewood's breath in his nose, the drift of warmth from her skin. "You, on the other hand, Miss Harewood . . ."

"I . . . *what*? I'm treacherous?" She laughed. "Surely not. I'm straightforward to an absolute fault. I'm a living monument to straightforwardness. Why, my sister would be *delighted* if I were less straightforward. *You must strive to obtain a few wiles, Abigail*, she tells me, *or you'll never catch yourself a husband.*"

"Oh, you've wiles enough," Wallingford heard himself growl. Almost as if . . . good God, it couldn't be so. He couldn't be *flirting* with her, could he? He wanted to jump back, but his shoes seemed to have glued themselves to the flagstones.

"Wiles enough for what, Your Grace?" Her voice twinkled in the shadows. "For a husband?"

"For anything you damned well please. Isn't that right, Miss Harewood?"

She laughed. "You have a great deal more confidence in my abilities than I do, Your Grace. Why is that?"

"Because I have seen them at work. Now tell me, Miss Harewood, in the plain, straightforward language of which you own yourself proud: Exactly *what* is going on in that *library* right now?" He spoke forcefully, putting a feral snap into the words *what* and *library*, and looming over her so closely that scarcely an inch or two of empty space remained between their respective bodies.

"Oh," she said breathlessly, "how I adore it when you speak like that! Towering over one like a colossus! It gives one the most delicious shivers, straight the way down one's back."

"Answer the question, Miss Harewood!" he thundered.

"It's the same way you spoke at dinner tonight, and—I speak in confidence here, Your Grace—it was all I could do then, not to fling myself in your arms and insist you ravish me, right there on that enormous old table. Well, once you'd ordered all the others out of the room, of course. I am not so depraved as *that*."

Wallingford opened his mouth and found he had not the smallest word to say.

"Now tell me, Wallingford," Abigail continued, with perfect composure, "what you meant by all this business of raising the stakes? Of ousting us from the castle, lock, stock, and all that? It seems so excessive."

Wallingford's brain, still reeling, returned no answer.

"And smacking rather of hypocrisy, if you don't mind my saying so. After all, strictly speaking, you and I are the guiltiest parties of all. Are we not?" She placed her hand on his sleeve, so gently he might not have noticed the pressure at all, except that this was Abigail and Wallingford's every available faculty recorded her movements, her words, her expressions, in minute detail.

Not that many of Wallingford's vaunted faculties were available at the moment. At the words *ravish me, right there on that enormous old table*, an image had leapt into his brain of such voluptuous depravity, such extravagant sensuousness, such luscious sexual possibility, it rendered him helpless as a newborn.

"Guilty?" he mumbled, fastening on a word at last. He wished she would take a step or two backward, to allow a little space between her tempting warm body and his. Perhaps then he could gather his wits about him.

"Quite guilty. If I hadn't made that silly comment upstairs in your room—for which I am deeply sorry, Wallingford, I should *never* think of our liaison in such terms, *never*—why, I daresay I shouldn't be standing here now, as I am."

"As you are?"

"As a maiden, of course. You would have quite despoiled me, and I should have been very glad of being despoiled, and we would probably be upstairs furthering my ruin at this very moment. I say, are you quite all right? I haven't been too *straight-forward* with you, have I?"

"I think, Miss Harewood," he said at last, in a strangled voice, almost a whisper, "you had better lead the way to the library directly, and I shall endeavor to forget this conversation ever took place."

"I *have* shocked you, haven't I?" She sighed. "You see? No wiles whatsoever. Here you are, a notorious seducer, and here am I, quite willing to be seduced, and yet somehow . . ."

"Miss Harewood," said Wallingford, working frantically to stave off the imminent explosion of his brain, "the *library*!"

"Oh!" Her hand dropped away from his sleeve at last. "The library. Of course. Do you think it might be better to head 'round the bottom of the main staircase, or to . . ."

He was going to kiss her, Wallingford realized in horror, if only to stop her mouth. With heroic effort, he forced his shoes to separate from the flagstones, stumbling backward with the force of his momentum.

"Careful!" she sang out.

He didn't answer. The narrow Gothic windows beckoned, outlined with moonlight, guiding his footsteps across the great hall to the passageway to the west wing. The library lay beyond, a great two-story cavern of a room, lined with ancient leather-bound volumes in a fine state of mildewed neglect. A warm room, despite its high ceilings; it caught all the afternoon sun through its windows (not a favorable location for a library, in fact, but perhaps the builder had not been a lover of books) and trapped it like an oven. Wallingford had spent many a well-intentioned hour there with a book sitting promisingly in his lap, only to fall promptly asleep.

Perhaps that was the case with Roland, too. A clever chap, his brother Roland, beneath all that laziness, but since the precocious days of his youth, he had seemed to settle into an intellectual somnolence that few books could penetrate.

Abigail's footsteps tripped lightly behind him down the stone passageway. "Wait, Your Grace!" she called. "A word with you!"

He could not ignore her. Ass he might be—he admitted it freely—but certain breaches of etiquette were impossible even for him. He stopped and turned, warily. "Yes, Miss Harewood?"

The passageway was even darker than the great hall, without

any moonlit windows to speak of, and only the distant glow at either end to lighten the shadows. Abigail was panting a little, from the effort of keeping up with him, and his fevered imagination fastened at once on the undoubted heave of her breasts— God, such breasts, he could feel their echo on his palm even now—beneath her dress.

"You never answered my question, Your Grace. Why change the terms of the wager? Are you so eager to see us away?"

"You and your friends, Miss Harewood, are an entirely unnecessary distraction," he said, "quite antithetical to the purpose of our . . . our *sojourn* here in Italy." The word *sojourn* sounded so pompous; he shuddered as he said it. "And what's more, I strongly suspect that you're attempting to do the same thing by us, only with rather more subversive means. It's an act of preemption, nothing more."

"But I don't want you to leave at all. I've told you so."

He hesitated. "Perhaps you don't, Miss Harewood, but your sister does. And Lady Morley is even more inclined to have her own way than you are, isn't she?"

A delicate pause settled between them, and then, quite unexpectedly, Abigail drew nearer, put her hand beneath his elbow, and spoke in a gentle voice. "Please, Your Grace. All this—it isn't necessary. Can we not simply try to get along with one another? Must everything be battle and conflict?"

Her voice was so low, so sweet. Her hand cupped his elbow caressingly. He could not resist her like this, soft and pleading. He could not resist her elfin form with its graceful curves, her generous warmth reaching out to surround him, to breathe life into the stiffened cells of his body. *Yes*, he wanted to tell her, *I should be miserable if you left, more miserable than before; I should wither and die.*

Wallingford took a step closer. His hand reached up to enclose the curve of Abigail's jaw.

My dear boy, said the stern Duke of Olympia, *has the entire conduct of your adult life ever suggested your usefulness for anything else?*

"Wallingford," whispered Abigail, the smallest breath of a word.

He stood still, muscles locked, brain hammering. Abigail's face was dark and shadowed; his eyes couldn't seem to resolve a single detail of her, and yet he knew exactly how she lay before him, exactly how her eyes tilted, exactly how her ear curved beneath the soft chestnut wave of her hair. Her skin was pure warm satin beneath his palm.

He leaned his lips toward her opposite cheek. "Miss Harewood," he whispered, even softer than she. "The library."

Abigail walked as slowly as possible along the flagstones, feigning uncertainty. "It's so dark," she said. "I can't see a thing. I do hope Philip hasn't left any of his toys on the floor, or we shall be done for."

"For God's sake, Miss Harewood," Wallingford growled behind her, "hurry along."

How long had it been since Lilibet had crept downstairs to meet Lord Roland in the library? Abigail didn't dare check her watch, not that she could have made it out in the darkness. Half an hour, perhaps? An hour? How long had she been standing in the great hall with Wallingford, in the passageway with Wallingford, stringing him along while her nerves frizzled and her brain spun? Enough time for poor, lovesick Lord Roland to work his magic on poor, lovesick Lilibet?

The irony, of course, was that Lilibet actually *expected* Abigail to march through the library door and surprise them. That was the plan, after all, as Abigail had presented it to her cousin: Seduce Penhallow, and then Abigail would catch them in the act, and the gentlemen would be dispatched out of harm's way before any attention—say, that of beastly Lord Somerton—could be brought to bear on the Castel sant'Agata.

Lilibet, therefore, would not be surprised to hear Abigail and Wallingford pound on the door to interrupt her in flagrante with Lord Roland Penhallow on the library sofa. She would be ready to claim that Penhallow had come after her while she looked for a book, and Penhallow—dear honorable gentleman that he was—would immediately accept all the blame and that would be that.

According to plan.

Except that Abigail had not actually intended to interrupt them. She had intended to let nature work its undoubted course on the two of them, and then at least one loving couple under the roof of the Castel sant'Agata would be well on their way to reversing the ancient curse.

Until the Duke of Wallingford had blundered into things.

"Oh!" Abigail feigned a desperate stumble. "Oh, my ankle!"

"Shall I lead the way, then?" came Wallingford's dark voice, unsympathetic.

"Of . . . of course not." She limped on with gallant head held high, more slowly than before. "I can manage. Just. Only a little strain of the sinews. I shall be right as rain by morning, I'm sure, though I shall perhaps need some trifling assistance on the stairs."

The end of the passageway drew near. Just around the corner lay the door to the library. A glow spread out along the stones, from the large window at the entrance to the library wing, which caught the moonlight at a perfect angle. Abigail put her hand on the wall and held up her foot like an injured hound. "Oh, how it twinges!" she said.

"Shall I carry you, then?" Wallingford's voice nearly bowed under the weight of his sarcasm.

"Oh, how kind of you! I should like that very much. Shall I put my arm around your neck, like this, or can you manage without it?"

Wallingford's skin quivered under her fingers, just above his starched collar. He removed her hand with great care. "I assure you, Miss Harewood, I was only making a joke. We both know how unsuitable it would be, were I to carry you unchaperoned through the castle at night. A clear breach not only of the terms of our wager, but of propriety itself."

"Yes, of course. I . . ." She swallowed and pushed back a lock of her hair, which had fallen from its pins to curl below her ear. Her fingers smelled ever so faintly of bergamot from the contact with Wallingford's neck. She nearly swooned. "What was I saying?"

"We were going to visit the library, Miss Harewood, to arouse my brother from his academic stupor."

"Yes, of course. Though I rather think he won't be pleased to be disturbed, now that I reflect on it. In fact, he's sure to be quite cross. I know *I* should be, if somebody interrupted me while I was reading something I particularly liked. It's like a slap to the face. I'm certain that's why he locked the door in the first place."

"No more certain than I am." Again, the dripping weight of sarcasm. "Come along, then, Miss Harewood. Better to face trouble straight on, don't you think, rather than delaying the inevitable? Particularly for someone of your *straightforward* nature?"

"Oh, quite," she said. Her back seemed to have settled helplessly against the wall. "All part of being straightforward. Let me just . . . pin up this silly hair of mine, which has got quite loose . . ."

Wallingford sighed, straightened, and turned around the corner in a single long stride.

"Wait!" she called, scrambling upward, forgetting to limp.

"Well, well." Wallingford's voice rumbled to her ears.

Oh, God.

Abigail whipped around the corner. The library doors stood open, moonlight spilling faintly from the shadows. Wallingford towered before them, hands on the door handles, wool-covered arms magnificently outstretched.

He turned his head to her, and his expression wasn't dark and thunderous, as she'd feared, but rather admiring. Almost . . . *amused.*

"It appears we were both wrong, Miss Harewood," he said. "The library is quite empty."

NINE

When the Duke of Wallingford had entered the sacred gates of Eton College at the age of thirteen, he had noticed Phineas Burke at once. A difficult chap to ignore, Burke, with his great height and his astonishing head of red gold hair ablaze in the September sun; he had been clutching a satchel under his sticklike arms, and was flanked on one side by a black-clad servant carrying a large leather-buckled chest, and by a woman of eye-watering beauty on the other. Wallingford had poked his companion in the ribs and said, in the offhand way of thirteen-year-old boys discussing something vitally important, "Who the devil's the ginger?"

The other boy—heir to the Earl of Tamdown—had followed his nod and laughed. "Why, don't you know, old boy? That's your own bloody uncle."

Wallingford had blackened his friend's jaw, of course, as was only proper in affairs of libelous insult, but when he'd gone out for a walk early the next morning, he had been astonished to encounter his grandfather, the august Duke of Olympia, standing on the Thames footbridge, under the very shadow of Windsor Castle, engaged with the lanky ginger-haired newcomer in what appeared to be a discussion of an intimate fatherly nature.

The sort of discussion in which Wallingford's own father had never once seen fit to engage with him.

On alternate Mondays, when the weather was dour, Wallingford fancied he could still feel the burn of bile in the back of his throat.

But today was a Tuesday, and the weather was as fine as only an Italian spring morning could be, and Wallingford had long since come to regard Phineas Burke with a sort of bemused affection, and a great deal of concern for the state of his common sense.

Not that Wallingford's own common sense was in the best of shape these days. He ran his palm over the smooth curve of his saddle, picked up the cloth, and began to rub in small meditative circles. He had no idea, in fact, if this was the proper way to oil one's saddle. He'd never witnessed a saddle being oiled, and had only the faintest notion that saddles were oiled at all. But he imagined it was rather the same case as one's boots, which were also made of leather, and he had come to terms with the regular oiling of such several weeks ago. Like everything else, one simply rolled up one's sleeves and plunged in.

If a valet could figure it out, by God, a duke should have no trouble at all.

Wallingford rubbed a little harder, and saw with satisfaction that the leather was growing shinier, turning butter soft and supple beneath his oily cloth and oilier fingers. That was something, anyway. After a night fraught with erotic images of Miss Abigail Harewood atop the massive dining table, awash in candlelight; after waking at dawn to saddle Lucifer for a twenty-mile circuit about the hills; after hours spent swinging wildly between the ecstasy of succumbing to mad passion and the satisfaction of withstanding it, Wallingford welcomed the tactile reality of the softening leather. The usefulness of it. That he could point to this saddle and say to himself, *See there, I have done something right today. I have returned my saddle to its former glory.*

He could master himself. He *would* master himself.

Still, the mastering bit would be a damned sight easier if there were no elfin-faced, round-bosomed temptresses about the castle, plotting his moral downfall with cheerful straightforwardness.

The sun shone pleasantly on Wallingford's back. He had set the saddle atop the fence rail in order to both enjoy the fine weather and to facilitate his work, and expected the cheerful voice of Abigail Harewood to deliver its straightforward observations into his ear at any moment. She did not, however. This ought to have been a relief, and was instead unsettling.

Wallingford rubbed furiously, until the high gleam of the leather burned his eyes. Unsettling why? Unsettling because of what Abigail might be planning, or unsettling because he longed, in fact, for her to arrive by his side? Longed to hear her voice, longed to feel her hand on his elbow?

Wallingford stepped back to admire his handiwork, and was rewarded by a chorus of vowel-rich Italian profanity, delivered in shrieking contralto.

"Giacomo, my good man," he said, turning. "By damn, you ought to have announced yourself. I might have injured you."

"Signore Duca, my foot, it is broken!" Giacomo clutched the appendage in question and hopped in an irregular circle.

Wallingford folded his arms. "Oh, I say. Hard luck, that. When you have caught your breath, however, perhaps you might condescend to explain why you were skulking over my left shoulder just now, in such a suspicious fashion? Take your time," he added, plucking a stiff black horsehair from the immaculate tweed of his jacket. "I am quite at leisure."

"Not this . . . this *skulking*, signore!" Giacomo gasped. He stopped hopping and placed his injured foot tentatively on the grass, toe first. "Is not *suspicious*." Slowly the foot eased flat; slowly Giacomo shifted his weight, ounce by ounce, to his ravaged tarsals. An aggrieved sigh marked each step of his progress.

"In your own time, Giacomo," said Wallingford. "Or perhaps I can save you the bother and divine your purpose myself." He tapped his finger against his chin. "If I should hazard a guess—and I'm not particularly a betting man by nature, though I'm known to dabble in the odd wager or two—I should imagine it has something to do with . . . now, let me ponder a moment . . ." He snapped his fingers. "The women."

"The *women*," Giacomo said scornfully, as he might say *the fermenting compost*. He sighed, with a trace of regret. "Is not the women."

"It's not? You astonish me." Wallingford could not help a

twinge of relief. God knew he was no particular champion of the sex, but Giacomo's relentless whining and plotting in re the female inhabitants of the Castel sant'Agata made him feel positively chivalrous. No one but Wallingford, after all, should have the right to insult Abigail Harewood.

Giacomo shook his head. "No, Signore Duca. The women, they are cleaning the castle today. Is the visit of the priest."

"The priest is coming? The devil you say!"

"*Signore Duca!*" Giacomo crossed himself. "*Si*, signore. The priest. For to bless the house for the . . . the spring . . . the come to life of our Lord . . ." He snapped his fingers frantically.

"Easter?" Wallingford hazarded. Good God, was it Easter already?

"For the Easter! *Si!* The women, they are busy today, *grazie a Dio*. But Signore Burke . . ."

"Burke? What the devil's the matter with Burke?" Wallingford demanded. Lurid images filled his head: gas explosions, engine combustions, tea spilt over the battery. Anything might happen when one was tinkering with infernal machines all day long.

Giacomo put his hand to his heart. "He is needing help, signore. He has the wires, the . . . the batteries . . ." He leaned forward. "And that Signora Morley, that devil-woman, she like for to visit him, to *torment* him . . ."

"Aha! So it *is* the women!"

Giacomo shrugged. "Who can say, Signore Duca? But is better to be safe, no?"

Wallingford pictured Burke's workshop, filled with sunshine and machine parts, with the masculine scents of oil and metal and leather, with the sound of Burke's little grunts and snarls of concentration. A place of purpose, of genius and invention.

Also a convenient and secluded place for Lady Morley to play her tricks. In the struggles of last night, he had almost forgotten that Burke had his own troubles; clever, steadfast Burke, a gem of a chap, really, easy meat for the Dowager Marchioness of Morley.

And finally, and perhaps most importantly, the last place in the world Abigail Harewood would visit, on a fine spring morning.

Wallingford swung the saddle over his arm.

"Say no more, old fellow. I shall be down to buck him up directly."

Abigail cocked her head and gazed at the plate on the dining room table. "Are you quite certain?" she asked.

"*Si*, signora. Is the tradition. The priest, he bless the eggs, for to make the castle full of life." Signorina Morini bobbed her headscarf—white today, presumably in honor of the purity of Our Lord, and of His earthly representative, due at the Castel sant'Agata in a scant few hours—and ran her hand over the rounded tops of the half dozen or so eggs on her most festively decorated plate.

"And you really believe that sort of thing?"

Morini turned to her with a reproachful slant to her eyes. "Signorina, you believe the other, the great curse, and you are not believing the eggs?"

"But they seem so . . . complacent." Abigail stared once more at the smooth white shells, which indeed had not the smallest scrap of magic attaching to them. "Quite ordinary, in fact. I only fetched them this morning, straight from the coop, just like any other eggs."

"Is not what is happening to the eggs *now*," said Morini confidently. "Is *after* the blessing."

"And you're quite certain this priest of yours knows what he's doing? Won't accidentally cast some different blessing altogether? Our plans are fragile enough as it is, Morini." Abigail drummed her worn fingernails against the wood. "I had the most difficult time with the duke last night; he's really dead set against any sort of amorous activity whatsoever, let alone the transcendent curse-defying love of which we're in desperate need. Why, he nearly caught Lord Roland and Lilibet in the library himself, which would have brought an end to everything!"

Morini smiled and shook her head. "You are not worrying about the duke. You are not worrying about the priest. Is fate. I know this, the very first minute I see you in the hall. This time, the fate is with us."

"*This* time?" Abigail turned. "You've had others here before?"

"Of course we have had the others. Every thirty years, fifty years, it is all to try again. The ladies, the gentlemen of the blood. But . . . *pfft!*" Morini made a dismissive noise. "Nothing. Is only to wait and try again."

"Oh, Morini." Abigail reached out and patted the housekeeper's hand. "I shall try my best, really I shall. I believe Alexandra is down at the workshop with Mr. Burke this instant, and how can he possibly resist her? And I'm quite sure something went on between Penhallow and Lilibet last night. She blushed like a . . . like a . . ." Abigail groped.

"A rose?"

"Yes, a rose! Quite! The sweetest pink rose, really lovely, when he came swinging through the door in that dashing way of his. It won't be long there, I'm sure of it." Abigail gave a dreamy sigh and leaned back against the peeling plaster wall.

"And you, signorina? You and the Signore Duca?" asked Morini, in a soft voice.

Abigail closed her eyes and laid her palms against the rough-smooth pattern of the plaster behind her. "Oh yes. The duke. I was going to speak to you about that."

"Signorina."

"Yes, well, as I said, I think we're nearly there with the others, they're quite in love, and all of them of the marrying sort. Eternal love, faithful love. All right and tight. But you see, Morini . . ."

"Signorina."

Abigail opened her eyes and met Morini's gaze earnestly. "It's not quite the same with Wallingford and me. There's a great deal of physical attraction, of course, not that His Grace seems inclined to consummate it, but I don't think . . . Morini, you must understand, it's not in his *nature*."

"His nature, signorina?"

"I mean that certain people aren't *suited* for married life. For faithful married life, I should say; anyone's capable of existing in a state of marriage, everything else being equal. But the duke . . . even if he were to fall in love with me, Morini, which . . . well, it would be difficult to tell, because he isn't exactly forthright about that sort of thing, but even if he *did* fall in love with me . . ."

"He love you, signorina," Morini said quietly, motionlessly. "Is no doubting he love you."

A sharp pain bit into Abigail's palms; she looked down and realized it was her own fingernails. "Even if he did love me, he simply couldn't be true to me. In six months, in a year, the novelty would wear off, or some seductive widow would catch his eye . . ."

Morini shifted forward and took Abigail's hand between hers. "I think you are not seeing the duke with your true eyes."

Abigail gathered herself. "So you see, you mustn't get your hopes up. Even if Wallingford loves me, loves me enough to wish to marry me, it's not enough. He's not a suitable husband, and I'm certainly not a suitable duchess, and we should make each other quite miserable. Either way, the curse wouldn't be broken."

A flurry of noise overlaid her last words. Footsteps rattled down the hallway, and the door to the dining room sprang open before Morini could reply.

"Signorina!" burst out Maria in eager Italian syllables, sparkle-eyed, gripping her apron with both hands. "Don Pietro is here. And his acolyte, oh, signorina! The most beautiful young man in the world!"

"Of course he is." Abigail rose from the chair with a deep sigh. "Exactly what the castle needs. *Another* handsome chap sworn to chastity."

The two cups sat side by side on the worktable, both plain and white, handles turned away from the other, as if they were enjoying a confidential chat. A pot of honey squatted a foot or two away, like a round-bellied chaperone.

Burke's voice rose from behind Wallingford's back, in response to the question the duke had just posed. "*Two* teacups? How extraordinary. I suppose . . . well, I wanted another cup."

Wallingford stepped forward and peered into the cups. Triumph flooded his veins: the heady sensation of having one's worst suspicions confirmed by the facts on the ground. He turned to face Burke and brandished an accusing finger. "Half full, both of them. You didn't think simply to refill the first?"

Burke rolled his eyes. "Oh, for God's sake, old chap. You're like a detective from one of those dashed sensational novels. I suppose I forgot about the first cup. One tends to get a bit distracted, fiddling with machines all morning."

Already, Burke's composure had returned. His arms were crossed against his chest, and his face had relaxed into annoyed boredom. His right foot twitched, in preparation for an impatient tap against the worn wooden floorboards of the workshop.

Wallingford wasn't fooled, not for an instant. He cast his eyes about the room, speculating, considering, until his gaze fell upon the large wooden cabinet next to the counter fixed to the opposite wall.

Just the right size for a contraband female.

Wallingford strode across the floor, past the automobile, and reached for the knob of the cabinet door with tingling fingers. By God, Lady Morley must be shaking in her boots by now.

"Look here!" Burke exclaimed.

Wallingford flung open the door and shouted: "*Aha!*"

The hinges squeaked in astonishment, unnaturally loud against the empty stillness of the cabinet. A pot of paint, upset by the intrusion, toppled from the shelf at the top and landed with a ringing crash on the floor.

"You see?" Burke said triumphantly. "Nothing there."

Wallingford whipped around. "Oh, she's here, all right. I know it. I can feel her, sneering at us." His every sense had prickled to life, sweeping the sunlit dimensions of Burke's workshop with a surveyor's eye for detail. He stalked the perimeter, examining each chest, each stack of parts and machinery. The leaning tower of pneumatic tires, inside and out. He cocked his head toward the rafters, in case her ladyship should be swinging by her marsupial tail.

Burke stood next to the automobile, not quite resting himself on the smooth metal frame of one door, his arms still crossed. "Wallingford, you're boring me. Can you not learn to control this . . . this clinical paranoia of yours? Find some other baseless obsession. Resume your goose feather flirtation with young what's-her-name. Oh, *really*. I assure you, she's not in the damned *sink!*"

Wallingford turned and sniffed the air. Was he mistaken, or did the faint hint of lilies hover about the air?

Lilies. Lady Morley's scent.

He scowled at Burke, who stood with legs planted and arms crossed next to the machine in the center of the room, green eyes narrowed against the sunlight now shafting through the window.

The *machine*. In the center of the room.

Burke's automobile sat guilelessly on its blocks, without wheels or seats, its smooth metal returning the gleam of the sun. It was long and sleek and narrow and quite unlike any other automobile Wallingford had encountered in his limited experience, dashing almost, even denuded of any obvious signs that it was an automobile at all. Burke was immensely proud of it. Not three days ago he had said, over breakfast, and without a trace of immodesty, that it would change the entire course of automobile design, provided he could get the damned electric battery to do its duty.

Burke adored that machine.

Wallingford whispered, "Yes. Of course."

"You're mad," snapped Burke. He took a step.

Wallingford swallowed the distance to the automobile in two eager strides. He curled his hands around the metal edge, where he presumed the door should be, and tilted his body with a deliberate flourish to peer inside.

The floorboards stared back up at him, polished to liquid honey smoothness, containing not a trace of a cowering dowager marchioness.

He looked forward and back, into the shadows, just to be certain she had not shrunk herself to rodent size and scurried beneath the steering column.

From some nearby tree outside the silent workshop, the squirrels had set to chattering. Wallingford felt a growl of frustration rise up in his throat. "Empty," he said, turning back to Burke. He was seething, razor sharp with suspicion, like a hound whose quarry had darted into the thickets at the last instant. "Where is she, then?"

Burke spread his hands innocently, palms upward. "Haven't the slightest. Back in the castle, perhaps?"

The solution was here somewhere. Lady Morley could not have dissolved into the air. Her tea still sat right there in its cup, with a trace of warmth. How had she escaped? Not by the front door, clearly.

But the carriage doors at the back?

Wallingford stared at the old wooden portal, hands on hips. His mind reviewed the chain of events, went over the details of his own arrival a short while ago. Penhallow had been chatting amiably with Burke. He had been on the point of leaving, in fact, with no marchioness in sight. "She slipped out, didn't she? When Penhallow arrived."

Burke threw his hands up in the air and groaned.

Wallingford stomped toward the carriage doors. Wood warped, bars coated with dust, they looked as if they hadn't been opened in decades, but who was he to judge such things? He grasped the bolt, yanked it from its socket, and flung open the right-hand door. The immediate burst of noontime sun stung his eyeballs.

He looked about the little clearing behind the workshop. "The question is whether she's gone back to the castle or lingered about, waiting for us to leave."

"Search away," said Burke, behind him.

Wallingford stepped forward into the dappled sunshine. The scent of apple blossom surrounded him, warm and delicate, from the orchard on the terrace above. His boots sank into the soft new grass. "My guess is that she's still about. She's a persistent woman, after all. Tenacious." He glanced back at Burke. "Come along. I'd like to keep an eye on you."

"You bloody dukes. You don't understand the first thing about actual work. How, for example, it requires hours of uninterrupted concentration . . ."

"Humor me."

Up went Burke's arms again. "Bloody hell, Wallingford." But he followed anyway, in grudging steps, coming to rest at last against a gnarled and ancient olive tree, his ginger head nearly losing itself in the new-laden branches. "I'll wait here," he said grimly.

Wallingford did not give a damn for Burke's grimness. Dukes were not in the business of pleasing others, after all. He meant only to find Lady Morley, to roust her out of whatever hollow she had hidden herself in until his departure from the workshop, and from there to roust her and her companions out of the castle itself.

For Burke's sanity, and his own.

He raised his head and sniffed the air, searching for the telltale hint of Lady Morley's lilies, but smelled only the sweetness of the apple blossoms, the gentle hints of sunshine and grass, as he paced about the clearing in measured steps. What had Lady Morley been wearing today? Blue? Yellow? He couldn't remember, couldn't even recall seeing her. Surely those endless skirts would be difficult to hide outdoors.

But he saw only the brown of the trunks and limbs, the green of the leaves, the endless springtime blue of the sky above the trees.

Burke called out from his olive branches. "There, you see? She's not here. Now would you mind taking yourself off?"

Wallingford circled slowly back to the door. His mind, accustomed since childhood to the split-second adventure of hunting, turned keenly over the possibilities. She was not in the clearing, likely hadn't been in the clearing. She was not in the workshop itself. What had he missed?

He glanced at his uncle, who stood firm next to the olive tree, his face set in stern lines. "Well done, Burke," he said. "Admirably played. But next time, I assure you, I'll be ready."

"Whose blasted side are you on?"

"Yours, though you may not believe it." He put his hand on the latch.

Burke started forward. "Look here, man. You've already searched the damned cottage!"

"Only retrieving my hat, for God's sake." Wallingford pushed open the door and stepped through, blinking, his eyes adjusting to the dimness after the unchecked sunshine outside.

"I'll retrieve your hat!" said Burke, dashing in behind him.

Wallingford turned around. "For God's sake . . ."

Burke stood with the sunlight at his back, hands flexing at his sides. Wallingford could not see his face properly, but there was no mistaking the wideness of alarm in his eyes, the taut set of his shoulders and arms.

The *devil*.

Wallingford smiled, a slow and satisfied smile. For a moment there, a brief and rather horrifying moment, he'd wondered whether his instincts had truly been scrambled by the befuddling effects of Tuscan sunshine and Abigail Harewood, and not necessarily in that order.

"Aha," he said softly. "She's still here, isn't she?"

Burke's feet shifted. "She was never here. You and your damned imagination."

Wallingford turned in a slow and calculating circle. The details of the workshop slid past his eyes, the same as before, the cabinet and chests and machine parts, the automobile in the center of the room. What had he missed? He rubbed his fingers against his thumb, as if to draw out the answer from his own skin. "Now, if I were a lady, caught in flagrante . . ."

"In flagrante, my arse."

". . . where would I scurry to hide my shame? A slender lady, mind you. And one with plenty of nerve. None of your missish airs about Lady Morley, I'll say that."

Burke said nothing, merely stood there by the carriage doors, crackling with expectancy. His hair, poor chap, seemed actually to stand out from his head, like a ginger thistle.

Wallingford came to a stop. No use looking where he'd looked before. He'd searched up, he'd searched north and south, west and east, inside and outside. But he had not looked . . .

His gaze, roaming about the vacant machine, slipped downward.

"By God," he said. "You damned clever thing."

"Wallingford, you're mad."

Just like the end of a long day's hunt, when the fox had led them a merry chase across half the county, and they were wet and tired and muddy, and the drizzle had moved in and spoilt his coat, and the infernal hounds had lost the scent time and again, and at last, at *last*, as if by the hand of some magnanimous Creator, the old devil fox made some critical error. Had grown overconfident and shown himself.

Wallingford took his time, walking across the floor to the automobile on its blocks. There was no point in rushing the moment. Such intense pleasure must be savored.

"Do you know, Burke," he said, "I almost admire this Lady Morley of yours. It takes a certain amount of fortitude, not to say cheek, to lie beneath an automobile for such a considerable period of time. I do wonder whether she's sincerely in love with you after all."

He stopped, mere feet away from the sleek metal box that contained all Phineas Burke's dearest hopes. Something stirred in his chest, some unfamiliar sensation, something that another man might perhaps have called . . . what was the word?

Sympathy.

"Are you, Lady Morley?" he asked softly. "Are you in love with my friend Burke?"

No reply came. Naturally, a Harewood woman would never be so accommodating as to essay a direct answer to a direct question.

Wallingford eased himself down into a catlike crouch and put one hand on the floor. His riding boots creaked with indignation. "Although," he said, leaning his face beneath the bottom edge of the machine to peer into the shadows, "I daresay she wouldn't recognize the emotion if it slapped her on her pert little . . ."

Daylight. Nothing but daylight and . . . was that a spider?

He struck the floor with his fist. "Bloody hell. She's gone!"

TEN

Wallingford was halfway back to the first terrace when the answer struck him.

The cabinet.

He staggered to a halt and slapped his hand against his thigh. Good God. Of course. She'd slipped out from under the automobile when they'd gone outside, and then darted into the empty cabinet when the carriage doors had rattled open again, the clever devil.

He slapped his thigh again, this time with his closed fist. A child could have figured it out. How they must be laughing at him now, absolutely doubled over at his witlessness. If they weren't already locked in a passionate embrace, of course.

A pair of squirrels raced across the faint beaten-down grass on the path before him, squabbling angrily over some purloined delicacy, or else madly in love. Together they scampered up a towering cypress, one chasing the other, until Wallingford lost them in the branches.

The castle lay beyond, mellow red roof tiles against the blue sky.

A movement caught his eye, down among the trees: a flash of yellow, dipping in and out of view. A golden brown head, bobbing above the budding leaves, the unfolding bounty of springtime.

Roland, by God. Roland and Lady Somerton, deep in a tête-à-tête, oblivious to the world.

What the devil was going on around here? Was the entirety of bloody Tuscany falling in love before his eyes?

Wallingford looked up at the cloudless sky, at the sunlight pouring down from the heavens, and sighed.

What an astonishing shade of blue it was, this Italian sky. Depthless, concentrated, impossibly pure. On his leaving England two months ago, the sky had hung down like iron, quite impenetrable. He remembered leaning against the railing aboard the packet steamer for Calais and staring at the departing coastline until the drizzle had enfolded it whole, and the entire horizon had become one immense block of gray, from sky to shore to sea.

How distant it all seemed, against this landscape of blue sky and green hills and blossoming trees.

Joint by joint, his fisted hand began to relax against his leg, until his palm had fully opened and his fingers drummed lightly against his trousers. The noontime sun caressed the back of his head. After all that, he'd left his hat behind in the damned workshop. If he never set foot in it again, he should count himself happy.

Happy.

He sighed deeply, closing his eyes. For an instant, and for no particular reason, he found himself thinking of Phineas Burke's face, eyes round with terror, as he'd stalked forward toward that dashed automobile.

A chuckle escaped him, without warning.

Are you, Lady Morley? Are you in love with my friend Burke?

The poor fellow.

Another chuckle, and another. Wallingford's back began to quiver, his sides began to burn. The laughter built in his chest, exploding at last into the fragrant air, rattling the leaves in hearty gusts. He bent over and braced his hands against his knees, laughing without restraint.

"Signore?"

Wallingford started and looked up, expecting to see Giacomo's face, compressed with disapproval.

"I beg your pardon. You are English, are you not? The English visitor?"

Wallingford straightened. It was not Giacomo at all. The man was of medium height, dressed in a well-tailored suit of summer flannel, hair neatly trimmed beneath his straw boater, dark eyes grave. His low voice carried hardly any trace of an accent.

"I am indeed," Wallingford said. His mouth couldn't seem to stop twitching. "Can I help you at all?"

"I beg your pardon. My name is Delmonico, a colleague of your friend Mr. Burke. I understand his workshop lies this way?" The man's eyebrows rose in polite inquiry. He carried a small satchel beneath one arm, more of a portfolio, really. He shifted it to the other arm and straightened his hat with a nervous twitch of his hand.

"Why, yes. Yes, it does." Wallingford turned and made a motion with his arm. A chuckle rose again in his throat; he managed with great effort to restrain it. "Straight down this path, through the clearing. A small building, a sort of old carriage house. You can't miss it. But Signore Delmonico?"

The man was already tramping down the path. He turned and cocked his head. "Yes?"

"I'd advise you to knock first, my good man. Knock first, and sharply."

The priest had just begun to pass his crooked fingers over the eggs in their bowl when Abigail felt Wallingford's hand on her arm.

She knew it was his, of course. She knew it in the instant before it cupped her elbow, large and warm and light. She had felt him steal up next to her, among the servants and villagers filling the dining room. She had felt the tingling warmth of his body and the electric crackle of energy that seemed always to surround him, that was so essentially Wallingford.

"What's this?" he asked in her ear.

"It's the priest," Abigail whispered. She was conscious of Alexandra, standing nearby on her other side, watching the ceremony with hypnotic fascination. So hypnotic, in fact, Alexandra hadn't noticed Wallingford's arrival in the slightest. "He's blessing the eggs."

"Blessing the *what*?"

"Shh. It's a very solemn ceremony."

Wallingford had been swimming, Abigail realized. He smelled of dampness, of clean water and fresh air. His hand remained at her elbow, light and respectful. What the devil was it doing there? Had they not parted last night on the iciest of terms?

Next to the table, Don Pietro reached for the holy water, borne on a tray by his server. Maria had been right: The young man was beautiful, golden haired and blue eyed, an archangel sent to earth. He had followed the priest obediently about the castle, keeping the water at the ready as the rooms were sprinkled, hither and yon, without regard to the decidedly Anglican bodies who resided among them. Nearby, Maria interrupted the stillness with a wilting sigh.

The eggs seemed to strain against one another, yearning for Don Pietro's holy—if rather gnarled—hands. Abigail watched the water trickle from his fingers, to roll in delicate tracks down the fragile white shells. The faint sunshine caught on the droplets, making them glitter.

"Extraordinary," murmured Wallingford, next to her ear.

"I gathered them myself, just this morning," Abigail heard herself say, and nearly smacked her forehead with her palm over the inane statement. Inane? *Her?*

"Blessed indeed." The hand dropped away from her elbow, leaving it cold, and then he was gone, idling through the small crowd of villagers, his dark hair still damp and shining above them all.

Abigail's legs wobbled beneath her. What the devil had he meant by that? What the devil was he doing here at all?

Don Pietro was stepping away from the table. His assistant held out a stiff white linen cloth; he wiped his hands and handed it back and turned to Alexandra and Abigail. "*Ora abbiamo il pranzo*," he said gravely, and turned away to greet the villagers. Wallingford stepped forward and made a brief bow. His face had set into careful formality, the Duke of Wallingford greeting an honored guest, dark eyebrows low and sharp on his forehead.

"What did he say?" Alexandra whispered.

For an instant, Abigail thought she meant Wallingford.

She gathered herself. "Oh, he's just invited himself to lunch, of course!" She patted her hair beneath its modest scarf. "I do hope his assistant stays, too. Do you expect I shall burn in hell for it?"

But the eternal fires remained quite safe from the threat of Abigail Harewood's occupation. When luncheon was laid, she could not take her eyes from the Duke of Wallingford.

He sat at the head of the table, Don Pietro at his right and the acolyte at his left. The young man, who had looked so golden and radiant as he passed about the house with his delicate pewter pitcher of holy water, seemed to pale into childishness next to the broad shoulders and severe features of the duke. Despite his lack of a valet, Wallingford managed to appear with flawless jacket and crisp collar, with his necktie folded credibly, and all the gravity in the room seemed to sink somewhere into the beating heart of that well-tailored chest. He was every inch the lord of the castle. He was magnificent.

Abigail, for the first time in her life, was unable to say a word.

Not that Wallingford spent the luncheon in stony silence. No, despite his magnificence, he acted the perfect host, chatting with the priest, in Latin of all things, showing himself an absolute master of classical grammar. Abigail had never heard his Latin before, had assumed him to have only the usual schoolboy proficiency, and his fluency astonished and rather humbled her. At one point, he turned to Alexandra, who sat next to the elderly priest, and troubled her for the salt; the seamless shift into English made Abigail start from her chair.

Alexandra laughed her obliging little laugh and said *yes, of course, Your Grace*, just as if they were not mortal enemies, and handed the salt in his direction. Without a pause, she turned back to the village mayor, who sat on her other side, and resumed her halting half-English, half-Italian conversation with him, using her long, elegant hands to illustrate what their limited common vocabulary could not.

Abigail looked down at her plate, at her broken-nailed fingers holding her knife and fork. She cut her roast lamb into small pieces, and placed each one in her mouth with quiet deliberation. Who was this polished and polite Wallingford? Was this his true character? Or was he simply a good actor, his manners gleaming from years of formal experience?

Did she really know him at all?

"Signorina?"

The whispered word made her start once more. She turned her head over her right shoulder. "Yes, Morini?"

"After the luncheon," Morini said. "I must see you, after the luncheon. Is very important. We have the plans for tonight."

"Of course. What plans?" Abigail said listlessly.

Morini put her finger to her lips and drew away.

"I beg your pardon," said the man next to her, a burgher of some sort from the village. "You are speaking to me?"

The lamb was finished, and the artichoke leaves lay in a neat pile at the edge of her plate. Abigail picked up her wineglass and smiled over the rim. "I was not," she said, in Italian. "But since we are speaking now, perhaps you can tell me, my dear sir, something of the history of this castle. The more I learn, it seems, the more questions I have."

ELEVEN

The blossoming peach orchard glowed silver white in the
moonlight, reminding the Duke of Wallingford of nothing
so much as a threatening bank of London fog, or else his great-
aunt Julia's feral French poodle.

Not the most romantic fellow, the Duke of Wallingford, as
he was the first to admit.

And yet it was not a romantic assignation for which he was
bound, he reminded himself sternly, though the note burned in
his waistcoat pocket with a distinctly amorous flame. *Ten
o'clock, the peach orchard*, it had read simply, which might
mean anything, might come from anyone. Burke, perhaps,
wanting to conduct some sort of interview far from the eaves-
dropping ears that filled the Castel sant'Agata.

Oh, very well. Perhaps that wasn't the likeliest scenario. But
he had no reason to believe the note came from Miss Harewood,
either. The writing had borne a distinctly masculine tilt, for one
thing, and for another . . .

He couldn't think of another reason.

He didn't *want* to think of another reason. In every cell of his
hardened and unromantic brain, he admitted, he wanted Abigail
Harewood to be waiting for him in the peach orchard with the
moonlight gilding her skin, just as he had longed to see her

when he returned to the castle after his harrowing experience in Phineas Burke's workshop this afternoon. He had longed for a deep fresh gulp of Abigail; he had longed to be like Roland and Finn and the blasted Italian squirrels and walk with the object of his desire in the vineyard, or kiss her next to a beaker of battery acid, or chase her up a bloody cypress tree. When he had seen Abigail in the dining room, watching that bowl of eggs with rapt attention, her chestnut hair shining from beneath her modest headscarf, he had hardly been able to stop himself from gathering her up and carrying her upstairs with him. He had savored the simple curve of her elbow into his palm as he had once savored a vintage port.

Of course, such yearnings were both impractical and impossible. Even if Abigail *were* waiting for him now, she likely meant some sort of trick. Meant to catch him in some incriminating act, or perhaps not to meet him at all. Perhaps she was watching right now from her window upstairs, giggling with delight at the success of her little subterfuge.

I don't think I've ever enjoyed winning a wager so much.

A wrenching movement came from some hidden muscle in the center of his chest.

Perhaps he was a fool, after all.

Darkness began to close around him, as the soft glow of lights from the castle windows dissolved into the night. He had reached the meadow now, and strode across the dampening grass with his long and purposeful stride, guided by the moonshine incandescence of the peach blossoms ahead. The wrenching alarmed him. With every step, he placed a brick next to that hidden muscle, shoring it up. He would not hope for Abigail's appearance. He would not, if she *did* appear, reveal any chinks in the brickwork, as he had in the dining room. He would be stern, and hold firmly to his vows, and mistrust her every word.

The trees of the peach orchard had been planted conveniently in long rows, almost the entire width of the terrace. Long before Wallingford reached the first brown trunk, the first heavily laden limb, he could smell the blossoms in the clear night air. The scent drew him in, rich and dulcet, until he was surrounded by the hushed rustle of the branches in the air, the delicate touch of the petals as they brushed his cheek. Where in this otherworldly stillness was Abigail?

Wallingford brought himself to a stop. The blossoms absorbed the moonlight; he could see only shadows around him.

"I know you're there," he said, booming out the words to make the trees tremble around him. "You may as well come out."

His voice died away into the evening. From some distant tree came the faint trill of a nightjar.

Too rough. He had spoken too roughly: a fault of his, when he was uncertain of himself. He forced his voice to soften.

"I have your message," he said. "There's no need to hide. No need for any more tricks."

Tricks. There he went again. No chance of coaxing her into the open with words like *tricks.* Scheming Abigail might be, but she also had a streak of fatal tenderness for him, a genuine desire for him. Not nearly so much, alas, as he had for her; but then he was used to women longing to bed a duke, particularly a duke with a reasonably attractive physical presentation. He knew how to use that desire to his advantage.

He bent his voice still lower, until it rumbled in his chest and rounded out of his mouth. "Now look here. You asked me to meet you tonight. Don't be afraid, my brave girl."

Snap, snap.

Wallingford whipped around.

A shadow emerged from the trees, catching the hint of moonlight, crackling the fallen twigs with its footsteps.

His breath caught, suspended like a bubble in his throat.

The shadow took another step, directly into some unexpected gap between the trees, and the moonlight fell upon its modest white headscarf and the face beneath.

Wallingford's breath left him at last, in a gust of utmost pain. The brickwork in his chest crumbled into dust.

But that was all inward. Outwardly, of course, he remained exactly the same.

"Lady Morley. This is charming indeed." He maintained perfect control of his voice: not a waver. He folded his arms and swept his gaze up and down the elegant curve of her body, exactly as one expected of the Duke of Wallingford.

What the devil was she doing here? Accident, or design? Had she written the note? Or was her appearance here an extraordinary coincidence?

Lady Morley gave no sign. Her voice was perfectly clear,

perfectly smooth. "Your Grace. You're looking well. Courting the moonlit shades for your studies, perhaps? Or a dalliance with a village girl?"

"I might ask the same of you, Lady Morley."

She made a shallow laugh. "Village girls are not in my preferred style."

"Ah, more's the pity. You're a lover of nature, then?"

"I walk here every evening," she said. "The cool air braces one wonderfully before bed. Dare I hope you're picking up the same habit? You'll find it puts you to sleep directly."

God, the cheek of her.

"Now why do I have trouble believing this charming tale?" he said.

"Because you've a fiendish mind, I suppose." She spoke without a hint of censure, as if fiendishness were a trait to be admired, or at least expected in a man of his rank. "You're a devious fellow, and you can't imagine that everyone else isn't scheming just as you are. I expect you think I'm meeting Mr. Burke here tonight, don't you?"

The thought had not yet crossed Wallingford's mind, despite all his speculation. Immediately the hackles of suspicion lifted at the back of his neck. "Since you asked, yes. I do."

"Then tell *me*, Wallingford, whom *you're* meeting here tonight."

He lifted one hand and examined his fingernails. "Perhaps I came to catch you out."

"That won't do at all," she said, with another shallow laugh. "Even if I were meeting Mr. Burke tonight, I shouldn't be so careless as to let anybody else know of it. No, the shoe is quite on the other foot. I've caught *you* out. The question, of course, is whom."

"There is no question. I've no meeting at all."

"Your Grace, I should never be so indelicate as to call into question a man's command of the truth . . ."

His voice darkened. "I should very much hope not."

"Though of course, in affairs of the heart, one's allowed a bit of rope. After all, it would be far more shabby to expose one's sweetheart to disgrace than to insist on an exact adherence to the facts. Wouldn't it?"

Of all his reasons for coming to the orchard tonight, crossing verbal swords with Lady Morley ranked dead last on the list. It was time to end this interview. Wallingford drew a deep breath and said, "We have strayed, Lady Morley, rather far from the point at hand. Are you meeting Burke here tonight?"

"I'm not under any sort of obligation to answer your question. Why don't you ask him?"

"He's not here, at present."

"Isn't he?" She looked about. "But I thought you said I was meeting him! Dear me. What a dreadful muddle. Perhaps I got my times mixed up. Or perhaps it was the seventh tree, twelfth row instead of the twelfth tree, seventh row. I burnt his note, you see, in the fireplace."

Wallingford gazed at her shadowed face, at the pale and dark of her in the moonlight, impossible to read. "Well played, madam. I commend you. My friend Burke, I must concede, is an exceptionally lucky man."

"Mr. Burke is twenty times the man you'll ever be, Your Grace."

The words hit him in the chest. He opened his mouth, but there was no air with which to make a sound. He could almost hear his own grandfather's scorn-soaked voice, could almost hear the Duke of Olympia repeating those very words.

Has the conduct of your entire adult life ever suggested your usefulness for anything else?

The nightjar trilled again, sharp and lonely in the rustling dusk.

"So I perceive," he said at last. "What now, then, Lady Morley? We seem to be at an impasse. Do we await his arrival together?"

"Do as you like, Wallingford. I shall continue with my walk." She started forward.

He could not say what devil made him reach out his hand and snare her arm, just as she brushed past. He looked down at the moonlit curves of her face, this face now beloved by the worthy and honorable Phineas Burke, his grandfather's natural son. "A shame, Lady Morley, to waste this lovely evening," he said softly, not really wanting her, not even liking her at the moment, and certainly not liking himself.

She shrugged off his hand. "I don't intend to, Your Grace. Good evening." She walked on a pace or two, and then stopped and turned back to him. "Tell me, Wallingford. Why does it mean so damned much to you? Can you not simply let people do as they please? Can you not simply look to your own affairs for happiness?"

He stared at her shadow among the blossoms. "No. It appears I cannot."

Lady Morley turned and dissolved into the night.

Wallingford stood still, listening to the tiny sounds around him, the movements of animals and the soft rush of the wind among the trees. The temperature was falling; already the air chilled his burning cheeks, penetrating the wool of his jacket and waistcoat.

He ran a hand through his hair. He ought to have worn a hat, he supposed.

At last he turned and walked through the trees, down the terraces, past the apple trees and the vineyard. As he walked, he took the folded note from his waistcoat, ripped it into neat tiny squares, and let them flutter from his fingers into the breeze.

Fifteen minutes later, when the coast was finally clear, Abigail Harewood slipped down, branch by branch, from her post among the blossoms, not six feet away from where the Duke of Wallingford had run his fingers through his sleek dark hair.

Her limbs were trembling, and not just from the effort of perching motionless in a peach tree for well over half an hour, hardly daring to breathe, as the air grew damp and chilly and the inhabitants of Castel sant'Agata came, one by one, to hide among the trees and rendezvous with one another.

You must go to the orchard! Morini had told her frantically, when Abigail finally found her that evening, so confused and addled by her preoccupation with Wallingford that she had entirely forgotten the housekeeper's whispered message at luncheon. *It is all a great mess! They will all do the bumping in the night together! Signore Penhallow, he is leaving too early, and that rascal Giacomo, that sneaking scoundrel, he has . . .*

Say no more, Abigail had told Morini, and off she went, spirits restored by the notion of a secret assignation in the peach orchard.

But no sooner had she scaled the branches and settled herself into her blossom-scented arbor, when Phineas Burke had settled himself against the very trunk of the tree into which she'd climbed.

She was trapped, trapped like a . . . well, like a cat in a tree.

Then Lord Roland had come along, muttering poetry, apparently waiting for Lilibet. Then everyone had run into hiding as Wallingford crashed through the branches with his glorious, heedless stride.

And then Alexandra had appeared.

Wallingford had left in the downhill direction, away from the castle. He might, of course, be going anywhere, but Abigail knew as she knew her own bones that the duke had gone to swim in the lake.

The moon was not full, but what surface it offered shone clear and bright over the terraces of the hillside. Abigail made her way down each one, finding the steps in the walls by moonlight and instinct, until she reached the fringe of olive and cypress that surrounded the lake like a bristling belt. Through the branches, she heard the faint sound of splashing water, mingling with the calls of the night birds.

She settled herself on a boulder to wait for him, near the neat pile of his clothing on the rocks, not far from the boathouse, while over and over her mind saw again the little jolt of Wallingford's body at Alexandra's words.

Mr. Burke is twenty times the man you'll ever be, Your Grace.

Abigail doubted Alexandra had noticed. It was only a small jolt, really, hardly more than a flinch. But to Abigail it had the same effect as an earthquake.

Wallingford, vulnerable. Wallingford, in pain.

Abigail clenched her fists in her lap at the memory.

She had remained in her tree, unmoving, biting her own arm with the effort to keep still. Her skin had grown wet with her tears, and then she had been afraid lest one should fall down and give her away.

Oh, where was he? Was he going to swim all night?

Abigail tucked up her knees under her chin and wrapped her arms around her legs. Beneath her bottom, the boulder cast a numbing chill that spread up her back and into her legs. The evening was already cool, and the breeze from the lake was even colder. He would catch his death if he weren't careful.

A single cloud passed before the moon, like a wraith.

The splashing grew louder and more distinct. Regular, like a metronome. It must be Wallingford.

She couldn't stifle the gust of relief that left her body as he rose from the water. He didn't see her at first. The moonlight caressed the planes of his body, turned him to silver, even his dark wet hair, which he wrung out in swift motions of his hands.

He was so beautiful, made in such exquisite proportion, lean and strong, glittering with water, his shoulders flexing and his quadriceps curving in tight arcs into the tendons of his knees. He reached for his shirt, gleaming white under the moon, and rubbed himself dry with it; he slid his drawers up his legs and tied the string at his waist, his body set in magnificent profile to hers, perhaps twenty feet away.

He bent to the rocks and reached for his trousers.

And froze.

A little gust of wind brushed Abigail's skin, making her shiver.

"Miss Harewood," Wallingford said, in a low voice, "is that you?"

She cleared her throat. "Well, yes."

"Ah." He put one leg in his trousers, and then the other. "And I suppose you've been sitting there for some time?"

"Quite some time, in fact."

He drew up the trousers and buttoned them, neither slowly nor hastily, his eyes fixed on the rocks before him. "You followed me down from the orchard?"

"Not quite." She cleared her throat again. "Burke was there, you see, and Penhallow turned up . . ."

"Penhallow!"

"Yes, it was all rather . . . rather like a comedy . . ." She choked. "I came down when I could. I knew you would be here."

"How did you know that?" He put his wet shirt over his gleaming shoulders and began to button it.

"I've seen you swimming here before."

"Of course you have. I should have expected nothing less." He tucked the shirt into the waistband of his trousers and picked up his waistcoat. He seemed impervious to the chilling effect of wet cloth on a breezy night. "I suppose you realize this must constitute a violation of the wager. I could demand the ladies' forfeit this instant."

"You could," she said. "But that was the flaw in the wager all along, wasn't it? We never actually laid out the rules. What was permissible contact, and what was not."

"Watching a man dress himself is permissible, in your notion?"

"I closed my eyes at the crucial moment," she lied.

He had his jacket on now; he was straightening his sleeves. He turned to her.

The tears welled up in her eyes again. Even in the darkness, she could pick out the severe arrangement of his features, could see how cold and hard he was.

She blurted out, "You're beautiful."

"You're mad."

"Please, Wallingford." She rose from the boulder, limbs stiff, and held out her hands. "I never meant to hurt you. I hope I haven't."

"Hurt me? I beg your pardon?"

Oh, he was so cold. She stepped down from the boulder and tottered toward him.

"Are you all right?" he asked suddenly.

"Yes, only stiff."

"How long have you been sitting there?"

"Not that long, but the tree . . ."

"The tree?"

She smiled and stopped, a few feet away from him. She counted it a victory that he had held his ground. "The tree above you, in the orchard."

A strange expression crossed his face: a softening, a relaxing of the muscles about his jaw and his eyes. "Then it *was* you who sent the note?"

The *note*? What note?

No one could ever accuse Abigail Harewood of slow wits. She hesitated only an instant before she answered, "Yes. Yes, I sent you the note," and held out her hands.

Wallingford snatched them with his own. "Thank God," he said, looking at her fingers.

"I wanted to meet you, away from the others," she went on,

hoping to God she was getting it right, "but then everybody began turning up, and I didn't want to embarrass you . . ."

"Oh, God, Abigail." He took one hand and pressed it to his lips. "I thought . . . I thought it was all a trick . . ."

"It was never a trick. Please believe that of me. Please, Wallingford. Look at my face."

"No, I can't."

"But you *do* believe me. Say you do."

He sighed. "I don't know. I think I do. My God, your hands are frozen."

"I'm quite all right."

"You're shivering. You've brought no shawl with you, foolish child, nothing at all." He released her hands and took off his jacket. "We must get you back."

"No! No, not yet." The jacket settled around her shoulders, warm and heavy, dwarfing her. She was shivering, from cold and from excitement. Wallingford's hands lingered at the collar of the jacket, drawing her a step closer, and another step.

His breath was fanning across the top of her head now. His chin touched her hairline. Her face hovered in the warm nook beneath his jaw, where the skin of his neck lay so close to her nose and lips, so damp and alive, smelling of nothing but sweet fresh water.

Abigail lifted her arms and laid them against his waistcoat, from elbow to fingertip. "If I ask you a personal question, a very impertinent question, will you answer me truly?"

"Miss Harewood, when have you ever asked me anything else?"

She laughed into his neck. They were not quite embracing; Wallingford's hands remained at the collar of the jacket, bracketing her between his arms but not altogether enfolding her. Still, she felt deliciously secure in this intimate space between their two bodies; almost a part of him. His heartbeat crashed beneath her hands; his breath warmed her hair. She felt as if she could say anything, do whatever she wanted; she was his prisoner, and yet more free than she had ever been in her life.

"You and Mr. Burke. You're related, aren't you?"

"Hmm."

"I noticed it at dinner last night. I don't know why I never saw it before. Your coloring's quite different, of course, but you're both tall and lean . . ."

"I'm not quite so tall and lean as Burke."

"No." She laughed. "It's as if he's taken your body and stretched it longer. And your faces, they're built alike, Penhallow's, too, those same cheekbones and jaw, and the way your brows meet your eyes . . ."

"You were studying the matter a great deal."

She gave him a nudge with one hand. "Tell me the truth."

Her arms rose and fell with the depth of his sigh. "Burke's natural father is the Duke of Olympia, my mother's father."

"Oh," Abigail breathed out. The information was shocking, of course, but even more shocking was that he had told her this fact at all. Perhaps it was common knowledge among a certain set, acknowledged wordlessly in aristocratic hallways, but it remained a delicate family secret, a matter of trust. "Then he's . . . he's your . . ."

"My uncle, yes." His tone was dry, and just faintly amused.

She laughed into his throat, almost a giggle. "Your uncle!" She laughed again, bubbling over, until her back was shaking and Wallingford's hands slid around her shoulders at last and held her, cradled her against his big body. "Your uncle," she said again, and this time he laughed, too, vibrating under her hands.

She laid her head against his chest. "But it must have been rather hard for you."

"Not at all. He's a fine chap, Burke. I'm proud to own him. Every family needs a genius, and . . . well, he's an absolute legend, as you know. A colossus in his field."

Abigail thought of the little jolt of Wallingford's body, back in the peach orchard. "He's a darling fellow, of course. But I believe I like *you* best."

Was she mistaken, or did his arms tighten around her, a fraction of a degree? He bent his head to press his cheek against her hair. "Then you've no sense at all, as I suspected," he said.

"I have much more sense than anyone gives me credit for."

"And what about my charming Adonis of a brother? You haven't considered him?"

"He's a darling as well, I quite adore Penhallow, but . . . well . . . there's something missing . . ."

"A dukedom, perhaps?"

She snapped her fingers. "Oh yes, of course! That's it." The buttons of his waistcoat lay beneath her hand, smooth and covered with cloth. She touched one gently, circled it with her finger. "Besides, my cousin Lilibet owns him, body and soul."

"I fear you're right."

The water lapped against the nearby shore. Outside the circle of their arms, the breeze was picking up, chilled and restless. It was late, midnight at least, but Abigail didn't want to move, did not want to budge a fraction of an inch away from this spot and this man.

She inhaled deeply.

"Wallingford, I want you to call off the wager."

He didn't move. She held her breath, waiting.

"Hmm," he said at last.

She drew back and tried to look up at his face, but his arms wouldn't loosen around her, and she only bumped her nose against the bottom of his jaw. "I mean it. It's pointless, can't you see? Nobody wants to leave the castle, there's room for everyone. And what possible harm does it do, letting people fall in love with one another, as they were meant to do?"

The instant she said the words, a flush began to spread up from her heart and into her face, until her cheeks absolutely burned with self-consciousness. *Say something*, she thought frantically, while the word *love* dangled like a pendulum between them, in rhythm with the slow, deliberate beat of Wallingford's heart beneath her hands.

"I suppose," he said, like a magistrate delivering a verdict, "if we were to let the matter drop, without saying anything . . ."

She flung her arms around his neck. "Oh, thank you! Thank you. Just think what *fun* it will be, without this dreadful sentence hanging over us. What *friends* we will all be."

Wallingford reached back, caught her hands, and brought them between his chest and hers. "Friends, Abigail?" He was looking at her now, his expression soft and serious, the moonlight glinting against the tiny droplets that still clung to his eyelashes.

Abigail was glad for the darkness, because it hid her blushes. Blushes! *Her!* Abigail had scarcely blushed in her life, and now here she stood, flushing and trembling like some silly debutante in a London ballroom, exactly the sort of girl she'd sworn never to become. And yet, the sensation was not altogether unpleasant. She felt rather . . . thrilled. As if one of her long shots, galloping along hopelessly at the rear of the pack, had turned for home and put on a dazzling kick of speed, hurtling past all the others, with the finish pole beckoning ahead.

That sort of dizzy elation, only better. As if she were the horse herself.

"Yes, friends," she warbled. "Men and women can be friends. We can study together, every afternoon. You're an expert in Latin; I heard you at lunch. We'll work our way through . . ."

"Abigail." He stopped her mouth with the gentlest of kisses. "Let's not get ahead of ourselves. It's a very long distance from embracing passionately in a stable to becoming friends."

Her eyes rounded with astonishment. Wallingford looked down at her, perfectly serious, almost stern, except for a minute fleck of muscle at the corner of his mouth.

"Oh!" she gasped. "Oh! How I adore you!" She flung her hands back around his neck, laughing, feeling with ecstasy the shaking of his chest as he laughed, too. He lifted her from the ground, and something pressed against her hair, and she knew he was kissing her.

"Listen to me," he said at last, "we must get you back. It's late and you're chilled, and everyone will wonder . . ."

"No one will wonder. They'll think I'm in my room."

"Abigail." He brushed a stray lock of hair from her face. "We're not going to do this, do you understand me? I may be a brute and a scoundrel, but I'm not in the habit of seducing virgins, even one for whom I . . ."

"Yes?"

He kissed her forehead. "Never mind. Come along."

He made no move to disengage, and neither did she.

"I don't want to go," she said. "Please. Just a little longer. I don't want to let it go."

He hesitated. "You'll be chilled."

His voice was impossibly gentle, an entirely different Wallingford, some true and hidden Wallingford. She wanted to capture it somehow, the way Mr. Burke might capture a sample of air in his scientific beakers.

Abigail drew back. "Wait here a moment," she said, and hurried across the damp rocks to the boathouse.

When she returned, arms laden with blankets, he was still standing there on the rocks, barefoot, arms crossed. "What the devil?" he asked, eyebrows high.

"I keep them in the boathouse, in case of picnics," Abigail said breezily. She laid a blanket about his shoulders and wrapped the other around hers.

"Picnics." He pulled her against him. "You mad girl." He kissed her hair. "My mad girl."

She drew him against a boulder and sank to the ground. "Just for a few minutes." His hand remained in hers, doubtful; she gave it a little shake. "Come along. I'm sure your reputation can withstand the scandal."

"It looks dashed uncomfortable down there."

"You can rest your head on my lap."

"God help us." He settled down next to her with a resigned sigh of theatrical proportions. Almost gingerly he put his arm around her and urged her head into the blanketed nook of his shoulder. "You're warm enough?"

"Mmm." She closed her eyes. "You're not a brute, nor a scoundrel, Wallingford. Why do you pretend to be?"

His hand drew long lines up and down her arm. "It's not a pretense. It's a part of me. It's you who insist on pretending otherwise."

"That's rot. Of course we all have baser urges. I daresay even Lilibet has them, from time to time."

"Yes, but I give in to them, far too often. My grandfather has often remarked on it. He believes it's because I've lived a life of unbridled privilege, denied nothing from the instant of my birth."

Abigail sat in awe, savoring the stroke of his hand, the warmth of his body, the astonishing intimacy of his words. He had probably never said as much to anyone before. Why her? She snuggled closer. "Is that why you're here? To prove you can exist without your dukedom?"

Wallingford's body went still. Even his heartbeat seemed to suspend in his chest, for just an instant. "What a mad girl you are, Miss Harewood."

"You really must decide what to call me, Wallingford. Either it's Abigail or it's not."

"Abigail, then." He kissed the crown of her head, where it rested beneath his chin. "Since you allow me the privilege."

She sat there quietly, listening to the slap of water, to the rustling of leaves. To the sound of Wallingford's breath, stirring her hair.

"If you were really a scoundrel, you'd ravish me now."

"Perhaps you've changed me altogether."

"No. I don't believe people can be changed, not in the essentials. You are simply as you are; it's only a matter of what you choose to do about it."

"Free will?"

"Yes, I suppose. If you want to call it that." She looked at her hand, which had nestled inside Wallingford's blanket to lie once more atop the hard buttons of his waistcoat. What would he do if she unbuttoned them? "Look at you. There's so much goodness in you, and you won't show it to anyone, you hide it away in that tender heart of yours."

"Tender *heart*?" he said, as he might say *tender boiled kitten*.

She patted it. "The tenderest I've ever known. Except tender hearts aren't allowed in almighty dukes, are they?"

"The practice is generally discouraged."

She was wrapped in warmth, wrapped in Wallingford. She had forgotten all about the curse, all about faithful love and faithless English lords; she simply existed in this state of perfect bliss, disconnected from everything else.

The moon shone down on the two of them, curled together by the lakeshore, breathing each other in, joined in peace at last. Her mouth stretched into an enormous yawn. "Well, you needn't hide it from me. I shall take the gentlest care of it."

"Will you, now?"

"I promise."

Her head felt heavy. She let Wallingford's chest take its full weight. Beneath the blankets, she drew up her knees to rest against his leg. His thick arm held her in place, as securely as . . . as a . . . as one of those . . . when one was . . .

She opened her eyes, because she was moving along in a carriage, and yet unlike any carriage she had ever known. For one thing, it was comfortable; for another, it was warm and rather muscular and possessed a distinct heartbeat, which thudded like a bass drum into her ear.

"Where are we going?" she murmured.

"To your room."

"Oh! That sounds lovely."

He laughed softly. They were outdoors somewhere; she thought she could smell the peach blossoms again. "*You're* going to your room, darling. To sleep."

At the word *sleep*, she must have dozed off again, because next he was laying her on a bed, drawing down her dress, loosening her stays.

"Take them off," she murmured. "Wretched things."

"I don't dare." But he did anyway, with shameful expertise, and her petticoat, too. He tucked her under the covers in her chemise and drawers.

"Wallingford," she whispered, just as he pulled away, "what's changed? Why now?"

His hand cupped her cheek: "I don't know. I suppose . . . I suppose you wore me down, the lot of you, all against me. *Especially* you, Miss Abigail Harewood: You who never give up on anything."

"Never." She covered his hand. "What do we do in the morning, then?"

"God knows. Good night, Abigail."

"Good night, Wallingford."

He kissed her forehead and stole away into the blackness.

TWELVE

Midsummer's Eve

The Duke of Wallingford stretched one booted foot to nudge Abigail's hip. "You're falling asleep again," he said.

She started beautifully. Her chestnut hair, loosened from its pins, fell against her cheek. "No, I'm not. We were right . . . right . . ." She tucked her hair behind her ear and flipped over a page in the volume of Plutarch that lay in her lap.

"Never mind."

"I've got it right here. Just a moment." She picked up the bread lying on the blanket beside her and tore off an absent hunk.

"Why the devil are you so sleepy this morning? Haven't got yourself a lover, have you?"

She tilted her head and looked at him sideways, through her upturned fairy eye. "And if I have?"

"I'd punch his lights out, of course." He took the loaf from her fingers and tore off a piece for himself. They were sitting in the shade, shielded from the sun, except for a single piece of morning sunlight, no larger than a sovereign, that landed on Abigail's chestnut hair and turned it a bright golden red.

She turned her head back to the book, and it was gone.

"You've no right," she said. "You hardly ever kiss me, and even then only when I've been very naughty indeed. It's no wonder I've found another fellow. You've driven me into his arms."

Wallingford smiled indulgently at her. Nothing could pierce his good humor this morning. He had awoken even earlier than usual, opening his eyes to the golden sunrise with the settled conviction that he was going to ask Abigail Harewood to marry him.

Perhaps even today.

The idea had been hovering in the back of his mind for some time, of course, though he hadn't acknowledged it, nor even put it into words. Since the early days of his manhood, when he had thought of marriage at all, he had put it under the heading of *Duties, miscellaneous*, and had some vague notion that he would find a suitable bride when he could put it off no longer, sire a few children, and carry on with the rest of his life more or less as before, albeit with a little more discretion. But falling in love, and asking that woman to marry him, to cleave only unto each other and all that rot? Such things were unspeakably bourgeois.

And yet here he was, falling in love, fallen already, doomed from the moment she'd kissed him in the rain-soaked stable of the inn. To place Abigail Harewood under the heading of *Duties, miscellaneous* was a sacrilege. He couldn't bear to think of carrying her back to Belgrave Square in a cloud of white tulle and proceeding to bed her once a week, according to ritual, while she carried on a life of charitable committees and afternoon calls, and he carried on a life of club dinners and afternoon mistresses. No, he wanted to keep her right here in this enchanted Italian castle, and make love to her in the sunshine and under the silver moon.

Except that he hadn't made love to her. He had scarcely even kissed her, and only then, as she said, when she had been particularly naughty and trapped—*trapped!*—him into it.

He had not made love to her, because she was an innocent, and he was not.

He had not made love to her, because he must first prove himself worthy of the privilege.

He had not made love to her, because he was waiting to be sure. He was waiting to wake up in the morning, open his eyes to the golden sunrise, and know that marrying Abigail was the right course, the only course, and the rest of it—Belgrave Square and *Duties, miscellaneous*—would sort itself out.

If she would have him.

A little wobble of worry overturned his smooth-sailing bonhomie. Abigail, after all, did exhibit a certain cynicism about the institution of marriage, and aristocratic marriage in particular. He might reassure her all he liked about Belgrave Square and *Duties, miscellaneous*, but whereas other girls would leap at the chance to be Duchess of Wallingford (it did have rather a nice ring to it, he thought affectionately, gazing at Abigail's creamy cheek), his mad little elf would probably much rather elope to a garret in Paris, suitably wretched and north facing, with some ghastly emaciated poet.

"In any case," she went on, turning pointedly back to her Plutarch and flipping another page, "he's a great deal more attentive than you are this morning."

By God, he would make her his duchess. And take her to live in a garret in Paris, if he had to, where they would keep their bohemian neighbors awake all night with the creaking of the bedsprings.

"Rubbish," he said. "I'm attentive to your every need. Picnics and Latin every day. Moonlit walks every night."

"Except when there's no moon."

"And I deliver you honorably to your door before midnight, a gentleman to my fingertips."

"I didn't take up with you for your gentlemanly fingertips. Quite the opposite."

God, she was perfect. Why hadn't he made this decision before? So right, so elegant a solution.

For one thing, well down on his list but a pleasant prospect indeed, marriage to Abigail checkmated his grandfather's scheme rather neatly.

Wallingford sprang forward, filled with glee, filled with certainty, and planted his hands on either side of Abigail's hips.

"What the devil, Wallingford," she began, but he leaned into her mouth and kissed her confusion thoroughly away. In an instant, she had cupped his cheeks with her hands, and kissed him back so ardently that desire flamed up like a torch in his belly.

She leaned back against the tree and he followed her, running his tongue along the seam of her lips until she opened them with a sigh and allowed him inside, allowed him to taste the curve of her mouth and the sweetness of her velvet tongue, while his hand crept up to caress her waist. Sometime in the heat of late May, Abigail had shed all but one of her petticoats, and her skin now burned so tantalizingly close he could feel every swell of her body through the barriers of her dress and stays and chemise.

"Tell me," she said, against his lips, "to what do I owe the pleasure of this wholly ungentlemanly conduct?" Her thumbs brushed against his cheek; her fingers caressed his hair.

Wallingford left her mouth to kiss his way along her jaw to her ear. "I can't leave the field entirely to my rival."

"Mmm. Yes, he's very skilled. I should think you'll need a great deal of practice."

"I am at your service."

She pulled back. Her eyes were wide in her delicate face. "Are you, Wallingford? Are you really?"

"Up to a point." He ran his finger around the curve of her ear.

"Oh! Only more of your teasing, I suppose. This pointless self-denial, when even my untrained virgin sensibilities can tell you're aching to have me."

He sat back. "For God's sake, Abigail."

"Good heavens, Wallingford. Are you *blushing*? Do you think I'm unaware of your aroused physical state? I *have* studied the functions of male anatomy, you realize."

"Yes, I realize that." He resisted the urge to glance down. He knew quite well that the male anatomy in question was straining desperately against the prison of his trousers, just as Abigail had observed.

"Why, you *are* blushing! And how lovely it looks on you. It brings your face quite alive."

"I didn't strike you as alive before?"

A frustrated sigh. "Look, must we go on exchanging clever remarks? I'd much rather kiss."

He leaned forward to oblige her, but before he had quite reached her lips she gave a gasp of dismay and pushed him away. "Stop a moment. How long was I sleeping? What time is it?"

Wallingford groaned and produced his watch. "Nine twenty-three."

"Oh, Lord. Already? I'm dreadfully sorry, my darling, but I

really must go. I promised Morini I'd help with the midsummer masks. We're quite behind, though I stayed up half the night working . . ." She was on her feet, picking up random picnic detritus and tossing it in the wicker basket in a series of dangerous crashes. The sun dappled her hair through the leaves.

"Midsummer masks?" Wallingford repeated stupidly, transfixed by the sight of her bosom as it ducked and lifted before his eyes.

"Yes, for the party tonight. You *do* have a mask, don't you?"

"Of course I have a mask."

She stopped and turned, a flask of water hanging from her hand. "You've forgotten entirely, haven't you?"

"Of course I haven't forgotten. I . . . my mask is . . . it's all ready. Quite . . . quite ready, and all that. With a"—he made a helpless motion with one finger—"a feather, you see, in one corner. Both corners, that is. Goose down, to be precise. I have a great fondness for the stuff." He grinned up hopefully at her.

She dropped the flask in the basket and clapped her hands. "Well played. You nearly had me, right up until *goose down*." She picked up the basket. "Now will you help me with the blanket?"

He took the basket from her and set it down in the grass, and then he picked up the blanket and folded it. In his present state of panting lust, it seemed a useful thing to do. Wallingford had learned, in the past few months, how to manage this constant simmer of passion, how to distract himself from sexual arousal with physical tasks, to discipline the cravings of his body. Not so different, really, from swimming to the middle of the lake and knowing there was nothing else to do but keep going, whatever his personal inclinations. He had learned simply to enjoy the flaring of desire, to take pleasure not in hasty consummation but in anticipation, in touches and glances, in Abigail herself.

Abigail herself, meanwhile, was no help at all. She simply didn't see the point. "I don't see the point, Wallingford," she said, picking her way through the trees by his side. They had walked around to the far side of the lake, as they did most days, where privacy was more certain. "We're far from the proprieties of London, after all. I'm willing; you're certainly willing. What the devil are we waiting for?"

He smiled to himself. "You've never heard of the virtue of self-denial?"

"What do you know of the virtue of self-denial? I'm sure you've never sampled it before."

"You sound cross, my dear."

"I *am* cross." She stopped and turned to him. "You've gone to bed with dozens of women, Wallingford. Why not me?"

How could he answer her? He hooked the basket handle over his elbow and touched her hair. "You know the answer to that."

Abigail slapped his hand away. "Yes, this tiresome and ridiculous prohibition against seducing virgins; or rather well-bred virgins, for I'm sure you gentlemen have no such scruples about the unprotected sort."

"That's not true. I've never . . ." He frowned. "In any case, it has nothing to do with scruples. It has to do with . . ."

She turned and resumed walking. "Convention? Doubts?"

"God, no. With . . . with wanting to do things differently." He said the last words in a mutter, almost to himself.

"With what?"

"With exactly the sort of sentimental rubbish you insist you despise. Tell me more about this midsummer whatever-it-is." He shifted the basket back to his hand.

"Oh, it's going to be splendid! You really must come, Wallingford; I'm quite serious. Masks and dancing, and all the villagers out in the courtyard with us. Lilibet and Alexandra and I shall be dressed as serving girls . . ."

"*Serving girls?*"

"According to Morini, it's traditional for the ladies of the castle to dress as maids on Midsummer's Eve. Of course, one's got to do the thing properly and . . ."

She went on pattering about anchovy paste and the local philharmonic, but Wallingford's brain had ceased functioning at the phrase *serving girls* and the image it conjured: Abigail in some low-necked frock, her breasts spilling over the bodice, perhaps even (oh, merciful God!) an apron around her swinging hips, as she offered him a tray of delectables. Words passed over his head, *olives* and *stuffing* and *tuba*, but his mental fingers were plucking at her mental bodice, and nothing made any sense until a sharp object bludgeoned his ribs and Abigail's indignant voice intruded on his vision: "I say, Wallingford, are you attending me?"

"Oh yes. Tubas. Awfully jolly. Shall perish of excitement."

How soon, he wondered, would the threatened tubas make their appearance? Was it possible to spirit Abigail away first, in costume of course, to serve him his olives privately, one by one?

Would she be wearing her mask, too?

He swallowed heavily.

"Tubas, *really*. You're not listening at all, Wallingford. I was discussing the significance of Midsummer's Eve."

"Midsummer, of course. Longest day of the year. A cause for celebration, certainly."

"To the *castle*, Wallingford. It's an enchanted night, the night of lovers, they say. And Morini and I have made such careful preparations. It won't go awry this time, I'm certain."

Just as the phrase *night of lovers* began to have the same arresting effect on Wallingford's brain as *serving girls*, something else snagged his attention.

He cocked his head, gave it a little shake, and asked, "What did you say?"

"Oh, the preparations. You can't imagine . . ."

"You said *this time*. As if there were some other time. That is to say, some other night."

"Did I? You know how I drop these silly remarks, Wallingford. They mean nothing at all." Her pace picked up, leaving Wallingford slightly behind, and causing the hem of her single petticoat to swish into view around her churning ankles. Her graceful ankles, of which he occasionally caught glimpses . . .

Stop.

He shook his head again. "No. Your silly remarks mean the most of all, Abigail Harewood." He lengthened his stride and caught up with her. "Out with it. What are you scheming?"

"Nothing at all. The absurdity. Do you think Philip needs a mask? I'm not sure I shall have the time . . ."

"Abigail," he growled, catching her arm.

She pivoted about his elbow with all the force of her forward momentum. He caught her just in time, rather neatly, so she was trapped between his two arms. He let the picnic basket drop to the ground. A blush was rising up in her cheeks, though it might have been the exertion.

Might.

"Tell me about Midsummer's Eve, Abigail," he said, in a silky voice.

Abigail cast her eyes down to the sliver of grass between them. Despite the morning hour, the weather was warm, with a baking quality already settling into the air, promising a hot afternoon. A few tiny dewdrops of perspiration shone on her upper lip. "I already told you," she said. "An enchanted night, a night for lovers. I had hoped . . ." She lifted one hand and laid her fingertips against his jacket, staring at them as she spoke. "You and I, Wallingford . . . oh, don't make me ask it . . ."

"Abigail."

"I know why you haven't touched me. I know you're trying to behave honorably, to prove you're capable of self-restraint. And I respect that, I do. But you see, Wallingford . . ." She looked up at him at last, and her face was pure longing. "You don't need to go on like this. I'm not a debutante, a conventional marriage-minded girl; I never wanted that. You know this. I don't expect promises and betrothals. I adore you, you know that, too, now more than ever, and I should so want . . . and I do believe you want it, too, that you care for me . . . I want . . . to *show* you, Wallingford. To *know* you, every bit of you. Without restraints or promises, simply two people who . . . who care for each other, and who . . ." She stamped her foot. "Oh, don't make me go on like this. *Say* something."

He was not capable of speech. He muttered something, some endearment, and kissed her forehead. At least that way he was safe from her penetrating eyes, her beseeching eyes.

She whispered, "You know I am untouched, Wallingford. With my whole heart, I want you to be the first man to lie with me. Won't you give that to me?"

When he could speak at last, his voice was a husk of itself. "Not the first man, Abigail." He kissed her again. "The only man."

"Don't say that."

"I'll say whatever I damned well please, Miss Harewood. I haven't denied myself the pleasure of your bed all these months only to pounce on you at the end of some village bacchanal . . ."

"When, then?"

"On our wedding night, by God!" he thundered.

"Our *what*?" She jumped away.

"Our wedding night! Don't look so surprised. You can't tell

me it hasn't crossed your mind." Even as he said this, a smug little voice at the back of Wallingford's brain informed him that he had possibly just made the most bloody balls-up of a marriage proposal in the entire history of romantic love.

Wallingford blamed Abigail, of course. The woman could drive the Black bloody Prince to unchivalrous acts.

"Of course it hasn't crossed my mind! Not for an instant! What the devil are you thinking, Wallingford? I'd make the worst duchess in the world. I'd embarrass you nightly. I'd have the whole damned aristocracy in ruins by Christmas!"

"For God's sake, Abigail, I've just offered you *marriage*!"

"And I've offered you my *innocence*!"

"It ought to be the same thing!"

"You mean on *my* side! On yours, the story is very different, isn't it?"

He threw up his hands. "I thought my debauched carnal history was all to the good, in your calculus! The more experience, the better, you said!"

"It is! I don't care how many women you've slept with. It's *you* who must marry a virgin, isn't it? And if it weren't for my virginity, that tiny bit of membrane that means so deuced much to you fools, you'd never have thought of marriage. You'd have bedded me long ago, and probably quite forgotten me by now."

A fine spray of fury fogged over Wallingford's vision, making Abigail's blazing face, her agonized eyes, blur and fade before him.

"How could I possibly forget you, Abigail," he said, between his closed teeth, "when you and your bloody women *refuse to go away*?"

A vast silence spilled out between them, like the breaching of a dam. From the vineyards up above them came a faint Italian voice, singing down through the trees. Someone answered, laughing.

"Oh!" Abigail said at last. She stamped her foot and opened her mouth to deliver some scathing retort in the classic Abigailian manner, but nothing came out. "Oh!" she said again, in frustration, and turned to her right and stomped three hard paces down the path toward the castle.

Then she stopped and whipped around. Before his horrified

eyes, she stomped back, kicked over the picnic basket, and marched off with her sharp elfin chin leading the way.

"He is an ass, Morini! A colossal ass, just as I always knew." Abigail stuck another feather on her mask with a fury usually reserved for defending one's homeland from attack by barbarian raiders.

"What is this ass, signorina?" asked Morini serenely.

"An ass, Morini. Like a donkey. A burro."

"Signore Duca is a donkey?" The housekeeper looked astonished.

"In a manner of speaking, yes. I mean, he has behaved like a donkey. A stubborn"—she stuck on another vengeful feather—"witless"—she pounded it in place with her fist—"ill-mannered donkey."

"He has offended you?"

"*Yes*, he has offended me! He has offered me *marriage*!" Abigail said, as she might say *offered me a rancid cheese*.

Morini clasped her floured hands together, setting the maids to coughing. "But this is wonderful news! Wonderful! We are breaking the curse at last!"

Abigail set the finished mask aside to dry and reached for another. She was sitting at the kitchen table, attempting the impossible task of decorating the rest of the masks before the celebration began at eight o'clock, while Morini and the maids were preparing the food. "We are not breaking the curse," she said, examining the new mask. Sequins, she thought. She was growing weary of feathers. "As I've told you daily, Morini, *daily*, your curses have nothing to do with the . . . the friendship between Wallingford and myself. That is quite separate. We are to concentrate on the others, who mercifully are falling into such appalling extremes of love that even a thousand scoundrelly Englishmen should be redeemed by them. I fancy tonight's celebration should just about do the trick."

"But you and the duke, signorina! Is so romantic. He love you so." Morini kneaded the bread, eyes closed in romantic contemplation.

"I assure you, Morini, as I believe I've assured you before, Wallingford is the last man in the world to rely upon for faithful love. I'm terribly fond of him, of course, and wish to God he would renounce this ridiculous vow of chastity for *one* night at least . . ."

A sigh came from Francesca, and Abigail cast a sharp look at her. Evidently the young woman's command of English was growing.

". . . and I do believe he has a great deal of good in him, good intentions in any case, but I . . ." Abigail's voice trailed off. The sequins blurred in a glittering collage before her eyes. Again, that magical night intruded in her mind, that night of the peach orchard, when she had seen him at last, had caught a glimpse of his precious soul. They had been so perfectly close in those hours on the lakeshore, wrapped together in blankets and moonlight, and while they had spent every afternoon together since, and often mornings as well, talking and studying and laughing, they had never quite replaced that sense of physical connection, that melting together of two bodies into a single and beautiful whole. And oh, God! How she longed for it! She lay awake longing in her bed every night, and every night the tears started from her eyes with the force of her desire for him. Not just the act of sexual union, which was still rather vague and unreal in her imagination, but the closeness to him, the oneness. He would never be her faithful lover. He wasn't made for it, any more than a stallion was made for faithful love, but she could at least have that moment of flawless union once more.

If only Wallingford would allow it.

"He love you so," Morini said again, pounding at her dough.

Abigail stood up. "These are far too many masks for me to manage by myself," she said. "I believe I shall find the others and ask them to help."

Morini's voice called after her. "Signorina! You are not forgetting the plans for tonight?"

"I assure you, Morini," said Abigail, hand on the kitchen door, "I shall remain your loyal accomplice. For the others, mind you, and not myself."

"Of course, signorina." Morini turned back to her dough. "For the others."

THIRTEEN

He was an ass.

"I am an ass, Lucifer," Wallingford said aloud.

To the horse's credit, he didn't snort in agreement. Instead he radiated a sort of man-to-man understanding as he ambled down the road to the village, as if to say, *Don't worry, mate, we're all asses when it comes to women.*

Or perhaps that was only Wallingford's imagination. The horse *had* had his stones removed at the tender age of thirteen months, after all.

For a brief mad instant, Wallingford almost envied him.

"But for God's sake! She *did* react rather unreasonably. I *did* offer her marriage. Duchess of Wallingford, by God! A duchess of Great Britain, which is rather more substantial than your empty European titles, godless chaps who haven't any notion of primogeniture, princes and dukes littering the streets like shopkeepers."

A man came ambling up the road, leading a goat, footsteps sounding crisply on the beaten dirt. Wallingford squared his shoulders, as befitted a duke of Great Britain, and nodded gravely at man and beast. "*Buon giorno,*" he added, at the last instant.

"*Buon giorno, Signore Duca,*" said the man, tipping his hat.

Maa, said the goat.

"I suppose I shall have to apologize, and that rubbish,"

Wallingford went on, when the fellow was safely out of earshot. "Women expect that sort of thing, or so I'm told. By God! Do you know, Lucifer, I don't believe I've ever apologized to a woman before, except for the odd bit of language, which don't signify. Perhaps that's been my trouble all along."

Wallingford knew, of course, that this was only the tip of the iceberg of his trouble: an entire mountain of arrogance and entitlement at which to chip away, piece by piece, until he became a decent human being. "Which is why I can't afford to chase her off," he said aloud. "She's the only one willing to arm herself with the necessary pickax to do the job properly."

The road began to curve, tracking back along the hillside, and a pair of rabbits made a flustered run for cover as Lucifer trotted into view. Beneath Wallingford's hat, a trickle of sweat ran toward his ear, emerging just at the point of his jaw. "I shall have to learn to control my tongue better, among other things," he said. "I shouldn't have said what I did. God knows, if they *had* left, if I didn't wake up every morning knowing she was near, I'd . . . I'd . . . well, I wouldn't be the same man. She takes my breath away, old boy. I don't mind saying it to *you*. Takes my breath away at times, with that innocence, my God. And I don't mean her physical innocence; it's the way she sees the world. The way she sees *me*." He paused and added, in an almost embarrassed mutter, "The trueness of her."

He heard his own words fade away in the air, and gave his head a rueful shake. What banal sentiment, and from him! The Duke of Wallingford! Well, but there it was. He supposed it served him right, after all the women he'd made miserable over the years. Comeuppance, that was the word.

When he reached the village, he made straight for the house of his man of business, the only retainer he had allowed to follow him to Italy. In the early days of his occupation, Wallingford had gone here nearly every day; all his business correspondence was forwarded here, and he preferred, even in his absence, to keep a close watch on the estate he had worked so hard to recover from the excesses and mismanagement of his father's tenure. Now, as he strode through the door, he was struck by the expression of surprise on his agent's face.

"Your Grace!" he exclaimed, rising from his desk.

"No need," said Wallingford, waving him down. "I'm only

here for a short while, as it happens. Anything critical needing my review?"

"Why, no, Your Grace. All is in order. I received the papers you sent back yesterday. Have you any further instructions for me?"

"As it happens, Beveridge, I do." Wallingford removed his hat and set it upon a corner of the desk, together with his gloves. "I have asked a young lady to marry me, and I should like all the necessary contracts to be drawn up, pro forma, to forward the happy event as expeditiously as possible, should I prove so fortunate as to receive the honor of her acceptance."

The agent's jaw swung into his necktie. "Straightaway, Your Grace."

An hour later, having mastered a solid grasp of the fundamentals of British and Italian marriage law, and feeling an immense self-satisfaction at the size of the settlements he, in his unbounded generosity, was prepared to provide his heedless elf, Wallingford was on his way home, and rounding the first switchback almost directly into the path of Lord Roland Penhallow.

"What ho!" said his brother, sheering his horse to the right.

"Good God!" exclaimed Wallingford, sheering left.

The horses, who had better sense, managed to disentangle themselves without injury. Wallingford, however, was rather cross. "You ought to have turned to your left," he said.

"I say, old man, we *are* on the Continent now, if you hadn't noticed."

"One doesn't need to adopt vulgar customs, simply because one finds oneself in an uncivilized corner of the globe."

"I daresay not, unless one's keen to avoid collisions on the road, in which case it's rather dismally essential." Lord Roland flicked at an insect with his riding crop.

"Only if one happens to encounter one's harebrained brother along the road in question. Which brings me conveniently to the point: What the devil are you doing here? Business in the village?"

Lord Roland tilted his head to the sky, as if considering the weather. He had gathered the reins in one hand, and the other lay gloved upon his thigh while the horse danced underneath him. "You'll never believe this, old man, but I came out after you."

"After me?" A jolt of alarm hit Wallingford's gut. "Nothing's happened, has it?"

"Happened? At the Castel sant'Agata? You must have the wrong century, brother." Roland laughed his easy laugh and turned the horse around, back up the road. "I'll ride along with you, if you don't mind."

"Not at all."

The sun beat against Wallingford's hat as they traveled, making his hair simmer underneath the woven straw. Not a single thread of wind made its way along the hillside, as if the entire broad valley were holding its breath, waiting for the exact instant of the solstice. Wallingford glanced up at the sky, just as Roland had, and laughed.

"Something amuses you?"

"I was only thinking," said Wallingford.

"Egad, old man. You had me frightened. For an instant, I thought you said *thinking*." Roland swatted at another insect, perilously near Wallingford's left hand.

"Ass. What I meant to say was this: The last time we were riding along like this, it was March, and we were making our way to the damned castle with the drizzle and the mud and the wretched ladies underfoot, and now look." Wallingford gave a sweeping nod of his head to indicate the changed state of affairs, from weather to landscape to ladies underfoot.

"A vast improvement, wouldn't you say?"

"At the very least, we've exchanged one set of difficulties for another."

They rounded the elbow of the last switchback, and the castle leapt into view, yellow gray stone warm against the luminous blue sky.

"At least you've had the good sense to drop the matter of that silly wager," said Roland.

"I haven't dropped it at all," Wallingford said. "Only . . . only biding my time."

Roland laughed. "Biding your time? Is that what you call it?"

"Look here, old fellow. Unlike you with your libertine ways, *I've* behaved as virtuously as a monk."

"And we all know what went on in those medieval monasteries."

Wallingford felt a wholly unreasonable flush of anger spread upward from his belly. "At least I can claim, with perfect certainty, that Miss Harewood remains virgo intacta. Can you say the same of your lady?"

The lazy summer air between them snapped into tautness.

Roland gave a low whistle. "I say."

"Look here, I apologize, that was quite . . ."

"Say no more. I quite understand you." Roland paused. "Virgo intacta, eh? Well done of you."

A flush of an entirely different nature struck Wallingford's cheeks. He looked down at his hands, holding the reins, and mumbled, "You appear shocked."

"Shocked? No. Awed, is more to the point. I didn't know you had it in you."

"I'm as capable as the next man of self-restraint, when . . ." He let the sentence hang.

"When you intend to marry the girl in question?" Roland asked, with inexpressible gentleness.

Wallingford gathered himself. "Not your business."

"I declare it is my business, when my brother means to kick me several rungs down the ladder of inheritance. I had thought the dukedom quite mine."

"Don't give up hope, old fellow," Wallingford said darkly.

For a long stretch of road, the sound of the hoof beats measured out the time, thudding companionably against the hard dirt, the occasional stone. The castle grew larger, and the long vineyard rows resolved into detail, now rampant with leaves and close-packed fruit. In the rear courtyard, figures were scurrying about, setting out tables and benches. Wallingford glanced at his brother, who was staring thoughtfully at the activity, his golden hair flashing below the brim of his hat.

"You had something to tell me, didn't you?" Wallingford asked.

Roland turned. "What's that? Oh yes. The damnedest thing. I was just thinking on it again, in fact. Wondering how it all fits together."

"Wondering how what fits together?"

"I was in the library this afternoon, thumbing through the old account books . . ."

"What, the *castle* account books?"

"Yes, an idle curiosity," Roland said, with a too-casual flick of his hand, which Wallingford took to mean an idle curiosity of young Philip. Since Abigail Harewood's afternoons were now taken up with Wallingford, Roland had stepped in to see to the boy's tutoring, in an act of pure cunning that Wallingford could only applaud. After all, what mother could resist a man who took such an interest in her son?

"Go on," he said.

"Well, it was fascinating stuff of course, went straight the way back to the Medici, as I'd always suspected, and double-entry bookkeeping, if you can believe it! I was positively floored, but there it was. You wouldn't believe the outlay on silver . . ."

"For God's sake, Roland. What's the point?"

"I'm coming to the point, you impatient old bugger. In any case, one thing led to another, and I came upon the old deeds of ownership, and do you know what I found?"

"Obviously not, or I should never have sat through your tiresome meanderings."

"I found," Roland said, with dramatic emphasis, "a rather curious fact. Namely, our fellow Rosseti, whoever he is, don't own the old pile after all."

"Doesn't he?" Wallingford's brain scrolled back to the horrific moment he'd stood there in the drizzle, outside the castle, with the two identical lease documents in his gloved hands. "But the lease stated quite plainly . . ."

Roland shook his head. "Doesn't own it. Saw the deed written out quite plainly."

"Good God." Wallingford's back went as rigid as a fire iron. They were nearing the crest of the hill, with the stable a quarter mile away. Lucifer's steps began to quicken, his eager head pulling against the duke's stiff fingers.

"Aren't you going to ask who *does* own the castle?" Roland said, after a moment.

"Is it relevant? I presume this Rosseti must be an agent of some sort, though I can't begin to imagine how the legality . . ."

"Oh, it's relevant, all right. Deuced relevant."

Wallingford looked at him, frowning. "And why is that?"

"Because." Roland lifted one hand to rub the corner of his mouth with his thumb. "The castle deed was transferred in the year 1591 to the Earl of Copperbridge."

A current of pure ice water flooded the channels of Wallingford's body. "Copperbridge! But that's . . ."

"Yes, quite. Now a courtesy title, with which we're both all too familiar." Roland heaved a deep sigh and shook his head. "It's the awful truth, I'm afraid. The owner of the Castel sant'Agata, dear brother, is none other than . . ."

Wallingford's fist landed squarely on his thigh. He looked up at the sky and howled into the blazing sun, "The Duke of bloody *Olympia.*"

A bigail Harewood looked down and gave her bodice a final minute adjustment before attending to Lilibet.

"There," she said, tugging her cousin's neckline a strategic half inch lower, until the lace of her chemise peeked out from beneath an enthusiastically laced corset. "You look perfect. You've filled out so beautifully with Morini's cooking, I'd hardly recognize you."

Lilibet's gaze rested heavily on her for an instant or two, before dropping down to contemplate the overflowing bounty of her own bosom. Considerably more bountiful, in fact, than the bosom with which she'd ridden into the castle over three months ago; what a difference a well-trained cook could make in a woman's attractions! Abigail shook her head in awe.

Lilibet picked anxiously at the trifle of lace shielding her nipples from general public admiration. "You don't think I've grown too plump?"

"Lord Roland certainly doesn't seem to mind." Abigail gave Lilibet's apron strings a last constricting tug, to emphasize the curve of her waist and hips. Not that her figure needed much in the way of artifice; not that Penhallow needed anything at all in the way of encouragement. Still, Abigail and Morini had vowed to leave nothing to chance. "The way he looks at you! You might take a little pity on him, you know."

"How do you know I don't?" Lilibet said, with some asperity, brushing Abigail's hands from her waist.

"Darling, your room's next to mine. If I can hear Mr. Burke bringing back Alexandra at the crack of every dawn, I'd certainly notice you." Abigail made a little twirl. "Does mine look all right?"

"Quite adorably fetching. You'll have to keep your distance from poor old Wallingford."

"I doubt poor old Wallingford will be in attendance," Abigail said, as carelessly as she could. She was thankful for her mask, which allowed her to grimace unchecked, though it did itch like the devil. All afternoon she had looked out for Wallingford: first in lofty disdain, certain he would crawl back like a beggar; then in idle concern, as evening began to approach; and now in fatalistic resignation, in abject despair. She had behaved like a child, snapping back at him like that, kicking over the picnic hamper, for heaven's sake! He had offered her marriage—*marriage!* The most confirmed bachelor in England!—quite needlessly, and rather unwelcomely, but still it was a lovely gesture, showing a gratifying attachment to her, and moreover it was a gesture that had probably cost him a great deal to make. And what had she done? Thrown it in his face, of course! His poor tender heart was undoubtedly shattered, just like the picnic plates, which had made an ominous series of crashes from underneath the overturned wicker.

He had a right to sulk. She conceded him that. If only he didn't have to sulk tonight, of all nights.

Midsummer's Eve.

"Signorina, is ready," said Morini, next to her elbow.

Abigail turned. Trays of stuffed olives covered one end of the kitchen table; several joints of meat were roasting in the enormous fireplace. The heat was immense, though all the windows were open to the evening air, cooling at last as the sun slipped down. She picked up a tray of olives and handed it to Lilibet. "Off you go! I'll find Alexandra and join you in an instant."

"But I . . ."

"Or shall I send Francesca out with the olives? I believe Penhallow's already roaming about . . ."

Lilibet whirled around and marched out of the kitchen. Through the window came the whine of the violins and the low throb of the tuba, tuning up.

Abigail turned to Morini. "There you are. It's begun. I do hope you know what you're doing."

Morini gave her a wise smile. "Trust in me, signorina. Is all coming together tonight. Is the Midsummer, is the night of enchantment. Is . . ."

At that instant, the Dowager Marchioness of Morley swept through the doorway and stopped before them. With one elegant finger she plucked at the lacing of her bodice, which was nearly invisible under the rampant overhang of the exposed Harewood Chest.

"This is *so* undignified," she said.

By ten o'clock, the Duke of Wallingford had still not made an appearance.

The thing to do was to keep oneself busy, and Abigail kept herself busy with a vengeance. She pushed the duke firmly from her mind. Her arms dangled from their sockets with the effort of ferrying endless courses of food and wine between kitchen and courtyard; her feet throbbed through the sturdy leather of her shoes.

"Signorina, you must rest, you must sit," said Morini, emerging into the open air of the courtyard, wiping her hands on her apron. The dessert had been laid out on the trestle tables, and the musicians were striking up an energetic polka beneath the emerging moon.

"Rest? Sit? On such a lovely evening?" Abigail drew in a long breath, as if sampling the festive air, and indeed it was festive enough: A cooling breeze gusted gently along the hillside, and from the kitchen drifted the sugared scent of macaroons and *panettone*, of warm baking bread. Already the villagers were pushing aside the trestle tables and forming lines on the flagstones, throwing aside somber Tuscan good sense to assemble, laughing men and giggling women, for the dancing.

Only a single figure remained sitting at the tables. Her white mask glinted gold in the firelight, her firm chin rested in her elegant hand, and her gaze traveled longingly into the kaleidoscope of shifting dancers.

Her breasts swelled precariously over the bodice of her dress.

"Alexandra, my dear." Abigail let her hand fall lightly on her sister's shoulder. "Why aren't you dancing?"

"Oh." Alexandra seemed to gather herself. "I daren't. If I take another step, I shall probably spill free altogether, and I don't believe these Tuscan chaps would ever recover."

"Nonsense. In the first place, you've at least another inch standing firm between you and infamy. In the second, all your Tuscan chaps have made themselves thoroughly drunk, and won't remember a thing."

Alexandra laughed and put her hand atop Abigail's.

"If you're pining after a certain ginger-haired scientist of our acquaintance," said Abigail, "I understand the best cure for that sort of melancholy is to go off and amuse yourself regardless."

"I'm not pining after anyone. And in any case, I've no one to dance with."

Abigail ran her hand down her sister's arm until it gripped her palm. "Come along, you ninny."

Dragging Alexandra into the dance proved roughly comparable to dragging Percival the goat into his pen, but Abigail had managed this feat nearly every morning since her arrival at the Castel sant'Agata, and eventually experience told. "I don't think you need to know the steps," Abigail called, over the relentless *oom-pah* of the tuba and the shrilling swing of the violins. "Nobody else does."

"Rather like London, then," Alexandra called back.

The torches flickered; the band played. The last of the sunset disappeared behind the hills to the east. Alexandra's cheeks flushed with the effort of the dance, lurching back and forth from partner to partner. When her smile crested at last over the top of her lips, when her eyes sparkled with pleasure, Abigail slipped quietly away from the throng and found Morini in the kitchen.

"Alexandra's with the dancers," she said. "I think she's ready. Though where the devil Finn's gone, I can't . . ."

Morini looked up. She was sitting at the table, before a tray of six small glasses, which she studied intently. Each was filled to exactly three-quarters with a clear liquid; a collection of bottles and herbs lay scattered around the wooden surface.

"Morini," Abigail said, in a dark tone, "why are there *six* glasses before you?"

"Signorina, listen . . ."

"I've told you, Morini, on numerous occasions—of which you appear to take no notice at all—Wallingford has *nothing* to do with tonight's plans. Or any plans at all, for that matter."

"Signorina, what is the difference? There is no harm in

giving the nature a little push." Morini made a short wave of her fingers, illustrating a friendly helping hand to nature's design.

"No harm? No *harm*? When I might wake up to find myself shackled to the most notorious libertine in the British Isles?" This was not perhaps fair, or even factually accurate, but Abigail saw no reason to let such a trifling detail as the truth derail her argument, which was sound in the fundamentals.

"The duke, he loves you. He is not this libertine."

Abigail pointed an accusing finger at the glasses on the tray. "I daresay you've been imbibing this stuff yourself, if you really believe that! No, I'll have none of your love potions, addling my brains and doing God knows what to my ordinary human reasoning."

Morini rose and closed her fingers around two of the glasses. "Signorina, you are not listening. You wish to have the night with the handsome duke, it is so?"

Abigail eyed the two glasses and said, warily, "If the opportunity should arise, I wouldn't say no."

Morini held out the glasses. "Then here is your chance, signorina. The duke, he is proud, he has the honor, he does not make the try to seduce you. *This*, signorina. *This* will make him forget these things. This will open the arms of the so-handsome duke."

The lamp flickered on the table next to the tray, giving the liquid an oily gleam, almost iridescent. Morini gave the glasses a little swish.

Abigail crossed her arms. "What's in it, then?"

"A little of the limoncello, a little of other things."

"What other things?" Abigail narrowed her eyes at the jars on the table.

"Is a secret, signorina. Is nothing harm." She jiggled one glass enticingly near Abigail's fingertips.

Abigail watched the drink catch the light. She ran her tongue along the roof of her mouth, which had gone strangely dry and thirsty. With unsteady fingers she plucked the glass from Morini's fingertips and held it up to her eyes. "Nothing harmful? Are you certain?"

"Is pure, signorina. It give only the love."

"I suppose," Abigail said, stretching her words to the limit, "there are no priests nearby, should my intellect be overturned."

"No, signorina. Is only for the love."

"And it's such a beautiful night, such a perfect night, a night for . . ."

". . . the lovers," Morini finished for her.

Abigail turned the glass this way and that, admiring its clarity, its brilliance, almost lit from within. The faint scent of lemons drifted into her nose. She tilted the glass closer and inhaled more deeply, lemon and something else, something lovely, and at once a sense of peace overcame her, a delicious, languorous anticipation. "Oh, that's nice," she breathed.

"You see, signorina? Is no harm. Is destiny."

"Destiny. Yes. I shall take this to Wallingford at once." Abigail turned on her heel.

"Wait, signorina! Is not working, just for one." Morini held up the other glass and dangled it gently, back and forth, between her fingers. "There must be two. One for the gentleman, one for the lady."

A little frisson of warning snaked across the haze of delight in Abigail's brain, and then disappeared. "One for the lady?"

"Is so. There must be two, signorina. There must be equal."

It seemed to make sense. Everything seemed to make sense at the moment, an absolute exquisite rightness, all the way through the world. Abigail plucked the glass from Morini's fingers. "Very well. If I must."

"You must, signorina. Now go find the handsome duke. Give him the great desire of his heart."

"I will, Morini! I will!" Abigail exclaimed, and she danced on air across the kitchen and through the door, holding her precious burden in each hand.

An instant later, she poked her head back through the doorway.

"Ah, Morini. Just a slight . . . a little detail. I don't suppose you know . . . of course, there's no reason you *should* know . . . that is to say, I was rather wondering . . ."

Morini was already picking up the tray from the table. Without turning, she said, "In the library, signorina. The duke, he is in the library, all the evening."

FOURTEEN

The tuba pounded through the open window of the library, the same two bloody notes, over and over again, until the Duke of Wallingford would willingly have given up one of his lesser estates for the chance to stuff a full-grown male pheasant down the bell, feathers and all.

He had tried closing the window at first, but the old glass hardly blocked the sound, only filtered out the obscuring effect of the other instruments. Moreover, he soon realized he had cut off the only source of fresh air in the stuffy book-lined room, which had been baking in the sun through most of the afternoon.

Suffocation, or slow descent into madness? The choice was his.

At last he opened the window again, reasoning that he was already far down that well-beaten path to insanity, and might as well finish the journey in style.

He returned to the desk, removed his jacket, slung it across the back of the chair. Hardly had he straightened his shirt cuffs and resumed his seat when the doorknob rattled, and into the library danced Abigail Harewood.

At least it seemed to be Abigail. A white feathered mask

obscured her face, and her dress—what there was of it—had been cut so low in front and so high at the leg, Wallingford could not quite focus his eyes on any remaining identifying features.

"Oh, hullo," she said. "There you are. May I come in?"

Wallingford lowered his eyelids to eclipse the sight of her overflowing bosom, but it was too late: The image was seared on his brain, in flawless photographic negative. "I would rather you didn't," he said.

"Disturbing your studies, am I? I do apologize."

She sounded not the slightest bit contrite. Wallingford looked back up. She was balancing a pair of small glasses in her hands, and she glanced at him with a smile he might have described as shy, if he hadn't known better from long experience.

She looked at him expectantly, and he realized he hadn't answered her. "You are, as a matter of fact. What the devil are you doing here? Aren't you supposed to be serving olives to the villagers?"

"Oh, the olives were finished long ago. They're dancing now. The villagers, I mean, not the olives. What are you studying?" She wandered across the room toward him, looking . . . hesitant? Not Abigail Harewood. Surely not.

Wallingford slid the sheaf of papers back into the leather portfolio. "Nothing of particular interest."

She laughed. "Why on earth are you studying nothing of particular interest?"

"You mistake me. What I'm studying is of no particular interest to you, Miss Harewood." He sat back in his chair and steepled his fingers, rather like one of his more pompous tutors at Oxford. "It is, however, of immense interest to me."

She stopped a few feet away, holding the glasses before her. The lamplight shone like a nimbus on her chestnut hair. "I see. You're still angry with me."

Wallingford sat in his chair, regarding her, trying to ignore the lush picture she made in her mask and her provocative costume, trying to set aside all that he knew of her and felt for her. The effort was immense, like pushing a boulder away from the mouth of a cave to look inside. "Tell me something, Miss Harewood," he said, in a soft voice.

"Don't say that. Don't call me Miss Harewood, in that tone of yours, that dreadful distant tone. You sound exactly like a duke."

"I am a duke."

She stepped forward, set the glasses down one by one, and curled her hands around the edge of the desk. "You know what I mean."

He pinned his gaze firmly to her face, to stop it from wandering fatally downstairs. "Tell me, Miss Harewood, exactly how long you've been acquainted with my grandfather, the Duke of Olympia."

Her start of astonishment was so instant, so profound, it nearly buckled his chest.

"Your grandfather? I beg your pardon. *Do* I know your grandfather?"

"You tell me."

"I . . . I don't know. I don't think I do, but then Alexandra's always introducing me to chaps at dinner parties, and I can never keep them straight. What does your grandfather look like?"

Wallingford wanted to place his elbows on the desk and lean forward, but as Abigail's bosom happened to be overflowing its bodice exactly at eye level, he forced himself to remain at ease. "Pale gray hair, quite tall, overbearing disposition."

"You in fifty years, then, more or less."

Wallingford's mouth twitched. "Breeding will out."

"Well, I can't say for certain. Half the fellows down the pub might be your grandfather, on that description, and the other half are merely too short. Does he dress well?"

"Exceedingly."

"I suppose that rules out a few. But in all seriousness, Wallingford, if I *have* met him, I can't recall his face, let alone a single conversation. Why the devil do you ask?"

Because I suspect my grandfather has played me for a fool.

"You're certain?" he asked.

"Didn't I just tell you I *wasn't* certain? What are you driving at?" Her eyes, behind her mask, looked as if they were narrowing at him.

Wallingford pressed the pads of his thumbs together with bone-crushing force and said, in a conversational tone, "You haven't, for example, met him over the course of the winter, and concocted a scheme with him, whereby you gain yourself a ducal coronet, and he brings his licentious disappointment of a grandson to heel at last?"

The instant the words were out of his mouth, he recognized their absurdity. He reached forward and placed his hand on the portfolio, as if to reassure himself of the reality of what he'd studied throughout the afternoon and evening. Without so much as a bite to eat, his stomach reminded him, with a decidedly undignified growl.

Abigail, meanwhile, was laughing without restraint. "A ducal coronet? You're not serious. A scheme with your *grand-father*?" She collapsed helplessly into a nearby chair. "Are you quite mad, or are you only having a laugh?"

"Certain facts have come to my attention . . ."

"And after I rejected you so gracelessly just this morning. Really, Wallingford!"

"No lady accepts the first proposal."

Abigail's laughter trailed off. She leaned forward in her chair and twisted her hands together. "You *are* serious. You *do* mean it."

Something about her bewildered tone made his chest give off that infernal buckle again, that crumbling of the brickwork. "I only thought . . ."

"Was it what I said this morning? I *am* sorry, Wallingford. I didn't mean to throw it back at you like that. You took me by surprise, that's all. I should never have hurt you like that."

"*Hurt* me?"

She rose with her fairylike grace and flew to his chair, sinking to her knees beside him. "Yes, your tender heart. You're so abominably ill behaved at times, my darling, I forget just how tender it is. Do forgive me." She put her hand on his leg, just above the knee. "You know I adore you."

Wallingford's mouth had gone shocked and dry. His every muscle was paralyzed with indecision: whether to embrace her, or to dash away. "Mad girl," he managed at last.

"Yes, I am. I'm *your* mad girl. It's just that it simply wouldn't work, marriage. We are so much better off as we are."

"As we are? As *this*?" He made a helpless motion: the library, the castle, the *oom-pah* of the tuba outside the window.

"Exactly like this." She took up his hand from the arm of the chair and kissed it. "Don't think for an instant I'm not honored, terribly honored. You're the Duke of Wallingford; you have this extraordinary gift in your power, to raise some fortunate young lady to the highest in the land, and you have offered it to *me*, you dear and thoughtless man." She kissed his hand again. "It's magnificent, and there *is* some lovely girl in England right now, some sweetly perfect rose of a girl, who longs for that gift, who longs to be your duchess. She'll be so much better at it than I would." She laid his hand against her cheek. "But you have my *heart*, Wallingford. You must believe that."

He opened his mouth to speak, but she laid her finger over his lips.

"Hush. Don't say anything. You don't need to make up any sentimental rubbish. It does tax you so." She rose in a sinuous motion and picked up the two glasses from the desk. "I missed you tonight. I was looking so much forward to serving you dinner."

"Abigail, I . . ."

"But you must at least share this with me. It's traditional."

He took the glass and frowned at it. "What is it?"

"Oh, I don't know. Some concoction or another, a special recipe of Morini's. Limoncello, I think, and a few other things." She lifted her own glass. "Come along, my love. Buck up. To . . . oh, let's see. To love affairs. Long may they prosper."

The scent of lemons rose up from the glass to surround his intellect. "To love affairs," he heard himself say, and he clinked his glass with hers and drained it.

The liquid burned delicately down his throat to his belly, spreading a lemon-scented warmth into each individual corpuscule of his body. He looked up and found Abigail's bright eyes gazing at him adoringly from behind her white feathered mask. The entire world seemed to sigh and settle around him. "Oh, that's very good," he said.

"It's perfectly lovely, isn't it? Even better than I dreamed."

"I want to kiss you, Abigail. May I kiss you?"

She took the glass from his hand and set it down, together with hers, back on the desk. She turned back and placed her long-fingered hands along the sides of his face, framing him with herself like a work of art. "It's all I want in the world, Wallingford."

Her lips tasted like lemons and enchantment. He wanted to devour them, but instead he kissed her gently, inquiringly, savoring each movement of her mouth, each movement of his. With one arm he reached underneath her and hoisted her into his lap.

"Oh, it's divine," she whispered. Her body melted against his; her arms twined around his neck. He could feel her in every nerve, his pulsing, living Abigail, more beautiful than air. Her feathers tickled his nose; her hair fell against his cheek as he kissed her, and when he rubbed it between his fingers he could not imagine a silk more fine, more perfect and unbreakable than Abigail's chestnut hair.

I love you.

She drew away, and for an instant Wallingford was afraid he'd said the words aloud, and then—because the world around him had mellowed into such a lovely and forgiving place—he was *glad* he'd said them aloud.

But if he *had* said the words, Abigail gave no sign. She only caressed his cheek and said, "Wallingford, let's go down to the lake. It's such a beautiful evening."

"The lake?" He had been thinking more along the lines of the library sofa, which was certainly wide and well built enough to take on an amorous encounter, though the cushions might resent the abuse.

"Oh, please?" She lifted herself away from his chest and tugged at his hands. "There are so many people in the court-yard, and I want to be alone with you, perfectly alone. Don't you?"

At that instant, the tuba intruded with a particularly emphatic series of notes, attempting a kind of ambitious grandfatherly arpeggio. The old windows buzzed in alarm.

Wallingford rose from the chair in a single effortless heave, carrying Abigail upward with him.

"Let's go," he said.

T he moon lay high and bright, cradled by the velvet sky. "I believe I could count every star," Abigail said. "Look at them all, glittering like a diamond mine! Don't you love the stars in Italy?"

Wallingford jumped down the terrace wall and held up his arms to her waist. "Every one of them," he said, and swung her down to the grass beside him. The blood sang in his veins. He bent his neck to kiss her—he couldn't resist—and when she laughed and flung her arms around him he picked her up and twirled her about in mad circles until they were staggering, laughing, nearly collapsing in the grass.

At last he took her hand and led her between the rows of grapevines, half running, like two foolish lovers in the blush of youth. The sounds of music and laughter died away behind them, until there was only the soft thump of his feet against the grass, Abigail's whispers against his skin, the rustle of the warm breeze in the trees nearby.

When they reached the end of the vineyard, Wallingford turned to her. "Where to? Not the boulders, I hope."

"The boathouse," she said.

"The boathouse?"

"I've a surprise for you."

He didn't question the existence of her surprise. He didn't question anything. She might have suggested a balloon ride to China and made it seem like the most natural idea in the world. The rightness of Abigail, the rightness of this night with this woman, surrounded him with certainty.

He kissed her hands, one by one. "Right-ho, the boathouse."

He felt fifteen again, scampering through the moonlit trees, clasping Abigail's warm hand. Ahead glimmered the lake; they spilled onto the shore at exactly the spot where Wallingford had risen from the water in April to find Abigail waiting and watching. He spared a glance for the enchanted rock where she had curled her supple body into his, had fallen asleep against him in her innocence. Abigail, *his* Abigail, who thought herself so daring and independent, had tucked her head into his dissolute shoulder, his faithless and unreliable shoulder, and slept like a child.

She had trusted him.

The boathouse loomed ahead, a smudge against the trees. Wallingford turned to her, and in the full tide of the lemon-soaked bliss coursing through his body, he found himself putting his hand to her cheek to ask, "Are you certain, darling?"

She tilted her face upward, and he caught his breath at the

way the moon made her white feathers glow, made her eyes
glow. "For God's sake, Wallingford. Do I strike you as the sort
of girl who isn't certain?"

Wallingford bent and gathered her up in his arms, making her
gasp and clutch his waistcoat. He carried her to the boathouse,
kicked open the door, and staggered into the darkened room.

"Oh!" She slid to the floor and pulled his head down for a
kiss. He could hardly see her in the faint shaft of moonlight
through the open door. "That was magnificent! Close your eyes."

"Close my eyes? What difference would that make?"

She put one finger to each eyelid, and he closed them
obediently.

"Don't move," she said.

He stood there with his eyes closed, grinning like an idiot.
He could hear her rustling around the room, could smell the
stuffiness of old dust and warm wood. A soft scratch, a few
thumps, Abigail's careful breathing. "What the devil are you
doing?" he asked.

"Open your eyes."

He opened them and caught his breath.

A pallet of wool blankets lay on the wooden floor before
him, ringed with cushions. Abigail stood nearby in her mask
and her outrageous dress, lit by perhaps half a dozen candles
scattered about the floor and the worktable and the stool. The
glow turned her skin to living gold.

"What do you think?" she whispered.

"You planned this."

"Not this night exactly," she said, "but I hoped that sometime . . . if I could lure you in somehow . . ."

She stood there so diffidently, so almost shy, her masked face
ducking in a most un-Abigailish way. Her right hand plucked at
her apron; the other lay behind her back.

"Oh, Abigail." He was molten inside, hard as stone on the
outside. His fingers shook, he wanted her so.

"Is it all right?" The candlelight shadowed her cheekbones,
making her look almost unearthly in her fairy beauty. "I don't
know much about seduction, practically speaking, and what's
required."

The room wasn't large. In three strides Wallingford stood
before her, reached his hand to the back of her head, and untied her

mask. He drew it away and saw that her eyes were wet, that her skin was flushed along her cheekbones and the tip of her dainty nose.

"Abigail, my love," he said. "I think you know everything about seduction."

"Don't refuse me this time, Wallingford. I'd die if you did."

"*You'd* die?" He kissed her cheeks, her nose. She smelled of the kitchen, of smoke and sweetness and lemon. He untied her apron and let it drop to the floor. He wanted to give her words, loving words, to fill her ears with everything a woman like Abigail deserved to hear on a night like this; but he couldn't think of any. Instead he kissed her, long and thoroughly, back and forth, until she gasped under his lips and her fingers traveled up his chest to find the buttons of his waistcoat.

"Let me see you," she said. "I want to see you."

"You've already seen me."

She laughed. "I want to touch you." She tore at the buttons, fumbling each one through its hole, kissing him feverishly as she went. The brush of her hands against his chest burned into his center. He touched her neck; he cupped his hands at the back of her head and loosened her hair until it gave way in unimaginably lustrous waves, spilling over his forearms.

All those long weeks of abstinence crumbled into dust. "Oh, God, Abigail," he said, and tugged at her sleeves until her shoulders were bare. His fingers scrambled for the buttons at her back, but there were none. "What the devil? Are these hooks?" he demanded, working at the fastenings. Her breasts glowed between them, the tips barely contained by the fabric of her bodice, and he couldn't think for the lust billowing into his brain at the sight of them.

"Wait." She lifted his waistcoat away and tugged his braces from his shoulders.

"I can't wait. You don't know."

She laughed and pulled his shirt free. "No, you first. How does this fasten?"

Wallingford pushed her hands away and unfastened his trousers, letting them fall to the ground in a shameless plop. He kicked them free, tore off his stockings, his drawers. His arousal tented the billowing linen of his shirt.

"Oh." She took a step back. Her eyes, round and large, shot upward to his face.

"Yes." He took her firmly by the shoulders. His groin felt as if it might burst. Already his ballocks were tingling with eagerness. If he was not inside Abigail Harewood in two minutes, he might disgrace himself. Four months of abstinence, and he could not take the strain of self-restraint anymore, not an instant longer.

"Turn around." He must have used his commanding voice, because she turned at once and lifted up that impossibly heavy mane of hair above her shoulders. Her neck curved sinuously in the candlelight, wisping with tiny hairs at the top. He ran his finger down its length to the top of her dress, until he found the fastenings and his hands wrenched desperately at each one, exposing her chemise and stays and petticoats, all the layers of Abigail he must uncover before he could have her.

At last the dress gave way. He took off her petticoats, grasped the top of her corset and unhooked that, too, until her flesh burst free and she sagged back against his chest, nearly naked, wearing only her delicate chemise.

"Oh, God, Abigail." Wallingford slipped his hands upward and closed them around her breasts at last. "Oh, God," he whispered again, weighing her fullness, heavy and firm in each palm. He brushed his thumbs against the tips, and even through her shift he could feel their hardness, the tiny nubs rasping against his skin.

"Wallingford!" Her head fell back against his shoulder. "Oh! That feels . . . my God . . . oh . . ."

He pulled down the neck of her chemise and her nipples popped into view, pink and erect. At the sight of them, right there between his own tanned fingers, Wallingford's prick gave a warning throb.

Abigail's breasts. Abigail's body in his arms. The hollow of Abigail's back, cradling his own aroused flesh.

He spun her around. Her hands worked at the buttons of his shirt; he tried to brush them away, he couldn't wait another instant for her, but she said, "Please!" and when the shirt was loose enough he yanked it over his head himself and stood before her, fully naked, as he had not stood before any woman in his life since boyhood. He watched her face, her expression of wonder, her eyes dimmed with lust, and thought he might crack down the center.

"Wallingford, you're so beautiful, like a statue, only warm and . . . and . . ." She ran her hands along his quivering chest, around the curve of his shoulders, down his back.

"Touch me." His voice was inhuman, like a growl. He was a beast, a craven beast, while her fairy fingers smoothed his skin and curved around the sinews of his body. "Touch me, Abigail. Do you see how much I want you?"

"Yes." Her hands slipped around his buttocks and found his cock. She touched it lightly, stroked it, and he let out a cry. She looked up. "Am I hurting you?"

"God, no." He closed his eyes and forced the words between his teeth. He could hear his pulse in his ears, counted off each beat to steady himself while Abigail's hands encompassed him, closed around him, ran up and down his length and then touched his tightened balls as if with a feather.

At that, he reached down and snatched her hands.

"I'm sorry," she said, but already he was lifting her up and laying her down on the blankets, raising her chemise over her stockings and her silk garters, over her curving thighs. She gasped and put her hand over the apex, but not before he had caught a glimpse of chestnut hair, short and crisp and curling, a delicate triangle pointing suggestively between her snugly closed legs.

"Don't hide." He drew her hand away and nudged her legs. "Open for me, sweetheart. Help me."

Her legs loosened. He mounted above her and looked down at her face, wide and desperate, longing and uncertain. Her innocence awed him. He bent and kissed her. "Ready?" he asked.

She nodded and put her hands around the back of his head.

How did one make love to a virgin? He had no idea. The usual way, he supposed, except she would be tight and perhaps afraid, and might bleed at first. He must treat her tender flesh with care; he must let her know that he would take care of her, that she had nothing to fear from him. All these thoughts he tried to encompass through his lust-fogged brain, and then her hips shifted beneath him, and her legs opened a brave fraction more, and the motion brought the head of his prick right up against the curls guarding her virgin passage.

"Oh, God," he said, and in that instant he forgot everything except the need to be inside Abigail, to make her his, to claim her.

He put one hand down between his body and hers, guiding himself, until he felt the tip lodge in her soft notch.

"Oh!" she bit out.

"It's all right, love. Let me in. Open for me."

Her legs opened, and then stiffened. He moved his hips, as gently as he could manage, but he could not get inside her, could not quite find his way.

"Oh!" she said again. Her fingers dug into his arm. He checked his aim and lunged again, harder this time, his blood pounding in his ears. The friction of her slick skin drove him wild. In another moment he would spend, inside her or not. He braced himself above Abigail's lush candlelit body and looked into her frantic face. "Oh!" she gasped.

Or perhaps *"Ow!"* He couldn't quite tell.

He gathered himself and shoved with mighty effort, and this time he heard her give a little cry, felt her give way, felt something tighten around his knob and then loosen, and he was gliding up her, buried in her, clasped from tip to root by Abigail's untouched flesh.

A tingling rose up from his ballocks, a rush of perfect power, unstoppable. He sank down, bent his head, and thrust again, and the thundering climax engulfed him, pulsing through his loins in welcome throbs, blessed relief at last. On and on it went, as if he were emptying himself into her, all his sins and imperfections, as if he could simply give himself into Abigail's keeping and be born anew.

He sank his head next to hers and listened to the roar of blood in his ears, the staggered rasp of his own breath.

"Abigail," he whispered, as the pulses died away, and she made a sound in reply, a tiny half sob. His hands had somehow become tangled in her hair, trapped as if by a web. He had no desire to free them.

For long moments he lay atop her, savoring the way her body embraced him, the way her soft flesh encompassed him, the way his damp skin melted into hers. His brain spun with the enormity of what had just occurred. Never had he imagined he could join with a woman like this; never had he imagined such consummation. He turned his head and kissed her cheek, her throat; he lifted himself on his elbows and kissed her breasts. His cock was still as hard as iron, still lodged deep inside her. By the living God, he could go another round.

He kissed her again.

Her eyes were closed. She didn't move. Senseless with rapture, no doubt.

"Darling. Abigail." He kissed her lips. "My darling love. Are you all right? Happy?"

Her eyes cracked open. He pressed a featherlight kiss on each lid. He was full of love for her, full of tenderness for what she'd just given him.

He would tell her, by God. Women liked that.

"Abigail, my love, never in my life have I imagined such joy. You . . ."

Her hands moved at last, landing on his shoulders. "Would you mind," she said, very quietly, "getting off me, please? You're rather heavy."

"I'm sorry."

She pushed with her hands, and reluctantly he slid himself out of her warmth and rolled to the side. He unwound his hands from her hair to reach for her, to gather her next to him. "Darling," he began again, but she was already sitting up, looking dazed. "Darling, lie down with me. It's too soon for that; we have all night. You . . ."

She pushed his arm away and turned to him. "Too soon? Too *soon*?"

A warning bell began to jingle in the fog of Wallingford's enraptured brain. He struggled to sit up. "What's the matter, darling? Was I too rough? I'm sorry, I tried to be gentle, but I didn't realize how . . ."

"Gentle? You were a *battering ram*!"

"Well," he said modestly, "I wouldn't go quite that far."

"That was not a *compliment*! You were a *brute*! I felt no pleasure at all! I should have been in *transports*! You should have . . . this was supposed to be *lovely*!"

"No pleasure?" He stared at her in astonishment. Her loosened chemise was falling from one shoulder, exposing her breast; her hair tumbled about her flushed face. She looked the picture of a well-loved woman. "No pleasure at all?"

"None!"

"You must have felt *something*, surely!"

"I felt a battering ram!" She rose to her feet, stopped, and looked down. "And look at me! I'm a mess!"

"Oh, damn. So you are. My poor love. Here, I have a handkerchief. Let me." He scrabbled for his waistcoat on the floor.

She snatched the handkerchief from his fingers and turned her back toward him. "I chose you *specifically* for your experience! *Specifically* because I thought you knew how to give a woman pleasure!"

"I *do* give women pleasure!" He stood up behind her.

She tossed the handkerchief on the floor and picked up her stays. "And how do you know this?"

Without thinking, he helped her fasten the corset, the way he had refastened corsets in so many similar moments. "I've never had any complaints, have I?"

"Of course you haven't had any complaints! You're the Duke of almighty Wallingford! Who would dare complain about your performance in bed?"

"*You*, obviously!"

"You've no idea how to bring a woman to crisis, do you? I suppose you just heave away and assume your partner is enjoying herself."

"I do not!"

Did he?

Her stays were fastened. She pulled away and found her dress. "I'll wager you don't even know where to touch a woman, to give her pleasure."

"I most certainly do!"

Abigail turned around to face him. Her eyes blazed in the candlelight. "Where, then?"

"Why . . . well, the breasts, of course, and . . . and . . . between the legs . . ." He was stammering like a schoolboy, flushed to the crown of his head. He made a vague illustrative motion with his fingers.

"*Where* between the legs?"

"Well, obviously. Where the . . . where the male organ . . . that is . . . the female passage . . ." He tried to think of the polite term.

"Wrong!" she said.

"Wrong?"

"Wrong, wrong, wrong! You really don't know, do you? You

have no idea! Well, I'll give you a hint, my dear duke, my supposed expert in the arts of love. The seat of a woman's pleasure is not her *vagina*." She threw out the term without a hint of embarrassment and tossed her dress over her head.

"Good God, Abigail!" he cried. The candles flickered in shock. He became conscious that he was utterly naked, and she was not. He folded his arms across his chest. "Where, then?" he mumbled.

"I'm not going to tell you. It's no business of *mine* to tell you."

"What the devil does that mean?"

She fumbled with the hooks at the back of her neck. "It means, Your Grace, you may rest assured I shall not seek a repeat performance. You are quite free to seek your pleasure elsewhere."

"I don't *want* to seek my pleasure elsewhere!" he roared, uncrossing his arms.

"Then I'm afraid you shall simply have to do without." She picked up her mask from the floor and tied it around her head in swift jerks.

"Do *what*?" he roared, even more loudly, but Abigail was already storming across the floor, flinging open the door, dashing out into the darkness.

"Abigail!" The old timbers rattled at the boom of his voice. "Come back here!"

The moonlight poured silent and unchecked through the open door.

Wallingford stood stunned. He glanced down at the disordered blankets and cushions, the flickering candles, Abigail's discarded apron. His own clothes, scattered and crumpled.

The handkerchief on the floor, stained with her blood and his seed.

I'm afraid you shall simply have to do without.

With a loud oath, he put out the candles, gathered up his clothes, and ran out the door.

FIFTEEN

In her younger years, Abigail had often dreamed of storming away from the arms of some darkly handsome lover and into the moonlight.

The reality was rather less romantic. The feathers tickled Abigail's nose abominably, her shoes scrabbled against damp pebbles of the lakeshore, and her dress was coming undone in the back. She felt neither fleet nor graceful nor passionate, and to make a sorry situation worse, her nose was running, too.

"Damn it, Abigail!"

Wallingford's roar floated in the air behind her. Wallingford, that beast, that rutting boar. He hadn't even fully undressed her, had he? Simply pushed up her chemise and shoved away, no preliminaries, no caresses, no loving exploration of her anatomy. Two thrusts, two heaves of his massive body, and he was groaning out his release, while her torn flesh still burned with pain, and her body still arched for more.

More. Just . . . *more*. More of that sweet melting sensation, as he had unfastened her dress and held her breasts in his warm hands. More of that thrill, as he'd swept her up and placed her on the blankets, and his hungry gaze had enveloped her, and his rigid organ had searched out her tender flesh. More of those mighty thrusts, of the way even in the shock of pain she had felt an impossible pressure that made her hips tilt and her body strain to meet him.

"Abigail! Stop right now, by God!"

No! *Not* more. What was she thinking? Never, ever again. No more romantic illusions, no more dreams of transcendent sexual union, no more Wallingford heaving atop her with sinews flexing and face desperate. The dream lay shattered, the scales had fallen from her eyes, the . . . the . . .

The muscles between her legs ached like the devil.

The lakeshore gave way to the grass and the olive trees, the gradual slope upward to the castle. Abigail slowed her steps and picked her way through, trying to discern the path in the shadows. Somewhere ahead lay Mr. Burke's workshop, her customary landmark; she looked for its dark shape amid the trees. Wallingford's voice still echoed behind her, a little fainter. Perhaps he'd lost her in the darkness.

There it was! A great dark mass, moonlight glinting from the stones. The path should lie just to the left.

She plunged forward and stopped.

A light shone from inside, a flickering light. Which was not odd in itself; Mr. Burke often kept late hours, tinkering about on his machine, Alexandra at his side.

But tonight the workshop should be dark. Tonight Mr. Burke should be deep in Alexandra's arms, his body coursing with Morini's lemony drink, vowing eternal and faithful love to break the ancient curse.

And what was that smell? Odd and chemical. Rather like . . . Gas.

Abigail took a step closer, and as her foot touched the ground she felt a percussive jolt shudder through the air. An instant later, a bright flash filled her vision, and she went flying to the ground.

For a moment, she lay stunned. She was not hurt, except for the ache between her legs and the buzz in her ears, but she could not quite seem to move.

"Abigail!" Wallingford's voice rang frantic in her ears. His hands took her shoulders, turned her over. "Abigail!"

"I'm all right!" she gasped. "I'm all right! The workshop! Quickly!"

He looked up. "Bloody hell!"

They scrambled up together. Flames shot out from one of the windows; the stones around it were already black with soot, and glass covered the grass outside.

"Your shoes!" Abigail said. "Put on your shoes!"

She didn't stop to make sure he had. She ran forward to the pump, the blessed pump, which sat to the side of the building with bucket in place. Mr. Burke had always been particular, with all his chemicals and batteries about. She grabbed the handle and pumped with all her might, and when the bucket was full Wallingford appeared at her side, trousers and shoes fastened, and snatched it from her.

"Find another bucket!" he shouted over his shoulder, and he ran forward and tossed the contents into the flames.

Buckets. Buckets. Near the back door, perhaps? She ran around and saw two of them sitting next to the double carriage doors. She snatched them and ran back around to the pump, where Wallingford was already heaving, his shoulders bunching with effort, gleaming wet in the moonlight.

"I'll pump! You throw!" she screamed.

He took the bucket and ran, and she put the next one down and began to pump, and a new pair of hands grasped the handle just as the water hit the rim.

Alexandra's hands.

"What the devil . . ." she began, but Alexandra was already off with the bucket, and Abigail started another. She looked up and saw Mr. Burke was there, too, breaking down the wooden door with a massive thrust of his shoulder. Another bucketful, taken by Alexandra, handed off to Wallingford, and Burke came bursting through the door with a stack of blankets. He dumped them at her feet and ran back inside, together with Wallingford.

"Oh, you clever brute!" She took one of the blankets and began pumping, wetting it thoroughly, and then she lost track of the sequence of it all: buckets and blankets, the men and Alexandra running back and forth, Alexandra taking over when her arm tired of pumping.

She took a wet blanket and ran to the workshop. Everything was wetness and soot and heat. Wallingford handed her an empty bucket and snatched the blanket from her. "You're not going in!" he shouted at her. His face was gleaming and blackened, like a chimney sweep, and his voice was raspy with smoke.

"Oh, God! Are you all right?"

"I'm fine! Get more water!" He turned away and ran into the workshop. Through the window she saw him standing next to Burke, side by side, beating away the flames, and something rose in her throat and choked her.

She ran back to the pump, snatched a full bucket from Alexandra, staggered back with it. The flames were nearly gone, but the smoke still snaked through the window and from the roof. A pair of hands took the bucket from her and handed her an empty one.

Back and forth, again and again, until the urgency seeped at last from the air. The fire was out; the workshop still stood, its stones black with soot, reeking of smoke. A bucket lay on its side near the doorway. She picked it up, and another. The third sat next to the pump. She stacked them neatly, one inside the other, and straightened.

The window was shattered. Through the open frame, Alexandra and Mr. Burke stood in the darkness, hardly visible, speaking quietly. Burke's head hung downward, its ginger color obscured by darkness and damp and soot. As Abigail watched, transfixed, Alexandra's white arms slipped around Burke's lean waist, and his hand rose to cover hers.

She loves him, Abigail thought in wonder. Amid the debris and the grime, the water puddling in the grass about her feet, she felt a curious tranquility steal over her.

And without warning, her belly heaved, and she turned and vomited thoroughly into the grass.

E arly one fine crisp October morning, many years ago, Wallingford had been making his way to the Eton playing fields for a bout of honor, when he had encountered none other than the ginger-haired bastard son of the Duke of Olympia in the footpath. The familiar bile had risen in his throat. "Move aside, you whoreson bastard," he'd said—as one did—and young Burke had demanded immediate satisfaction for libel, and Wallingford had told him straight-out that it wasn't libel, and that as

Burke's mother accepted money and gifts in exchange for acts of carnal gratification, and as the Duke of Olympia had not in fact been married to her at the time of Burke's birth, Wallingford had only been speaking the truth.

Burke's right fist had shot out with reflexive speed to connect with Wallingford's eye, and before Wallingford could so much as stagger backward into the grass, Burke had followed up with a punishing left to the lip. Blackened and bleeding, Wallingford had shaken hands, called him a good sport, and brought him home to Belgrave Square at Michaelmas to meet his bemused father.

Since then, they had stood by each other through thick heads and thin company, not giving a particular damn for the opinion of society. When Wallingford had once found himself fleeced at Oxford by a publican running a racing book, Burke had come to his rescue and slipped a fierce chemical purgative in the house ale.

When Burke's workshop caught fire in the middle of the night, risking everything he'd labored over his entire adult life, Wallingford picked up a bucket and ran into the flames.

By the grace of God, the workshop was built of stone and they'd caught the fire quickly. Wallingford had helped Burke roll the automobile through the carriage doors and out of harm's way, and both Lady Morley and Abigail had pumped water and carried buckets like heroines.

In half an hour, the flames were out. Burke stood at the remains of what had once been the long counter, near the cabinet where Lady Morley had hidden herself all those months ago. A large black hole split the wooden surface in two, right near the window.

"It was the gas ring," Burke said quietly. "I must have left it on."

"Nonsense. You'd never have left it on," said Wallingford. He glanced around the room and shook his head. Most of the space had been spared, but the corner where the flames had burst out was charred and blackened, the contents irreclaimable. He cleared his throat. "I'll clean up the glass outside, before someone comes to grief."

Burke said nothing. Wallingford found a broom and went outside, where Lady Morley still pumped frantically into a bucket. Her hair was loose, her dress soaked and streaked with black. "That's it," he called out to her, but she didn't seem to notice, simply went on pumping.

He went to her and put his hand on her arm. "Alexandra, it's out. You can stop now."

She looked at him blankly. Her eyes had that glassy look of a prizefighter at the end of the bout, not quite certain who has won.

"It's out," he said again.

She turned to the workshop and stared at the broken window, the hole gaping in the roof. She pushed back a lock of hair and tucked it behind her ear. "Where is he?" she asked huskily.

He gave her arm a little squeeze. "Inside. I'm awfully sorry, Alexandra. We did the best we could."

"Thank you." She gave his hand a pat and hurried into the workshop.

Wallingford looked down at his bare chest and went to retrieve his shirt and waistcoat from the spot where Abigail had fallen. He put them on swiftly, closing his eyes at the memory: the flash of light, the crash of sound, Abigail landing in the grass. The bolt of pure terror in his heart, until she'd lifted her head and met his gaze.

He picked up the broom and walked back toward the workshop and stopped. Abigail stood there in the grass nearby, bent over, one hand braced on the pump, sick as a dog.

In an instant he was at her side.

"My God! Are you all right?" He took her by the shoulders.

"Yes, I'm quite . . . just . . ." Abigail straightened and patted herself, as if searching for a handkerchief.

His own handkerchief was long gone, of course. He tore off a strip from the bottom of his shirt instead. "Here."

"Thank you." She wet it from the pump and wiped her face, not looking at him.

"I'll take that," he said, shoving the linen in his pocket.

"I was just gathering the buckets, and . . . all that smoke and excitement, I suppose . . ."

"Abigail, I . . ."

"But I'm quite all right now. Thank goodness we found the fire in time. Was Mr. Burke able to save his machine?"

Her voice was false and bright, and her eyes lay fixed on the stone walls of the workshop, avoiding him. Wallingford's throat ached. Had he really made love to this woman, not an hour before? Had he really held her in his arms, kissed her, laid atop her, and taken her innocence? She spoke to him as if he were an acquaintance in a ballroom.

"Yes," he said. "We managed to roll it out back, through the carriage doors."

"Oh, good." She looked at the broom in his hand. "Shall I sweep up the glass, then?"

"I'll do it. Sit and rest."

"Oh, but I . . ."

"Abigail, you must. You must rest." He put his hand to her cheek, and she drew away instantly.

Cleaning the glass was the work of a moment. When he finished, she was sitting on a stack of buckets, staring at her hands.

"Come," he said. "I'm taking you to your room."

She rose. "We must say good-bye first."

Inside, Burke and Lady Morley were standing together, embracing quietly in the darkness. "I've stashed the buckets and swept up the glass outside," said Abigail. "How are things in here?"

Lady Morley disengaged from Burke. "Absolutely buggered, but we'll manage. The automobile's all right."

Burke stood still, arms empty. Behind him, the cabinet was a charred ruin, the long counter all but obliterated. But the rest of the room had been largely spared, Wallingford saw. He couldn't tell if the blackness were soot or shadow, but the furniture was intact, the machinery and tires still standing.

"Burke, old chap," said Wallingford. "What a damned nuisance. Are you all right? Anything I can do?"

Burke made his way across the puddles and debris and held out his hand. "You've done more than enough, my friend. I can't begin to thank you."

"You know damned well there's no such thing as thanks between us." Wallingford grasped Burke's hand and met his gaze. A steady gaze, a living gaze; no signs of shock, thank God.

Burke spoke up briskly. "I'll just tidy up a bit. You head on back to the house and let the stable lads know. I shall require carts to haul off the rubble, that sort of thing."

"Done. Lady Morley?"

She lifted her chin and smiled at him. It rather suited her. "I'll stay and help. But I'd be much obliged if you'd see my sister safely back to the house."

Abigail made a little snort. "I should think I'd be much safer without his help."

"Oh, for God's sake." Wallingford took her firmly by the elbow and led her outside.

"That's not necessary." She drew her arm away and increased her pace.

"Abigail! You will not run away from me again!"

Abigail stopped and turned. They were standing in the trees, shaded from the moon, and Wallingford couldn't see the expression in her face, couldn't tell if she were angry or tired or sorrowful. He wanted to touch her, but the air around them bristled with her disinclination to be touched. "I am not running away," she said.

"You are."

"I'm simply going back to my room to sleep. It's late, it's been a trying day, and I'm eager to go to bed."

"Very well. And I shall see you there. It is both my duty and my right."

Her chin snapped up at that. "It's neither your duty *nor* your right."

"Do not pretend, my dear," he said quietly, "as if nothing has passed between us."

"Do not pretend, *my dear*, as if what passed between us gave you any right over me, any dominion over me."

"By God, it does!"

"It was brief, and unpleasant, and I would prefer simply to forget it occurred at all."

A curious ringing began to sound in Wallingford's ears. He clenched his fists at his sides, to prevent them from closing around Abigail's shoulders, from holding her to him as securely as she held him. "But it *did* occur, Abigail. We lay together, you and I, and it does *not* mean nothing. It means everything. It has bound me to you in honor, if not in fact."

She folded her arms. "Has it, now? What a string of brides you must have collected by now. You might set up your own harem with them, like those marvelous Persian chaps."

"Don't pretend you don't understand me. A gentleman does not take a young lady's innocence without . . ."

She turned and began to stride up the path. "Oh, don't recite that rubbish to me! You know I wanted a lover, not a husband. I made that clear from the beginning. You have no obligations whatsoever."

"We might have conceived a child. Have you thought of that?"

"No doubt you have dozens of natural children running about by now. One more won't make any difference."

"I have none, as it happens."

She hurried between the trees, tossing her words at him as she went. "Oh, rot. I do know my pistils from my stamens, Wallingford, and I assure you, you can't have spread your seed about so freely without some sort of harvest, unless you're incapable of children altogether."

He took in a steadying breath. The air smelled of smoke, everything reeked of smoke: his clothes, his hair, his skin. What a sight he must be. No wonder she wouldn't look at him.

"I may or may not be incapable," he said. "That remains to be seen, I suppose. But I have not spread my seed about, as you so candidly put it. Until tonight, I have taken the greatest possible care not to do so."

Abigail walked on steadily. "I don't believe you. Why would you care?"

"Because." He hesitated, then said softly, "I made a pact, long ago."

She did not reply. The terrace wall loomed ahead; she found the steps in the moonlight and climbed them, her loose hair swinging around her shoulders and back. Wallingford followed her up, watching the curve of her backside slide beneath her dress, wanting her again with a kind of agonized soul-deep desire.

They were halfway down the first row of vines before she spoke. "With Burke, I suppose. You promised Burke, because he's illegitimate, because he knows what it means."

"Yes." He wondered if she knew he'd just delivered her a piece of his soul.

Silently they climbed the terraces together, walked down the rows of vines. The grass was soft and silent beneath their feet, dampening slowly in the night air. Wallingford breathed in the lingering reek of smoke, the lazy hint of ripening fruit, and thought how much he should like to draw Abigail down into the sweet-smelling turf, to lie with her in the enchanted Italian midnight, to watch the glow of her skin as the moon crept across the sky.

The courtyard was empty and quiet, the trestle tables removed, the musicians and villagers gone home. Abigail crossed the flagstones without looking and found the door.

"Wait," Wallingford said, and she turned with her soot-smudged fingers on the latch. "I must go to the stables and tell Giacomo what's happened. May I walk you to your room first?"

"Of course not. If I can find my way around Tattersalls on auction day, I can find the way back to my own bed. Do excuse me."

He tried again. "Look here, Abigail. Are you really all right? Let me . . . let me do something for you. Warm water, or . . . or perhaps tea . . ." He had no idea how to make tea, but surely it couldn't be that difficult, if kitchen maids could manage it.

A flash of white from her eyes. "Don't worry. You haven't rendered me an invalid, I assure you."

He placed his hand on the doorjamb and leaned against it. He felt as if someone had taken a sledgehammer to his innards and demolished everything inside. "Abigail, I'm sorry. I was a brute. I'd been waiting so long, I was blind with it. I *do* want to please you, if you'll allow me another chance. If you'll *show* me how to please you."

"I shouldn't *have* to show you. That was the point."

He closed his eyes. "For God's sake, Abigail. I'm only a man."

Something warm and soft landed on his cheek, and he realized it was Abigail's hand. He reached up to cover it with his own, but it was already gone.

"Yes, you *are* only a man, Your Grace," she said. "But you see, I was hoping for so much more."

SIXTEEN

Two weeks later

Abigail set the jugs of goat milk on the kitchen table with a significant clatter. "We have guests," she called out.

Morini emerged from the scullery, wiping her hands on her apron. "*Che cosa?*"

"Guests. Or *a* guest. I'm not certain which, because of the dust. Alexandra's receiving them in the library, as soon as she's cleaned the goat droppings from her shoes. I expect she'll want tea." She turned to leave.

"Wait, signorina!"

"I haven't time, Morini."

"Signorina, please."

Morini's voice floated quietly behind her. Abigail paused, with one hand on the door. "Make it quick, Morini. I really am frightfully busy."

"Signorina, this is not true. You only make yourself busy. You are making busy, so you do not have to do the thinking."

Abigail turned around and crossed her arms. "I don't know what you mean. I do a great deal of thinking, very lofty thoughts indeed."

Morini stood perfectly still next to the open window, and the warm morning breeze stirred the tiny black hairs around her temple. "Talk to me, signorina. Tell me what is happening on the midsummer night. Why you and the Signore Duca walk around with your unhappy eyes."

"I'm surprised you need to ask, Morini. I thought you were the all-seeing, all-knowing sort of person. In any case, there's nothing to tell. We discovered we don't suit, as I told you we shouldn't. It was all a great waste of limoncello."

"Signorina, listen. I have a plan . . ."

Abigail held up her hand. "No more of your plans. No more of your wretched curses. It was all great fun, a right old romp and all that, but you see how it's ended. Disaster hither and yon. Mr. Burke's bolted off to his automobile exposition in Rome, without a word to poor Alexandra. Heaven only knows where Penhallow and Lilibet have scampered, but I expect it's something to do with that beast Somerton, which means pistols at dawn at the very least. Besides, we've run out of time, haven't we? Midsummer's been and gone."

"Is not quite gone, signorina."

"Close enough, I daresay."

"You are not having much hope, signorina," Morini said.

"Really, what is there to hope for? This is what comes of meddling in the occult, or in matters of love, which is much the same thing."

Morini shook her head. "I never think to hear these words from you, signorina. Your sister, maybe. But you are so . . . so fresh, signorina. So full of the fun. Where is this fun now?"

"Where, indeed?" Abigail muttered.

"Oh, signorina." Morini stepped forward, skirts swishing, and put her hands on Abigail's shoulders. The air around her was warm with the scent of baking bread, of the familiar kitchen with its banked fire and old wooden table and worn flagstones. "You are so young, you are in love. The duke, he long for you, he ride about on his great black horse, he sit in the library with the books, with his head in his hands."

Abigail's heart gave its usual reflexive heave at the word *duke*. The silly organ had disclosed a singular and most unnatural streak of sentimentality in the past few weeks. It *would* ache so, whenever she thought of Wallingford's soot-streaked face in the courtyard on Midsummer's Eve, or whenever she caught sight of him about the castle or riding down the road. She told herself the ache came only from her conscience, for she *had* been rather hard on him that night, rather cold. He hadn't meant to disappoint her. He had simply carried on in his usual selfish ducal way, which she ought to have expected if she hadn't been so blinded by lust and by Morini's talk of destiny and transcendent love and that sort of rot, and how could she blame him for acting according to his nature? It was her own fault for developing such an unwarranted tenderness for the man. For having expected so much from him.

But she would soon recover, and so would he. It was only her girlish infatuation that was wounded, after all, and his aristocratic pride. If she continued to keep out of his way, and he continued to bar himself in the library and avoid all contact, why, they should both be quite indifferent in another week or so.

Yes, quite indifferent.

If only life weren't so bloody empty without him.

Abigail gave her heart a sharp knock to recall it to its duty, and gave her head a careless toss to show how indifferent she'd already become. "He is *studying*, signorina. Shocking, I know, but that *is* why we're all here, in case you're unaware. To study. Free from the distractions of the other sex, sapping our little beans dry. I admit, we all had a touch of the spring fever, caught up in the headiness of it all, but by God's grace we've all recovered our proper wits."

"Your wits, signorina?"

"Yes. Lovely things, wits. Indeed, I'm delighted, *delighted* to hear that His Grace has picked up his Livy at last. His mind could certainly use the improvement."

"Is not the Livy, signorina."

"Well, whatever it is. I'm sure it's most instructive. Most . . . most edifying."

"*Instructive*, signorina." Morini tasted the word. "*Si*. Is instructive."

Abigail narrowed her eyes. "You're *twinkling*, Morini. You're cooking something up. I can tell."

"*Si*, I am cooking." Morini lifted her hands away from Abigail's shoulders and gestured to the fire. "I am cooking the tea for the Signora Morley and her guest."

Abigail looked in bemusement at the teakettle hanging above the hot embers. "Already? How did you . . . ? Oh, never mind. I'd rather not ask. In any case, I didn't mean *actual* cooking.

I mean that you still think there's hope for us all, that you think you can wave your ghostly fingers and make us all fall crashing into each other, like witless human ninepins."

"I am not ghost, signorina," Morini said, in an offended tone.

"You know what I mean. Occult whatever-it-is." Abigail twirled her finger. "In any case, you can keep your mad schemes to yourself from now on."

"But signorina, only listen! The visitor, he . . ."

Abigail clapped her hands over her ears. "Not listening!"

"But signorina!"

"Not listening. Not listening. You can scheme all you like, Morini, but *I*"—she straightened herself into dignity, or as much dignity as could be achieved when smelling of goats and holding one's ears—"am going to change clothes."

"Is good!" Morini called. "Change the clothes! And while you are in the room, changing the clothes, perhaps you wish to take out the trunk for to carry them?"

Abigail poked her head back around the doorway through which she'd just disappeared. "What's that? Trunks?"

Morini smiled, smoothed her apron, and went to attend the whistling teakettle in the fireplace. "Because, signorina. I think it is maybe possible you and the signora are soon leaving."

"Leaving? Why should we leave? Where on earth would we go?"

"Why, for Roma." Morini poured the hot water into the teapot and looked up, still smiling. "For Roma, signorina. How do they call it? The city of eternity."

The next day

I say, Giacomo, old fellow," called out the Duke of Wallingford, swinging from his horse into the hard-packed dirt of the stableyard, "the geese appear to be scampering about the grounds unchecked. Have you any notion . . ."

"Signore!"

Wallingford found his hands seized, his frame turned about this way and that. Lucifer gave a snort of astonishment.

"Good God, man." Wallingford disengaged himself with

some effort and brushed the sleeves of his riding jacket. He peered at Giacomo, who, undiscouraged by his loss of a dance partner, proceeded to heave and jerk his body about the stable-yard like a drunken marionette. "Remember your dignity."

"Is a miracle, signore! A miracle!"

Lucifer was beginning to look alarmed. Wallingford snatched the reins. "A miracle? What sort of miracle? Has the stable roof begun to leak wine instead of water?"

Giacomo fell to his knees and looked up at the sky.

"I say, are you quite all right, old man?" Wallingford took a concerned step toward him.

The groundskeeper lifted his hands, palms upward. "This day, I give the thanks. I pray at the throne of Our Lord, who give us at last the great blessing."

"The goats have learned to milk themselves? One of the geese has perhaps laid a golden egg?"

"No, signore."

Wallingford considered. "*Two* golden eggs?"

"Signore. Is the *women*!"

Wallingford loosened Lucifer's girth and led the horse to the fence. "The women? Is *that* all? I rather thought you disliked the women. I rather thought, in fact, you jolly well hated them."

"Is not jolly at all, signore. The women, I hate them seriously. They are so much the trouble," Giacomo said, following at his elbow. "This is why I am today so happy." He kissed his fingers.

"So they've kept indoors all morning and left the goats to your tender care?"

"No, signore. Is better than that." Giacomo held up his hands to his Creator. "They are gone!"

Wallingford, in the act of sliding the saddle from Lucifer's broad black back, turned into stone. "What's that?" he said at last, through his frozen lips.

"Gone, signore! They leave at the sunrise, in a cart from the village, with the trunks and the hats. They are gone! Gone at last!" Giacomo hugged himself and twirled about like an ancient bandy-legged ballerina.

"Are you certain, Giacomo?" The saddle pressed into his arm. Lucifer sounded an uneasy whuffle.

"I see them myself, Signore Duca. I wave the good-bye."

Giacomo made an illustrative wave, back and forth, adding a flirtatious wiggle of his fingers for effect.

"Quite gone?"

"Gone, the two of them. The devil-sisters."

"They are not devils, Giacomo. Merely high-spirited."

"Signore." Giacomo was reproachful. "You know the women. You have seen the trouble. Your heart, it is light now, yes? Light of the great burden." He sighed and pressed one hand to his chest. "My heart, it feels full of the gas."

"The *gas?*"

"The gas that we breathe." Giacomo breathed. "Ah. So light."

"*Air*, my good man. Your heart is full of *air*. Lighter than air, I believe, is the proper English phrase." Wallingford tossed the saddle atop the fence with unusual disregard for the condition of the leather—unusual, that is, since he began caring for it himself. Lucifer nudged the small of his back with a gentle muzzle.

"Aha! You see! You, too, feel this thing, this air in your heart."

Wallingford turned. "What I feel, my good man, is a strong desire to see to my horse and then see to my luncheon. You will forgive me?"

Giacomo returned his hand to his heart and made a happy little bow. "I forgive you, Signore Duca. I go now, I leave you in the peace, to savor the joy."

"Oh, that's right," said Wallingford, fetching a brush. "Go on, take the rest of the day off to celebrate. I daresay I can't jolly well stop you, as I'm not paying your wages."

He brushed Lucifer's coat in long, steady strokes, erasing all signs of saddle and girth. He checked the hooves for stones. He removed the bridle, added a halter, led the horse through the gate and into the paddock. For a moment, he stood at the fence and watched Lucifer canter to the end and back, kicking his heels once or twice with the joy of being alive.

Gone.

The sun burned quietly, right over the crown of his head, penetrating the snug weave of his straw hat with all the strength of an Italian July. It would be very hot, riding in a cart, along the rough road to Florence and the nearest train connection. He hoped the ladies had brought parasols and water.

He picked up the tack and took it inside the stable, to its proper place.

Though his stomach hurt with hunger, Wallingford did not go to the empty dining room, with its enormous old table, on which a cold luncheon was usually laid out by noon. He went instead to the library, where he'd spent many long hours in the past two weeks. With Roland and Burke gone, with the memory of Abigail's wretched cold eyes burned on his brain, he had had no other company to distract him.

He had first gone through all the old paperwork, the account books and the estate documents, making careful notes where appropriate. When he felt he had the facts straight, had a solid grasp of the legal and financial history of the castle, he turned to sex.

More specifically, the female anatomy; still more specifically, where its seat of pleasure might be found. He had begun with this single and rather idle goal—merely to satisfy his curiosity, he told himself—but once he had discovered the proper Latin terms, the anatomical descriptions, the degrees of natural variance, he had found himself intrigued. One thing had led to another, and all at once a dizzying new world had opened itself up to Wallingford's eager mind: a world, moreover, that seemed to have been thoroughly studied and catalogued by the provisioners of the Castel sant'Agata library.

Almost as if they had anticipated his requirements.

By the time he had finished all the anatomical studies, all the titillating Continental memoirs, all the exotic Oriental handbooks, a tiny flame of hope had flickered to life in Wallingford's breast, among other areas of his body.

Except now, it felt quite extinguished.

Wallingford walked across the threadbare rug to the desk, over which Abigail had bent her abundant torso to such glorious effect on Midsummer's Eve. He sank into the chair. On the baize-lined surface of the desk, smelling of ink and old paper, a book lay open to a page of illustrations that would cause an immediate run on the market for smelling salts, should it magically appear in a London drawing room at half past four in the afternoon. He gazed for a moment at the entwined figures, at the helpful Latin descriptions below each engraving, and reached out his large hand to close the book.

Just that morning, he had met with his business agent in the village. Just that morning, the fellow had said, *I have those marriage contracts drafted for your approval, Your Grace. Should you like to look them over and make amendments?*

The clock had ticked off a few silent seconds, and Wallingford had replied, *Perhaps another time. I've a great deal to do today.*

But as he had ridden through the hot air back up the hill, and the sun-soaked castle had appeared around the bend in the road, he had damned himself for a coward. For two weeks, he had hidden himself from Abigail Harewood. For two weeks, he had let the awful memory of her final words beat over and over in his mind, paralyzing his resolve. He had watched her go about her business with her light step and her delicate fairy face: the face that had become so beautiful to him, it made his heart ache whenever she passed by the library window.

It was time to stop hiding, he had thought, riding up the hill. It was time to stop acting like a mere man. That hadn't achieved much at all.

It was time to act once more like the Duke of almighty Wallingford.

Now, in the warm somnolence of the library, he gazed down at the cover of the book, which was of tooled brown leather, plain and bland. Even its title suggested no more than a dry scientific study on matters of human biology.

Wallingford rose from the chair and walked back out of the room.

He climbed the grand staircase, two steps at a time, the crack of his riding boots echoing from the empty stone walls. He went directly to the ladies' wing, which he had last visited months ago. He tried each door; they were all unlocked, the hinges well oiled. The first room contained a trundle bed, clearly where young Philip slept with Lady Somerton. The second was a little smaller, tidy, shadowed from the noontime sun. He went to the wardrobe and opened it: nearly empty, except for a blue dress he recognized as one Lady Morley wore, from time to time.

The door to the third room swung open with a faint whoosh. He recognized it at once. He could feel Abigail's lingering presence, as if some magic elfin dust had been scattered carelessly about the walls. Or perhaps it was the books, which sat on every available surface, even the foot of her narrow bed. Abigail's bed, Abigail's cool linen pillow, on which she rested her head every night and slept and dreamed. What did she dream of?

What did she wear, in bed at night?

A washstand sat against the wall, next to the chest of drawers. He stepped toward it. The pitcher and bowl were empty, but a small cake of soap sat on the edge. He picked it up and sniffed it, lemons and blossoms, and his heart hollowed out of his body, his breath stopped. He sank into the chair and put his head in his hands.

Wallingford had never visited the kitchen of the Castel sant'Agata before. He had only the vaguest notion where it lay: somewhere down the corridor past the dining room, he supposed.

In the end, he let his nose guide him, let the scent of baking bread draw him down the hall and through the half-open door. The kitchen was empty, but a kettle hung above the fireplace, and a loaf sat cooling on the large table in the center of the room. A slight hot breeze wafted through the open window.

Wallingford stopped in the center of the room and turned in a slow circle.

"You're here, aren't you?" His voice was low. "Morini, isn't it? The housekeeper. I've never seen you, just as Abigail can't seem to see Giacomo, God knows why. But you're here. I can feel it. It's like a tingling in my head, at the back of my neck."

The room was so quiet, he could hear his own breathing.

"You know where she's gone, don't you? I daresay you know everything."

His boots scuffed against the stones as he turned again.

"I wish . . . I wonder if you could tell me where she's gone. I'm all alone here, of a sudden, and while I suppose that's a triumph of some sort, the last man standing and all that, I can't help feeling that . . ."

His words trailed away. Outside the window, the geese honked indignantly, and an instant later Giacomo's voice let loose a string of lyric Italian curses.

"The thing is, I love her. I love her so much, I can't think, I can't sleep. And you know how she is: She's like a sprite, impossible to catch, and yet I must try, I *must*, because there's no living without her." He took a breath, and went on, more calmly, "If you know where she's gone, Morini, whoever you are, you must tell me. Find a way to tell me. I'll keep her safe, I swear it. I'll devote my life to making her happy, because . . ."

The breeze gusted in, stronger now, making the teakettle swing above the embers of the fire with a little rhythmic squeak.

"Because she's my last hope."

His words bounced lightly from the walls. The scent of the cooling bread tantalized his hungry belly, reminding him that it was an hour past luncheon, and he was talking sentimental rubbish to an empty room, like a madman.

He turned on his heel and walked out the door, down the stone hallway, to where a lunch was laid out on the massive dining room table, set for one.

Wallingford had just finished an excellent artichoke tart and a glass of wine when the door opened and a maid slipped into the room, straightening her headscarf nervously and not quite meeting his gaze.

"Maria, isn't it?" he said, grateful for even a trace of human contact.

"*Si*, Signore Duca." She made a little curtsy and held out her hand. "A note, signore."

His heart crashed against his ribs. "Thank you, Maria."

He unfolded the note with care, because he didn't want his shaking fingers to be noticed by Maria, who stood still by the doorway as if waiting for a reply.

He read the note with care, because the handwriting was difficult to decipher, and the words themselves had an odd syntax, as if the writer were not a native speaker of the English tongue.

He refolded the note with care, because he knew he would have need of its details again, and slipped it into his waistcoat pocket.

"Thank you, Maria." He folded his napkin and rose from the table. "It appears I shall be leaving the castle within the hour. Would you please send a message to the stables, that my horse should be saddled and ready. And Maria?"

"*Si*, signore?" The maid looked a little panicked, as if she hadn't quite understood his every word.

"Give Signorina Morini my best compliments, and assure her that the Duke of Wallingford will endeavor not to disappoint her."

SEVENTEEN

Borghese Gardens, Rome

Abigail handed her sister the wide leather-trimmed goggles and helped her to ease them around her head, atop her billowing white scarf. "This is so thrilling," she said, tightening the buckle. "I want you to know, I've laid twenty lire on you with the chap running the book at the hotel café."

"Where the devil did you find twenty lire? Really, Finn," Alexandra said, to the man hovering over the bonnet of the automobile, "that's quite enough. These men are really most frightfully competent. You should see to your own machine."

Mr. Burke straightened. He looked terribly dashing, Abigail thought, so very tall, with his long duster coat swirling about his legs and his peaked driving cap shadowing his creased forehead. His own goggles hung about his neck, and a light sheen of perspiration shone on his temples. From the heat, no doubt, which hung like a sticky wool blanket against the skin, but also from worry: Mr. Burke, Abigail gathered, was not particularly happy to see his beloved Alexandra competing in a motor-race against him and his beloved automobile.

Abigail glanced at William Hartley, the owner of their own machine and a nephew of the late Lord Morley. He lounged against the side, his belly resting comfortably against the gleaming metal, a foot shorter and a foot rounder than his ginger-haired rival.

Really, there was no comparison.

"You're certain of the course?" Mr. Burke asked, in a disapproving growl that reminded Abigail exactly of his nephew.

"Perfectly," said Alexandra. "Around the gardens, down to the Colosseum, back up to the gardens. I tracked it yesterday. And it's marked."

Mr. Burke stared at her a second or two longer, and Abigail thought she could feel the very air throb between the two of them.

"Be safe," he said.

"And you," whispered Alexandra.

He turned and walked to his motor-car, circling it with attentive care. Abigail watched him tenderly for a moment, thinking how his stern profile reminded her of Wallingford, and so great was her sense of Wallingford's essence that the sound of his familiar voice did not, for a fraction of an instant, surprise her.

"Lady Morley."

A shadow loomed on the gleaming metal of Alexandra's steam automobile.

Abigail whipped around. "Good God! Wallingford!"

"Wallingford!" Alexandra exclaimed. "What on earth?"

He stood there glowering at her from his magnificent height: Wallingford, unmistakably Wallingford, right here next to her in the middle of the hot Roman morning, wearing a light gray suit and straw boater. The sunlight flashed in his dark eyes, revealing the blue in them. Abigail's heart soared straight upward, as if some invisible weight had lifted away from her chest. She opened her mouth and couldn't speak.

"You might have told me where you were going, you silly fools," he said.

"And why is that, exactly?" demanded Alexandra.

He glanced at her. "Because I woke up four days ago to find myself the only damned resident in the castle, and the entire pile gone silent, without a word of news from anyone, and . . ."

Abigail found her voice at last. "I'm so terribly sorry. How were the goats?"

Wallingford returned his gaze to her and spoke between his clenched lips. "I don't give a damn about the goats."

"Such language, Your Grace!" said Alexandra. "In front of

Miss Harewood! I'm shocked. Shocked and appalled. Moreover, I've a race that begins in"—Alexandra consulted her watch—"five minutes, and I beg leave to point out that you're a most unwelcome obstruction."

Wallingford started. "You're *driving*? In the *race*?"

"Certainly I am."

He turned to Abigail. His eyes were wide with shock. "But you can't simply leave your sister alone in a crowd of . . . of *Italians*!"

"Of course not. Mr. Hartley will protect her from any insult."

Abigail looked again at William Hartley. He stood now a few diffident yards away, hat in hand, scratching his ear, mechanics idling at his side. He seemed to hear his name, for he looked over at them, replaced his hat, and worked his jowls.

Wallingford stared, too. He turned back to Alexandra. "You're not serious."

"Well, watch her yourself, then. Though I'd be more concerned for the poor Roman fellow who dared to accost her. Mr. Hartley!"

He straightened. "Yes, your ladyship?"

"I believe it's time. Is the steam up?"

"Yes, ma'am," said one of the mechanics. "Full steam. She's ready to go."

As he spoke, a loud noise like a pistol shot cracked through the air, and Abigail found herself flung to the grass, with Wallingford's heavy body covering her own.

O h!" said Abigail faintly. "Has the Prime Minister been assassinated?"

Wallingford's cheek lay against hers. He wanted to keep it there, but lifted his head instead. He saw first the hard rubber of the automobile tire near his nose, and then, farther up, the inquisitive face of Lady Morley.

"No," her ladyship said cheerfully. "Only a bit of an explosion, it seems. These dashed petrol engines."

Abigail lay quite still beneath Wallingford. He looked down at her squashed hat and her chestnut hair, covering her face.

"Are you all right?" he asked desperately.

She stirred, and he gave way with an odd reluctance. Even

with a few thousand people in attendance, and the threat of further catastrophic engine explosions, he had rather enjoyed the feel of her warm body beneath him once more. "An explosion, you say? Where?"

"Over there, I suspect," said Alexandra, pointing. "The one with the blood all over the bonnet. The poor fellow."

Wallingford followed Alexandra's pointing finger. He considered himself a man of strong stomach, of sound British phlegm, but this sight before him—swarming already with doctors and stretchers and bandage rolls—made his belly go strangely sickish. He put his hand on one side of Alexandra's automobile and studied his fingers as the sweating minutes ticked away. Was it his imagination, or had his skin gone rather green?

"Oh, right-ho! Jolly lurid," Abigail was saying. "Is that his arm?"

"Damned hand cranks on these petrol engines," Alexandra said, with a knowing shake of her head. "Those petrol automobiles. Nuisances, the lot of them."

Burke wandered over, his hair showing in a bright ginger line underneath his cap. "Everyone all right?" He saw Wallingford and started. "What the devil are you doing here, old man?"

"The same as you, I expect." Wallingford nodded at the sisters, whose crisp white dresses nearly blinded the eye in the Roman sunshine. "Are you certain this is quite all right?"

"Wallingford, old fellow," Burke said, "if you can find a way to stop them, you're a better man than I am."

The doctors arrived with a stretcher, and with surprising efficiency they had bandaged up the compound fracture and the dislocated jaw, and mopped up the blood from the bonnet. Wallingford tried to maneuver himself next to Abigail, but she and Alexandra had their heads together, chattering in that altogether intimidating feminine way, and Burke drew him aside to discuss the cause of the explosion, and the superiority of the electric engine in safety and performance and overall smell.

Wallingford looked again at the gory scene, at the ten or more automobiles lined up at the start, at Lady Morley in her goggles and her white scarf, and finally at Phineas Burke. "Look here. You'll be all right, won't you? It seems to me like a dashed dangerous business."

"I'll be all right." Burke glanced at Lady Morley. "But I'll tell you, Wallingford, I rather wish the next hour or so were over with."

"Hmm."

Burke checked his watch and began to circle around his own machine. "Looks as if they've got things cleaned up, anyway. We'll be starting soon."

Wallingford followed him and leaned against the doorframe as he climbed into the seat. "Anything I can do for you, old man?"

"Just keep an eye out, won't you? If something happens, if she finds herself in trouble . . ." Burke looked down at the steering tiller, as if checking the mechanism.

"Done," said Wallingford. A cheer rippled across the assembled crowd, as the stretcher was hoisted up and the injured man carried off. "You mean to marry her, don't you?" he asked quietly.

"If she'll have me." Burke gazed forward, both hands on the tiller, leather gloves glowing dully in the sunshine. "And what about you?"

"If she'll have me."

Burke laughed and shook his head. "By God, that's the last time I'll answer a newspaper advertisement."

The drivers were once more climbing into their seats, the petrol engines cranking to life. Wallingford stepped away. "Good luck, old man."

"And you, by God. And you."

Wallingford went around the back of Burke's machine and grasped Abigail firmly around the arm. She looked up in surprise.

"*You*, Miss Harewood," he said, in the commanding voice he knew she loved, "are coming with me."

"Oh! Where?" Her eyes sparkled, as if she expected him to say *to my room*, or *to a nearby bawdy-house*.

"Out of harm's way," he growled.

She stepped back with him willingly enough, into the crowd of spectators. The sultry smell of petrol exhaust drifted through the air. All the hundreds of throats had ceased moving; all eyes were on the starter, who stood at the end of the line, consulting his watch, his pistol raised.

"That's a jolly fine pistol," Abigail whispered in his ear. "Do you suppose it's actually loaded?"

The starter looked up and down the line. The very air had

gone utterly still. Not a sound, except for the roar of the engines; not a movement, except for the starter swiveling his head, watching the automobiles with his keen eyes. Inches away, Abigail's body seethed beneath its layers of ladylike white chiffon. Her gloved hand slipped into his.

A puff of smoke came from the end of the pistol, and an instant later a bang shattered the air.

Alexandra's car lunged ahead, matched Burke for a second or two, and then passed him. The ends of her white scarf fluttered in the backdraft, and the last Wallingford saw of her was the wide smile splitting her face in two.

"She's ahead!" Abigail squeezed his hand like a nutcracker. "She's ahead! Oh, hold me up, so I can see!"

What else could he do? He put his hands around her trim rib cage and hoisted her upward. "There they go! She's ahead, she's going around the corner, there's Mr. Burke chasing her, and oh! *Oh!*"

"What is it?" Wallingford could see nothing but white chiffon.

"Some chap's lost his tiller! Good God! Oh, watch out!" She gave a delicious shudder and slid down in his arms. "Directly into a fruit stand. Bananas, I believe."

Bananas. Wallingford closed his eyes and inhaled her, sweet, living Abigail, just before she stepped away with a laugh.

"Well, that's that, I suppose! When are they expected at the finish line?"

Wallingford consulted his watch, as if that would give him the answer. "Burke said something about an hour." He felt a little dizzy, not quite himself. The old Abigail had returned, lighthearted and charming, inserting herself willingly between his two hands, as if the night in the boathouse had never occurred. It couldn't possibly be this easy.

Could it?

He took her by the shoulder and turned her toward him. "Abigail, I . . ."

"There you are, Miss Harewood!" A portly gentleman appeared next to them, standing a good deal too close: the same gentleman who had been hanging about Lady Morley's automobile before the start. He stuck his thumbs cheerfully into his waistcoat pockets. "Lady Morley asked me to keep a bit of an eye on you, during the race."

"Oh, that's quite unnecessary," Abigail said, with equal cheer. "A dear friend of mine has turned up, quite unexpectedly." She patted Wallingford's arm. "He's a splendid chaperone, frightfully protective. He often reminds me of a particularly keen bloodhound."

The gentleman's eyebrows rose as he contemplated Wallingford. He tipped back his hat in an indolent way. "A bloodhound, what? I say, old fellow. You look dashed familiar. Have you a handle of some sort?"

Wallingford stared down his nose. "I am the Duke of Wallingford, *old fellow*. And who the devil are you?"

The gentleman went quite pale. He turned to Abigail, as if she might possess better information on the matter than he did.

"Oh, I beg your pardon! Wallingford, this is William Hartley, my sister's nephew. By marriage, of course. He's the owner of the automobile she's driving."

Wallingford did not move his gaze a fraction from Mr. Hartley's round face. "And why isn't he driving the machine himself, in that case?"

"Because it makes him sick, I believe. Isn't that so, Mr. Hartley?"

"Quite so." Hartley dabbed at his pearling forehead with a handkerchief. "Quite so."

"I see," said Wallingford.

"Mr. Hartley came to see us at the castle, on his way down to Rome," Abigail went on. "I believe he convinced Alexandra to make the trip. Didn't you, Mr. Hartley?"

"I . . . I hope I have that honor," gasped out Hartley.

A shimmer of activity swept through the milling crowd.

"Oh, what's going on?" Abigail craned her neck. "Is it a brawl? Oh, do say it's a brawl. I've been in Italy nearly five months without a brawl."

A shout, and a voice raised in jabbering outrage. Wallingford shifted his body next to Abigail, overlapping her, his feet planted a little apart.

"Have no fear, Miss Harewood," said Hartley. "My mechanics will protect you from any insult."

Abigail clutched Wallingford's arm and rose up on her toes. "If it *is* a brawl, you must lift me onto your shoulders at once. I don't want to miss a single blow."

Wallingford was at least half a head taller than any of the spectators nearby. He tilted his chin to avoid a particularly intrusive ostrich feather and peered across the shifting sea of hats.

"It isn't a brawl," he said at last, relaxing his stance. "It's a chap running about with a steering tiller."

Six hours later

So there I stood, Miss Harewood, everything in the balance, forced to make a split-second choice between the three-and-a-quarter-inch cylinder and the three-and-three-eighths-inch cylinder, and do you know what I did?" Mr. Hartley extended his middle finger and pushed away a greasy lock of hair from the center of his forehead.

Abigail gasped and put her fingers to her lips. "You chose the three-and-a-quarter!"

"No, I did not."

"The three-and-three-eighths?"

"No, no, Miss Harewood." Mr. Hartley's smile grew wide and smug.

"Oh, the suspense, Mr. Hartley! Do tell me. I can't stand another instant."

He tapped his temple. "I called for the engineer, of course!"

"You didn't!"

"I did. Your true leader, Miss Harewood, always knows when to delegate his duties to others." He paused and lifted his hair again, which seemed to insist on drooping, like an exhausted worm. "Are you quite well, Miss Harewood? Your eyes have been shifting about these past ten minutes."

"Quite all right, I assure you, Mr. Hartley. Scintillated, indeed. But the fact is, I do seem to have lost my sister in the crush." Abigail nodded her head to indicate the crush in question; namely, the crowd of motor enthusiasts gathered at the Villa Borghese for the winner's banquet. Or rather, what ought to have been the winner's banquet, were the winner not currently occupying a private corner of a Roman jail. Still, the celebration had gone on regardless, with Alexandra at the center of things in her usual style, and Abigail—who had risen early that morning—now longed for nothing more than the oblivion of her heavenly hotel bed.

The fact that the Duke of Wallingford had disappeared at some point during dessert had nothing, she told herself firmly, to do with her longing.

"Oh, Lady Morley left half an hour ago." Mr. Hartley patted his waistcoat pockets. "Didn't she tell you?"

"No, she did not." Abigail's heart drooped.

"Quite half an hour ago. I hailed her a cab myself."

"Well, that's rather odd," said Abigail. "I suppose I should make my way back to our own hotel, then."

"I shall of course accompany you."

"That's not necessary, I assure you."

"Miss Harewood!" Hartley let out a shocked gasp. "A young maiden, alone on the streets of Rome! It wouldn't do."

"I should be in a cab from door to door. It will do very well."

"No, no." He took her by the elbow. "I'm going back myself. Frightfully late, after all. I'm absolutely"—a theatrical half-stifled yawn—"conked."

"Mr. Hartley, I'm quite capable . . ."

But he was already forging a path through the crowd, and there was little else to do but follow him with a sense of settling despair. How could an evening that had started out with such promise end so miserably? She had sat next to Wallingford at the banquet, and he had been exactly like the old springtime Wallingford, with his dry humor and sly innuendos and his large hands grasping his wineglass with enough coiled strength to shatter it to pieces. He had been a sleek-limbed tiger next to Mr. Hartley's well-fed sloth.

Now Wallingford was gone, and Alexandra was gone, and even Mr. Burke had long since disappeared to tend to his machine. Which left only William Hartley to see her back to the Majestic Hotel. What a scandal that should be, back in London, but here in this crowd of scientists and engineers, there seemed to be no such notion as impropriety.

Hartley reached the door and stood aside for her to pass. The attendant gave them a wise look.

"Look here, Mr. Hartley," Abigail said, determined to try again, "I'm not at all certain this is quite the thing. Perhaps we can determine where my sister went and . . ."

"No, no. We're practically related, Miss Harewood. Taxi!" He lifted his arm as a cab appeared down the drive, trotting along at a brisk pace.

Abigail rolled her eyes upward. "Mr. Hartley, we are not remotely related, and . . ."

Hartley stepped forward to intercept the cab. The horse began to arc toward the steps, slowing to a walk. "You see, Miss Harewood? Right and tight. Best of all, along the way we'll have time for me to finish my story about the cylinders."

"Do you mean to say that wasn't the end?" asked Abigail faintly.

"Not at all, not at all!" The cab stopped. Hartley stepped back with a flourish. "Miles to go. You haven't heard what the engineer said to me. Your chariot, my dear."

He opened the door of the cab with a little bow, and out sprang the Duke of Wallingford.

"Wallingford!" Abigail nearly lurched into his arms with relief.

"Why, Miss Harewood! Mr. Hartley!" Wallingford turned to Hartley and raised his eyebrows in that terror-inducing ducal way. "Were you off somewhere?"

"Mr. Hartley had very kindly offered to see me to my hotel, though I *insisted* it wasn't necessary." Abigail put a delicate emphasis on the word *insisted*.

"Gallant fellow," said Wallingford. "However, you needn't bother. Before she left, Lady Morley asked me to see to Miss Harewood's welfare, and I have just returned with my own vehicle."

"Your vehicle?" Hartley asked, looking at the cab.

"I leased it for the week, cab and driver both. So much more convenient than hailing for one. Shall we be off, Miss Harewood?"

"See here," said Hartley, "this is quite improper. I'm one of the family!"

Abigail shook her head sadly. "It's true, Wallingford. He is my sister's late husband's nephew by marriage. Almost a brother."

"All very well, but I, as you see, am in possession of both Lady Morley's direct order and a waiting cab. Miss Harewood?"

Wallingford swept her into the cab before Hartley's swinging jaw. He rapped the roof and said, through the opening, "Majestic Hotel, if you please."

When she had finished laughing, Abigail found she had not a word to say. Wallingford sat next to her, impossibly large, filling every last cubic inch of the cab's interior with his black evening suit and his brilliant white shirt and his infinite dignity. Abigail, who had conversed so easily with him in company, went mute in the intimacy of the closed space.

For his part, Wallingford made no effort at conversation, either. He sat still, staring through the window at an idle angle, moving not a single finger of his broad and endless body.

The way to the Majestic Hotel was not long. Hardly five awkward minutes had passed before the cab slowed, the lights shone through the window, and Wallingford was swinging through the door to hand her out.

"I'll see you to your room," he said, in a tone that brooked no opposition.

Up they went, in the Majestic's modern mechanical lift, the attendant standing between them like a grave red-suited statue. What the fellow must think, Abigail thought, with an inward smile. Really, it was dreadfully careless of Alexandra to leave her in Wallingford's care for the night. Her rendezvous with Mr. Burke—for of course it could be nothing else—must have been of the most desperate nature.

The lift came to rest with a clang. The attendant opened the grille. Wallingford stood aside for her and walked by her side down the corridor without a word.

"Here we are," she said, taking out her key. She held out her other hand. "Thank you so much for saving me from that fellow Hartley. If only every damsel could be plucked from the jaws of boredom so effectively."

"Abigail." Wallingford looked down at her with liquid eyes. "I must speak with you."

Thump-thump, went Abigail's heart.

"Oh no. Most improper. I've no idea what Alexandra told

you, but I'm quite certain your orders don't go so far as tucking me into bed at the Majestic Hotel."

Wallingford placed one hand on the doorjamb, right next to her ear. "And I am equally certain that Miss Abigail Harewood gives not a fig for the opinions of others."

Abigail moistened her lips, which had gone quite dry. "Oh, there's where you're wrong. I hate being caught out. Most unnerving. I . . ."

A series of loud thumps came from the direction of the staircase.

"You'd better make up your mind," said Wallingford.

Abigail swallowed, turned, fitted her key into the lock, and thrust the door open.

The room was dark. Hurriedly Abigail reached for the electric light switch, and a dim yellow glow illuminated the furnishings.

Wallingford removed his hat and gloves and placed them on the table next to the lamp. "Ah, modern accommodations."

"Yes, it was built only last year." Abigail positioned herself behind a chair. "Running water, such a treat. Have you a room here, too?"

"Yes."

"I expect it's twice as large. I expect you have the imperial suite."

"Something of that sort, yes. Would you like to see it?" He turned to her.

Abigail gripped the back of the chair. The room was a small one, and the two narrow beds loomed unnaturally close. "Look, Wallingford, I hope you don't mistake my earlier friendliness for a desire to resume our . . . our . . ."

"No, I do not."

Her shoulders heaved, whether with relief or disappointment she couldn't say. "Well, that's that, then. I bid you good evening."

"I don't *mistake* anything at all, Abigail." He leaned his shoulder against the wall and watched her patiently. "I know very well how you feel. I feel the same."

"Which is?"

"That we belong with each other. That this ridiculous

estrangement of the past fortnight must end at once, before we both go mad."

"Well!"

"I will not give you up, Abigail. I will not let your misguided notions of independence and freedom destroy this promise of happiness between us."

"I say! That's rather high-handed of you."

He smiled. "You like my high-handedness."

"I find it novel and exhilarating, like Mr. Burke's motor-car. And like Mr. Burke's motor-car, I should not wish to live with it every day." Her head was a little light, watching him lean against her wall a few feet away, his face turned to gold by the incandescent light from the modern electric lamp.

"Abigail," he said softly. "Abigail. What are you afraid of? Do you think I wish to clip your wings? I love your wings. I love everything about you. I would cut off my own arm before I forced you into some London drawing room full of chattering nullities."

She closed her eyes. "Wallingford, this is all very well, but I believe we established in the boathouse that we don't suit. We don't . . . we don't connect, on a physical level, which I consider . . . I consider essential to . . ." She lost her train of thought. His words kept repeating in her head: *I love your wings. I love everything about you.*

She heard the faint brush of his shoes on the plush new carpet, drawing close.

"My dear girl, I will apologize one more time for my boorish behavior that night. It was inexcusable."

"It was dreadfully disappointing."

"The next time we meet in bed, I shall endeavor not to disappoint you."

"There will be no next time."

"Yes, there will. Open your eyes, Abigail."

She opened them and gasped. He stood not two feet away, enormous and black-shouldered, his hand next to hers on the back of the chair, his dark blue eyes enclosing her. The warmth of his body irradiated her skin. He moved his hand to cover hers.

"Despite appearances, I have always considered myself a man of open mind, Abigail. One not too proud to learn from his mistakes."

"I own myself astonished."

"In that spirit of inquiry, I have taken it upon myself to learn a few things, during the course of our separation." He bent close to her ear and whispered. "I have learned, for example, where the seat of a woman's pleasure truly lies."

"Oh." Abigail's pulse crashed in her throat. Her middle seemed to be turning disgracefully into jelly.

"I have also learned the twenty-six different copulatory positions in which it is best stimulated." His finger ran along the slope of her jaw.

"How . . . alphabetical," she gasped out.

"And finally, Abigail, I have learned the most important technique of all. The one element guaranteed to enhance all others, to deliver the most profound ecstasy experienced by mortal man. Do you know what it is, my very dear love?"

His mouth stopped a hairsbreadth away from hers. She parted her lips and took in his breath, took in his scent and his crackling heat, until her every nerve throbbed with him.

"Bergamot?" she asked breathlessly.

He laid the tip of his finger against her open lips.

"Anticipation."

He stepped away, and she sagged forward, only just catching herself on the back of the chair. "Wallingford, wait!" she called, but he had already turned for the door.

At that instant, the knob rattled.

"Abigail! Abigail, darling!" Alexandra's voice floated through the wooden door. "I seem to have forgotten my key."

Wallingford went still.

"Abigail, are you there?" Another rattle. "Oh, there it is, dash it. My other pocket. How silly."

Wallingford dove under the bed.

The knob turned, and Alexandra burst into the room. "Oh, there you are! Why didn't you answer?"

"I was . . . I was . . . I was on the telephone, ringing for the hotel maid to help me undress."

"Never mind that. Abigail, I've the most tremendous news. I'm going to be married!" Alexandra threw her arms around Abigail's waist and twirled her in a circle. "Isn't it marvelous?"

"Oh, marvelous! To Mr. Burke, I hope?"

"Yes, of course to Mr. Burke! Oh, I'm so happy, I'm positively delirious." She threw herself backward onto the bed and laughed. "Just think! Mrs. Phineas Burke! Doesn't it sound splendid?"

Abigail stared at Alexandra, whose shoes dangled inches from Wallingford's nose. "Splendid!" she choked.

Alexandra sat up. "You shall be my bridesmaid, of course. We'll have the wedding as soon as possible, days if we can manage it, a small affair of course. What, are you getting ready for bed?"

"No! I mean yes, of course." Abigail paused. "Are you?"

"I can't decide. I've half a mind to speak to the hotel manager at once, to see about the details. Whether we can obtain a private room for the ceremony on such short notice."

"Yes, do that! No time like the present," said Abigail.

"Though I'm dreadfully tired." Alexandra put her hand to her mouth. "It's been an enormously stimulating day. Perhaps we should simply ring for the maid after all."

"No, no. Really, I'm in such transports! I don't think I could sleep. Let's go downstairs and share a bottle of champagne, shall we?"

Alexandra looked shocked. "Really, Abigail! In a public hotel! What the devil are you thinking? We'll have one sent up, that's all. We can strip down to our chemises and dance about the room, just like when we were little."

"I think," said Abigail, a little faintly, "I may be a trifle more fatigued than I thought."

"I'm not surprised. I daresay it's been a long day for you as well. Did Wallingford see you back, as I asked him to?"

"Yes, he did. Just in the nick of time, too. I was about to be abducted by Mr. Hartley."

"Such a gentleman, that Wallingford!"

"Yes, he was. A thorough gentleman. Though the entire episode was really devastating for my nerves. I don't suppose you could see if they have any sort of . . . of elixir downstairs, could you?"

"Your nerves!" Alexandra laughed. "And when did you acquire these *nerves*, Abigail?"

She put a hand to her heart. "I'm quite serious, Alexandra!"

Alexandra was still laughing. "Why don't you use the telephone and ask yourself?"

"It . . ." Abigail glanced at the telephone. "It isn't working."

"Nonsense. Weren't you just using it to ring the hotel maid?" Alexandra rose and walked toward the wooden box on the desk.

"No, don't touch it! It's . . . it gave me an electric . . . a charge of some sort . . . there must be a faulty wire." Abigail cast a desperate glance at the bed.

Alexandra jumped back. "Good heavens!"

"Yes! It's quite dangerous! You should go straightaway and ask for someone to repair it, before we're burnt to a crisp in our beds." Abigail rested her forearm against her brow. "I'd go myself, but my teeth are still buzzing."

"Oh, my poor dear! Of course I shall run down at once. I shall simply *demand* another room. Would you like a damp cloth?"

"No! No, thank you. Just, if you please . . ." Abigail made a waggling motion with her fingers.

"Very well. I'll be straight back." Alexandra made for the door in a swish of white skirts.

"Don't forget your key!" called Abigail.

"In my pocket!" sang back Alexandra, drawing the door shut behind her. Just before the latch clicked, she poked her head back through. "Oh, and Abigail, my love?"

"Yes, dear?"

"Do tell Wallingford not to forget his hat and gloves when he leaves."

EIGHTEEN

Three days later

Wallingford found her at last in the hotel café, arguing with her bookmaker. She was still dressed for the wedding breakfast, which had not really been breakfast at all, having started at five o'clock in the evening. Her shoulders were almost bare, glowing under the lamps, and her hair was gathered up high on her head with an artful little feather. If he'd been the bookmaker, he'd have given her whatever she asked for.

"What the devil's going on here?" He arrived at her side and touched the small of her back.

Abigail turned to him. "I can't make this fellow give me back my twenty lire for the motor-race, which was clearly fixed. He claims that since Alexandra's motor didn't finish, the rest of it doesn't matter, the rascal."

"Oh, is that all?" Wallingford turned to the man, who sat insolently at his table with a tiny cup of strong black coffee before him. "Give the lady back her twenty lire, sir, or I shall be obliged to haul you outside and drag you before the nearest magistrate." He skewered his fingers into the top of the table, leaned forward, and spoke softly. "By the lobes of your ears."

"That was splendid," said Abigail, a few minutes later, tucking the banknotes into her bodice. "How do you manage it?"

"It's my birthright. Everything squared away upstairs?"

"Oh yes. I helped the maid move Alexandra's things into Burke's suite whilst everyone was eating cake, and we put flowers everywhere, and laid out a bottle of champagne. Do you think he carried her over the threshold?"

"Burke? I daresay he did. Hideous romantic, that one."

"Well, lovely! That's that, then."

"That's that."

Abigail looked down at the marble floor. They were standing in the hall, just outside the magnificent hotel ballroom, where a party of some sort was in full swing. Laughter spilled through the door, and raised gay voices, and an expert orchestra playing a waltz.

Wallingford held out his arms. "Dance?"

"Here? In the hall?"

"Wherever you like."

She smiled and took his hand, and he waltzed her gently along the grand corridor, surrounded by pale marble and vaulted ceiling and intricate moldings. Her body was light and strong beneath his fingertips. She moved intuitively with him, gave herself up wholly to his lead, smiling at him as they swayed and spun. A couple walked by, giggling, not noticing them at all.

"Married," she said. "I can't believe it. And yet they looked so very happy. I've never seen Alexandra so happy."

"Nor I Burke. The chap absolutely beamed as I walked her down. There's no accounting for taste, it seems."

She slapped his arm. "*I* think he's a very lucky man."

The orchestra wound up the waltz with a grand flourish. Wallingford pulled back and took both of Abigail's hands. They were warm and firm beneath her gloves; her delicate face was overspread by a fine pink blush. He didn't dare look farther down, where her breasts curved voluptuously from the low lace-edged neckline of her dress.

"Come with me," he said.

"Wallingford, I . . ."

He kissed her hands and led her down the corridor to the staircase. She said nothing, but he could feel the tremors of her body through her hand, which he kept in his. They climbed the silent staircase, floor after floor, meeting no one, until at last she began to flag under the weight of her dress and petticoats, and he lifted and carried her up the final curving flight.

"But Wallingford, my room . . . my things . . ."

"Hush." He maneuvered his key from his jacket pocket and opened the door.

"You're going to ravish me, aren't you?" She sighed dreamily.

"If I must." He kissed her neck and closed the door with his foot. "Anticipation cuts both ways, after all."

He eased her to the floor and turned her around, until her back rested against his chest, and the heave of her gasp sent waves throughout his body.

"What's this?"

"For you."

She turned her head slowly, taking in the vases bursting with flowers, the champagne in its bucket, the little table laid out with fruit and sweets. The low glow of lights beckoned from the doorway into the bedroom.

"Much more comfortable than a boathouse, don't you think?" he whispered into her hair.

"Oh, Wallingford." She turned and clasped his face. Her eyes were wet. "I had no idea. When did you do this?"

"When everyone was eating cake. When you were busy upstairs in Burke's room."

"Oh." Her hands slipped down and went around his waist. She tucked her face into his chest. "What am I to do with you?"

"Whatever you like, Abigail. I'm at your mercy." He kissed her hair. "There's only one rule."

"What's that?"

He cupped the back of her head and turned her face upward. The pale skin below her eyes shone with dampness. "No one leaves this room until morning. No more running from me, Abigail. You can rail away, tell me I'm a brute, insist on whatever conditions you like, but you're not to *leave* me."

She laughed through her tears. "I won't. I promise."

Her lips were so round and pink, parting just slightly to reveal the white tips of her teeth. Wallingford bent his head and kissed her, as softly as he could, relaxing his mouth and his eager impulses in order to take in every sensation of her, to relish every movement and every detail of her. She tasted of champagne from the wedding breakfast, sweet and golden, effervescent in his arms, and he simply opened himself and drank her up, this endless, life-giving glass of Abigail.

It was the champagne, Abigail thought. She should never have swilled back that final toast. On the other hand, what could one do, when the minister kept calling for more bottles?

Or perhaps it was simply Wallingford himself, who kissed her with irresistible patience, as if he were savoring every drop of her; a marvelously sensual Wallingford, all warm slow skin and stroking tongue. He stood so tall and so close, she had to bend her neck to meet him, but his two hands were right there to support her: one caressing her back, and the other encompassing the curve of her head. He held her firmly, and under his kind lips and his strong arms, her body loosened and accepted him, leaned back and allowed him to take her weight.

What a delicious sensation, to be held so securely, without fear of falling.

She couldn't refuse him. She didn't want to. She had been tamping down her desire for him for days, as they toured about Rome with Alexandra and Finn; for weeks, really, as she'd moped about the Castel sant'Agata, missing him in every fiber. Did it matter if she experienced the earth-shattering rapture of her dreams? Somehow, it didn't seem important any longer; she only wanted *him*, his skin against hers, his weight and substance, connection with Wallingford, union with Wallingford, and afterward, his voice in her ear and his kisses on her breast.

That was what mattered now.

She slid her hands up the sleek black wool of Wallingford's chest and thanked God for him.

His lips pulled away. "*Yes*, Abigail?"

"Yes."

He bent, picked her up, and carried her into the bedroom with that effortless movement of his, as if he'd been slinging women about since the dawn of time. The champagne bubbled up in her veins and she laughed.

"What is it?"

"You. Your flowers and your kisses. Carrying me about. You're a romantic, aren't you?"

He set her down and began to work the fastenings of her dress. "Bite your tongue."

She laughed again and closed her eyes, because the brush of his fingers down her back lightened her blood and made her unsteady. The dress sagged downward, aided by Wallingford's hands, and she stepped out of it and kicked it aside.

His hands came up around her middle, over her stays. "Do you know how beautiful you are?" he murmured in her ear. "How your skin glows in the light, like gold?" He brushed the lace of her chemise, just above the firm clasp of her corset, raising tiny goose bumps across her chest.

She leaned her head against his chest. His gaze traveled across the curve of her bosom; she felt its weight, its admiring thoroughness. His fingers went once again to her back, drawing down her petticoats, unlacing her stays, removing each layer that separated him from her bare skin, until she stood before him in her chemise and drawers.

"You're shivering," he said.

"I can't seem to stop."

He wrapped his arms around her and brought her against his big body. His hand moved in her hair, taking out the pins one by one, pulling the feather away, until it tumbled down her back. "Shy, Abigail? You?"

"Astonishing, isn't it?"

"Why are you afraid of me now? You never were before."

She didn't answer. She couldn't; she had no answer for him. All she knew was that she wanted him, his hands on her skin, and yet at the same time she wanted to stay safe inside her chemise, where he couldn't see her fully, couldn't see every mark and shadow of her body.

"If you knew," he said. "If you knew how beautiful you are to me."

She made a noise against his chest. "You've seen far more beautiful women than this."

"My love, I have not." His hands slid down to gather up her chemise. "May I, Abigail?"

She didn't resist as he brought the thin linen up her waist and over her chest. She tilted back and raised her arms, and in a whoosh of whiteness it was gone, and she was bare to the waist before Wallingford.

"My God."

"The Harewood Chest," she said ruefully. "Not so impressive as my sister's inheritance, but . . . well, she is the older sister, after all."

"My God," he said again.

"Rather a nuisance to bind up, you perceive, when one needs to pass as a young man. As one does, from time to time."

"As one does," he agreed. A little smile brushed the corner of his mouth, though his eyes didn't so much as flicker up to her face. Instead he rubbed his thumb against the tip of her right breast, very lightly, sending a long shiver into every corner of her body. He bent and kissed the hollow of her throat, and then he lowered his enormous frame, kissing his way in a line down her center, until he knelt before her with his face buried in her belly and his palms cupping the curve of her bottom. She rested her hands on his smooth black shoulders.

The room stood still around them, lit dimly by the electric lamp: the soft white walls, the forest green curtains, the large, comfortable armchair angled companionably next to the lamp table. The bed stretched from the center of one wall, covered in matching forest green velvet with a neat heap of pillows at the head. Wallingford's warm breath spread from her belly. His shoulders rose and fell beneath her hands.

Remember this moment, she thought.

Wallingford's fingers stirred at her back, slipping inside the waistband of her drawers and around to her front. He found the ribbons and untied them and, still kneeling, allowed the last of her barriers to slide down her legs to the ground.

He kissed her curls and rose to his feet.

"And now?" she whispered. Her hands still lay atop his shoulders.

Wallingford shrugged off his formal black jacket and tossed it expertly to land on the back of the chair. "And now, I have the very great honor of applying all this academic theory into delightful practice."

She loved his starched white shirt, his crisp white tie, his gray silk waistcoat: so very formal and well-tailored, so perfect a contrast with his shining dark hair and wicked eyes. She touched his lips with one finger. "And how do you propose to begin?"

Without warning, he sucked her finger into his mouth and caressed it with his tongue. His eyes never left hers. "We begin," he said at last, giving her finger a final kiss good-bye, "as such lessons always begin: with a thorough examination."

"Oh no." She took a step back.

"Oh yes."

He swooped her up, arranged her on the chair, and settled on his knees between her legs. "Don't hide from me, Abigail," he said, and gently pulled her hands away. She tried to close her legs together, but his shoulders had wedged firmly between her knees.

"Now, then," he said. "Unclench your limbs, my dear. This may take some time."

"Oh, God." Abigail closed her eyes and let her head fall back against the back of the chair, cushioned by the sleek black wool of his dinner jacket. She felt the crispness of his shirt between her knees, the solid muscle of his arms beneath. His palm touched her gently, somewhere atop the mound of curling hair, and her breath sucked sharply inward.

"You're perfect," he whispered. "Look at you. Each beautiful piece of you, exactly in its place, pink and shining." With exquisite slowness, his finger drew downward until it brushed her inner flesh and ran along each lip, with such lightness it felt simply like a slender wand of heat passing over her.

"Wallingford, please. I can't stand it." She was melting, exposed, restless. Her legs moved urgently against him.

"Hush." His finger moved, inserting just the very tip inside her. "You're wet, love."

"For God's sake! Of course I am."

"I understand that indicates the presence of physical desire?"

"Of course it does!" She tugged at his hair.

He ignored her tugs and absorbed himself utterly in his examination of her. "These are your nymphae," he said in wonder, touching each one.

"Is that what they're called?" she gasped.

"Yes. Except yours are much prettier than the illustration."

"You're disgraceful. Let me up, do."

He didn't answer. She felt his warm breath, and then the firm pressure of his lips, and she jumped.

"Hush, love." The words brushed intimately inside her. His hands moved atop her thighs, holding her down.

"Oh, don't. Oh, don't." Her mind seemed to be levitating above her body.

"Your scent, Abigail. I can't describe it; I want to drown myself in it. You're divine." His tongue flicked across her, hot and wet, and she let out a little scream. "Does that hurt?"

"Yes! No!"

"Shall I do it again?"

"No! I . . . Oh yes. Yes!" Her hands worked in his hair.

His head bent down, and his tongue flicked again, over and across, up and down, exploring each fold and crevice, everywhere except where she most wanted it. The delicate movements eased into strokes, longer and lusher, and she writhed and panted, pinned like a butterfly under his searching mouth, every nerve in her body gathering and expanding between her legs.

I can't stand it, I can't stand it, no one could stand this, she thought, but her mouth could form no words, and her voice caught deep in her throat. She gripped his hair instead. She heard herself make a mewling noise, not even human.

"Look at you, so plump and rosy," he murmured. "Look right here. You've turned vermillion."

"Wallingford, please!"

"Please stop, or please go on?" He kissed her. "Now let me concentrate, darling. I'm searching for something, something terribly important. Though as I'm such a brute and a novice, I shall require your expert guidance. Is it here?" He flicked his tongue.

"No . . ."

"Here?" He flicked again.

"No . . . oh, God, oh, *God*, Wallingford . . ."

Another flick. "Here?"

"I shall *die*!" she gasped. "And you will have . . ."

". . . Here? . . ."

". . . the very *devil* of a time . . ."

". . . Not here, surely? . . ."

". . . explaining yourself to my sister . . ."

". . . Here, perhaps? . . ."

"Higher, damn you!"

"Ah." His voice grew warm and rich. "Thank you. Then it must be *here*."

And her breath left her body, and her body itself was engulfed, and there was nothing in the world but Wallingford's stroking tongue and the swirl of perfect sensation building in the tender vortex between her legs. On and on he went, his large hands holding her in place, keeping her trembling limbs from losing hold altogether, until the mad swirl reached its flood and rushed toward her and sent her flying, crying his name, clasping his head between her hands.

Wallingford held still, breathing against her throbbing flesh, murmuring words she couldn't hear through the roar of blood in her ears. His scent drifted up from the jacket behind her head, clean and masculine, a hint of smoke. Gradually, the roaring ebbed away, and Abigail sank gently back to earth, cradled by the chair and by Wallingford's caressing hands. She opened her eyes to the intricate plasterwork on the ceiling. The endless pattern fascinated her. She felt as if she were floating up toward it, and yet her limbs were heavy, limp, satiated. A curious paradox, she thought.

Wallingford stirred. She rolled her chin down, and saw him smiling at her, his lips gleaming and his navy eyes crinkled with masculine smugness.

"I expect you're pleased with yourself," she said.

"Immensely."

"Any half-wit could have found it."

"Still, I'm deeply grateful for your direction." He was still smiling.

She leaned forward and kissed him. "Thank you. That was marvelous. More than I ever imagined."

He laughed. "Darling, I haven't even begun."

"Haven't you?"

In answer, he rose and unbuttoned his gray silk waistcoat, unfastened his gold cuff links and placed them under the lamp. The deliberate movements dissolved her lassitude. She sat up and helped him with his shirt. His trousers, she saw, were sporting a dramatic bulge.

She looked up. "May I?"

He nodded.

She stood and pulled down his braces, one shoulder at a time, and then she tried to unfasten his trousers but her fingers had lost their dexterity and he, urgent, pushed her hands away and undid the buttons himself. Drawers, shirt: He removed each one, until he stood as naked as she, his staff jutting forward from his dark hair, his eyes fierce.

She took his hands and backed toward the bed, drawing him with her, until the velvet brushed against the backs of her legs. "Your turn," she said.

He drew back the covers and laid her on the bed, among the pillows, and kissed her long and passionately, a possessive kiss. She ran her hands over his smooth back, over the hard contours of his muscles, over the hairs springing from his chest. "You're beautiful," she said. "Did I tell you that, last time?"

"I don't remember." He kissed her neck, her collar.

"It's true. You're like a statue, sculpted from stone, only real and alive. You're beautiful. I could admire you forever."

He shook his head, as if he didn't believe her, and traced his lips to her breasts. He took her nipple into his mouth, and everything flared up again, her entire body bursting into heat. Her hips strained upward to find him. He suckled her tenderly, rolling the other nipple between his finger and thumb, and her back arched beneath him.

"Shh," he said. "Wait, my love."

"I don't want to wait."

His hardened organ pressed into her leg. She tried to wriggle her bottom, to bring herself closer to that tantalizing weight, but he laughed into the skin of her breasts and held her steady. "All in good time."

She made a frustrated noise. She craved him so much, all of him; she was aflame with it. His hand slipped downward, across the plane of her belly, down her mound to find unerringly the dear little button he'd lavished earlier, even more tender now, aching with intensity. "Oh," she groaned, and went limp.

Wallingford lifted his head. "Is that all it takes to render you compliant?"

"Yes," she said honestly.

He circled her, rubbed her delicately, and up it built again, her beautiful swirling of sensation, even more effortless this time, as if her body recognized his touch and knew exactly how to respond.

"Please," she said. "I'm ready. Please."

Wallingford lifted his head from her breast and looked in her face, and his eyes were glazed over with the same passion she felt.

He mounted her. His thick staff, his battering ram, pressed

between her legs. Abigail clenched herself for his thrust, but it didn't arrive; instead, he lowered himself atop her, resting on his elbows, until his face hovered only inches from hers. "Listen to me, darling." His voice was rough, as if he were fighting to hold it steady. "Tell me truly. Is there any possibility of a child?"

"No," she said at once.

He kissed her. "And this time. Shall I take care, or not?"

Her mind went blank at the enormity of his question, at the gift he offered her. "Isn't that a hardship for you?"

A little shrug. "One I'm accustomed to bearing, as necessary."

"Oh, Wallingford." She stroked his cheeks. A child, *his* child. Could she accept that risk? If she bore his child, he would insist on marrying her. She knew that beyond any question of doubt. Marriage to Wallingford? Her heart shrank in fear. And yet something else rose inside her, something primeval, something that craved his seed and his life, craved a total union, craved every possible bond between them. Craved *him*, all of him.

He kissed her again. "Take your time, darling. I'm only out of my mind with desire, knocking at the very gates. There's no hurry at all."

No, she thought.

"Yes," she heard herself say.

"You're certain?" He pressed against her entrance, lodged the tip inside her. He felt enormous, too impossibly large to take in. How had they done it before?

No. "Yes." *Oh, God.*

His back flexed, and she braced herself, but there was no pain, only a long and marvelous stretching as her flesh parted, as her body took him in, as the battering ram glided up inside her without opposition.

"Oh!" she said in surprise.

He rocked against her, working himself deeper, smiling at her. "I'm inside you, little elf," he said, lowering his lips to kiss her. "*Inside* you."

He was. He *was* inside her. He was part of her, and it was beautiful. She felt as if she were blossoming from the inside out, in lush petals of Wallingford. She curled her hands around his shoulders and kissed him back.

"Raise your knees," he said.

She raised her knees. "Oh, that's nice."

"How nice?"

"*Very* nice. Oh!"

He lifted himself a little higher. "Like this? Faster?"

"Yes! Oh!" She could hardly breathe. He filled her to bursting, hitting some exquisite nerve at every stroke. Pressure built inside her; impossibly intense pressure, like the swirling tide he had wrought for her just a short while ago, only more profound, more solid and dimensional. "Like that! Oh, God!"

He kept moving, thrusting over and over in an unstoppable rhythm, watching her face for every flicker of response, and she loved him for it, loved every powerful movement of his body into hers.

"Oh my God, my God . . . almost . . ." She dug her heels into his legs, dug her fingers into his back, forced him harder, and without warning a fierce packet of energy burst over her, radiating through every pore of her body in hard and eager waves.

At her cry of joy, Wallingford's body went rigid above her. She heard him groan her name from deep in his chest, and she clutched him to her, absorbing the shudder of his body, until she could actually feel the rising pulse of his own flesh meeting the ebbing pulse of hers.

He sank slowly down, damp with sweat, and this time she welcomed his weight, welcomed the mindless crush of his bones and sinews. His breath rushed hard and fast against her ear: Wallingford's breath, the precious air from his lungs. She buried her fingers in his hair. "Arthur," she whispered. Her brain was hazy, floating like a cloud. She kissed his wet temple.

"What's that?" he whispered, not moving.

"*Arthur.*" She kissed him again. "I like it."

A rthur.

He had never particularly liked his given name, but he loved the sound of it from Abigail's lips, intimate and loving. Her body felt delicious beneath him, full and delicate all at once, but he remembered the last time and shifted himself.

"No." She clenched her legs around him. "Stay."

So he remained atop her, inside her, taking weight on his

forearms to spare her. He drew the lemony scent of her hair into his nose and stroked a nearby curl with his fingertips.

She whispered, "You're still . . ."

"Yes."

"Is that . . ."

He chuckled and lifted himself up. "Because I love you, and because I'm a devil in full rut who's kept himself chaste for a longer stretch of time than he ever imagined possible."

"Except the boathouse."

"That, my dear"—he kissed her—"was hardly enough to take the edge off."

Abigail said nothing. He kissed her again, her lips and her soft cheeks, the tender nook behind her ear. "Was that satisfactory? Have I redeemed myself?"

"You know you have."

Wallingford tried to quell himself, but it was no use: Her full breasts brushed against his chest, and her skin smelled so exquisitely like Abigail, and her wet sheath surrounded him like heaven itself. His erection swelled hungrily inside her.

Brute, he told himself.

He slid himself out and fell into the sheets at her side.

She turned with an air of surprise. "Why did you stop?"

He kissed her nose. "Because I daresay you've been ravished enough for one night, haven't you?"

Abigail searched his face with her wide and knowing eyes, as if his thoughts were imprinted across his head and she could read them. Her hair tumbled about her flushed skin, curling around the generous curve of her breast. One nipple poked through the chestnut silk, hard and rosy brown. Abigail's hair, Abigail's breast. He thought he might crack apart.

"Do you know, I don't believe I have." She reached down to encompass his prick in her hand, to caress the tightened sac beneath. "You see, we both have so much to learn."

He rolled onto his back, taking her with him.

Her eyes widened. "Like *this*?"

"Like this."

Abigail rose above him and took his rigid cock inside her with a groaning sigh, took him so deep his balls nestled against her arse, so deep he knocked against her womb at every thrust.

He inhaled her womanly musk, the voluptuous scent of her, the commingling of his essence with hers, and his blood fizzed in his veins.

She rode him with eager joy, with her breasts hovering before his eyes and his hands balanced on her hips, with her head thrown back in delirious pleasure. She reached her climax first in a throaty cry, and he followed directly after, spending into her with the explosive strength of a first release.

This time she collapsed atop him, and the brand-new sensation of her weight, the idyllic curves and softness of her, her sweet champagne-scented breath drifting across his face filled his hungry soul to overflowing, made him pray to God in grateful thanks.

NINETEEN

Abigail felt his arm first, lying across her belly and curling around her waist. A brilliant shaft of sunlight pressed against her eyelids, but she didn't open them. She didn't want to move a single hair.

In the first place, she couldn't. Every muscle ached, even the ones she hadn't known she possessed. She had lost count of the number of times she and Wallingford had come together in the night: four or five perhaps, tender and compulsive, both of them unable to fathom the freedom of it; and in the spaces between he had brought her to climax repeatedly with his mouth and his hands, in every possible attitude, as if he wanted to learn just how much pleasure she could bear.

A great deal, it had turned out.

The light against her eyes became too much, and she opened them and turned her head to the man in bed next to her. He lay sprawled on his stomach like a little boy, his hair dark and tousled against the white sheets, his lips parted. How relaxed he looked, how happy. The sunlight gilded the curves and planes of his muscled back with watered gold.

Her lover, the Duke of Wallingford.

She had no illusions. Yes, he loved her, or thought he did; she meant more to him than any woman had before. Yes, she had his heart, at least. But eventually he would stray; eventually some other woman would snare his passion, even for a moment, even if he still loved her devotedly. He might resist at first, but one day his strength would fail him. It was inevitable. The habit of promiscuous mating was stamped in his bones and blood. She had known this from the beginning, had told herself repeatedly that her interest in Wallingford was largely carnal, tinged with affection. An infatuation, at the very most. She had deliberately protected herself from any deeper emotion.

But there was no use pretending anymore. She loved him, his magnificence and his hidden tenderness and his human failings. She loved him with every filament of her body and heart. She would have him on any terms, even marriage, if he absolutely insisted. She would wring every joy and every pleasure she could from him, until he strayed. And it would hurt when he did, because she loved him so; but if that was the price, then she must pay it.

She had always wanted a grand passion, and now she had it. She ought to be thrilled. How often did one have the chance of a grand passion, in this modern age of steam engines and electric lamps?

Wallingford's eyes cracked open and blinked, sleepily. "Abigail."

"Good morning."

He lifted his head and rose up on his elbow. "Darling, what's wrong?"

"Nothing," she whispered.

"You're weeping."

"Only happy." She wiped at her eyes.

"Mmm." He gathered her up and kissed her. "Not nearly so happy as I am. I feel like a new man. A redeemed man."

"Yes, you've redeemed yourself thoroughly. All is forgiven."

He laughed. "I don't mean that, exactly, though I'm deeply relieved I didn't send you away screaming this time."

"I did a great deal of screaming. So did you." She nestled herself against his chest. The sunlight warmed the back of her head; Wallingford warmed her front. All she wanted was a little coffee, and the world would be perfect.

Simply perfect, she told herself.

Wallingford stroked her arm. "Abigail, I realize you despise the very mention of the word *marriage* . . ."

"Oh, don't."

"And I won't mention it again, for now. But I want to make my intentions clear, Abigail. I want you to be my wife. I consider us already bound in honor, after last night." He picked up her left hand and kissed it. "Just so you know."

"I know."

"I won't push you, Abigail. But that's how it is. And I won't give up, not ever. If I have to marry you on my deathbed, God help me, I will."

She said nothing.

"You don't believe me, do you?"

"You're talking such rot, Wallingford. Marriage and deathbeds, *really*. Must you take everything so seriously?"

Wallingford sighed. "Abigail, you have my faithful love, I swear it. I promised Morini . . ."

Morini.

She jumped up as if electrocuted, in an agonized flash of protesting muscles. "You *what*?"

"Back at the castle. I promised her that if she told me where to find you, I'd make you happy . . ."

Her body shook. "You *saw* her? You saw Morini?"

"No." He propped himself on his elbows. "She's a ghost, isn't she? But I felt her there. I stood there talking into the walls like a madman, because I couldn't think of anything else. Are you all right, darling? You're trembling." He took her shoulder and drew her back into the pillows. "My God! You're like a leaf in a breeze. Did you think I didn't know?"

"I thought you didn't believe in them. I thought . . ." She shook her head, trying to make sense of his words. "Did she speak to you? Did you hear her?"

"She sent me a note, through the maid."

"And that's all. You didn't see her, you didn't hear her."

"No. I can't, can I? Any more than you can see Giacomo. Are you all right?"

"Yes, I'm fine." She forced her fists to unclench. "Of course you can't see her. There's no reason you should. Nothing's changed, after all. Do you still have this note? May I see it?"

"If you like." He kissed the top of her head, swung out of bed, and groaned. "Good God. You've done me in."

"Whilst you're up," she said, in a small voice, "would you mind having coffee sent in?"

"Of course."

He strode naked out of the room with his pantherlike grace. Abigail lay back in the pillows and pulled the sheet over her body. The faint trace of bergamot drifted into her senses; she wrapped her arm around Wallingford's pillow and buried her nose in the warm, clean linen. From the other room came the sound of the telephone crank, of Wallingford's rich voice issuing orders.

He had admitted his love for Abigail. He had told Morini of it, and the curse hadn't lifted. He still couldn't see her, couldn't hear her.

What did that mean? That he didn't really love her? Or that his love wasn't of the faithful, eternal sort necessary to appease the wrath of Signore Monteverdi?

Unless there was no curse at all. Unless they were simply the playthings of Morini and Giacomo, of idle ghosts with nothing else to do except to meddle in the lives of gullible English houseguests.

"Here we are." Wallingford appeared in the doorway, lit by the golden streak of morning sunshine through the crack in the curtains. He set his knee on the bed and handed her a sheet of folded paper. "The coffee will be up directly."

"Thank you." She sat up against the pillows. Wallingford reclined next to her and kissed the ends of her hair, kissed her neck, toyed with her breasts. *Her lover,* she thought in wonder. Her body warmed beneath his touch. She unfolded the paper and tried to bring the crooked words into focus.

Signore Duca

> *You ask where is to find the signorina. She travel to Rome with her sister, for to see the ottomobil of Signore Burke. You must find her and tell her . . .*

Wallingford bent his head to suckle her breasts, and her breath whooshed from her chest. The ink blurred before her. "Stop that," she said. "I'm trying to read."

"Can't stop."

She lifted the paper high above his dark silk head.

> *. . . tell her of your love, and you must promise always to be her faithful love. You must then give her a message from Signorina Morini. You must . . .*

"Oh! Do stop. I can't . . . oh!"

Wallingford's finger slipped between her legs. "Don't mind me. Only refreshing my memory. How wet you are, love. Do you always wake up like this?"

"Wallingford . . ." She groaned. Her head fell back. "This is important."

"Vital." His tongue trailed across to her other breast, while his fingers kept moving in the same clever little circles that had sent her out of her mind last night. "Carry on reading, darling. Have you got to the part about my faithful love yet?"

Her hand crumpled the side of the paper. She forced her eyes to open again.

> *. . . You must tell her that the Signorina Monteverdi live now in the Convento di San Giusto in the city of Siena. She has the instruction for the Signorina Abigail, before the . . .*

"*What?*" Abigail shot up.

"What the devil are you doing? Lie down." Wallingford nudged her.

"No! We must leave at once! Oh! Where are my clothes?" She tried to scramble away from him, but his hands grasped her shoulders.

"We're not going anywhere. Good God. What's the hurry?"

"It's *important*, Wallingford!" She tugged at his hands.

"I'm making love to you, for God's sake. What could be more important than that?" His voice was imperiously Wallingford, who did not take kindly to being thwarted, even in bed.

"*This!*" She shook the paper at him. "We must go to Siena at once!"

"*Siena?* Why the devil Siena?" He snatched the paper.

"Because *Signorina Monteverdi* is there! She's really *there*! At the convent!"

"Who the devil's she?"

"Didn't you even *read* this?"

He looked at the writing. "Of course I did. I was to find you in Rome, and . . . oh, that's right. Monteverdi . . . Siena . . ."

Abigail gave his shoulder a push. "Why didn't you tell me earlier that Morini had a message for me?"

"Because it rather slipped my mind, with everything else going on, races and weddings and seducing you. Besides, as the note quite clearly states, I was first to declare my undying love to one Signorina Abigail." He brandished the paper triumphantly.

"But you said all that last *night*! We could be halfway to Siena by now!" she said desperately.

Wallingford dropped his hand and stared at her. "Are you mad?"

"I am quite, quite sane." She swung her legs over the edge of the bed. "I must go to my room and pack, and while I'm there you must call for your cab to take us directly to the station . . ."

His hand snared her arm. "Calm down, Abigail."

"I *am* calm!"

"You're completely overwrought."

"This is important, Wallingford."

He kissed her shoulder. "*This* is important. And this." He kissed her neck.

"You don't understand," she said, but she allowed him to draw her backward into the sheets.

"It can wait a half hour, Abigail. The coffee's on its way. You can't go anywhere without breakfast, can you? You need your strength." He was above her now, kissing her ravenously.

"My things . . ."

"I'll have the maid pack your things. The chap downstairs will arrange the cab and the train."

"You don't understand." Oh, his languorous lips, his caressing fingers. She couldn't think, could hardly remember what was so important. How did he do that to her?

Something about the note. What had she read, at the end? *Before the* . . . Before the what?

"Be easy, sweetheart. We've all the time in the world. Let me into you, let me make love to you again." He nudged at her, stiff and gentle all at once, making her swollen parts sting and her thoughts swim into delirium. "I promise I'll make it worth your while."

She opened her legs and put her arms around his neck. "Five minutes. No more."

Thirty minutes later

A bigail."
    She moved her head.

"Abigail, sweetheart. Your coffee."

"Hmm?" She lifted her head. A curtain of hair fell away from her eyes, revealing Wallingford, who stood by the bed in a dressing robe, holding a steaming cup and grinning ear-to-ear with an unmistakable expression of male satisfaction.

"Oh." She scrambled up and took the cup. Something nudged at the back of her mind, some important reminder, lost in a frenzy of tangled limbs and Wallingford's driving body and . . . and the headboard . . .

Oh, God. The headboard.

"I've checked with the fellow at the desk," Wallingford was saying calmly, quite as if he hadn't just made her scream with ecstasy up against the headboard of a substantial Italian bed, with the morning sunlight streaming through the window and her hands pinned against the wall. "There's a train leaving in an hour. Someone's packing up your room right now. You can wash and . . ."

Train. Siena. The note.

"Oh!" She scrabbled around the sheets. "The note! Where is it?"

"Right here. What's the matter? You're as jumpy as a hare."

She snatched the note from his fingers.

. . . ottomobil . . . faithful love . . . Monteverdi . . .

There it was.

She has the instruction for the Signorina Abigail, before the first full moon after the Midsummer.

Morini.

"Good God!" Of course! What had Morini said, that day in the kitchen? Something about a midsummer moon. The end of midsummer. Abigail's mind stumbled over itself, racing with calculations. How many days since Midsummer's Eve? How full had the moon been that night?

"What's the matter?"

"The *moon*! When's the next full moon?"

He blinked. "The moon?"

"Moon! Glowing orb in the night sky!" She shook the paper.

"Oh, do you mean that odd bit in the note, at the end? I don't know. Another day or two, I suppose." He shrugged and picked up the newspaper on the coffee tray.

Abigail's shoulders sagged with relief. "Thank heaven. Then we still have time." She eased her aching limbs out of bed and looked down. "Good God! The sheets!"

Wallingford glanced over from the newspaper and laughed. "That should give the laundry maids something to gossip about."

"You're so terribly amusing. You forget I'm an unmarried woman."

"Well, whose fault is that?" He brushed her cheek and nodded at a door across the room. "There's a bathroom en suite, if you'd like to wash. Your clothes will be here any moment."

"Thank you." She felt suddenly shy, standing there naked, conversing with Wallingford about baths and laundry.

He must have seen her consternation. He leaned over and kissed her head. "Shall I join you?"

"No, thank you. I can manage."

His thumb brushed her cheek again. "You're safe from insult, you know. If anyone says a word against you . . ."

She tilted her chin. "It's my choice, Wallingford. I am quite prepared for the consequences."

"There's my girl."

She kissed him and went to the bathroom. She scrubbed herself thoroughly in the enormous white enamel tub, until the steam rose from her very pores to cover the mirrors, and then she skipped back out into the bedroom, wrapped in a thick Turkish towel.

"Oh, it was divine!" she exclaimed.

"Was it? You *look* divine, all pink and clean. My turn, then." He kissed her, tossed the newspaper on the bed, and strode for the bathroom door, from which a thin vapor of steam still escaped. Just before his hand reached the knob, he turned his head over his shoulder. "Oh, and I was mistaken about the moon."

She choked on her coffee. "What's that?"

"I checked in the paper. The full moon's tonight."

TWENTY

The dun stone walls of the Convento di San Giusto glowed gold in the late afternoon sun, crowned with familiar crumbling red tile. It looked no different from its neighbors, all of them clustered cheek by dusty jowl in a narrow street near the cathedral.

"You're certain this is the place?" Wallingford asked the driver.

"*Che cosa?*" asked the man, addressing Abigail. She translated quickly, and he nodded with vigor. "*Si, si. Il convento, signorina.*"

"He says this is it." She looked at Wallingford. His face was damp and slightly flushed beneath his straw hat; the July sun beat down without mercy on the black roof of the cab they'd hired from the train station. Both windows were open, but the breeze drifted through them like the draft from an oven. "You'll wait outside for me, won't you?"

"The devil I will. I'm going in with you."

She made a little snort of laughter. "Wallingford, my dear, it's a convent. They're not going to *let* you inside. Foxes and henhouses and all that."

"We'll see about that." He prepared to rise. "I'm not going to allow you behind some locked cloister gate to cavort with bloody *ghosts*, Abigail. Not without some sort of protection."

"Have you ever met a nun, Wallingford?"

He paused. "Not a real one."

"Then you've no idea. Your vicious despot is nothing compared to an abbess defending her flock. You might be the Emperor of Wallingford, and it would make no difference at all. They won't let you in. Besides," she added, rising from her seat, "there's eternal damnation to consider."

He grumbled something about eternal damnation and his arse, and jumped up to help her out of the cab. "I'll be waiting right here," he said.

"I won't be long. I only need to speak with her."

"I don't see why. I don't see how some woman of three hundred years ago has anything to do with you, or us, or my damned ancestor. It all sounds like an elaborate hoax." He folded his arms and stared down at her, willing her to challenge him.

Should she have told him the story, after all? But what choice did she have? On the train to Siena, before she had fallen into a dramatic and exhausted sleep on Wallingford's shoulder, he had demanded to know what errand could possibly be important enough to roust them both out of a perfectly satisfactory bed of sin. There was no resisting him. She had sketched out the history of the castle and the curse of the long-ago Monteverdi family. At the mention of the English lord, he had turned pale. *Next you're going to tell me his name was Copperbridge*, he'd blurted out, and Abigail had searched her memory and said *Copperbridge! That's it exactly!*

He had told her, with reluctance, about his grandfather owning the castle, and the revelation had flashed in her brain like an illuminating light.

Is destiny, Morini had said.

The cathedral bell tolled the quarter hour with a slow and dignified clang. Abigail looked up at Wallingford's grim face. "Think about Giacomo and Morini. Think about your grandfather owning the castle."

"Some natural explanation, I'm sure. Some trick of Olympia's, the old scoundrel, God knows why. To marry me off somehow."

She put her hand on his arm. "Don't try to talk me out of this. Just let me see if she's there, if it's really her. What's the harm?"

"All sorts of possibilities come to mind," he said darkly.

"They're not going to recruit me, if that's what has you worried." Abigail went up on her toes and kissed his cheek. "I'll be careful, I promise."

"Oh, right-ho. My worries have flown."

"I promise to be back in an hour. Will that suffice?"

"At least let me see you to the gates." He took her arm in a proprietary gesture.

They walked to the thick wooden door, which interrupted the flow of stone like the portal of a medieval fortress, topped by a grille of old iron. Wallingford lifted the knocker and let it fall with a crash.

"Salubrious sort of place, isn't it?" he observed, peering through the grille.

There was no sound from within. Wallingford crashed the knocker again, three good knocks this time. "Hello!" he called through the door. "*Buon giorno!*"

"Anything?" Abigail asked, rising on her toes to look through the grille. She could not quite get enough height.

"Nothing. That's that, then. Shall we head off to the piazza and find ices? Dashed warm day." He turned away and took her arm.

"Don't be silly. All this way and all this trouble for nothing?" She nudged him aside and slammed the knocker against its plate, sending the echo of outraged metal down the street and into the courtyards beyond. "*Buon giorno!*" she called, with equal strength.

"*Si, si!*" came a voice from beyond the grille.

"Someone's coming!" Abigail hissed at Wallingford.

He glowered at the door. "Evidently."

"I'm coming, I'm coming," said a peevish voice, making the iron bars of the grille bend with its shrillness.

"You speak English!" Abigail said in astonishment.

"*Si, si,* I speak the English." A pair of bright black eyes appeared with unnerving abruptness in the center of the grille. "We have no visitor."

"Oh, we're not visitors," said Abigail.

"We're not?" said Wallingford.

She stuck her elbow firmly in his ribs. "We're pilgrims, of a sort. We have come to . . . to pay our respects to the . . . the holy Signorina Monteverdi."

"Suor Leonora!"

Hope burst to life in Abigail's breast. She was here! "Yes! Suor Leonora. We have . . ."—her mind raced—". . . we have heard of her . . . her holy goodness. We wish to . . . to pray with her." Abigail cast down her eyes with what she hoped was a look of piety.

"Quite," said Wallingford. His six feet two inches of muscled limbs and black hair looked anything but pious.

"This, you cannot. Suor Leonora, she is in seclusion. Good day." The eyes disappeared.

"Wait! We have traveled very far!" called Abigail.

"The Lord God will remember you for it."

"We have a message for her!"

"You write her a letter." The voice grew fainter.

"It's urgent! It's . . . it's from Lord Copperbridge!" Abigail said desperately.

No answer.

Abigail rose up and strained against the grille. A faint sound of tinkling water seemed to drift in the air.

Wallingford put his hand to her back and spoke softly. "I suppose that's it, then."

The door jerked open without warning.

"Oh!" Abigail staggered forward.

A woman stood before her in a loose black habit, her face creased and sharp. The air whooshed through the doorway around her with welcome coolness. "You come inside."

"Oh, thank you, *sorella!*" Abigail said. Wallingford's arm closed protectively around hers.

The woman pointed a bony finger in the center of the duke's broad chest. "You stay."

"This lady is my wife. I will not leave her side." Wallingford's voice rang with the full force of ducal authority.

The woman's finger did not budge. "She is not your wife. You stay."

Wallingford looked down at the finger, and then at Abigail's face. She shrugged. "I *did* warn you. Now you'll have to do penance, of course."

"For what?"

"For lying to a nun."

She swept past him and followed the woman into the courtyard.

The corridor was so dark, Abigail could scarcely see the nun as she followed her down the flagstones. Only the thin white line of her wimple bounced in the blackness.

Had the full moon risen yet? Surely not. Didn't full moons rise around sunset? Several hours away, at least. And perhaps it wasn't even moonrise at all. Perhaps they had until the full moon set to . . .

To do what?

The floor was hard and cold beneath the thin soles of Abigail's shoes. The nun turned a corner before her, disappearing for an instant, and Abigail rushed to follow. A faint glow appeared at the end of the new hallway: an open door, perhaps? A rush of warmth brushed her cheek, like the air outside.

Abigail's heart beat furiously in her chest, making her blood feel light and unsteady in her veins. Be sensible, she thought. Be patient. There was no danger, no crisis. Whatever this instruction from Signorina Monteverdi—if indeed this *was* that unfortunate lady, by some occult miracle—they would not be struck down by some avenging bolt of lightning, surely, if Abigail failed to carry it out. If Leonora chose to ask the impossible. If they were already too late for whatever she asked.

The curse, if it really existed, was three hundred years old. Why should she, of all people, be chosen to break it? The idea was ludicrous. Only curiosity drove her now.

But why, then, did this feeling of unease shadow her pounding heart?

Already the air was filling with light. It came from a door near the end of the corridor, left ajar, sunshine pouring from the wedge of open space. The nun came to a stop and beckoned her.

"Suor Leonora, she is in the garden." She laid her finger on her lips. "Now is the time of her prayer, as the sun falls down in the sky."

"How dramatic," Abigail murmured. She peered through the doorway. A tiny square garden sat quietly in the sunlight, paved with old gray flagstones and rimmed in green. A lemon tree nestled into one corner; in the other, a golden cross fixed against the wall, above a small black-clad figure knelt in prayer. A gentle scent of lemon and eucalyptus drifted through the air.

Abigail waited for the nun to announce her, but nothing came. She craned her head and saw a black skirt whisking around the far corner, out of sight.

"Well! There's hospitality," she said, sotto voce, and at her words the kneeling figure stirred.

Abigail's breath suspended in her chest. The figure rose slowly to her feet: not with the stiffness of age, but with a fluid deliberation. The folds of her wimple spread across her shoulders.

"Hello, there," Abigail said, and then, hastily, "*Buon giorno.*"

"*Buon giorno.*" The woman did not turn.

Abigail cleared her throat. "My name is Abigail Harewood."

"Abigail Harewood." The nun tested the words. Her voice was clear, young, familiar with the English syllables. "I have been expecting you today."

"Have you?"

"Is three hundred years. Is the first full moon after the Midsummer. You are the English lady, are you not?"

The air seemed to fall around Abigail's face, in small soft pieces of light. "I am. You are Signorina Monteverdi?"

The woman turned, and Abigail gasped. She was extraordinarily beautiful, almost unearthly, with rich dark eyes and a face of impossibly delicate symmetry. She held out her arm, indicating a small stone bench. "I am. Sit, please."

Abigail sat. What else could she do? Signorina Monteverdi settled next to her, like a lark into its nest. "So you are the one," she said.

"The one?"

"The one who is sent to break this curse, my father's curse." Her voice remained steady and clear, conveying no particular emotion, no excitement.

"I . . . I don't know. I have heard something of the curse. I don't know if I can break it. I'm only . . ." Abigail took a deep breath. She could not quite believe that she was sitting here on a stone bench in a Sienese convent, speaking with this woman, with Leonora Monteverdi. The very air around her seemed to bend and warp with the unreality of it. "I'm only an ordinary woman."

"But you are in love with the heir of Copperbridge?"

"I am," Abigail said softly.

"And he loves you?"

"I . . . I think he does. As much as he's capable of it." Abigail wet her lips. "Is that all that's required?"

The woman sighed deeply. She did not look at Abigail, but rather at the lemon tree, burgeoning with round yellow fruit.

"Signorina Monteverdi?"

"You call me Leonora."

"Leonora, tell me what happened to you. I must know everything, if I'm to help you at all. All I understand is that you meant to elope with Copperbridge, that the pistol went off, that your father was killed. That he cursed you all."

"It is so."

"But then what? Did you flee here? What about Copperbridge?"

Leonora smoothed the heavy black cloth in her lap. She spoke so quietly, Abigail had to strain to hear her. "Yes, we flee. We take the horse, we ride all the night, here to Siena. My love, my Arthur . . ."

"Arthur!"

"*Si.* He have a friend at the cathedral here, who give us the peace, the protect . . ." She rubbed her fingers together impatiently.

"Sanctuary?"

"*Si.* The next day, my grandfather arrive, the Medici, the father of my poor mother, the friend of my father. He has his men, he surround the *convento.* He demand to see us, to have the revenge, but we are safe inside."

"Hostages, though, in effect."

She shrugged.

"Was there anything you could do?"

Leonora seemed lost in reminiscence. A bird sang out quietly from the lemon tree, in long, lonely notes. She stirred at last. "I beg my Arthur to leave, to go back to England. But he insist to stay, because of the baby."

"The baby! Of course! You were with child."

Leonora looked back at the lemon tree. "I was with child,

and Arthur, he would not leave us, he vow to stay and protect. The months go by, and my grandfather take a house here with his men, and he wait and wait."

"Like a spider," Abigail whispered.

"He wait and wait, and at last my time is come. I feel the pain, and I come to the garden and the cross, and I pray."

Abigail made a startled movement. "*This* garden? *This* cross?"

"*Si.* I pray for my Arthur, for my child. I say to the Lord, if you see them safe to England, if you watch over their days, I will take the curse upon me, I will do the penance. I will wait and pray, until our sins are redeem."

"Good God."

"The pain is great, and I go to my bed, and I labor in the night. The pain comes hard, and the nuns, they help me, but I bleed, I am desperate, I am near the death. I open my eyes, and I see the angel by the bed."

Abigail could not say anything. She reached out and picked up Leonora's hand, where it lay atop her black nun's habit.

"The angel," she whispered, "the angel, he tell me he will see my Arthur and my baby home to England, he will watch over their days, there to live a long and happy life. And I am to stay here at the convent, to pray and to wait for three hundred years, until the heir of Copperbridge return to pledge his faithful love before God. That is my penance."

"Oh, Leonora." Abigail's eyes swam.

"The next morning, we are blessed with a boy, a son, strong and beautiful. I take him to my breast, I kiss his little head, so warm. Then I wrap him in the cloth, and I give him to the sister. I turn my head to the pillow so I do not see his hair, his small dark eyes that blink to me as he goes."

She bowed her head. Abigail could not speak.

"Then I write a note to my Arthur, my Arthur who wait outside the room for me all the night, while I labor," Leonora said at last. "I tell him he must go to England, to take our son with him, there to raise him. Arthur, he will not accept this, he pound on the door, he beg and he weep. I hear my baby cry in his arms, such a hungry little voice. But the sisters, they will not allow him in. So at last, he leave."

"And you are left alone, for three hundred years."

"No, signorina," said Leonora. She laid her other hand atop Abigail's. "I am not alone. There is my brother."

Abigail gasped. "Your brother? He found you after all?"

"*Si*. He is my kind, my loving brother. He argue with our grandfather, he try to make him see the reason, but is no use. So he take instead the vow for the monastery. He help Arthur to leave with the baby, in the night, and he come to me. My brother, he will share my penance, he say. He will take on the curse with me, the two of us of one blood, until we are redeem together."

"My God. And . . . and Morini, and Giacomo . . ."

She nodded her head. "They keep the castle."

"Morini was your maid, wasn't she? The one who helped you meet Arthur."

"*Si*," Leonora said quietly. "She is my faithful one."

"And Giacomo?"

"Him, the manservant of my brother. They helped to pass the secret notes, you see. My father, he curse us all."

"Well! That explains why Giacomo's such a bitter old chap. And they have kept the castle, all these years? For three hundred years, they've watched over the travelers?"

Leonora nodded again. "Since my son first come to the castle, when he is a man. He go, his father send a bride, but is not enough, the curse is not broken. The love is not faithful, they are not happy in each other. When my son has a son, he send him, and still the curse, it does not break."

"Good God," whispered Abigail. A feeling of mortal dread began to insinuate in her chest. "Generation after generation, and none of them, not *one*, can break the curse? These lovers, they are all faithless?"

Silence settled between them, thick and warm and scented with lemons from the burgeoning tree. Abigail thought of Wallingford, waiting outside in the heat for her, so full of tantalizing promise, if only he knew it. Wallingford, telling the nun she was his wife. Wallingford, lavishing himself on her in the night, bringing her coffee in the morning. Wallingford, her lover, her love. Was it even possible that he, of all the descendants of Lord Copperbridge, should prove the one capable of true and faithful love?

"What happens if the curse is broken?" Abigail asked. "Do you . . . you turn mortal again?"

"So I have faith." Leonora bowed her head. "I have faith that my life become real again, that I grow old and I die, that my time in purgatory is done here on earth, that I go to heaven to see again my love and my son."

"And if it isn't broken? Do you keep waiting?"

Leonora took her hand from Abigail's. "Signorina, there is no more waiting. The angel, he has give three hundred years, no more. There is no more chance. We are redeem now, or we have this purgatory on the earth, until the end of the world."

Again, the sweet silence, the slow stir of the afternoon air. The lark spoke again, and this time Abigail saw him, hopping from one branch of the lemon tree to another, cocking his head and watching them with a steady black eye. Abigail looked down at her hands, and saw they were shaking in her lap.

"I will do my best, Leonora. I will do whatever you ask. I'll marry him, if I must. I will pledge myself to him faithfully."

"Oh, signorina." Leonora lifted her head. Her glittering eyes seemed to hold all the sadness of the world. "Is not for you to do. Is not you who can break the curse. Is not you who redeem us."

"It's not?"

"No, signorina. Is the heir of my love, my lord of Copper-bridge. Is the heir of our blood, of our curse, of Arthur and Leonora. Is he alone who redeem us."

TWENTY-ONE

The interior of the cathedral was dark and cool, a different world from the stone-baked heat outdoors. Wallingford paused for a moment in the entrance, waiting for his eyes to adjust from the blinding glare of the afternoon sun.

An extraordinary building, this cathedral, planned by some extravagant Gothic architect in alternating stripes of black and white stones, like a great holy zebra. He remembered visiting it once, several years ago, touring about the Continent with his brother one year, though he had spent as little time as possible inside. He had never quite liked cathedrals. The immense space, the cool, profound quiet always made him uneasy.

Why, then, had a strange yearning seized his heart, at the sight of that ambitious black-and-white tower against the vivid blue sky, as he wandered about the nearby streets, waiting for Abigail? He had found himself on its front steps without even realizing where he went.

He was not alone here. A few dark figures knelt among the pews, heads bowed and covered. A small group of tourists lingered underneath the dome, gesturing upward and speaking in low tones, red Baedekers flashing from their hands. Above him, between the crisscrossing ribs of the ceiling, a thousand gold stars twinkled from a rich blue sky.

He walked slowly around the back of the nave, to the left, his shoes clacking on the inlaid marble. So much decoration, such a glorious profusion of art and color on the floor and walls, and yet his eyes traveled continuously upward to the soaring ceiling, the immense cavern of the dome. What had inspired the medieval imagination to such impossible heights? Mere men, sinners all, facing the same earthly temptations as he did. But still they looked to heaven, still they raised their eyes to their Creator. Each man of clay found hope in the sublime.

The black-and-white columns passed by, one by one. Ahead lay the white marble pulpit; to his left, a small chapel, bright with gilding. On a whim, he entered, and saw that it was consecrated to John the Baptist; a fine bronze statue loomed above the back of the chapel, and a baptismal font sat in the center. Near the altar, a man knelt praying.

Not wishing to intrude, Wallingford took a step back, but the man rose and turned to him. He was dressed in a friar's robe, brown and woolen, belted at the waist by a plain length of rope. He pulled down his hood, and it seemed like a greeting.

"*Buon giorno*," Wallingford said guardedly. The hair stirred at the nape of his neck.

"*Buon giorno*, signore. You have come to pray?" The friar gestured to the altar.

Wallingford held up his hand. "Oh no. Merely a tourist." He paused. "You speak English well, sir."

"I know a little. Come, sit. Is a beautiful chapel, no?"

"Beautiful." Wallingford made a polite circle, taking in the elaborate decoration, the Renaissance font, the statue at the back.

"The statue, he is by Donatello," said the friar.

"It's magnificent." Wallingford walked forward a step or two, as if to examine it more closely. His heart, he realized, was beating rapidly.

"You have come to Siena alone, signore?"

"No. I'm visiting with . . . with my fiancée."

"Ah! You are to marry! Is good, signore. A wife, she bring great joy, she has the price above rubies."

Wallingford turned, amused. "And how would you know this, my good man?"

The friar was smiling. A handsome young fellow, really,

though his hair was cropped close and his ears extended boldly from the sides of his head. "I see many men in the confession, signore, and the one who has the good wife, he sin less. Is happy."

Wallingford turned back. "You must hear a great many extraordinary things in confession."

"I hear this and that. But the sin, it is all the same. We are all men, we all face the same temptation."

The friar's words echoed his own thoughts so closely, Wallingford gave a little start. "Yes, it's so," he said softly.

"Do you confess, signore?"

"No. I'm English, of course, and there is no confession, as such."

"Ah. Is a shame. Is good, I think, to say aloud the sin, to have the forgiveness."

Wallingford laughed. "I'm afraid my sins are too numerous to count, let alone relate in detail. I shall have to take my chances, I suppose."

"Are they, signore? You are a good man, I think. You think to marry, to have the family." The friar paused. "Your lady, she is good?"

"She is an angel," Wallingford said instantly. "A mischievous one, I'll admit, but free of vice, free of any thought of wickedness, as pure and loyal as . . ." His breath ran out of his body. "Ah, God."

"What is it, signore?"

Wallingford sank slowly onto the pew beside him. "I don't deserve her, of course, but what man does?"

"This is not so, signore. You are good; if you are not yourself good, you see not the goodness in her."

"She is an angel, she exists in an almost impossible state of grace, and I have led her into sin. I have taken her to bed."

The friar was silent.

Wallingford leaned his forearms on his knees and looked down. "She was a maiden, and I took her in pleasure, because I couldn't resist her."

"This is a sin, of course," said the friar, "but you will marry her, yes?"

"I will, I've sworn it before God. I should not have taken her otherwise." He lowered his voice. "But there have been others,

Father, many others before her. I have lain with women since I was fifteen, without marriage, nor yet a word of love between us. I have seduced other men's wives. I have coveted and lusted. I have been ruled by my own wants alone." He fisted his hands against his eyes. "Is it too much to hope, Father, that I can change?"

"My son, for the change, is need that we see the error of the past, and seek a better way." The friar's voice was infinitely kind.

"I do. I mean to be faithful to her. I would not hurt her for the world."

"Then why do you fear, my son?"

"Because I have never resisted temptation before. I don't know if I can." A sob burst out from his tortured throat. "How can I promise her fidelity, with these lips that have kissed so many others? How can I offer her this hand, that has drawn women into adultery?"

"My son, you have the will to act, or not to act. This will, it is God's true gift to man. He can choose to sin. Every sin, he make the choice."

Wallingford said nothing. The candles flickered next to the altar, rippling golden light across the intricacy of marble and gilding. A weight came to rest on his head: the friar's hand.

"I can offer you the forgiveness of God, my son. But I think first you wish to forgive yourself, yes?"

Wallingford closed his eyes. "I suppose so."

From the air above him came a few murmured words of Latin, so low as to be unintelligible. The weight lifted from his head. He had been blessed, Wallingford knew, but when he rose some time later to leave the chapel and stride back down the nave, he did not feel a bit different.

Outside, the light blinded him, reflecting from the white marble of the facade in the full horizontal glare of a falling sun. A falling sun?

He pulled his watch out of his pocket, stared at the face, shook it, stared at it again.

Three hours. He had been inside the cathedral for three hours.

He went on staring stupidly at the watch face, unable to comprehend what it told him. He spun around in a circle, looking for a public clock, but saw none. Only the sun dipping down below the hills, below the faded red tiles of the rooftops.

"*Gran Dio!* Wallingford!"

He jumped and turned.

"You! In Siena! Ah, *mio caro*, I cannot believe it!" A woman stood before him, veiled, dressed in black, a young boy clutching her hand.

He cast his eyes over her in astonishment. Who the devil was she? The voice was familiar, intimately familiar, but his disordered mind could not connect it with a living person.

"Ah, you devil! You do not know me." With her free hand she lifted her veil, and her dark eyes sparkled out of her lovely pale face.

"Isabella!" The name burst like a reflex from his lips.

"*Si*, it is I, though I see from your face I have made much change." She made a deprecating gesture with her hand. "You have not met my son."

"I have not. *Buon giorno*, young man," he said, sounding as awkward as he felt.

"My son is five years old in September." Isabella gave him a significant look.

He met her eye squarely. "My felicitations to you both. His father must be very proud of such a son. But I regret to say I'm in a very great hurry. Perhaps another time?"

She laid her hand on his arm. "Ah, Wallingford, you are always so cold. Have you no kind word for me? You, who have make me suffer so."

Her dark eyebrows came together in genuine longing. Had he really caused her to suffer? He had left rather abruptly, of course, but such affairs always ended abruptly. Had he inspired genuine affection in her? He hadn't tried to, hadn't wanted to.

Wallingford glanced down at the boy, who was looking up at him with shy curiosity, his hair as dark as Wallingford's own. But this was not his son; he knew that. He had taken the greatest care, after all; and by his own careful calculations, this child had been conceived at least a month after their short liaison.

"I'm sorry for your suffering," he said softly. "I never meant to cause you pain."

"Wretch. But is all forgiven, to see you now. You are staying in Siena?"

"Yes, and in fact . . ."

"You must have the dinner with me, this minute! I am all alone here. My friends, we came here for the Palio, and I have stayed on for a matter or two of business. My husband the marchese, he died a year ago, and there are still the papers and the business." She waved her hand. "You must dine with me."

"I cannot," he said. "I have urgent matters of my own, I'm afraid."

"Ah! A lady, perhaps? But she is not more beautiful than me, yes?" Isabella looked up at him through her magnificent eyelashes, full of hope and something more, something lonely and almost desperate. "You tell her you have the engagement already."

Wallingford felt the weight of the friar's hand on his head, an echo of memory, and a wave of compassion washed over him. "Isabella, my dear, it won't do. I . . ."

"Wallingford?"

Abigail's voice floated across the steps.

He jerked around, and there she was, her white dress almost invisible against the pale marble. She hurried toward him, one hand clasped firmly on her hat, the other holding her skirts from her eager legs. A few strands of hair escaped from beneath her hat brim, and Wallingford wanted to fall on his knees and hold them to his lips.

"There you are!" He held out his arms.

"Where have *you* been, for heaven's sake?" She put her hands in his, and he kissed each one, pressing hard with the force of his relief.

"I was in the cathedral, keeping cool, and I . . . I don't know, I expect I fell asleep, though I don't know how. I am so sorry. Thank God you're all right."

"I'm quite all right. I've been turning the city inside out for you. We must hurry, Wallingford!"

"Wallingford, *mio caro*." Isabella's voice appeared at his shoulder. "You are not introducing me to your little friend?"

Christ.

Without relinquishing Abigail's hands, he said, "How unforgivable of me. Abigail, my dear, I give you the Marchesa Attavanti, late of Venice. Signora Marchesa, I have the very great honor"—he turned slightly toward her—"to present to you Miss Abigail Harewood, my affianced bride."

"*La vostra fidanzata!*" Isabella's voice was shocked and brittle. "Is a great surprise you give me, Wallingford."

"I am delighted to make your acquaintance, Signora Marchesa," said Abigail. Her cheekbones were tinged with pink, but her eyes were sincere and steady. Wallingford could sense the energy strumming through her body: hurry, or agitation? He gripped her hands firmly.

"Tell me, when is the happy day?" asked Isabella.

"Why, today, as it happens," said Abigail.

"Today!" said Isabella.

"Today?" said Wallingford.

Abigail smiled at Wallingford. "Isn't it lovely? That's why I came to fetch you, darling. They're preparing the ceremony right now." She glanced at the lowering sun. "We must hurry, I'm afraid. The moon will be rising any minute."

The steps of the cathedral gave way beneath Wallingford's feet. He wavered, planted his left shoe desperately on the step below, and for a horrifying instant it seemed the only thing holding him up was the steely grip of Abigail's hands.

"Moonrise," he said, rallying. "Of course."

"Moonrise," Isabella echoed. Her face was ashen. "Is so romantic."

"Wallingford is such a dear romantic soul," said Abigail. "All flowers and champagne and that sort of thing, aren't you, darling?"

He released one hand and kissed the other. Was her hand shaking, or his? "The more the merrier."

Abigail smiled at Isabella. "Isn't he a dear? But we must be off, I'm afraid. The moon waits for no man."

"Is true," said Isabella. "I wish you much happy. Good day to you, signorina, and to you, Your Grace. I hope one day to see you again, with much love and many child."

She gripped her son's hand and lowered her veil, and walked away with her chin tilted toward the pale lengthening sky.

The sun had fallen fully behind the surrounding buildings, and the black eyes were almost invisible inside the iron grille.

"It is Signorina Abigail," she said. "I have returned."

The door swung open. "This man, he is much trouble," grumbled the nun.

"I quite agree, Suor Giovanna, but I'm afraid he's all I have. You are so kind to allow him in." Abigail stepped through the doorway, pulling Wallingford along behind. His limbs seemed curiously heavy, almost unwilling. She hoped it was only the shock, and not some reluctance insinuated in his heart by the lovely flashing eyes of the Marchesa Attavanti.

"Fifty years I have lived inside the walls, and there is no man. Is only for the Suor Leonora, may God bless her days." Suor Giovanna turned to Wallingford. "You! The eyes are to close."

"Close my eyes?" asked Wallingford, incredulous.

"*Si*. And the head is to think holy things, signore. Eyes close, head holy. You understand?"

"I understand," Wallingford said humbly. He closed his eyes. "Quite holy."

Abigail took his hand. "I'll lead you. But do hurry."

"It's rather difficult to hurry when one's eyes are closed," he complained, but he followed her along as they raced down the corridors, with hardly a misstep. Abigail's heart beat with unnatural speed, as it had since she had spotted him on the steps of the cathedral, engaged in deep conversation with the shapely woman in black and her little dark-haired son.

Two hours ago, she had emerged from the convent in a haze of love and hope, expecting Wallingford's arms to lie open and waiting outside the door. Instead, there was only the empty cab, and the driver who said that the signore had walked off some time ago, and promised to be back in an hour.

She had waited and waited, panic growing in her heart, and at last she had set off looking for him in the cab. She had gone to the hotel in the Piazza del Campo, where they hadn't seen him; she had gone back to the convent; she had begun to search the streets, one by one. Perhaps he had gotten lost; perhaps he had been waylaid for his gold cuff links and the folded lire notes in his inside jacket pocket. Wallingford hurt, Wallingford kidnapped, Wallingford dead: All these possibilities had struck her, one by one, each more horrifying than the last. And all the while, the sun had dropped in the sky, in the full blinding glare of the approaching sunset, while the Signorina Monteverdi waited patiently for them in her little garden with the lemon tree.

At last Abigail had seen him, his head bowed solicitously to the woman in black, whose hand lay on his arm in a gesture of unmistakable intimacy. Her body had gone limp with relief, and then charged instantly with a burst of emotion. Anger, jealousy, helplessness: She had concealed them all as she stood there, exchanging greetings. She had done her best to sound exactly like Abigail, to inform Wallingford of their approaching nuptials with the same careless glee as she had informed him of their approaching first kiss.

He and the marchesa had been lovers, once. There was no doubt of that.

Abigail turned the corner of the convent hallways, and the door to the garden lay open ahead, flooded with dying light. She stopped, so abruptly that Wallingford crashed into her.

"I beg your pardon," he said.

"Wallingford, open your eyes."

"I can't. That terrifying nun will thrash me, I'm sure."

Abigail took both his hands in hers. "Open them. Look at me."

His eyes opened, black and opaque in the dim corridor. "What is it? What's going on?"

"Wallingford, if you don't want to do this, if you have any doubt at all, you must tell me."

His eyebrows lifted. "Doubts, Abigail? Are you mad?"

"I saw you on the steps with the marchesa. You were lovers, once; don't deny it. Is that your son?"

"Good God! Of course not. Not a chance of it, I promise you solemnly."

"But you were lovers."

He paused. "Yes. Many years ago."

His hands felt hot in hers, like coals. "Wallingford, you must be certain. You must be absolutely certain. The Signorina Monteverdi waits in there, and if you don't love me truly, if you can't pledge yourself in sacred vows—*sacred*, Wallingford—then there's no point at all."

Wallingford drew one hand from hers and cupped her cheek. "Abigail, the question is not whether I'm certain. Of course

I am. I've known for months I wanted you for my wife. The question, my love, is whether *you're* certain."

She returned his gaze steadily, searching his face in the shadows. "I *am* certain."

"Will you, Abigail, allow me to be your husband?" He kissed her hand. "Allow me the very great honor of calling you mine?"

"Your duchess."

"My duchess. Can you do that?"

Abigail felt the inexorable tick of the passing seconds, the weight of the sun sinking below the horizon. "I must," she said. "I can't do without you."

Wallingford's thumb brushed her cheek. "Then let's go."

This time, he led her by the hand down the corridor, and turned through the door into Leonora's walled garden.

It was not empty. Leonora was there, of course, standing beside the golden cross in her black habit, her dark eyes shining in her pale face. But from the stone bench rose Alexandra, and next to her stood Mr. Burke, holding her hand; and next to Mr. Burke stood a tall white-haired man Abigail recognized at once.

"Why, Harry!" she exclaimed. "What the devil are you doing here?"

TWENTY-TWO

H arry?" Wallingford turned to her. "Who the devil's
Harry?"

Abigail shook him loose and ran forward to take the hands
of Harry Stubbs between her own. "I can't believe it! How did
you know I was here? How on earth did they let you out of the
country, with that forgery conviction?"

Harry gave a great sigh from his great height—almost as
high as Mr. Burke himself—and opened his mouth to speak, but
Wallingford broke in instead.

"Harry Stubbs," he said, laden with irony. "Harry Stubbs,
down the pub. What a devil of a coincidence."

Abigail turned. "Why, do you know Harry, too?"

Wallingford folded his arms. "As a matter of fact, I do. But
our friend Harry Stubbs, unprincipled scoundrel that he is, has
a number of aliases. Among them, I believe, is the character of
the Italian, Signore Rosseti. Another is the august title of Duke
of Olympia."

Abigail gasped. She turned back to Harry. "Harry! It's not
true. You taught me how to pick horses! You taught me how to
render a man unconscious!"

Harry glanced at Wallingford and back at her. "My dear," he
said, in a voice quite different from the one he employed down

the pub, "I thought it might be wise to ensure you had every possible defense at your disposal, given your nature."

"Well, well." Wallingford's voice was deadly behind her shoulder. "It appears my grandfather has managed to pick himself out a bride for me after all. Well played, old man. I stand in awe. I suppose you placed that advertisement ·in the *Times* yourself?"

"Oh, I say!" exclaimed Mr. Burke. "Damnably clever. I can't thank you enough." He lifted Alexandra's hand to his lips and kissed it.

"Like a damned puppetmaster. And you!" Wallingford pointed to Leonora. "I suppose you picked me out in the cathedral. Plucked out all my secrets like an expert."

Abigail whirled toward him. "How dare you! Leonora is an angel! And she's been here all along, preparing for the ceremony."

"Leonora?" Wallingford looked at her in confusion. "I mean the friar. We met in the cathedral, not an hour ago. Didn't we, sir?"

Abigail turned to Leonora, mouth open.

Leonora stepped forward. "My brother. He is here, beside me. He perform the vows."

The air seemed to whirl in a dreamlike circle around Abigail's head. She stared at Leonora and the empty space next to her.

"Abigail? Are you all right?" Wallingford touched her shoulder.

Abigail stepped forward and reached out her hand to the empty space. "You're Signore Monteverdi, aren't you? But I can't see you, or hear you."

Leonora said quietly, "He say to tell you yes, he is here."

"Do you mean to say you can't see him?" asked Wallingford.

"No." Abigail went on staring at the empty space. "No more than you can see Signorina Monteverdi, who stands next to him. Until the curse is broken, I suppose."

"She's *here*? Right here?"

Leonora held out her hand. Her eyes glimmered wetly. "My son, the son of my blood. I am here."

"You can't see her," Abigail whispered, "but she's here."

Alexandra's voice broke the stillness. "I don't understand. Do you mean you can't see the nun, Wallingford?"

Abigail brushed her eyes and turned to her sister. "It's too much to explain, dearest, but yes. Do you remember, I told you once about the curse on the castle?"

"As a very great muddle of fathers and pistols and lovers, yes."

"Until this curse is broken, the women can see only Leonora, and the men can see only her brother. The men and the women, you see, are eternally separate."

Alexandra's face was white. She was clutching Mr. Burke's hands with great force. "Good God. I suspected . . . I thought . . . Good God."

"And how is this curse to be broken?" asked Mr. Burke. His face was equally pale.

"We hope . . ." Abigail looked at Wallingford.

The duke's eyes were round and soft in his handsome face. He stepped to Abigail and took her hand. "If I pledge myself in faithful love, isn't that right? I, the last prodigal son of Copperbridge."

A breeze drifted across the garden, making the leaves rustle in the lemon tree.

"Is late," said Leonora. "The moon, she is rising. Signorina Abigail, who give you in marriage?"

"I . . . I don't know . . ."

Leonora turned to her right and spoke softly. A short pause, and then the Duke of Olympia stepped forward. "I do."

I am going to be married, Abigail thought wildly. *Right now. To Wallingford*. She looked up and met his eyes. Something light and vibrant flew through her blood, thrilling and frightening all at once.

"My brother, he speak the words to the duke," said Leonora. "I give them to you. Take your hands, the both of you."

Another pause, and Wallingford picked up her other hand.

The words began to pass between them: Leonora's low tones and Wallingford's rich voice, steady and reassuring, promising to love and to cherish her, to be faithful only to her. And Abigail's own voice, high and strange in her own ears, promising the same extravagant fidelities.

"The ring," said Leonora. "There is a ring?"

The Duke of Olympia stepped to his grandson and offered him a small gold band. Leonora gave a little gasp, as if she recognized it.

"With this ring," said Wallingford, sliding it on her finger, "I thee wed, with my body I thee worship, and with all my worldly goods I thee endow: In the name of the Father, and of the Son, and of the Holy Ghost. Amen."

He leaned forward and placed a gentle kiss on her lips. Above his dark head, the full moon nudged its yellow rim into the evening sky.

The air went still, except for the lark in the lemon tree, who sang out with joy.

"It is done," said Leonora. "You are wed."

Wallingford kissed Abigail's hand, right above the wedding band, and the warmth of his lips traveled up her arm to cradle her heart.

"I love you," Abigail whispered.

Someone sighed deeply to her left. Alexandra, she thought. Her eyes blurred.

She turned to thank Leonora, to see Signore Monteverdi for the first time. But the space next to the nun remained empty, and only the golden cross showed through the arriving twilight.

There is no explanation," said Wallingford. "These are mysteries we can't begin to comprehend."

Abigail sank into the armchair. "I wanted so much to free her. You should have seen her face, Wallingford."

He loosened his tie, unbuttoned his waistcoat. The room was small and provincial, no telephones and electric lamps and gleaming en suite facilities, but this was his wedding night and only two things were essential: a bed and his wife.

His *wife*.

She sat in the ancient armchair, staring not at him, her new husband, but at the wooden floor. Her delicate fairy face was not radiant with joy, but heavy with disappointment. "Perhaps it takes time. Perhaps it's not an instant thing. Or perhaps it's because Olympia hasn't got any sons, any legitimate sons . . ."

Wallingford knelt before the chair and placed his hands on her knees. "Darling, look at me."

She looked up.

He smiled at her. "Your Grace. My own dear Duchess of Wallingford." He touched her nose. "My wife. I have pledged you my hand and my heart today, and I meant every word. Isn't that enough?"

She smiled faintly. "For me, it is. Evidently not for Leonora."

"We have celebrated with my family and yours. I've endured your damned sister leering triumphantly over me and calling me her *dear nephew.* We have made our toasts, and eaten our cake . . ."

"And very nice cake it was. So rich and dense, and all those lovely currants . . ."

"I've carried you once more across a threshold, nearly causing my back to spavin. And now, my love, my adorable bride, I want nothing more than to take you to bed and consummate our marriage properly." He kissed her hand. "Do you have any objections?"

She put her arms around his neck. "None at all, Your Grace. Consummate away."

He undressed her with care, beginning with the pins in her hair, and placed each item carefully on the chair as he removed it. He wanted to test himself, to keep himself in rigid check, to prove to her he was master of himself.

She stood patiently, almost passively, as he uncovered each radiant inch of her skin. Only her eyes glowed, watching him with that curious knowingness of hers, that innocent elvish wisdom that seemed to penetrate his soul. Silently she helped him with his buttons, drew off his shirt, put her hands against his chest. The room was still hot from the afternoon sun, and only a faint breeze stirred from the crack in the window. Her hands felt cool against his skin, though her cheeks wore the bright flush of arousal.

How was it possible that one little person, one delicate female form, could have conquered *him*, the mighty Duke of Wallingford? He was her willing slave, her supplicant. She could send him to the ground with a flick of her fingers.

He took her hand and led her to the bed. He pulled back the thin summer covering. The sheets, at least, were clean and white. A large bed: Abigail looked pale and small in the center, sitting up with her legs tucked under her, looking up at him. She was trembling, he realized.

He set his knee down, and his hand. "I believe we have at least twenty-three positions left to try. What do you wish?"

She put her arms around him. "I want to see your face. I want to feel your belly against mine. I want to hear your voice in my ear."

"Done." He kissed her slowly, caressed her soft body, laid her in the pillows. When she was ready, when her breath came fast from her chest and his finger was covered with her miraculous wetness, he mounted her and drove inside her, watching with wonder her changing expression, her noises of pleasure. Passionate Abigail, she was already approaching her peak, he could feel it, and it was too soon. He wanted more for her.

He pulled back, drawing her with him, arranging her, until they were sitting upright on the bed with limbs overlapping, still joined.

"Oh," she said in surprise, rocking gently, as if to test their connection.

"Open your eyes, Abigail."

She opened them.

He took her hand from his shoulder and guided it downward. "Feel it, Abigail. Feel us."

Her fingers touched him, touched herself, circled around the intimate point of their merging.

"Do you see what I mean?" he whispered. He wanted to say more. *Do you see how we connect? Do you see that I'm yours, entirely yours, that by this physical act I have joined us into one inseparable flesh?* But the words wouldn't form.

"I see," she whispered back. "I know." She slipped her hands around the back of his head and kissed him, and the sultry scent of her arousal drifted into his brain. She rose up a fraction and sank down, in a sweet rocking motion, and then said, "*Oh!*" with widened eyes, as some point of pressure came to bear on her.

"Like this?"

"Yes!" She rocked harder and rose up, coming down again with an explosive little sigh. Wallingford felt as if he were going to burst at the sight of her, at the feel of her breasts sliding against his chest and her wet flesh sliding along his cock, as she used his body for her own pleasure. The candlelight turned her body to gold, shadowed her every delicious curve, and as her movements grew more urgent he buried his face in her neck and drew in her sweet scent, her lemons and blossoms, until she was crying out in his arms, convulsing, his passionate Abigail.

He set himself free at last in a long and voluptuous spend.

Consummation.

She dropped her head against his shoulder and rested. Her heartbeat slammed against his, slow and immeasurably strong. "I lied to you before," she whispered.

"What's that?" His befuddled brain trudged slowly through her words.

"When I told you I didn't care how many women you'd had. I *do* care. I care passionately." Her voice ebbed, and he realized she was nearly in tears. "I hate them all, every one. I can't bear to think of it, and I can't help thinking of it. I can't help picturing you doing this to some other woman, in some other bed. Touching her the way you touch me. And it hurts my heart, Wallingford."

"Hush."

"It hurts my heart so, because I love you, and *this*, when we do this . . ." She raised her head. "It's so precious. I don't want to share it with anyone. I don't want to share *you*."

What could he say? His heart ached, too, ached for her pain. And anything he could say would have the ring of banality, would be nothing but cheap appeasement. *It meant nothing. I never loved them. I regret it all.*

But she was his wife. He had to try.

"Would it help," he said carefully, "if I told you that all those women belong to the past, before I knew you? And that I didn't really exist back then, not as I do now. It seems like another life. It *was* another life."

"I suppose it helps a little. But then I see you with a beautiful marchesa on the cathedral steps, after you've been missing for hours; or perhaps, one day, I'll see a lady in a London drawing room, some lover of yours, and the past isn't really past, is it? It's not another life at all. It's *your* life, and there are living women who have been to bed with you, who know you like this, and I have to find a way to accept that. To accept the possibility that one day, there may be others."

He held her tightly and rocked her. "Abigail, never."

"We didn't break the curse, Wallingford. We've failed them."

"It means nothing." He said it with all the conviction he could muster.

My dear boy, has the entire conduct of your adult life ever suggested your usefulness for anything else?

The failure was not *theirs*, was it? It was *his*, his alone. His vow was not enough.

She was clinging to him, her head buried in his shoulder, her damp skin stuck to his.

"How many are there, Wallingford? Just so I know. What are my odds, at any given party in London, that you've been up someone in the room?"

His chest was wet with her tears. "Abigail," he said softly, comforting her as best he could, holding her against him.

"I don't blame you, exactly. It's simply a fact, a part of you, and I don't know what to do. I love you so. If I didn't love you like this, it wouldn't hurt. I can't have one and not the other."

"We could live here in Italy, if you like. Anywhere you want. Whatever you want, Abigail."

"Run away, you mean."

"If it makes you happy. I only want your happiness, Abigail."

She looked up, and her eyes were awash: Abigail, who never cried. "I know you do. I know you do *now*. But tomorrow?"

"Every tomorrow."

She went on looking at him with her wet eyes, gazing upon his face with such love and sadness he thought he would break apart. Her hand came up and touched his cheek, ran across the emerging stubble on his jaw. "At least I have you now," she said. "At this moment, in this present minute, there are no others. I have you *now*, don't I?"

"You have me now." He eased her into the pillows and drew the sheets over them, and he held her close, because he knew that was all he could do. After a while, he made love to her again, lavished her with every possible pleasure, told her again how he loved her, until her body arched and trembled with the force of her climax, and this time she fell without words into an exhausted slumber, tucked into the circle of his arms.

Wallingford was exhausted, too, but his eyes remained stubbornly open, staring at the moonlit shadows on the ceiling. Somewhere in the room, a clock ticked away in loud scratches, in time with the beat of his heart.

He looked down at Abigail, at her trusting head nestled under his arm. He stroked her hair, her shining chestnut hair that he loved. She was deeply asleep; she didn't even flinch. Poor Abigail, he hadn't allowed her much rest in the past thirty-six hours.

He disengaged from her slowly, doing his best not to disturb her, though he suspected an elephant might have wandered across the bed without causing her to wake. Silently he found his clothes, dressed to his waistcoat, and opened the door with a soft click of the latch.

The full moon was low in the sky, nearly dipping behind the rooftops. Wallingford longed for a drink or a smoke, something to do with his fingers, and in the absence of either he stuffed his hands into his trouser pockets and walked across the empty Piazza del Campo, up the hill toward the striped cathedral, around the deserted streets. The air was still languid, still bearing a trace of the midday heat. His eyelids began to grow heavy at last, and he turned back for the hotel.

As he reached the awning, a voice stopped him. "Rather an odd place to find a man on his wedding night."

Wallingford sighed and turned in his grandfather's direction. "Afraid I haven't done my duty for the dukedom, are you? Let me assure you to the contrary."

Olympia emerged from the shadows, his bare white head catching the moonlight. "As it's not my dukedom, I don't really give a damn. Except I have rather a fondness for your new bride, and I should hate her to be disappointed."

Wallingford leaned against the wall and studied his grandfather. "It was all very neatly done, wasn't it, Grandfather? Tell me, how long ago did you pick her out?"

"A year or two, I suppose. You must admit I chose well."

"I won't deny it."

"And the others? Roland and Burke?"

Olympia came to rest on a nearby pillar. "In fact, it all started with your brother. I had done a bit of meddling, in earlier days . . ."

"I am shocked to the core."

". . . and I decided it was time to put things right. I was simply fortunate in the matter of cousins."

"Better to be lucky than clever, so they say."

Olympia tapped his long fingers against his trousers. "You love her, I see."

"More than I ever imagined. I would die for her." Wallingford spoke plainly.

"Given up your philandering ways and all that?"

"That is my firm intention."

Olympia raised a single eyebrow at that. "One couldn't help noticing, at the conclusion of the ceremony," he said, "that this so-called curse has apparently not been lifted."

Wallingford shrugged. "As to that, I can't say. I meant every word of my vows to her. I would cut off my right arm before I looked at another woman."

"And still."

Wallingford said nothing, because to say anything would give voice to the doubt in his chest, the doubt of himself.

"You don't think yourself capable, do you?" Olympia said at last.

"*You* certainly don't think me capable. You never have."

"Then I suppose, for the sake of that inexpressibly dear girl who sleeps upstairs in your bed," said Olympia, straightening from the pillar, "you had better find a way to prove to yourself that you are."

For some time, Wallingford sat in the armchair, watching her sleep. The rise and fall of her chest mesmerized him. He studied the curve of her cheekbone in the last of the moonlight, the dark pool of her hair on the pillow, the warm white swell of her breasts. He wanted to bury his face in them once more, to taste her skin, but he held himself in check.

She stirred; her eyelids flickered. He put his face into his hands.

"Why are you dressed?" she asked sleepily.

"I went for a walk."

The sheets rustled. "Look at me, Wallingford."

He raised his head. She sat in the bed, her lovely body shrouded by a white sheet, watching him with her wise light brown eyes.

"You're not certain, either? Whether you can do this.

Whether you can be faithful for the rest of your life. That's why the curse isn't broken."

"Rubbish. I would never stray from you, Abigail. I would never hurt you."

"You're only saying that to reassure me, because you want so much for it to be true. But a rake doesn't really reform, does he?"

He rose from the chair and went to the window. "I am not a rake."

"Still, you've behaved like one, all your life. That's why you came to Italy to begin with, after all. To prove that you were more than that. To try to get along without women and wine. And then I came along."

"Yes, you came along."

"So you don't really know, do you? Whether you can resist all the temptation around you, all the temptation to which the Duke of Wallingford is subject."

"I can. I must. I love you too much to fail."

The sheets rustled again, and a moment later he felt her hand against his back, and then her smooth cheek. "Listen to me," she whispered. "I've been thinking, thinking a great deal. Wallingford, my love, my husband. Go from here. Spend a year on your own. The year of chastity you set out for yourself, the one I interrupted . . ."

He turned. "What the devil, Abigail? What are you talking about?"

"What's a year, after all?" She put her hands around the back of his head. "There's no more rush, no curse to be broken. I'll wait for you. I'll wait at the castle. Set off on your own, and scratch for your own worms." She bent her head and kissed his chest. "I'll keep your tender heart right here, safe between my hands."

He was falling, right through some gaping hole in the floorboards, into an abyss below.

He scratched out, "*Leave* you? You're sending me away?"

"I'll manage. I'm strong enough; you know I am."

"It's impossible. It's ridiculous. I could never leave you . . ."

"Darling, you must."

". . . to say nothing of the estate . . ."

"On my own, I should certainly bollox it all up, but I know

your brother will help me manage things. Roland's very clever, you know."

He bowed his head above her and anchored himself in the soft scent of her hair.

"Listen, my love," she said. "I know you, I know you to your bones. I understand everything. I know why you went out walking in the moonlight on your wedding night. I know what weighs on your heart. You need this. You needed it last March, and you still need it. Simply loving me isn't enough. We proved that today."

"Yes, it is. You're my strength, Abigail."

"No, I'm not. *You're* your own strength, Wallingford, and you must see that. It's there, it's in everything you do, and you simply don't know it."

Wallingford closed his eyes.

"You are so *full* of golden promise," she said.

He pressed his lips against her hair.

She went on. "And I need this, too. I need you to suffer a little, to try yourself at ordinary tasks as mortal men do. To learn how to be the true and faithful husband who will share my bed and board, who will father my children."

"Abigail, it's absurd. I can't leave you." Was that his voice? He hardly recognized it. A tear left his right eye and rolled down his cheek, disappearing into her hair.

"You can, Wallingford. You should. A year of chaste living: It's what you meant to do all along. You knew, you always knew what had to be done."

He gathered her hair in his hands, tilted up her face, and kissed her. "Go back to bed, darling. You're making no sense at all."

"I'm not sleepy."

"Yes, you are. God knows I am. We'll both feel better in the morning."

He led her back to the bed and stretched himself next to her, with his shoes still on, and in an instant she was asleep on her side, facing him, his slumbering angel. He lay watching her, taking her breath into his lungs. His heart crashed painfully against the crumbled walls of his chest.

At last he rose and found a sheet of paper in the desk. In the light of the moon, he wrote down names and addresses: his solicitor, his banker, his man of business in the village. He took the marriage certificate from his jacket pocket and laid it out beneath a paperweight. He wrote a letter such as he had never written: words of love, of abiding faithfulness; and having used up all his store of sentiment, signed it simply *Arthur*.

She would know what it meant.

He packed nothing with him, not even a razor. He took only a few lire notes from his pocket and left the rest on the desk. Satisfied, he went to the bed and looked down at his wife. He drew the blanket over her; without his body curled around hers, she might be chilled, even in this warm room. With his finger he touched her hair, her cheek, her breast, her belly, marveling at her softness. He longed to touch the turned-up elfin tip of her eye, but he was afraid to wake her.

At last he turned and left the room, not daring to look back.

Outside the window, the moon disappeared below the horizon.

TWENTY-THREE

Midsummer's Eve, 1891

Alexandra Burke leaned back against her husband's chest and tossed her sister a self-satisfied smirk. "How disappointing you haven't got any serving outfits that fit me this year."

"There's always next year," said Mr. Burke, drawing his hand rather suggestively to where his wife's chest strained the boundaries of both propriety and possibility, to say nothing of the seams of her once-demure yellow gown. His other hand remained atop her belly, which was itself large enough to apply for independent statehood.

Alexandra patted his fingers. "With luck, you shall put me in this condition every midsummer, just to annoy Abigail and her schemes. Oof!" She grimaced and put her hand on her other side. "On the other hand, perhaps one child is more than sufficient."

"I hope for *your* sake there's more than one baby in there," said Abigail, "or else we shall have to send out for a much larger cradle." She set her tray of stuffed olives on the table. "There you are, sister dear. Shall I bring another platter for your husband?"

"For my husband? Don't be ridiculous." Alexandra reached for an olive and popped it expertly into her mouth. "I'm more than capable of eating two platters of Morini's stuffed olives without Finn's assistance. Look here, Penhallow!" She slapped Lord Roland's hand as it attempted an olive from across the table. "If you want olives, send for your own wife."

"But she's off serving everybody else," said Lord Roland, with the long face of a man accustomed to having his wife's ministrations entirely to himself.

"Shall I find her for you, Papa?" Philip swiped a pair of olives from the tray and squirmed off the bench.

"Splendid idea!" Roland called after the boy, as he disappeared into the crowd of villagers. "And I recommend you start by taking a running lap or two around the castle itself, just to be certain she's not off hiding in a corner somewhere." He turned back to the others. "Helps them go right to sleep," he explained knowingly.

"I shall keep that in mind," said Burke.

Abigail picked up the empty tray and wove her way back to the kitchen, nearly colliding with Lilibet on her way out. "Philip is looking for you," she said. "Though he may not find you straightaway. Roland's sent him running around the castle."

"Oh, that boy. If Roland told him to build a ladder to the moon, he'd do it."

"I daresay he's only happy to have a real father at last," said Abigail.

Lilibet's face softened. "Yes, of course. Oh, Abigail . . ."

"I must be off. They're frightfully busy in the kitchen."

Abigail swept into the kitchen, where Morini stood smiling, humming to herself as she arranged a plate of antipasti. "Morini," said Abigail, squinting, "is that a locket about your neck?"

Morini put her hand to the hollow of her throat and smiled. "Is nothing, Signora Duchessa. Is a trinket."

"A trinket from whom?" Abigail leaned in to peer. The locket was small and golden, with some sort of vine motif etched on the case.

"From nobody, signora."

"It's from Giacomo, isn't it? I knew it! You've mended fences at last, have you? That's a lovely locket."

"*Si*, signora. Is having much meaning. Is the same locket . . ." Morini stilled her active hands and glanced out the window with a wistful smile.

"The same locket . . . ?" Abigail prodded.

Morini drew a deep breath and turned back to Abigail. "Is the same locket Giacomo give me, many years ago. Is the locket I give him back, many years ago, when the sadness come, and he is so much angry. Now he give it back."

Abigail raised one eyebrow. Undoubtedly there was rather more to the story than that. "I shall have it all out of you, you know," she said, hoisting a tray.

Morini laughed and returned to her antipasti. "I am expecting you, signora."

Abigail made her way back into the courtyard. The musicians were tuning up already, the moon was rising. For a moment, the strength left Abigail's body. She leaned against the wall, holding her tray, looking out across the courtyard to where the terraces dropped away down the hillside. A gentle blue light filled the air, the arrival of dusk. Someone was lighting the torches, and the faint scent of smoke drifted to her nose.

The crowd parted, and there under the torches sat Alexandra and Finn. His arm was still wrapped around her, and the flames lit his ginger hair into gold. He said something in Alexandra's ear, and she laughed and looked up at him with adoration.

Across the table from them, Lilibet had paused near her husband, stretching one shapely arm to snatch a drink from his glass of wine. Roland caught her wrist in mock outrage, and she bent down and kissed him on the lips, distracting him just enough to free her hand and dart away, laughing, with the wine. He rose to run after her, and Abigail lost them among the throng.

I am so happy for them, Abigail told herself, deep in her aching throat.

So happy.

She straightened from the wall and turned her head to wipe her eyes on her shoulder. There was no use in self-pity. She herself had proposed this purgatory; she must bear it without flinching.

She had endured eleven months without Wallingford, eleven months without his dry laugh and his warm body, his bluster and his humor, his rigid strength and his unexpected tenderness. While the others had laughed and loved, throughout the cold Tuscan winter and the blossoming spring, she had waited and prayed. She could endure one more month, four little weeks. He would come back to her then. Surely, in the heat of July, he would return.

She must keep her faith and trust. She must believe in him.

She squared her shoulders and lifted her chin. A torch flickered behind her, and in the next instant, a pair of arms reached around hers and plucked the tray from her hands.

"This looks altogether too heavy for such a delicate little fairy as Your Grace, the Duchess of Wallingford."

Abigail's legs gave way. She closed her eyes.

"Good God! You're back!" someone said, and the tray was lifted away, and the arms wrapped around her so tightly she couldn't breathe.

"He's back!" It was Philip's voice, raised with excitement, running past her legs. "He's back, everybody! I helped him put his horse in the stable."

"You're back," she whispered, eyes still closed. Her back rested against his chest, his solid, impervious Wallingford chest.

"I'm back."

"There you are, old chap! Thought you were still tramping about Outer Mongolia," said Finn, and a shudder went through them both as Wallingford's back was delivered a hearty slap.

"So I was," said Wallingford, in a rumble against her spine. "But I got fed up, decided enough was enough, and came home to make love to my wife."

"Very sensible," said Alexandra, and Abigail opened her eyes at last.

"Good God!" exclaimed Wallingford. "Look at you, Alexandra! How the devil do you get her upstairs at night, Burke?"

Roland's voice: "Look here, my prodigal brother, I don't mean to point out the obvious, but have you perhaps noticed your wife is turning rather blue?"

Instantly Wallingford's arms loosened, and everybody began talking and laughing at once. Abigail found herself half dragged, half carried to one of the trestle tables, and settled on a bench in the crook of Wallingford's arm. Lord Roland swept up the tray of food. "I'll play serving maid tonight," he said gallantly.

Wallingford was plied with food and drink, which he ate

with one hand, keeping the other arm firmly around Abigail
while he answered a volley of rapid-fire questions from young
Philip, who had popped up on the opposite knee. Yes, he had
drunk the fermented mare's milk; no, it had not made him sick.
Yes, he had helped with the Ukrainian harvest, and yes, he had
ridden Lucifer most of the way, except when offered rides in
friendly hay carts. No, he had not climbed the Himalaya Mountains, but he *had* seen a tiger.

"A real tiger?" Philip asked in awe.

"Yes, a real one," said Wallingford, "though thankfully an
elderly one, who was quite as happy to let me go about my business as I was to let him."

"You should have written to let me know you were coming,"
Abigail said quietly, near his ear, when Philip at last slipped off
his knee. She still couldn't look at his face.

"I couldn't stop to write. I had to see you, to speak to you,
not to write words on a page. Look at me, Abigail."

"I can't. I shall lose control altogether."

"Now then," he said gently, taking her chin in his fingers,
"that's not the Abigail I know."

He turned her face toward him, and there he was: hair a little
shorter, navy eyes glowing in the torchlight, stubble dusting his
square jaw, thick eyebrows narrowed in concentration. He
smelled of dust and horses, of smoke and perspiration. She
wanted to lie against his bare skin and drink him in.

"Come upstairs," she said.

"With all my heart." He stood up and held out his hand. "For
one thing, I believe I hear that blasted tuba starting up."

She threaded him back through the crowd. The door stood ajar,
allowing a draft from the kitchen, fragrant with baking cakes.
Wallingford's hand curled warm and invincible around hers.

The corridor was empty. They turned the corner into the
great hall, where Wallingford pressed her up against the wall
and kissed her without mercy.

"Oh," she said, gasping for air, "oh, God, I've missed you so!
Every minute you were gone. Every second." She took his face
in her hands and stroked it with her thumbs. "Is it you? Is it
really you?"

"Of course it's me, dash it. I hope you haven't taken to kissing dark-haired strangers in hallways as a matter of habit."

She laughed. "It *is* you."

"It *is* me." He kissed her again, his hands at her waist. "Your faithful husband, Abigail, in thought and deed. I swear it."

"I never doubted you."

"Liar."

She laughed. She could not stop stroking him, could not stop running her thumbs along the high arc of his cheekbones, rubbing the short silk of his hair at the back of his neck. He was real. He was here. "Though I wasn't expecting you for another month."

"Well, I was going to stay the full year, just to prove I could. And then I thought, why the devil? I'd done what I meant to do. Why spend another month away from you?"

"I'm glad you came back." She slid her hands down his arms and grasped his fingers. "Come. I've something to show you."

"The sooner the better," he growled.

Abigail led him up the great staircase, past the women's rooms, through the passage into the west wing.

"We're going to *my* room?" he asked.

"Yes. Only it's not your room any longer."

"Isn't it?"

She pushed open the door and led him in.

"Oh, God."

Wallingford went still, his feet rooted to the floor. Abigail stood next to him, holding his hand, letting him take it all in: the soft furnishings, the clothes laid out on the drying rack, the two cradles sitting side by side.

The waves of noise radiating outward from one of them.

A woman rose up from the corner. "You are in the perfect time. Someone is hungry."

Abigail gave Wallingford's stricken hand a tug. When he didn't budge, she went forward by herself. "Look, I've brought Papa," she said.

"*Two* of them?" he gasped out. He put his hand on the wall.

"Don't worry. Only one of them is yours."

"*What?*"

"No, no. I mean Lilibet and Roland had a baby, too. A little girl. Poor Philip, he was so hoping for a brother."

Wallingford took a step forward, and another, until he stood next to her, looking over the cradles: at the cherubic infant fast asleep in one, golden curls catching the light in a halo; and the squalling little black-haired baby occupying the other, hands fisted and legs kicking.

Wallingford looked back and forth, and a deep sigh heaved from his chest. "Let me guess which one is ours."

Abigail lifted out the crying child, clucking and soothing. "He's only hungry. And he's four months younger, which makes a difference. There, now, my love." She put him up against her shoulder and turned her head to inhale the sweet baby scent of his hair.

"He?" Wallingford whispered.

"I named him Arthur."

"Why the devil did you do that?"

"Would you stop scowling at him, please? He's your son. He's very sensitive."

Wallingford swallowed. "My son."

"You can touch him." She shifted the baby in her arms. He gave a little sobbing heave and looked up into his father's face.

"Where do I touch him?"

"Anywhere you like. Put your finger in his hand."

Wallingford held out a hesitant finger and placed it against Arthur's tiny palm, which closed around him instantly.

"My God, what a grip!"

Arthur's red face crumpled.

"Oh, there," Abigail said. "Poor love. I've kept him waiting long enough."

"For what?"

"For his milk, darling. Babies drink milk; it's a known fact. Do you mind waiting? I know you must be exhausted." She tried to sound matter-of-fact, despite the devastation in her center, the wreckage in her breast at the sight of tiny Arthur clutching his father's finger at last. Of Wallingford standing there in awe and terror and—yes, she was certain—love, looking into his son's eyes.

"Waiting?"

"While I nurse him." Abigail settled into the rocking chair by the window and lowered her serving maid's bodice, which was a fairly straightforward matter, since there was very little bodice to speak of.

In the corner, the woman smiled and rose. "I will bring some tea."

"Thank you, Leonora," Abigail said softly, as Arthur's little mouth latched onto her breast.

Wallingford seemed not to notice her words. He leaned against the wall, arms crossed, watching his wife and son in silence. Abigail's heart lurched. She had forgotten how enormous he was, how he filled a room simply by standing in it. He had lost a little weight in his travels, she thought. He looked rangy, lean, his cheekbones standing out from his head. His travel-stained jacket hung from his sturdy shoulders. Abigail wanted to take it off, to enfold him in her arms, to enclose all his beloved, lean, travel-stained body with hers.

"I'm sorry," Abigail said. "I would have written after he was born, if I had had any way of reaching you."

Wallingford shook his head without speaking.

"It's not the most romantic homecoming, I know, but he's a fast eater. Rather like his father, in fact."

Wallingford turned his head into his arm against the wall, and his back shook with sobs in the quiet room.

Leonora returned with tea, pouring it into the cups as if she had been bred all her days in England. "He's nearly done," Abigail said, switching breasts. Wallingford had gone to the window, staring out into the moonlit darkness.

Arthur slowed and stopped, his head drooping sleepily against her skin, smelling sweetly of milk. Abigail rose and snatched a cloth from the drying rack. She laid it over Wallingford's shoulder.

"Here," she said, and handed him the baby before he could object.

"What do I do?" he asked.

"Pat him on the back," said Abigail. "Harder, for goodness' sake. He's not a butterfly."

Wallingford stood next to the purple-skied window, patting his son's back with one large hand and holding him in place with the other. His fingers were clean and calloused and deeply tanned, a laborer's fingers. He looked up and met Abigail's gaze, engulfing her whole, making her knees buckle. His face was tanned, too, she thought, as if he held the sun beneath his skin.

He spoke hoarsely. "Are you certain he's getting enough to eat? He's very light."

"For God's sake, *look* at me. Do you think he's missing any meals? He was twelve pounds nine ounces yesterday, which is quite enough for a two-month-old, I assure you."

As if to punctuate her words, Arthur opened his mouth and let out a resonant belch.

Wallingford nearly dropped the bundle in his arms. "Good God! Was that *him*?" He looked anxiously at his shoulder.

"There we are." Abigail lifted the baby from her husband's chest, trying to keep her hands from shaking. She took the cloth and dabbed at Wallingford's worn jacket. "Now we simply swaddle him up and put him back to bed."

Leonora drew close and held out her arms. "I do the blanket, Abigail. You take the good signore to his bed, to his comfort. He is looking like a man who has travel long."

"Quite," said Wallingford.

Wallingford walked down the familiar corridor in a daze. From the tiny arched windows came the faint sound of the revelry in the courtyard, the *oom-pah* of that wretched tuba. The worn old stones passed by his eyes in a blur.

Your son. He had a son. A tiny scrap of vibrant humanity, brought to life in Abigail's body by his own seed, in a precious act of love. His son. His brain caressed the unfamiliar word.

Wallingford stopped and shut his eyes, and little Arthur's blinking black gaze stared into his soul, his tiny warm head burrowed into his heart.

Something tightened around his hand. "You've nothing to say?" asked Abigail, very gently.

Abigail, his wedded wife, who stood beside him, fragrant with milk and warmth and candlelight, her hand holding his.

Wallingford shook his head, lifted her into his weary arms, and carried her without words down the corridor into the east wing. The ladies' wing, where Abigail's room lay.

The door stood ajar, exactly where he remembered it, tucked into the corner at the near end of the hallway, the farthest from the stairs. He began kissing her even as he kicked the thick wood open with his foot. She moaned and kissed him back, hard and impatient; her hands went to his hair, his back, his collar, dragging at his stained jacket. He staggered at her onslaught, and the door clicked shut against his back.

Abigail's lips slid across his face. "You came back," she said, and her voice was thick and choked. "You came back."

"You thought I wouldn't?"

"I didn't know. I didn't know. Oh, God, every day, every night I hoped . . ." She broke apart and cried quietly on his shoulder.

"Don't, love. Of course I came back." Gently he eased her down, holding her against him, until her slippers touched the stone. His body marveled at the shock of her, at warm, living Abigail crying into his shirt. He stroked her back and her hair, and his heart seemed to swell from his chest and surround them both. "Of course I came back. My wife. Of course I came back."

Abigail's hands stole around his waist. Her breasts pressed against his ribs, ripe flesh nearly bursting from the bodice of her absurd costume. A year ago, he had removed this same dress from her body in the boathouse, as the moonlight spilled across the lake; his fingers remembered, and found the hooks at her back.

The bodice loosened. Abigail's head fell back, exposing her beautiful throat to the faint silvery light from the window. He kissed her warm pulse, kissed her chin and ear, while his hands worked the dress from her body and fumbled with her stays.

The dress fell away, the stays dropped to the floor, and Abigail stood before him at last in her delicate chemise. The tips of her breasts were dark against the white linen. God, it had been so long! He wanted to savor her slowly; he wanted to ravish her in an instant. His hands shook with it.

Abigail's eyes opened. She reached for his shirt, yanked down his braces, tore at the buttons. "For God's sake, stop staring and take me to bed."

At the word *bed* Wallingford's thoughts snapped. He captured her mouth, and together they staggered across the floor, shedding clothes, laughing and kissing, crying out at the unfamiliarity of it all. They reached the bed; he tumbled naked atop her, his stiff cock brushing her belly, and bent his head to kiss her deeply. "Ah, God," he muttered, over the roar of his hot male blood.

Abigail's body shifted beneath him, spreading open. "Please. Oh, God, now!" she said.

He laughed against her lips. "What, already? I thought you liked me to . . ."

"Now, Wallingford!"

Well, one didn't dare disappoint one's wife, after all. Wallingford lifted himself on his elbows. Abigail's hands found him, cradled him, lodged his head just inside her.

He sucked in his breath. She was so slick, so slippery. Her hips tilted eagerly upward.

"It's all right?" he said, between his clenched teeth. "You're . . . you're healed?"

"God, yes!"

He thrust his hips and buried his prick inside her.

She sang out. "Wallingford! Oh, God!"

His brain reeled. A year, a year since he'd last occupied a woman's body. A year since he had felt her yielding flesh, the softness of her belly and breasts against his skin, her legs tightening around him, the sweet suck of her sheath as he drew back and shoved up her again. His balls prickled with urgency; he forced himself to slow, measured thrusts, to control the rise of pleasure in his own body. He watched Abigail's half-lidded eyes, heard her keening cries. "Every night," he whispered, "every night I dreamed of this. Every night, I thought of you. Only you, Abigail."

She made a desperate noise.

He drove harder, at the same deliberate rhythm. "Only you. My wife. My love."

"Yours," she gasped out, writhing, meeting his thrusts with her eager hips.

"You, Abigail. You."

Her tension rose up; he could feel it in the clutch of her gathering muscles. He lifted himself higher, angled his hips, quickened his pace. He drove into her without mercy, over and over, matching her desperation with his own. Her fingernails dug into his waist, and the pain combusted with the impossible concentration of pleasure to send him nearly mad. By brute force he held back the climax that thundered in his groin.

"*You*," he said again, and her body arched, she cried out, and at last, at *last* he set himself free, spending with almost violent intensity into the spasms of her release. A roar echoed in his ears, and he realized, as he sank shuddering downward, that it came from his own throat.

"Welcome home," whispered Abigail, a little breathlessly.

He couldn't move. He opened his eyes into the bedsheets and closed them again. He wanted to say, *It's good to be home*, but all that came out was the last word.

"Home," he groaned.

Her hands traced his back, like the wings of butterflies. "You've lost weight. You're as hard as a rail."

Wallingford turned his head. His heartbeat still slammed against hers. "And you're rounder. Full and soft." He shifted his body and laid his hand over her breast. "Delectable."

"You don't mind?"

"Mind?" Wallingford lifted his head. Abigail's eyes were wide and rather worried. "Mind? My God. Look at you. I leave you a girl, and now you're a woman. You're lush. You're perfect. The mother of my child." His voice, for some reason, cracked slightly on the last word. He was still inside her; gently he drew himself out and gathered her in his arms.

Her head burrowed against his chest. How exquisite, how unspeakably luxurious, to feel Abigail's silken hair again on his naked skin. "I wish you could have been there, when he was born," she said softly. "Finn was ready to ride out and scour the steppes to find you, but I told him . . . I told him . . ."

"What, love?"

"I told him there would be plenty of time when you got back. Newborns only eat and sleep, you know. And then . . . well, that . . . God willing, there would be more children after this one."

Wallingford stroked her hair, her shining moonlit hair, willing himself to stay in one piece. "You had faith in me."

"I had faith in you. I knew you. I knew how strong you are, how true you are. And in those darkest hours, Wallingford . . ." She stopped. He went on stroking. The noises from the party had died away; the musicians were perhaps putting away their instruments, the villagers fading in pairs into the orchards and vines. Abigail's back moved up and down beneath his forearm. "In those darkest hours, when I was so lonely, and I could feel our baby moving inside me, and I needed you so much I could hardly breathe . . ."

Another pause. Wallingford's tears rolled down his cheek and disappeared into her hair. He wanted to say something, to comfort her somehow, but he couldn't speak.

She whispered, "I remembered your face, your eyes, when you said those vows to me in Siena. And I said to myself, Wallingford would never break his word."

He kissed her hair, where the tears had fallen, and summoned his voice. "I would never break my word."

"Mmm." Abigail lifted her knee, crossing her leg possessively over his.

"I was too jolly tired, for one thing," he said, more lightly. "Earning one's bread is damned hard work, it turns out. Harvesting from sunrise to sundown. And tanning hides. I spent a month on that, in the winter. That was Poland. I don't know what I was thinking. Bloody near wore myself out."

A giggle. "Was it worth it?"

"Yes. I've got a fine pair of gloves for you, somewhere in my bags."

She turned to face him and put her arms around his neck. "Make love to me again."

He chuckled. "Already? You weren't properly satisfied just now?"

"Well, as a practical matter, Arthur will be needing another feed in a few hours, and I should try for a little sleep at least. So it's now or never until morning."

"Then rest, darling." He kissed her. "Rest for now. I'll bring him to you when he's ready."

"But I want you."

He laughed again. "And I want you. But we have a lifetime now. And you need your rest."

"So do you." She nestled back into his chest.

"So do I." He reached beneath his back, found the blankets, and worked them up to cover his wife and himself in the narrow bed. Her damp skin clung to his; his wetness mingled with hers. "We'll have a daughter next," he said.

Abigail snorted. "You won't know what to do with a daughter."

"Of course I will. Who better? Simply keep her under lock and key, and admit suitors only under rigorous application. And no bloody dukes, that's for certain."

"Horrid chaps, dukes. I quite agree."

Wallingford's cock was still stiff, but his brain was drifting pleasantly into sleep. Abigail's scent wound around him; her soft body curled into his under the warmth of the austere Tuscan blanket. His skin still radiated with the glow of long-sought sexual release. "Perhaps if we raise her here, out in the Italian mountains . . ."

"Mmm."

A faint trill of laughter drifted through the open window and then dissolved in the night. Wallingford's eyes wandered to the patch of dark sky. Probably the entire valley had heard him with Abigail a moment ago, in the noisy throes of passion.

He decided not to voice this thought.

Silence, heavy and peaceful. God, how lovely it was, to be falling asleep in his wife's bed, with the rattle of London omnibuses like a distant dream from another life. Perhaps they should live here, raise their children here. Perhaps . . .

Abigail shot upward. "Quite!"

"What's that?" he muttered sleepily. He extended one long and work-hardened arm to pull her back where she belonged.

She shrugged off his fingers. "You said *quite!*"

"I did?"

A pair of hands shoved at his shoulders. "Back in the nursery. You said *quite!* You did!"

"Abigail, go to sleep."

"When Leonora said she would take the baby, and you should go to bed because you were tired after your journey! You heard her! You *answered* her! You said to her, *quite!*"

Wallingford rose on his elbows, feeling rather cross. "Who the devil's Leonora? The woman in the nursery, you mean? The one who was looking after . . ."

His words froze in his throat.

"Yes," said Abigail. "Leonora. Signorina Monteverdi."

Wallingford fell back on his wife's pillow and stared at the ancient wooden beam above. He pictured her again: a lovely woman of some indeterminate age, surrounded by an invisible glow of tranquility, lifting his son from Abigail's arms in gentle reverence.

Her eyes, he remembered, were as dark as his own, and soft with love.

"Well, I'll be damned," he whispered.

Abigail sank down upon his chest, kissed his lips, and put her wet cheek against his.

"In fact," she said, "quite the opposite."

Turn the page for a preview of
Juliana Gray's next book

HOW TO TAME
YOUR DUKE

Coming soon from Berkley Sensation!

PROLOGUE

London, England
October 1889

At two o'clock in the morning, as a cold autumn rain drummed against the damask-shrouded windowpanes of his Park Lane town house, the Duke of Olympia was awoken by his valet and told that three ladies awaited him downstairs in his private study.

"Three ladies, did you say?" asked Olympia, as he might say *three copulating hippopotamuses*.

"Yes, sir. And two attendants."

"In my study?"

"I thought it best, sir," said the valet. "The study is situated at the back of the house."

Olympia stared at the ducal canopy above his head. "Isn't it Ormsby's job to take care of such matters? Turn the women away, or else toss them into the upstairs bedchambers until morning?"

The valet adjusted the sleeve of his dressing gown. "Mr. Ormsby elected to refer the matter to me, Your Grace, as an affair of a personal nature, requiring Your Grace's immediate attention." His voice flexed minutely on the word *immediate*. "The attendants, of course, are in the kitchen."

Olympia's ears gave a twinge. His sleep-darkened mind began to awaken and spark, like a banked fire brought back to life by a surly housemaid. "I see," he said. He continued to stare into the canopy. The pillow beneath his head was of finest down encased in finest linen, and cradled his skull with weightless lavender-scented comfort. Beneath the heavy bedcovers, his body made a warm cocoon into the softness of the mattress. He removed one hand from this haven and plucked the nightcap from his head. "Three ladies, did you say?"

"Yes, sir. And a dog." The valet made his disapproval of the dog apparent without the smallest change of voice.

"A corgi, I believe. And the ladies: two fair and one auburn?"

"Yes, sir."

Olympia sat up and heaved a sigh. "I've been expecting them."

Eight minutes later, in a yellow dressing gown rioting with British lions, with his whitening hair neatly brushed and his chin miraculously shaved, the Duke of Olympia opened the door to his private study in a soundless whisper.

"Good morning, my dears," he said cordially.

The three ladies jumped in their three chairs. The corgi launched himself into the air and landed, legs splayed, atop the priceless Axminster rug, on which he promptly disgraced himself.

"I beg your pardon," Olympia said. "Don't rise, I implore you."

The three ladies dropped back into the chairs, except the auburn-haired youngest, who scooped up the dog with a reproving whisper.

"Your Grace," said the eldest, "I apologize most abjectly for the irregularity of our arrival. I hope we have not put out your household. We meant not to disturb you until morning . . ."

"Except that wretched new butler of yours, Ormsby or whatever the devil his name was . . ." burst out the youngest.

"Stefanie, my dear!" exclaimed the eldest.

Olympia smiled and shut the door behind him with a soft click. He stepped toward the center of the room and stopped before the first chair. "Luisa, dear child. How well you look, in spite of everything." He took her hand and squeezed it. "A very great pleasure to see you again, Your Highness, after so many years."

"Oh, Uncle." A blush spread across Luisa's pale cheeks, and

her hollow blue-eyed gaze seemed to fill a trifle. "You're terribly kind."

"And Stefanie, my dear scamp. Do you know, I recently met another young lady who reminded me very much of you. It made my old heart ache, I assure you." Olympia reached for Stefanie's hand, but she instead sprang from her chair and threw her arms around him.

"Uncle Duke, how perfectly sporting of you to take us in! I knew you would. You always were such a trump."

Stefanie's arms were young and strong about his waist, and he patted her back with gentle hands and laughed. "You always were the most reckless girl in that damned cow pasture of a principality you call home."

"Holstein-Schweinwald-Huhnhof is not a cow pasture, Uncle Duke!" Stefanie pulled back and slapped his arm. "It's the most charming principality in Germany. Herr von Bismarck himself pronounced it magnificent. And dear Vicky . . ."

"Yes, of course, my dear. I was only teasing. Quite charming, I'm sure." Olympia suppressed a shudder. Bucolic landscapes made his belly twitch, or perhaps it was the rather charmless thought of *dear Vicky,* Kaiserin of Germany and his own sovereign's eldest daughter. He turned to the final princess of Holstein-Schweinwald-Huhnhof, the middle child, quietly soothing the corgi, who was yapping and whining by turns. "And Emilie," he said.

Emilie looked up and smiled at him behind her spectacles. "Uncle." She placed the corgi on the rug and rose.

How old was the girl now? Twenty-three? Twenty-four? But her eyes looked older, round and owlish, improbably ancient amid the clear skin and delicate bones of her face. Her hair gleamed golden in the light from the single electric lamp on Olympia's desk. The other two were handsome girls, constructed on regal lines that showed well in photographs, but Emilie's beauty was more subtle. It ducked and hid behind her spectacles and her retiring nature. A scholar, Emilie: She could parse her Latin and Greek better than Olympia himself. A strain of genius ran through the family blood, and Emilie had caught it in full.

"My dear girl." Olympia caught her hands and kissed her cheek. "How are you?"

"I am well, Uncle." She spoke quietly, but there were tears in her voice.

"Sit down, all of you. I have ordered tea. You must be exhausted." He motioned to the chairs and propped himself on the corner of his desk. "Did you make the crossing last night?"

"Yes, after sunset," said Stefanie. "I was sick twice."

"Really, Stefanie." Luisa was sharp.

"It was the licorice," said Stefanie, sitting back in her chair and looking at the gilded ceiling. "I never could resist licorice, and that little boy at the quayside . . ."

"Yes, quite," said Olympia. "And your attendants?"

"Oh, they were quite all right. Sturdy stomachs, you know."

Olympia coughed. "I mean, who are they? Can they be trusted?"

"Yes, of course." Luisa shot a reproving look—not the first—at Stefanie. "Our governess, who as you know has been with us a thousand years, and Papa's"—her voice quivered slightly—"Papa's valet, Hans."

"Yes, I remember Hans," said Olympia. He focused his mind on the memory: a burly fellow, not the most delicate hand with a neckcloth, but his eyes burned with loyalty to his master, whom he had served since before the Prince's marriage to Olympia's youngest sister. "I remember Miss Dingleby, as well. It was I who sent her to your mother, when Luisa was ready for schooling. I am relieved to hear she has escaped safely with you."

"So you have heard the tale." Luisa looked down at her hands, tangled tightly in her lap.

"Yes, my dear," Olympia said, in his kindest voice. "I am very sorry."

"Of course he's heard," said Emilie, in an expectedly brisk voice. Her eyes, fixed on Olympia's face, gleamed sharply behind her spectacles. "Our uncle knows about all these things, often before the rest of the world. Isn't that so, Uncle?"

Olympia spread his broad hands before them. "I am a private man. I simply hear things, from time to time . . ."

"Nonsense," said Emilie. "You were expecting us. Tell us what you know, Uncle. I should like, for once, to hear the entire story. When one's trapped in the middle of things, you see, it's all rather muddled." She looked at him steadily, with those wise eyes, and Olympia, whose innards were not easily unsettled except by bucolic landscapes, knew a distinct flip-flop in the region of his liver.

"Emilie, such impertinence," Luisa said.

Olympia straightened. "No, my dear. In this case, Emilie is quite right. I have taken it upon myself to make an inquiry or two, in hemi-demi-semi-official channels, about your case. After all, you are family."

The last word echoed heavily in the room, calling up the image of the girls' mother, Olympia's sister, who had died a decade ago as she labored to bring the long-awaited male heir of Holstein-Schweinwald-Huhnhof into the world. The baby, two months early, had died a day later, and though Prince Rudolf had married twice more, applying himself with nightly perseverance to his duty, no coveted boys had materialized. Only the three young ladies remained: Princess Stefanie, Princess Emilie, and—bowing at last to the inevitable four months ago—Crown Princess Luisa, the acknowledged heir to the throne of Holstein-Schweinwald-Huhnhof.

But their mother still hovered, like a ghost in the room. Olympia's favorite sister, though he would never have admitted it. His own dear Louisa, clever and handsome and full of charm, who had fallen in love with Prince Rudolf at court in the unending summer of 1863, during the height of fashion for German royalty.

Emilie, he thought as he gazed upon the young princesses, had Louisa's eyes.

"And?" she asked now, narrowing those familiar eyes.

The electric lamp gave a little flicker, as if the current had been disturbed. Outside, a dog barked faintly at some passing drunkard or night dustman, and the corgi rose to the tips of his paws, ears trembling. Olympia crossed his long legs and placed his right hand at the edge of the desk, fingers curling around the polished old wood. "I have no inkling, I'm afraid, who caused the death of your father and"—he turned a sorrowful gaze to Luisa, who sat with her eyes cast down—"your own husband, my dearest Luisa." This was not entirely a lie, though it was not precisely the truth; but Olympia had long since lost all traces of squeamish delicacy in such matters. "One suspects, naturally, that the murder must have occurred by the hand of some party outraged by Luisa's recognition as heir, and her subsequent marriage to . . . I beg your pardon, my dear. What was the poor fellow's name, God bless his soul?"

"Peter," Luisa whispered.

"Peter, of course. My deepest apologies that I was unable to attend the ceremony. I felt I would not be missed."

"By the by, that was a jolly nice epergne you sent," said Stefanie. "We absolutely marveled on it."

"You are quite welcome," said Olympia. "I daresay it has all been packed safely away?"

"Miss Dingleby saw to it herself."

"Clever Miss Dingleby. Excellent. Yes, the murders. I thought to send for you myself, but before I could make the necessary arrangements, word had reached me . . ."

"So quickly?" asked Emilie, with her clever eyes.

"There *are* telegraphs, my dear. Even in the heart of Holstein-Schweinwald-Huhnhof, I'm told, although in this case the necessary communication came from a friend of mine in Munich."

"What sort of friend?" Emilie leaned forward.

Olympia waved his hand. "Oh, an old acquaintance. In any case, he told me the facts of this latest crisis, the . . . the . . ."

Luisa looked up and said fiercely, "My attempted abduction, do you mean?"

"Yes, my dear. That. I was gratified to learn that you had defended yourself like a true daughter of your blood, and evaded capture. When the papers reported the three of you missing with your governess, I knew there was nothing more to fear. Miss Dingleby would know what to do."

"She has been a heroine," said Luisa.

Olympia smiled. "I had no doubt."

"Well then," said Stefanie. "When do we begin? Tomorrow morning? For I should like to have at least a night's sleep first, after all that rumpus. I declare I shall never look at a piece of licorice in quite the same light."

"Begin?" Olympia blinked. "Begin what?"

Stefanie rose from her chair and began to pace about the

room. "Why, investigating the matter, of course! Finding out who's responsible! I should be more than happy to act as bait, though I rather think it's poor Luisa they're after, God help them."

"My dear, do sit down. You're making me dizzy." Olympia lifted one hand to shield his eyes. "Investigate? Act as *bait*? Quite out of the question. I shouldn't dream of risking my dear nieces in such a manner."

"But something must be done!" exclaimed Emilie, rising, too.

"Of course, and something *shall* be done. The Foreign Office is most concerned about the matter. Instability in the region and all that. They shall be conducting the most rigorous inquiries, I assure you. But in the meantime, you must hide."

"Hide?" said Emilie.

"*Hide!*" Stefanie stopped in mid-pace and turned to him, face alight with outrage. "A princess of Holstein-Schweinwald-Huhnhof does not *hide*!"

Olympia lifted himself away from the desk and gathered his hands behind his back. "Of course, there's no point hiding in the ordinary manner. These Continental agents, I'm told, are unnaturally cunning in seeking out their targets. Simply sending you to rusticate in some remote village won't do. Your photographs are already in the papers."

Stefanie's hands came together. "Disguise! Of course! You mean to disguise us! I shall be a dairymaid. I milked a cow once, at the Schweinwald summer festival. They were all quite impressed. The dairyman told me I had a natural affinity for udders."

"Nonsense. A dairymaid! The very idea. No, my dears. I have something in mind more subtle, more devious. More, if you'll pardon the word"—pause, for effect—". . . *adventurous*."

Luisa drew in a long and deep breath. "Oh, *Uncle*. What have you done?"

"I admit, I had the idea from you yourselves. Do you remember, a great many years ago, when I came to visit your . . . er, your charming homeland? You were just fifteen, Luisa."

"I remember." Her voice was dark with foreboding.

"You put on a play for me, did you not? *Hamlet*, I believe, which was just the sort of melancholy rubbish a fifteen-year-old girl *would* find appealing." Olympia came to a bookshelf, propped his elbow next to a first folio, and regarded the girls with his most benignly affectionate expression.

"Yes, *Hamlet*," said Luisa warily.

"I remember!" said Stefanie. "I was both Claudius and the Prince of Norway, which proved rather awkward at the end, and Emilie of course played Polonius . . ."

Olympia widened his beneficent smile. "And Luisa was Hamlet. Were you not, my dear?"

The timepiece above the mantel chimed three o'clock in dainty little dings. The corgi went around in a circle once, twice, and settled himself in an anxious bundle at Stefanie's feet. His ears swiveled attentively in Olympia's direction.

"Oh no," said Luisa. "It's out of the question. Impossible, to say nothing of improper."

Stefanie clasped her hands. "Oh, Uncle! What a marvelous idea! I've always wanted to gad about in trousers like that, such perfect freedom. Imagine! You're an absolute genius!"

"We will not," said Luisa. "Imagine the *scandal*! The . . . the *indignity*! No, Uncle. You must think of something else."

"Oh, hush, Luisa! You're a disgrace to your barbarian ancestors . . ."

"I should hope I am! *I*, at least, have some notion . . ."

"Now, ladies . . ."

". . . who overran the steppes of Russia and the monuments of Rome . . ."

". . . of what is due to my poor husband's memory, and it does not require *trousers* . . ."

"My dear girls . . ."

". . . to create the very wealth and power that make us targets of assassins to *begin* with . . ."

"*Hush!*" said Olympia.

Luisa paused, finger brandished in mid-stab. Stefanie bent over with a mutinous expression and picked up the quivering corgi.

Olympia rolled his eyes to the ceiling, seeking sympathy from the gilded plasterwork. His head, unaccustomed to such late hours, felt as if it might roll off his body at any moment and into the corgi-soiled Axminster below.

Indeed, he would welcome the peace.

"Very well," he said at last. "Luisa rejects the notion, Stefanie embraces it. Emilie, my dear? I believe it falls to you to cast the deciding vote."

Stefanie rolled her own eyes and sat with a pouf into her chair, corgi against her breast. "Well, that's that, then. Emilie will never agree."

"I am shocked, Uncle, that a man of your stature would even consider such a disgraceful notion." Luisa smoothed her skirts with satisfaction.

Olympia held up his hand and regarded Emilie. She sat with her back straight and her fingers knit, thumbs twiddling one another. Her head cocked slightly to one side, considering some distant object with her mother's own eyes.

"Well, my dear?" Olympia said softly.

Emilie reached up and tapped her chin with one long finger. "We shall have to cut our hair, of course," she said. "Luisa and Stefanie will have an easier time effecting the disguise, with their strong bones, but I shall have to wear a full beard of whiskers at least. And at least we are not, taken as a group, women of large bosom."

"Emilie!" said Luisa, in shocked tones.

"Emilie, *darling*!" cried Stefanie. "I knew you had it in you!"

Olympia clapped his hands in profound relief. "There we are! The matter is settled. We shall discuss the details in the morning. Wherever has the tea gone? I shall have it sent to your rooms instead." He turned around and pressed a button on his desk, a state-of-the-art electrical bell he'd had installed just a month ago. "Ormsby will show you the way. Tally-ho, then!"

"Uncle! You're not going to *bed*?"

Olympia yawned, tightened the belt on his dressing robe, and made for the door. "Oh, but I am. Quite exhausted." He waved his hand. "Ormsby will be along shortly!"

"Uncle!" Luisa called desperately. "You can't be serious, Uncle!"

Olympia paused with his fingertips on the door handle. He looked back over his shoulder. "Come, my girls," he said. "You shall be well instructed, well placed in respectable homes. You are actresses of exceptional talent, as I have myself witnessed. You possess the dignity and resourcefulness of a most noble family. You have, above all, my unqualified support."

He opened the door, stretched his arm wide, and smiled. "What could possibly go wrong?"

The Duke of Olympia did not, however, make straight for his room. He walked in the opposite direction, down the hall toward the service staircase at the extreme back of the house. As he descended, the expressions of feminine outrage and excitement from the study died slowly into the walls, until the air went still.

Miss Dingleby was waiting for him in the alcove near the silver pantry. She made a little noise as he drew near, and stepped into the light.

"Ah! There you are, my dear," Olympia said. He looked down at her from his great height and placed his hand tenderly against her cheek. "Won't you come upstairs and tell me all about it?"

ONE

A ramshackle inn in Yorkshire (of course)
December 1889

The brawl began just before midnight, as taproom brawls usually did.

Not that Emilie had any previous experience of taproom brawls. She had caught glimpses of the odd mill or two in a Schweinwald village square (Schweinwald being by far the most tempestuous of the three provinces of Holstein-Schweinwald-Huhnhof, perhaps because it was the closest to Italy), but her governess or some other responsible adult had always hustled her away at the first spray of blood.

She watched with interest, therefore, as this brawl developed. It had begun as the natural consequence of an ale-soaked game of cards. Emilie had noticed the card players the moment she sat down in an exaggerated swing, braced her elbows, fingered her itching whiskers, and called for a bottle of claret and a boiled chicken with her deepest voice. They played at a table in the center of the room, huddling with bowed heads about the end as if they feared the spavined yellow ceiling might give way at any moment: three or four broad-shouldered men in work shirts, homespun coats slung over their chairs, and one stripling lad.

The stakes must have been high, for they played with intensity. A fine current of tension buzzed through the humid smoke-laden air. One man, his mustache merging seamlessly with the thicket of whiskers along his jaw, adjusted his seat and emitted a fart so long, so luxuriously slow, so like a mechanical engine in its noxious resonance, the very air trembled in awe. A pack of men at a neighboring table looked up, eyebrows high with admiration.

And yet his companions were so intent on the game, they couldn't be bothered to congratulate him.

At that point, Emilie had taken out a volume of Augustine in the original Latin and made an impressive show of absorption. Travelers, she had discovered early in today's journey from London, tended to avoid striking up conversations with solitary readers, especially when the book's title encompassed multiple clauses in a foreign language, and the last thing Emilie needed was an inquisitive traveling companion: the kind who asked one impertinent questions and observed one's every move. St. Augustine was her shield, and she was grateful to him. But tonight, at the bitter end of her journey into deepest Yorkshire, that godforsaken wilderness of howling wind and frozen moor, she could not focus her attention. Her gaze kept creeping over the edge of the volume to the table beyond.

It was the boy, she decided. Like her, he seemed out of place in this stained and battered inn, as if—like her—he had sought it out over higher-class establishments in order to avoid his usual crowd. He sat at a diagonal angle from her, his left side exposed to her gaze, illuminated by the roaring fire nearby. He was not much more than sixteen; possibly not even that. His pale face was rimmed with spots of all sizes, and his shoulders were almost painfully thin beneath a long thatch of straw-colored hair. He alone had not taken off his coat; it hung from his bones as if from an ill-stuffed scarecrow, dark blue and woven from a fine grade of wool. He regarded his cards with intense concentration behind a pair of owlish spectacles.

Emilie liked his concentration; she liked his spots and his long fingers. He reminded her of herself at that age, all awkward limbs and single-minded focus. Without thinking, she pushed her own spectacles farther up the bridge of her nose and smiled.

The boy was clearly winning.

Even if the stacks of coins at his side were not steadily growing into mountains, Emilie could not have mistaken the scowls of the other men at the table, the shifting in seats, the sharp smacks with which they delivered their stakes to the center of the table. Another round had just begun, and the dealer passed the cards around with blinding swiftness, not to waste a single instant of play. Each face settled into implacability; not a single mustache twitched. One man glanced up and met Emilie's eyes with cold malevolence.

She dropped her gaze back to her book. Her wine and chicken arrived in a clatter of ancient pewter, delivered by a careless barmaid with clean apple red cheeks and burly fingers. Emilie set down the book and poured the wine with a hand that shook only a little. The coldness of the man's gaze settled like a fist in her chest.

Emilie concentrated on the ribbon of wine undulating into her glass, on the chilly smoothness of the bottle beneath her fingers. Her wineglass was smudged, as if it had seen many other fingers and very little soap. Emilie lifted it to her lips anyway, keeping all her fingertips firmly pressed against the diamond pattern cut into the bowl, and took a hearty masculine swallow.

And nearly spat it back.

The wine was awful, rough and thin all at once, with a faint undertone of turpentine. Emilie had never tasted anything so awful, not even the cold boar's heart pie she'd been forced to eat in Huhnhof Baden two years ago, as the guest of honor at the autumn cornucopia festival. Only duty had seen her through that experience. Chew and swallow, Miss Dingleby had always instructed her. A princess does not gag. A princess chews and swallows. A princess does not complain.

The wine felt as if it were actually boiling in Emilie's mouth. Was that even possible? She held her breath, gathered her strength, and swallowed.

It burned down her throat, making her eyes prickle, making her nostrils flare. The atmosphere in the room, with its roaring fire and twenty perspiring men, pressed against her forehead with enough force to make her brow pearl out with perspiration. Except that princesses did not perspire; even princesses in exile, disguised as young men. She stared up at the ceiling, studied the wooden beam threatening her head, and let gravity do its work.

Her stomach cramped, recoiled, heaved, and settled at last

with a warning grumble. A buzz sounded from somewhere inside her spinning ears.

Emilie picked up her knife and fork with numbed fingers and sawed off a leg from her chicken.

Gradually her ears began to pick up sound again, her nose to acquire smells. To her right, a rumble of discontent ricocheted among the card players.

"Unless my eyesight is capable of penetrating the backs of your cards," the boy was saying, his voice skidding perilously between one octave and the next, "your accusation is impossible, sir. I must beg that you retract it."

One of the men shot upward, overturning his chair. "Not bloody likely, you cheating little bugger!"

"You are wrong on both counts. I am neither dishonest nor a practicing sodomite," said the boy, with unnatural calm.

The man flung out his arm and overturned the pile of coins next to the boy's right arm. "And I say you are!" he yelled.

Or so Emilie presumed. The words themselves were lost in the crash of humanity that followed the overturning of the coins onto the floor.

Emilie, who had just lifted the chicken leg to her mouth with a certain amount of relish—she had never, ever been allowed to touch a morsel of food without the intercession of one utensil or another—nearly toppled in the whoosh of air as a long-shanked figure dove from his seat near the fireplace and into the tangle of flailing limbs.

"Oh, fuck me arse!" yelled the barmaid, three feet away. "Ned! Fetch the bucket!"

"Wh-what?" said Emilie. She rose from her chair and stared in horror. A coin went flying from the writhing scrum before her and smacked against her forehead in a dull thud.

"I'll take that." The barmaid swooped down and snatched the coin from among the shavings.

"Madam, I . . . oh, good God!" Emilie ducked just in time to avoid a flying bottle. It crashed into the fire behind her in a shattering explosion of glass and steam, laced with turpentine.

Emilie looked at her wine and chicken. She looked down at her battered leather valise, filled with its alien cargo of masculine clothing and false whiskers. Her heart rattled nervously in her chest.

"Excuse me, madam," she said to the barmaid, ducking again as a pewter tankard soared through the air, "do you think . . ."

"Ned! Bring that bleedin' bucket!" bellowed the barmaid. The words had hardly left her lips when a thick-shouldered man ran up from behind, bucket in each hand, skin greasy with sweat. "About time," the barmaid said, and she snatched a bucket from his hand and launched its contents into the scrum.

For an instant, the scene hung suspended, a still-life drawing of dripping fists halted in mid-swing and lips curled over menacing teeth. Then a single explicit curse burst fluently from some masculine throat, and the fists connected with solid flesh. Someone roared like a wounded lion, a feral sound cut off short by a smash of breaking glass.

"You'd best fly, young sir," said the barmaid, over her shoulder, as she tossed the second bucket into the fray.

"Right," said Emilie. She picked up her valise and stumbled backward. She had already engaged a room upstairs, though she wasn't quite sure where to find it; but at least she knew there *was* an upstairs, a refuge from the brawl, which seemed to be growing rather than ebbing. Two men ran in from the other room, eyes wild, spittle flying from their lips, and leapt with enthusiasm onto the pile.

Emilie took another step backward, a final longing gaze at her chicken. She'd only had a single rubbery bite, her first meal since a hurried lunch of cheese sandwich and weak tea at the station cafe in Derby, as she waited for the next train in her deliberately haphazard route. She hadn't thought to bring along something to eat. What princess did? Food simply arrived at the appropriate intervals, even during the flight from the Continent, procured by one loyal retainer or another. (Hans did have a knack for procuring food.) This chicken, tough and wretched, pale and dull with congealed grease, was her only chance of nourishment until morning. The dismembered leg lay propped on the edge of the plate, unbearably tantalizing.

At the back of Emilie's mind, Miss Dingleby was saying something strict, something about dignity and decorum, but the words were drowned out by the incessant beat of hunger farther forward in the gray matter. Emilie ducked under a flying fork, reached out with one slender white hand, snatched the chicken leg, and put it in her pocket.

She spun around and hesitated, for just the smallest fraction of an instant.

"I've got you, you bleedin' little bu—" The shout rang out from the melee, cut short by an oomph and a splatter.

Emilie turned back, set down her valise, and wrenched the other leg from the chicken. The bone and skin slipped against her fingers; she grabbed the knife and sawed through until the drumstick came loose.

A half crown coin landed with a thud on the platter, at the bisection of leg from trunk, in a pool of thickened grease. "Oy!" someone yelled.

Emilie looked up. A man rushed toward her, his nose flinging blood, his arms outstretched. Emilie took the chicken leg, left the coin, and scrambled past the chair.

"What've you got there? Oy!"

A heavy hand landed on her shoulder, turning her around with a jerk. Emilie held back a gasp at the stench of rotting breath, the wild glare of the bulbous eyes. The chicken leg still lay clenched in her left hand, the knife in her right.

"Stand back!" she barked.

The man threw back his head and laughed. "A live one! Bleedin' little squeaker. I'll . . ."

Emilie shoved the chicken leg in her pocket and brought up the knife. "I said stand back!"

"Oh, it's got a knife, has it?" He laughed again. "What's that in your pocket, mate?"

"Nothing."

He raised one hamlike fist and knocked the knife from her fingers. "I said, what's that in your pocket, mate?"

Emilie's fingers went numb. She looked over the man's shoulder. "Watch out!"

The man spun. Emilie leaned down, retrieved the knife, and pushed him full force in his wide and sagging buttocks. He lurched forward with a hard grunt and grabbed wildly for the chair, which shattered into sticks under his hand. Like an uprooted windmill he fell, arms rotating in drunken circles, to crash atop the dirty shavings on the floor. He flopped once and lay still.

"Oh, well done!"

The boy popped out of nowhere, brushing his sleeves,

grinning. He pushed his spectacles up the bridge of his nose and examined the platter of limbless chicken. "I do believe that's mine," he said, taking the half crown and flipping it in the air.

"Wh-what?" asked Emilie helplessly.

"Freddie, you bleedin' fool!" It was the barmaid. Her hands were fisted on her hips, and her hair flew in wet strands from her cap.

"I'm sorry, Rose," said the boy. He turned to her with a smile.

Rose? thought Emilie, blinking at the broad-shouldered barmaid.

"You has to watch yer mouth, Freddie," Rose was saying, shaking her head. Another shout came from the mass of men, piled like writhing snakes atop one another on the floor nearby. Someone leaped toward them, shirt flapping. Rose picked up Emilie's half-empty wine bottle and swung it casually into the man's head. He groaned once and fell where he stood. "I've told yer and told yer."

"I know, Rose, and I'm sorry." Young Freddie looked contritely at his shoes.

"You'd best fly, Freddie, before yer father comes a-looking. And take this poor young sod with yer. He ain't fit for fighting."

Freddie turned to Emilie and smiled. "I think you've misjudged him, Rose. He's got a proper spirit."

"I have nothing of the sort," Emilie squeaked. She took a deep breath and schooled her voice lower. "That is, I should be happy to retire. The sooner"—she ducked just in time to avoid a spinning plate, which smashed violently into the wall an instant later—"the better, really."

"All right, then. Don't forget your valise." Freddie picked it up and handed it to her, still smiling. He was a handsome lad, really, beneath his spots. He had a loose-limbed lankiness to him, like a puppy still growing into his bones. And his eyes were pure blue, wide and friendly behind the clear glass of his spectacles.

"Thank you," Emilie whispered. She took the valise in her greasy fingers.

"Have you a room?" Freddie asked, dodging a flying fist.

"Yes, upstairs. I . . . oh, look out!"

Freddie spun, but not in time to avoid a heavy shoulder slamming into his.

"Jack, you drunken bastard!" screeched Rose.

Freddie staggered backward, right into Emilie's chest. She flailed wildly and crashed to the ground. Freddie landed atop her an instant later, forcing the breath from her lungs. The knife flew from her fingers and skidded across the floor.

"Right, you little whoreson," said the attacker. He was the first one, Emilie thought blearily, the one who had knocked the coins from the table to begin with. He was large and drunk, his eyes red. He leaned down, grabbed Freddie by the collar, and hauled back his fist.

"No!" Emilie said. Freddie's weight disappeared from her chest. She tried to wriggle free of the rest of him, but Freddie was flailing to loosen himself from the man's grasp. Emilie landed her fist in the crook of one enormous elbow and levered herself up, just a little, just enough that she could bend her neck forward and sink her teeth into the broad pad of the man's thumb.

"*Oy!*" he yelled. He snatched his hand back, letting Freddie crash to the ground and roll away, and grabbed Emilie's collar instead.

Emilie clutched at his wrist, writhing, but he was as solid as a horse and far less sensible. His fist lifted up to his ear, and his eyes narrowed at her. Emilie tried to bring up her knee, her foot, anything. She squeezed her eyes shut, expecting the shattering blow, the flash of pain, the blackness and stars and whatever it was.

How the devil had this happened to her? Brawls only happened in newspapers. Only men found themselves locked in meaty fists, expecting a killing punch to the jaw. Only men . . .

But then . . . she *was* a man, wasn't she?

With one last mighty effort, she flung out her hand and scrabbled for the knife. Something brushed her fingertips, something hard and round and slippery. She grasped it, raised it high, and . . .

"*Oogmph!*" the man grunted.

The weight lifted away. Her collar fell free.

Emilie slumped back, blinking. She stared up at the air before her. At her hand, grasping the tip of a chicken leg.

She sat up dizzily. Two men swam before her, her attacker and someone else, someone even broader and taller, who held the fellow with one impossibly large hand. Emilie expected to see his other fist fly past, crashing into the man's jaw, but it did not. Instead, the newcomer raised his right arm and slammed his elbow on the juncture of his opponent's neck and shoulder.

"Oy?" the man squeaked uncertainly, and sagged to the ground.

"Oh, for God's sake," said Freddie. He stood up next to Emilie and offered her his hand. "Was that necessary?"

Emilie took Freddie's hand and staggered to her feet. She looked up at the newcomer, her rescuer, to say some word of abject thanks.

But her breath simply stopped in her chest.

The man filled her vision. If Emilie leaned forward, her brow might perhaps reach the massive ball of his shoulder. He stood quite still, staring down at the man slumped on the ground with no particular expression. His profile danced before her, lit by the still-roaring fire, a profile so inhumanly perfect that actual tears stung the corners of Emilie's eyes. He was clean-shaven, like a Roman god, his jaw cut from stone and his cheekbone forming a deep shadowed angle on the side of his face. His lips were full, his forehead high and smooth. His close-cropped pale hair curled about his ear. "Yes," he said, the single word rumbling from his broad chest. "Yes, my dear boy. I believe it *was* necessary."

Dear boy?

Emilie blinked and brushed her sleeves. She noticed the chicken leg and shoved it hastily in her pocket.

"I was about to take him, you know," said Freddie, in a petulant voice.

The man turned at last. "I would rather not have taken that chance, you see."

But Emilie didn't hear his words. She stood in horrified shock, staring at the face before her.

The face before her: *His* face, her hero's face, so perfect in profile, collapsed on the right side into a mass of scars, of mottled skin, of a hollow along his jaw, of an eye closed forever shut.

From somewhere behind him came Rose's voice, raised high

in supplication. "Your Grace, I'm that sorry. I did tell him, sir . . ."

"*Your Grace?*" Emilie said. The words slipped out in a gasp. Understanding began to dawn, mingled with horror.

Freddie handed Emilie her valise and said ruefully, "His Grace. His Grace, the Duke of Ashland, I'm afraid." A sigh, long and resigned. "My father."